RED AFTER DARK

Elise Noble

Published by Undercover Publishing Limited

Copyright © 2020 Elise Noble

v6

ISBN: 978-1-912888-26-9

Edited by Nikki Mentges, NAM Editorial

Cover design by Abigail Sins

www.undercover-publishing.com

www.elise-noble.com

Knowing your enemy and yourself will help you to win; not knowing your enemy but knowing yourself means you are uncertain; knowing neither your enemy or yourself means you are sure to lose.

- *Sun Tzu, The Art of War*

CHAPTER 1 - BETHANY

IF TWO WEEKS ago, somebody had told me that I'd be sitting on a private jet heading for an apparently luxurious estate near Richmond, Virginia, I'd have died laughing.

But there I was, and quite honestly, there was nothing funny about the situation.

In fact, everyone on board looked tense.

Emmy Black was sitting at the table up front, pieces of gun spread out across the polished black wood in front of her. She'd been cleaning the thing since we left Northolt. When we hit turbulence half an hour ago, the bullets had all rolled onto the floor, and she'd cursed like hell while she crawled around retrieving them. Then she'd lined them up neatly on end again, exactly the same as they were before.

Sky Malone, her not-quite-eighteen-year-old sidekick, had downed a large glass of wine as soon as we levelled out, and now she was sprawled on the grey leather sofa, lips twitching. Even in sleep, she was unsettled. Could I blame her? Not really. She'd quit her whole life to work for Emmy, left everything she knew, and no way would Emmy give her an easy ride.

And then there was Alaric. My hot new boss. My hot new totally off-limits boss who rumour said had stolen ten million dollars from the FBI, then done a bunk. I was almost certain that he hadn't. *Almost.* There was still a tiny niggle at the back of my mind that wouldn't let me trust him completely. I knew he lied. I'd seen him do it, smoothly, convincingly, without a hint of guilt clouding those soft brown eyes.

The last passenger was Ravi, Alaric's friend and colleague, and now my colleague too. I'd just been hired as a PA at Sirius, the private intelligence agency they ran along with two others—Judd and Naz.

"Having second thoughts?" Alaric asked.

"Of course not," I lied.

How could I not be having second thoughts? I'd abandoned my old life too. First, I got fired from my job, and then I walked away from my family and my inheritance. My ex-husband as well, although I didn't miss him one bit. In the decade we'd spent married, Piers had turned from a slightly cocky trainee dentist into an obnoxious, philandering prick whose brain in no way matched the size of his overinflated ego.

The last fortnight had been fraught with drama—drama that started when Sky pinched my car. After that, I discovered I'd been inadvertently transporting stolen goods, which quickly got stolen again, and before we could think about recovering them, my friend got abducted by a psycho. Right now, my brain was still trying to catch up.

"Because I'd understand if you *were* reconsidering. Has your father called again?"

"Once this morning, but I didn't answer."

What would I say to him? I doubted very much he was calling to apologise. My father never said he was sorry. Not for selling my beloved horse behind my back, not for pushing me to stay with a man who'd cheated on me, not for his own extramarital affairs. No, if I spoke to him, he'd only pressure me to change my mind, to come back into the fold and toe the family line.

But no more.

Once I'd made the decision to go it alone, a weight had lifted. Yes, the future was daunting, but better to face the unknown than the certainty of being yanked back every time I made a decision that disappointed my parents, and threatened with being cut off financially if I ploughed ahead anyway.

"It gets easier, Beth. I promise."

I had to believe that. The same thing had happened to Alaric eight years ago, and he'd survived. I suspected that was partly why he'd given me the job with Sirius. Out of pity. That and guilt because he'd been instrumental in me getting fired from Pemberton Fine Arts—the gallery where I used to work—in the first place.

"Holy shit."

Emmy's quiet exclamation made everyone look up. Well, everyone except Sky because she was still fast asleep.

"What?" Alaric was at her side in an instant, looking over her shoulder at the phone in her hand.

"Irvine Carnes just endorsed Kyla Devane for his old senate seat."

Alaric gave a low whistle of surprise, so clearly that was unexpected, but I had no idea why. All I knew was that Irvine Carnes was somehow wrapped up in the disappearance of the aforementioned stolen goods, seeing as it was his assistant who'd picked up the package in London and then fled the country.

"For those of us who don't follow American politics, could you explain?" I asked.

"Carnes is a Republican, Devane's independent," Emmy said, as if that answered everything.

"Carnes recently retired from the senate," Alaric explained. "Said he wanted to spend more time with his family. Everyone expected him to throw his weight behind the next Republican on the ballot for the special election to replace him. Carnes is well-liked in Kentucky, so his opinion carries a lot of sway. For him to push Devane instead of David Biggs...that's huge."

"So why would he do it?" Ravi asked. "Does he have a problem with Biggs personally?"

"Not that I'm aware of. Their policies align, and Biggs seems like an okay guy."

Emmy snorted. "The term 'okay' being relative. Biggs is a lawyer turned politician. He checked his morals at the door."

Considering Emmy had thrown a man off a building two days ago, I wasn't sure she was the best person to make that argument, but then again, I'd had a hand in helping her. I kept my mouth shut.

"Maybe it was tactical?" Alaric suggested. "Devane's been surging in the polls, and Aidan O'Shaughnessy's been rising too. Perhaps Carnes figured that if Biggs was going to lose, Devane was the lesser of two evils."

"But is she though? I heard she wanted the US to pull out of UN peacekeeping operations."

"Where did you hear that?"

"From the horse's mouth. Her Twitter account. Apparently, the US military's just too expensive, and those countries should be fighting their own battles." Emmy gave her head a little shake. "No, Carnes's move doesn't make sense. If he'd publicly backed Biggs, Biggs's poll numbers would've gotten a boost."

"Then why do it?"

"Who knows? Maybe we're missing something."

"Like what?"

"If we knew that, it wouldn't be fucking missing, would it? But I'm curious. Aren't you curious? Let's add it to the list of questions when we talk to Carnes and his assistant."

I had to admit, I *was* curious. I'd long since learned from my father's cronies that when a politician did the unexpected, it was usually to benefit themselves rather than the country. Like the time Digby Bartrum, MP for Surrey Heath and Daddy's doubles partner, had awarded the contract for a new government computer system to a company my parents had invested in, despite it being more expensive than the other options. They'd split the spoils. I heard them bragging about it over drinks.

"Why not? Sure we can't fly straight to Frankfort?"

"Sky needs to go to Richmond. Plus I have a meeting, and it's already been rescheduled twice thanks to all the shit that happened in London."

Alaric sighed, and Emmy's tone softened.

"We've been chasing this painting for eight years, Prince. Another day won't make much difference."

Prince. Once again, I was reminded of Emmy and Alaric's past, of a time when they'd been close enough to give each other nicknames. Cinderella and Prince Charming. A hot bud of jealousy swelled in my chest, which was completely irrational since Emmy was happily married now. *Stand down, hormones.* Alaric had made it quite clear that he was focusing on his career for the moment, and I was getting over a messy divorce. Plus there was the whole lying/stealing thing.

No, I had to concentrate on work. My salary from Sirius was the only thing keeping me and my current horse off the breadline, and with my sketchy résumé, I couldn't afford to screw it up. Not with Chaucer's livery bill due in a week.

"I only booked accommodation from tomorrow night," I said. "If we go straight to Kentucky, I'll need to change the reservation."

Alaric straightened and came back to his seat beside me. "We'll go tomorrow. But this painting's jinxed, I can feel it. Just like *Emerald*. Every time we get a lead, it blows up in our faces."

The painting in question was *Red After Dark*, a modern masterpiece by Edwin Bateson valued at a cool million bucks. It had been stolen from the Becker Museum in Boston thirteen years ago along with four other paintings, and I'd left it in my freaking car while I nipped into Tesco. I wasn't aware of that at the time, obviously—my ex-boss had lied to me about the contents of the package—but my need to buy carrots for Chaucer had been the catalyst that led to the grand unravelling of my life and landed me on the plane today.

And *Emerald*? *The Girl with the Emerald Ring* was Alaric's nemesis. Believed to be the main target of the Becker raid, the oil painting hadn't been seen since the day it was stolen. Alaric had been on her trail eight years ago, ready to swap what was effectively a ransom for her safe return, when the pay-off had vanished along with his reputation.

See? We really were quite similar. I'd lost *Red*, and

he'd lost *Emerald*.

Then we'd both lost everything.

"That's the way of the world," Emmy told him. "If shit ran smoothly, neither of us would have jobs, would we?"

"I'd be good with that. Wouldn't you like to lie around on the beach all day, listening to the waves?"

"Nah, I'd get bored." The plane hit another rough patch, and her bullets fell over and rolled off the table again. "Fuck it. On second thoughts, the beach doesn't sound like a bad idea."

Wow.

Alaric had told me a little about the Riverley estate before we arrived, but I still wasn't prepared. Quite fancy, he'd said. I'd feel right at home.

Sure, if I were the Duchess of Marlborough.

My parents' mansion was "quite fancy." This...this was something tourists would pay money to gawk at. I could only imagine what the inside was like. And Emmy lived here?

When Ravi turned from the front seat of the chauffeur-driven SUV that had been at the airfield to meet us, his eyes were wide.

"This is a *house*?"

At least I wasn't the only one to be surprised.

"It's more of a playground for grown-ups," Alaric said.

Emmy's car had left us in the dust on the journey, probably because she'd shooed her driver into the back seat and taken the wheel herself. I spotted him when we reached the turning area at the top of the driveway, leaning against one of the stone pillars that flanked the massive front doors, hands on his knees as he tried to catch his breath. Mental note: don't get in a car with Emmy driving.

Sky didn't seem shaken, but she was staring up at the gargoyles that decorated the roofline with a dazed expression on her face. Glad it wasn't just me. Then she caught me looking at her and scowled as I climbed out of the car.

"What?" she asked. "We weren't all born with a silver spoon up our arse, okay?"

I was getting used to Sky now. To her snark and the somewhat abrasive personality she used as a defence mechanism. Underneath the prickly exterior, she had a good heart. I nodded towards the building.

"No, it seems some people were born with a gold spoon."

"Platinum, actually," Emmy said as she slammed the car door. "But that was my husband, not me. Need a hand with your stuff?"

"Uh... Yes, please."

Alaric had already started unloading the suitcases. One, two, three, four of them. And embarrassingly, they all belonged to me. He and Ravi had brought a duffel bag each, Sky carried a well-worn backpack, and Emmy had a laptop bag and nothing else. Until the others arrived at my flat to pick me up, I hadn't realised they were travelling so light, and by then, it was too late to repack. Whenever I'd gone on trips with Piers or my parents, it had been practically mandatory to take a mountain of luggage. A girl never knew when she'd need that third cocktail dress. But with hindsight, perhaps I could've left some of the shoes behind, and the yoga mat too. This place probably had its own gym. Heck, I bet there was even a personal trainer just waiting to whip everyone into shape.

I moved to grab a suitcase, but before I could extend the handle, a small man with orange hair bounced down the steps, his silver jumpsuit shining in the sun.

"Ooh, new people!" He scurried towards Sky but quickly veered in my direction when she took a step back. "You must be Bethany? I love your necklace." Oof. He squashed the breath out of me in a hug, then set his sights on Ravi. "Hey, hot stuff. I'm Bradley."

Behind his back, Emmy rolled her eyes. "Bradley, for fuck's sake let people get in the house before you start molesting them."

"I'm just being welcoming."

"Really? I pay your salary, and I didn't get so much as a hello."

"You live here. That's different." Now he headed for Sky again, and I noticed her fists ball up at her sides when he flung his arms around her. "So, you're Emmy's new project? I hope you know what you've let yourself in for. She's a real slave driver. I've barely had a day off since Christmas."

"Bradley, nobody made you go to every single fashion week. You also invited yourself to 'help' in Florida and then took it upon yourself to redecorate my house. Again. And you have an assistant now. Where is Izzy, anyway?"

"I sent her to the spa. Her manicure was chipped." He gave up on Sky, who was stiff as a board, and grabbed my hand instead. "Come on, I'll show you around. The guest house is ready for you and your men."

His wink told me exactly what he was thinking.

"My men? No, no, it's not like that." Both of them? Not even in my dreams. "Not at all."

"Sure it isn't. Oh dear, you need a manicure too. I'll book you in. Does tomorrow morning work?"

"Actually, we're going to Kentucky tomorrow."

"Tonight, then. I'll get a beautician to come over. Where's the rest of the luggage?"

"Uh, this is it. The cases are all mine."

"Well, at least somebody knows how to pack properly. Leave it, leave it, one of the men can put it in your room." He tugged me towards the front doors, and I pleaded with my eyes for Alaric to save me, but the cruel sod just grinned and waved. "The main house was built at the end of the nineteenth century, although it's been extensively modernised since…"

CHAPTER 2 - EMMY

PROBABLY I SHOULD have made more of an effort to rein in Bradley, but I didn't have the energy. The last week had left me drained. Not only the brush with death—although nearly following a lunatic off the roof of a high-rise was the closest I'd come to carking it so far this year—or even the dull ache from a broken nose, but part of my past coming back to haunt me.

And not just any old part.

Alaric.

We'd been together once, only for it to end in disaster when ten million bucks' worth of cash and diamonds had vanished from his custody. At the time, I'd been his fiercest defender. I'd put my job and my reputation on the line for Alaric fucking McLain, only for him to disappear as well. And I mean *disappear*. Poof. Gone. Believe me, I'd looked, and he'd given me nothing—not so much as a postcard—for almost a year. I thought he was dead. Hell, I'd even picked out an outfit to wear to his funeral.

Had I been in love? No, but I'd cared for him a great deal. His moonlight flit hurt.

Boy, did it hurt.

But deep down, I understood why he'd done it. The need to run from pain—mental pain, not physical—was ingrained in both of us, and I'd pulled a similar stunt myself a few years ago before I came to my senses.

What I didn't understand was why he hadn't told me about his daughter.

His fifteen-year-old daughter, a girl whose existence I'd only found out about by accident on Sunday. From Bethany, of all people, a woman he'd known for less than a week. Why had he trusted her with that knowledge but not me?

The question had eaten away at me for the whole flight back, and I was still no closer to an answer. Nor had I dealt with any of my emails or read the briefing notes for this afternoon's meeting. Should I just ask him? Once or twice I almost had, but there was clearly a reason he hadn't mentioned his offspring, and I didn't want to make things any more awkward between us. Somewhere over the eastern seaboard, I'd decided the easiest option was to pretend the girl didn't exist.

The problem was that before I found out about her, I'd offered Alaric the use of the guest house behind Riverley Hall as well as my help in finding *Emerald*. Finding *Emerald again*. Last time we'd gone after that damn painting, I'd ended up dodging bullets, so I was as keen to catch the thieves as him. Dish out a little payback, you know? But now I wanted to do it quickly. Get it over with.

Then the painting could go home to the museum, I could get on with my life, and Alaric and Bethany could head back to England and play happy families or whatever. As for the ten million bucks... I still wanted to believe Alaric was innocent, but my belief in him had wavered this week. If he'd lied once...

"Where are we going?" Sky asked. "And why are you walking so fast? Slap a number on your arse, and you could enter the Olympics."

"I don't like wasting time."

"Is that why you spent twenty minutes staring into space after dinner yesterday?"

Guilty as charged.

"Shut up." *Deep breaths, Emmy. Don't kill the brat.* She reminded me more of myself than I cared to admit. "We're going to meet the people you'll be working with while I'm in Kentucky. Then I'll give you a tour of the important parts of the estate and you can pick out a bedroom."

"I could've got a tour with Bradley. Does he always hug people like that?"

"You won't be spending much time in the hair salon or the movie theatre, which is Bradley's main focus. And yes, he always hugs people. Why? Does that bother you?"

She hesitated. Too long.

"I'm just not used to it, that's all."

Liar. It did bother her. "Lenny doesn't hug you?"

Lenny was her brother, the two of them bound not by blood but by circumstances. Lenny was also a junkie. As part of the deal with Sky, I'd agreed to pay for him to go into rehab while she was here, and we'd dropped him off at the private hospital before we left London. Which was another reason for my twitchiness. Because who else was an inpatient at the Abbey Clinic? My mother. I'd successfully avoided the bitch for over two decades, and I certainly hadn't wanted to cross paths with her this week of all weeks.

Sky just shrugged. "Sometimes he hugs me. Not much."

We reached the gym. I'd messaged Alex, my ex-

Spetsnaz trainer, before we left the plane, so he was in there waiting for us. I felt a little guilty for palming Sky off onto him right after she arrived, but I didn't have much choice. Bad guys didn't care about my schedule. And Blackwood, the security company I owned with my husband and two others, was in a very different place than it had been when I arrived stateside. Back then, there'd been three of us plus a handful of contractors, and now we had thousands of employees on six continents. Turnover was in the billions. Taking a couple of months off to train Sky myself just wasn't an option.

"Sky, meet Alex. He'll teach you how to fight as well as exhausting you on a daily basis. Alex, this is Sky. Watch out for your nose. She's sneaky."

He leaned down—and I mean *down* because he stood at six feet seven—and peered at my face.

"You should have been faster to block. You have been slacking, *da*?"

I should have known better than to expect sympathy. Alex didn't know the meaning of the word. I turned to Sky.

"Make him sing falsetto, honey. Go for the privates."

"I'll do my best."

See? *That* was why I liked her.

"You get the rest of the day off. Report here at five o'clock tomorrow for your first session."

"Five in the morning?"

"Yes, in the morning. This isn't a part-time gig. You'll do mornings with Alex, and in the afternoons, Carmen's going to teach you to shoot. Evenings are for tradecraft, plus my friend Sofia's gonna tell you all about plants."

"Plants? I'm meant to be training as a special ops whatever, not a bloody gardener."

"I'm well aware of that. You'll work with Black or me when we're available, and if we're not here, someone else will fill in. After a month, we'll change the evening and afternoon sessions so you work on languages and other skills. But you'd better get used to Alex's ugly mug because you'll be seeing a lot of him."

"What about weekends?"

"This isn't prison. You don't get time off for good behaviour." But I also remembered how frustrated I'd been to have no time whatsoever for fun and relented slightly. "If you perform in line with expectations, we'll schedule an afternoon off each week starting next month."

"That's...that's..."

"I never said this would be easy. If you want to leave, the door's right there. But if you want to be the best, you have to train the hardest. Do you want to be the best?"

She swallowed hard and faced up to Alex. "I'll see you at five." Then to me, "Who's Carmen?"

"Diamond."

I'd been waiting since dawn to hear that voice. Nobody else was in the living room at Riverley, so I flung myself into my husband's arms and got rewarded with a kiss that took my breath away. I didn't care. He could have it all. What was mine was his.

"I missed you," I finally managed to mumble,

balancing on tiptoes because he was only half an inch shorter than Alex.

He pinched his thumb and forefinger together. "I was this far from getting on a plane to London last week."

Because of Alaric. I already knew that. Black had a jealous streak that ran a mile deep, and even though I'd craved his touch, I was glad he'd stayed away. If he'd come, it would have meant he didn't trust me. And trust was everything.

"Me and Alaric are just friends now."

"I know that. But it doesn't mean I have to like it. Where is he, anyway? I thought he was coming back with you."

"He did. He's in the guest house with Ravi and Bethany."

Black raised one dark eyebrow a fraction. "Ravi, I'm familiar with. Who's Bethany?"

"The girl who worked for the dodgy guy that restored *Red After Dark*. After he fired her for asking too many questions, Alaric gave her a job as his PA."

"A pity hire?"

"Maybe. I think he also fancies her, so who knows?"

They'd gotten awful close, awful fast. Was *I* jealous? No, not really. Above all, I wanted Alaric to be happy the way I was with Black. Was Bethany the right girl for him? I had no idea. She seemed nice enough. Kind but nervy. Book-smart but naïve.

"And Sky? Where's she?"

"Asleep. She's not used to jet lag, and she's got an early start tomorrow."

"Which bedroom did she pick?"

"The Egyptian room at my place. The one with

hieroglyphics on the walls and those weird pots in the corner." Handmade by an artist in Luxor, apparently. Bradley had gone to pick them up personally, although I suspected that was just an excuse to hook up with his boyfriend, who happened to be running an archaeological dig out there. "Sky said she wants to see the pyramids someday."

Perhaps I should explain our living arrangements? I mean, how many couples had two houses next to each other? Well, Black had inherited the Riverley estate from his parents, but I'd always found it kind of dark. Gothic. We might have been married for close to sixteen years, but our original drunken wedding had been more of a scheme to help my citizenship application than a declaration of love, at least on my part. And back then, I'd made no bones about the fact I hated the house. So Black had bought me a plot of land next door as a birthday present and helped me to build my dream home. Little Riverley was the sun to Riverley Hall's shadow.

But being Mrs. Black had grown on me, as had the hideous old monstrosity of a mansion, and when Little Riverley had accidentally got blown up a few years ago, I'd moved into Black's house and never quite gotten around to leaving again. Sometimes, we stayed at Little Riverley for a change of scene, and I still kept my horse at the stables there. If Sky wanted to use the place, I was glad—it deserved to be lived in properly again.

Black pressed his hips into me, letting me feel the goods. "So we're alone?"

"Yes, but—"

"Why is there always a 'but'?"

I gave his ass a good squeeze. "More of a rain check.

I have a call with James in half an hour."

"What is this? Catch-up-with-your-exes week? Should I invite Nick over? Xavier? Jed? Luke? Is Gideon in town? How about Sofia?"

Yup, the green-eyed monster had reared its ugly head again.

"Chill, it's just work. Research stuff."

"What kind of research?"

"We think *Red After Dark* was brought to the US by Senator Carnes's assistant. *Former* Senator Carnes. And today, he endorsed—"

"One of his party's opponents. Yes, I know."

The video had been short and sweet, but Carnes had definitely given Devane his wholehearted backing.

"But do you know why?"

"No. Do you?"

"No, and that's why I want to speak to James. I bet he's been asking the same question. Don't you want to hear his take on this?"

"Yes," Black admitted. "If Kyla Devane wins that seat, the ripples will be felt across the whole country."

"Then sit in on the call. I should probably fetch Alaric too since this is his case. Let's get some answers."

Because if anyone could fill in the blanks on a political conundrum, it was the President of the United States.

CHAPTER 3 - ALARIC

"SHALL I MAKE dinner?" Bethany asked. "There's a whole load of food in the fridge. I presume we can use it?"

Alaric couldn't remember the last time a woman had cooked for him. Probably a decade ago at least. Emmy burned everything, and his parents ate out practically every night. That wasn't to say he'd always had to fend for himself—Judd was a budding chef, so he cooked if they were in London, and if Naz wasn't on yet another fad diet, he wasn't bad in the kitchen either. Ravi's cooking skills were on a par with Alaric's—neither of them would starve, but if they wanted to impress a date, they took him or her to a restaurant.

"Dinner would be great. But if you're tired, Emmy has a housekeeper, and she always leaves ready-made meals in the main kitchen."

With the amount of food on hand at Riverley, Alaric had never been able to work out how Emmy wasn't the size of a rhino. Certainly he'd put on weight every time he spent a few nights there.

"I'm tired, but I don't think I could sleep right now," Beth said. "Does that sound weird?"

"It's not every day you change your life completely. Your body's still adjusting."

And Ravi was dealing with jet lag too. He'd gone to

take a nap because in the morning, he'd be travelling to the Hamptons to snoop around a media mogul's mansion. Life at Sirius didn't stop just because Alaric decided to take off on a personal crusade.

"I guess. Any requests for dinner? I'd better get started."

"Don't rush. I have a conference call later and some research to do first, but I can eat afterwards if need be."

"Should I come and take notes for you or anything?"

"That's not necessary. Someone'll record the call. And it's not until ten o'clock."

"Ten tonight? Who's still working that late? Or is it a time zone thing?"

"The call's with James Harrison, and according to his public schedule, he's been busy all day. So I imagine he's fitting us in before he goes to bed."

"Oh, okay... Wait. You don't mean *the* James Harrison?"

"The president? Yes. If anyone can shed light on the situation with Senator Carnes, it's him."

"But...but... Are you joking?"

Beth was cute when she got flustered. Maybe Alaric *should* invite her along to take notes.

"No, I'm not joking. He's just a politician. I thought you'd be used to hanging around with that type of person. Doesn't your father run in those circles?"

"Yes, but his friends are crusty old MPs, not hot... uh..." Now her cheeks turned bright red. "Uh, the President of the United States is kind of a big deal. I don't understand how you'd even get a call with him. Er, no offence, I just meant... I'll stop talking now."

Alaric couldn't help laughing. "Emmy's husband

went to school with him."

And Alaric was ninety-five percent certain that Emmy used to fuck Harrison too, though she'd never openly come out and said so. But Alaric had seen how Harrison looked at her, and also the way Black glared at Harrison with open hostility whenever he caught him doing so. It was remarkably similar to the scowls the man shot at Alaric.

"Really? It's nice they've kept in touch." Beth spoke with a touch of wistfulness. "Have you spoken to President Harrison before?"

"A handful of times, but only once since he became president."

And that had been under awkward circumstances. When Alaric had heard that an unidentified female had been quarantined in the aftermath of a biological terror attack, Naz had ferreted out the details, and Alaric had known right away there was only one woman clever enough and crazy enough to get into that situation. Emmy. Breaking into the facility where she was being held had been his first step back into the light as well as a challenge to himself. Was his undercover game as good as it used to be? Could he still sneak into a heavily guarded military base? It turned out the answer was yes, but he hadn't realised Harrison would be there until he found himself facing off against a dozen Secret Service agents. It probably hadn't helped when he'd put two fingers to Harrison's temple and told him his security was fucked, but adrenaline had a lot to answer for, and hey, he'd lived to tell the tale.

That day, Harrison had looked like shit, clearly worried about Emmy. Black hadn't been in much better shape. It would be interesting to see the two men together again, to find out whether the dynamic between them had changed. In the old days when Harrison was a mere senator, Black had held all the power. Would he make any concessions to the president? Harrison still jumped when Emmy clicked her fingers. Alaric had glimpsed the message she'd sent him on the plane earlier—*Devane - WTF???*—and this late-night phone call was no doubt the result.

"Well, er, wow. Good luck. Is that the right thing to say? I'll make something you can reheat whenever you're ready."

Beth could act smooth and polished when she put her mind to it, but Alaric liked how she was so openly awkward in private. There was no second-guessing with her. She wore her heart on her sleeve, or at least, what was left of it after her prick of an ex-husband had done his worst. Alaric had messed up too when they first met—they'd gotten too close, too fast, and he'd taken a hasty step backwards before he ruined her. With his reputation still in tatters and his wanderlust unsated, he was in no position to consider a relationship. And Beth was too fragile for a fling.

That didn't stop Alaric from feeling like a shit for sleeping with Ravi two nights ago, though.

He blocked the memories out as he bent to kiss Beth on the cheek. "Anything you'd care to cook will be superb."

This wasn't a regular presidential phone call. Emmy, Black, and Alaric clustered around a tablet in a conference room at Riverley while Harrison was on a couch in what looked like his personal study, the space devoid of the usual hangers-on who sat in on his calls. Was anyone else listening from the situation room? Black got straight to the point.

"Is this a private call?"

"Does it look as if I'm on official business?"

Not in jeans and a faded Def Leppard T-shirt, no. Alaric noted that Harrison sidestepped the actual question, but Black seemed satisfied with the answer.

"You remember Alaric McLain?"

Harrison gave him a tight smile, a day's worth of light-brown stubble speckling his jaw. "How could I forget? You'll be pleased to hear the Secret Service has tightened up its procedures."

Good news for the country, bad news if Alaric wanted to bypass security again. "Excellent."

"And I never did thank you personally for the information about Likho."

Ah, yes. The supervirus Emmy had tangled with. The dirt had come from Naz, who was a treasure trove of secrets. When he quit his job at SVR—Russia's foreign intelligence service—he'd walked away with more than a stapler and a "Good Luck" card. The Russian government would still be trying to kill him if he hadn't faked his own death.

"Forget it."

One of Alaric's own sources had heard that the reason the FBI hadn't pursued Alaric to the ends of the earth was because Harrison had whispered in the director's ear. At the behest of Emmy, undoubtedly, but he'd still taken the pressure off. Alaric had owed the man a favour.

"It's late," Black said. "Shall we get on with this?"

Harrison shrugged. "Emmy? Why were you asking about Kyla Devane? Are you looking at her for some reason?"

"We're looking at Irvine Carnes, and Devane's name popped up as an oddity. Why'd he endorse her?"

"Why are you looking at Carnes?"

Emmy jerked a thumb at Alaric. "We're still after those bloody paintings from the Becker Museum raid, and we've got reason to believe Carnes's assistant picked one of them up in London the Wednesday before last. Either he's masquerading as an art thief in his spare time, or he was there on Carnes's behalf."

"Carnes was always a straight shooter. I can't see him getting involved in a robbery."

"You also couldn't see him endorsing Kyla Devane, right? And what would you say if I told you he once tried to buy this particular painting from the museum?"

"Shit."

"Yeah, that's about where we got to. I'm heading to Kentucky tomorrow with Alaric, but I want to get an idea of what we're walking into. Forewarned is forearmed."

"If I could tell you, I would, but quite honestly we're scrambling here. The Devane thing blindsided everyone. But holy shit, we need to keep her out of that seat."

"Why?" Alaric asked. He'd looked Kyla Devane up before the call, but he wanted to hear Harrison's reasoning. "Forgive me, I haven't been following that particular race. Isn't she running as an independent?"

Since Harrison was the country's first independent president, logic said he should be on her side. His victory had come after a vicious, mud-slinging battle between the Republicans and Democrats left the populace jaded, and a clever campaign coupled with people's apparent desire for change had enabled Harrison to slide through and claim the top job. Which was pretty much the path Devane seemed to be following. Oh, and it didn't hurt that both of Harrison's main rivals had been tainted by scandal right before the election. A call girl for one and association with a white supremacist group for the other if Alaric recalled correctly.

"She's unpredictable. Her policies are all over the place, and since the senate's split forty-seven Republicans, forty-eight Democrats, and four independents after Carnes's retirement, there are times when she could be the deciding vote."

"Playing devil's advocate, isn't that a good thing? She claims her wealth will allow her to listen to the people rather than corporate lobbyists."

"That's bullshit. She's not a politician, she's a party girl trading on her family name. Look at her history. Everything Kyla Devane does is to benefit Kyla Devane, nobody else, and she doesn't understand that if she's making decisions on a national scale, millions of real people are going to be impacted. Hell, she promised to hold Twitter surveys to help her decide how to vote."

"Or perhaps she does understand the impact of her decisions," Black suggested. "When her grandfather held that seat, he voted against the minimum wage, against the equality act, against tax breaks for lower earners. Yet he pushed forward legislation that reduced estate tax and increased the lifetime exemption." Black's lips flickered in a poor imitation of a smile. "I should have sent him a crate of champagne. The asshole saved me a fucking fortune." He quickly turned serious again. "But no matter. Kyla claims she's running in his memory, doesn't she?"

"Yes," Harrison agreed.

"And since she personally benefited from her grandfather's decisions, it stands to reason that she understands the influence she'd wield."

"That's worse than the alternative."

"It is. And she's not as clueless as you think. Power-hungry, yes. Narcissistic, yes. Devoid of empathy, yes. But not stupid."

James sighed long and hard and reached for a glass of wine. "She's running a smart campaign. Where her policies are unpalatable, she's using her gender to appeal to women and her looks to appeal to men."

Emmy burst out laughing. "Dude, look in the mirror. Do you have any idea how many women decided to vote for you after those shirtless pictures got splashed across the tabloids?"

"Why do you think I went surfing the weekend before the election? I froze my damn nuts off."

Another smirk from Black. "Which was why I advised you not to wear Speedos."

Why didn't it surprise Alaric to find out Black had been involved in that plan? Running a presidential campaign cost a fortune, and although Harrison had a lot of grassroots support, Alaric suspected some of Black's estate tax savings had also been funnelled in his old friend's direction. The men might have fought over Emmy, but they still shared certain goals. And Black understood the nuances of power better than anybody.

"Can we stay on topic?" Emmy asked. "I don't need to think about Speedos or shrivelled nuts tonight.

Irvine Carnes?"

"We spoke most weeks," James said. "He was Ranking Member on the Foreign Relations Committee, and I valued his advice. But he's sick. Cancer. That's why he stepped down. I wonder whether medication could be impairing his judgement, because I don't have any other explanation for why he's backing Devane over Biggs. I also hear he's made a number of poor investment decisions lately."

"What kind of cancer? Not a brain tumour?"

"It started in his lungs, but it's spreading. They caught it late. He thought it was bronchitis and put off going to the hospital, then *boom*. I doubt he has long left. When you ask about this painting, tread carefully. Whatever misjudgements Carnes might have made recently, he's still served this country well for over three decades."

Could things get any more complicated?

"I'll be polite," Emmy said, and James groaned. "Okay, maybe I'll let Alaric do the talking," she conceded.

Gee, thanks.

"I think that would be best. And I know I shouldn't ask, but if there's anything you can dig up on Devane..."

"I'll take my spade."

"Always comes in handy for burying the bodies," Black muttered.

James reached forward. "I didn't hear that. I'm going now."

The screen went dark.

CHAPTER 4 - EMMY

"WE'RE NOT TAKING the Corvette?" Daniela di Grassi dumped her bag next to my brand-new Range Rover and made a face. "What sort of a road trip is this?"

Originally, Dan had booked this week off to go on vacation with her family, but then Ethan, her significant other, got asked to produce a charity single to raise money for a recent earthquake in Haiti, and he didn't want to say no. And Caleb, their son, had been more excited about hanging out at the studio with a bunch of pop-star-rock-stars than taking a jaunt to Italy anyway, so they'd postponed the trip until summer. Caleb's principal would be happy—she hated when Dan snuck him out of school, never mind that seeing the world was more of an education than doing projects on the life cycle of woodlice or whatever he was working on this week.

And me? I was happy too. Dan had been one of my best friends for over a decade, and with so much going on in our lives, we didn't see enough of each other anymore. An adventure in Kentucky was just what the doctor ordered. Actually, I might need a whole hospital since Dan had offered to share the driving.

"No, we're not taking the Corvette. Firstly, I can't fit all my guns in the trunk, and secondly, if you're taking a turn behind the wheel, this is the vehicle I want to crash in."

"O ye of little faith."

"How many times have you crashed this year?"

She counted on her fingers. "Four? Five? Does the fox count? It ran right out in front of me."

"You needed a new bumper. Yes, it counts."

"Well, how many speeding tickets has Mack disappeared for you?"

Mackenzie Cain was another of my besties as well as being Blackwood's best hacker.

"Uh, two."

"Really? This year? That seems low."

"This month," I admitted. "Put your stuff in the car, Dan."

We'd considered taking the jet, but the helicopter was being serviced—first-world problems—so we'd have had to drive to the airfield anyway. And then we'd have needed a rental car to get around at the other end, and I wouldn't have had an excuse to road-test my shiny new toy. Kentucky really wasn't *that* far.

Bradley bounded through the back door, hauling my suitcase along behind him. "Everything's packed. Did you eat breakfast yet?"

Not quite everything—I hadn't paid a visit to the basement armoury yet. But Bradley had sorted out the boring stuff at least.

"I had coffee."

"You can't survive on coffee. Mrs. Fairfax made banana muffins, and they're a-ma-zing."

Mrs. Fairfax was my housekeeper, and yes, she was an awesome cook. But banana muffins sounded all too healthy. I'd planned to stop for a McDonald's breakfast en route, but then Toby, my nutritionist, materialised behind Bradley with a paper carrier bag.

"You get muffins *and* fruit salad, plus sandwiches for lunch. I wouldn't want you to starve on the way."

His tone said he knew exactly what I'd been planning. The dude was psychic. Last time I'd stopped for a cheeky cheeseburger on the way home, I'd paid cash and thrown the wrapper in a rubbish bin on the outskirts of Richmond, but somehow, he still knew what I'd done.

"Super, thanks."

Alaric was borrowing one of Blackwood's Ford Explorers for the journey, and now Bethany appeared with a single hold-all. Had she finally learned how to pack light?

"You guys ready to go?" I asked.

"Alaric's on a call, but he said he wouldn't be long."

Yeah, right. Alaric could talk for England *and* America when he got going. *Folks, this could take a while.* At least it gave me plenty of time to select my hardware, and I could probably fit in some shooting practice too.

"How's Gemma? Have you spoken to her?"

Gemma was the girl we'd helped out of a difficult situation earlier in the week. Bethany hadn't been keen to leave her alone in England, but Gemma had insisted she'd be fine. I wasn't entirely convinced—nobody recovered from what she'd been through overnight— but I had to look at the bigger picture. Gemma still worked at the gallery Bethany had been fired from, the same gallery that had handled *Red After Dark* and at least two other stolen paintings that we knew of. If our efforts in Kentucky failed, we'd have to try another tack, and having somebody on the inside who we could leverage wasn't a bad idea. Plus she could retrieve the bugs me and Alaric had planted a couple of weeks ago.

I'd asked Roxy, an acquaintance in London, to check in on Gemma regularly, and Alaric's buddy Judd had promised to keep an eye on her too. I'd walked in on the tail end of the conversation between the two of them, which was more of a warning on Alaric's part—*an eye, not hands, you asshole; Gemma's fragile*—and if Judd didn't do anything stupid, she'd be okay. Hopefully.

"I called her last night and offered the use of my flat if she doesn't want to go home straight away, and Judd's insisting on driving her to work tomorrow morning so she doesn't have to brave the Tube. He seems nice, doesn't he?"

Bethany hadn't seen Judd shoot a man between the eyes without flinching.

"Yeah, he seems nice." I shoved Toby's offerings into the back seat of the Range Rover—out of sight, out of mind. "Tell Alaric to get a move on, would you?"

Closure. I just wanted closure. To find *Red*, find *Emerald*, slam the door on that chapter of my past, and move on. I owed Alaric, but I didn't want to spend the rest of my days repaying the debt.

Down in the basement of Riverley Hall, I found the door to the weapons' locker ajar. The room was a terrorist's wet dream, and if the cops ever got a look inside, we'd probably all be arrested. Fortunately, the entrance was well-hidden.

Black was lurking at the back near a stack of Russian-made RPG launchers. We'd come across a whole bunch of goodies on a trip to Siberia a while back, and some of the stash might have made its way home with us. Not the nuke, though. We'd handed that over to the authorities. Ain't nobody wants to sleep on top of that shit.

"I've packed your electronics."

My husband waved at a black plastic case that looked more like carry-on luggage than a spy kit. I flipped back the lid and took an inventory. It wasn't that I didn't trust him—if I needed it, it would be there —but more that he'd spent nearly two decades drilling the importance of checking my own equipment into me. Cameras, burner phones, night-vision goggles, a nifty little device the size of a cigarette lighter that could download the entire contents of a smartphone in less than a minute...

"How many people are you expecting me to bug? We're trying to retrieve a painting, not discover state secrets."

"Yes, about that..."

Uh-oh. I knew that tone. I hated that tone.

"I'm just gonna back away slowly."

"Kyla Devane."

Shit.

I'd thought it was odd Black hadn't tried to stop me from going to Kentucky with Alaric. Arranged a meeting or a training exercise or a last-minute assassination, that sort of thing.

"She can't be allowed to win this election," he continued. "This government's got too much left to do to risk having progress derailed by some crank and her self-serving agenda."

"And by government, you mean James?"

Black just smiled. That didn't surprise me—he'd invested a considerable amount in James's campaign, and he wanted to get his money's worth.

"Businessman first, friend second?"

"Husband first, patriot second. Friendship and business come lower down the list. James needs to finish what he started, which means fixing what the last asshole broke, then winning a second term. America can't afford another four years of political infighting, which means he needs a clear path to do his job without being blocked by a woman more interested in sound bites and photo ops than global stability and a healthy economy."

Quite the little speech from a man as economical with his words as politicians were with the truth. But no matter how much I wanted a quick, no-nonsense trip to Kentucky, I couldn't pretend he was wrong.

"I'll take a look into what's going on."

"Give me a few days to get my current project sorted out, and I'll lend a hand if you need it."

Alaric and Black both in Kentucky? Brilliant.

"I'll keep you updated. Nate's already started researching Devane and Carnes." Nate was one of our business partners. "Check your messages."

Black handed me a suppressed Smith & Wesson . 22. "Don't forget this."

I took my previous "shit" and raised it to a "fuck." If Black wanted me to take that weapon, it meant wetwork was on the cards, and I wouldn't get much sleep until the job was over. So much for a fun road trip.

CHAPTER 5 - ALARIC

"THERE HE IS," Emmy murmured. "Smile, honey."

She raised a camera, and Alaric plastered on a cheesy grin and mugged for the lens. It could have been any old tourist photo in small-town Kentucky, but this one just happened to catch Stéphane Hegler as he paused to stub out a cigarette. A moment later, the man darted into a café.

Thankfully, all four members of the crew had made it to Kentucky in one piece. The trip wasn't so much of a problem in the drama-free tranquility of the Ford Explorer—Beth and Alaric had agreed on a radio station, shared the driving, and stopped twice for snacks on the way. The dream team of Emmy and Dan? Alaric's vehicle had passed the Range Rover fifty miles out of Richmond, pulled over at the side of the road in front of a state trooper. Two hours after that, following a brief period with no phone signal, he'd picked up a garbled voicemail from Dan. Apparently, she'd hit a guy, his dog was injured, and they were going to the veterinarian. Beth had gasped at the thought of a hurt animal, and Alaric had nearly bitten through his bottom lip as he watched her tearing up in the passenger seat.

He wanted to hit the brakes and give her a hug, but he didn't dare. Fucking Dan.

And then things got worse.

Somehow—*somehow*—the pair of crazies beat Beth and him to Kentucky, and the true horror of the situation became clear. Miracle of miracles, Dan hadn't had yet another fender bender. No, she and Emmy had stopped for their junk food fix at some diner in the middle of nowhere, and there they'd seen ol' Joe Bob booting his mangy old mutt across the parking lot. Emmy, of course, had asked him to stop, and when he gave her a mouthful in return, Dan had punched him in the face while Emmy slashed the tyres on his pickup. Then they'd stolen the damn dog and driven it to Lexington for a check-up. And now? Now Beth was feeding the skinny pooch cocktail sausages in their rented house while Alaric and Emmy tracked Irvine Carnes's assistant.

"Coffee?" Alaric asked after Emmy finished taking pictures.

He'd deal with Fido later. Right now, there were more important things to worry about.

"We've known each other for fourteen years, and you still feel the need to ask that question?"

Fair point. An old-fashioned bell jingled as he held the door to the café open for her, although the rest of the decor looked reasonably modern. A dozen tables were scattered haphazardly in a space large enough for twice that number—good if you wanted a private conversation, not so great if you wanted to listen in on somebody else's. Hegler ordered a chai latte and took a seat beside the window, paying more attention to his phone than the surroundings.

Alaric had learned his lesson. "One light coffee, one black coffee, and a chocolate muffin for the lady."

Emmy nodded approvingly. Some girls liked diamonds and pearls. She preferred caffeine and carbs.

They left a table between themselves and Hegler, keeping his back to them. He was a small man, dapper, dressed in a suit and tie even on Sunday in a town where the uniform seemed to be denim and plaid. Nobody gave him a second glance, which suggested he was a regular patron.

Emmy's camera hooked up wirelessly to her phone, and Alaric kept up a mostly one-sided conversation about local attractions while she sent the photo of Hegler to Richmond. Five minutes later, they had their answer.

"Sky says it's the same guy she saw collect the painting in London."

A finger of tension uncurled in Alaric's gut. They'd been almost certain this particular Stéphane Hegler was their man, but until that moment, there'd been a modicum of doubt. With Sky's confirmation, they could move on to phase two—interrogation.

"Good. That's good. How do we want to play this?" he asked, almost to himself.

"Hegler's most likely just a pawn. We need to scare him a little, but I'd vote against steaming in there with all guns blazing."

"Agreed. Go in too soft, and we risk them moving the painting again, but you catch more flies with honey."

As an FBI agent, Alaric had been expected to cultivate his own sources. In every interview he did, he'd wanted the subject to feel comfortable but just the tiniest bit intimidated at the start, and if he played his cards right, by the end of the chat, they'd *want* to help him. He employed the same philosophy with Sirius. Today's witness or even a suspect could become tomorrow's informant.

"If they've got the painting, then ten to one it's at Carnes's place," Emmy said. "He's coveted it for years, right? So he'll want to look at it, not hide it away in a vault somewhere, especially if he's on his last legs."

She was right. And back in the old days, it would've been easy to get answers. People tended to respect the FBI. Show a shiny gold badge, and... Hmm...

"Did Bradley pack you a pantsuit?"

"Knowing Bradley, he packed me everything from a bikini to a ballgown. Why? What are you thinking?"

"I still have my FBI shield."

In between defending his name and fleeing the country, Alaric had omitted to hand it back. They also had guns and a Ford Explorer. Of course, most agents didn't actually drive black SUVs, but thanks to the movies, the public thought they did.

"Oh, cool. I have a shield too."

"A fake one?"

"No, it's real."

"Where the hell did you get that?"

"I found it."

"Found it where?"

Emmy grinned behind her chocolate muffin. "In an FBI agent's pocket."

Alaric took a steadying breath. This was the Emmy who'd driven him crazy in both good ways and bad ways.

"You realise how wrong that is?"

"Stop being so pious, dude. You were the one who just suggested impersonating FBI agents. Oh, target's on the move." Emmy spread a tourist brochure out on the table and raised her voice slightly. "Hey, look, there's a candy factory we can visit. They make bourbon balls—chocolate mixed with whisky. Someone should try that with gin."

Hegler swallowed the last dregs of his coffee and stood, still engrossed in his phone as he headed for the door. What was so important? Was he running all of Irvine's communications? As he reached for the door handle, the screen tilted up and Alaric saw a telltale collection of coloured dots. Candy Crush. Rune had tried playing it last summer when a bunch of her school friends set up a league, but after a day or so, she'd gone back to reading science journals instead.

Emmy and Alaric didn't need to follow. They had Hegler's address—he both lived and worked at the Carnes property—and when he'd stopped at the gas station earlier, Emmy had stuck a tracker on his car. A good thing too. No way would Emmy have abandoned half a chocolate muffin in favour of a surveillance op.

Mid-morning on Monday, and Emmy slipped on a pair of aviators despite the cloudy sky. If the need arose, she'd play bad cop to Alaric's Agent Nice-Guy.

Fifty yards along the street, Stéphane Hegler strolled out of the pharmacy carrying the mother of all carrier bags. Prescription drugs? What state was Irvine Carnes in? Little information had leaked out about his condition in recent weeks. Somebody—Hegler?—was still posting to his Twitter account, but apart from a link to Friday's bombshell video, he'd been sticking to retweets of local news and the occasional arty photo of the Kentucky countryside. Seemed Carnes bred Arabian horses in his spare time. He certainly had plenty of space on the family ranch.

The origin of the video itself was hazy—several journalists had broken the story simultaneously, but all refused to reveal their sources. Rumour said they'd received flash drives in the mail. Who had sent them?

Alaric had stationed himself between Hegler and his car, and as the smaller man approached, he fell into step beside him.

"Mr. Hegler? Do you have a moment?"

Hegler didn't break stride.

"Who are you?" Did the supercilious attitude come with the job, or had he been born with it? His accent didn't help. There was a hint of French under the American, the remnant of a childhood spent in Switzerland.

Alaric pushed his suit jacket back just far enough to reveal the gold badge clipped to his belt. "FBI. I'm Special Agent Alec Lane with the Louisville field office, and this is—"

The guy stopped dead in his tracks. *Dead.* Emmy nearly walked into the back of Alaric, and her hand landed on his ass as she steadied herself. Perk of the job.

"It's about the painting, isn't it? I swear I didn't know what it was when I picked it up. I mean, yes, I knew it was *a* painting, but not *that* painting. I thought it was a portrait of Azira."

Well, this was unexpected. Alaric had never had a suspect confess to the crime in his opening sentence.

"How about we get a coffee? The street isn't really

the place for this conversation."

"Are you going to arrest me?"

"At the moment, I'm more interested in hearing your side of the story." Alaric motioned Stéphane towards a café. Not the one they'd been in yesterday, but a smaller joint farther up the street. "Who's Azira?"

Hegler's knuckles were white where he clutched the pharmacy bag, and the moment they sat at a table in the back corner, he dropped it and started picking at his cuticles. Charming.

"Ellen, would you mind getting the drinks?" Alaric asked Emmy. She nodded once and headed for the counter, pushing her sunglasses up on top of her head.

This place was as delightful as the other one. The table was stained, dust had settled on the faded prints that adorned the walls, and the faint smell of shit drifted from the nearby bathroom. Still, Hegler seemed cooperative. That was the most important thing.

"So, Azira?"

"She's Irvine's—Senator Carnes's—favourite mare. He's owned her for almost two decades, so of course she's getting on in years herself, but even last week, he still insisted on going out to groom her every morning. He told me he'd commissioned a painting of her, oil on canvas, and all I needed to do was pick it up from the artist."

"But you didn't pick it up from the artist. You collected it from an empty hotel room. Didn't that strike you as odd?"

The last hint of colour faded from Hegler's already pale cheeks as he ran a hand through short brown hair, leaving it ruffled.

"Y-y-you know about that?"

"Perhaps you could tell me what happened?"

"I don't... I can't..."

"Just start at the beginning."

"Will we go to jail?"

"Honestly? That's above my pay grade. But it'll depend on the exact circumstances, who knew what and when, and whether there are any mitigating factors."

"Cross my heart, I didn't have any idea what was in that package, not at first."

"From the top?"

Hegler took a couple of steadying breaths. He was either the world's worst criminal or the world's best liar. The jury was still out, but Alaric was leaning towards the former.

"I really don't know much. Just that Irvine asked me to fly to England to collect a package. Like I said, I thought I'd be meeting the artist, but when I got to the hotel, the concierge told me he'd had to depart early to deal with a family matter."

"So how did you get the painting?"

"He'd left the package in his room. The concierge gave me the key. It was all a bit chaotic. A lady guest was upset because there was a rather large spider in her bathroom, and the concierge had to dash off in a hurry."

Which was probably why Alaric hadn't seen the man when he arrived soon afterwards. "Did you pass anyone on your way upstairs?"

"Not a soul. At least, I don't think so. I wasn't really paying attention. I guess there might have been a maid."

Bad criminal, terrible eyewitness.

"Was there anything in the room apart from the painting?"

"Not that I saw. I mean, I didn't even see the painting. It was in a suitcase. The note said to take the case with the compliments of Massimo Slade."

Alaric didn't need to ask who Massimo Slade was. Slade's oil paintings sold for thousands, and a commission would have set Carnes back six figures if he'd genuinely wanted a picture of his horse.

"So you took the case and then you left?"

"Yes, for the airport."

"Did you open the case first?"

"Why would I? I assumed it was a simple errand."

Surely anyone with half a brain would have questioned that scenario? Or maybe Alaric had just spent so long swimming with the bottom feeders that anything out of the ordinary made him suspicious.

"Why did you take the back stairs?"

Hegler visibly started. "How do you know that?"

"I'm afraid I'm not at liberty to reveal sources."

Emmy came back with three black coffees plus sachets of sugar and powdered creamer. She never touched either. It had always puzzled Alaric how someone with such a sweet tooth drank her coffee straight.

"Here you go. Where are we?" She'd gone with a local accent today.

"Mr. Hegler was just filling us in on his stay in London. The back stairs?"

"Right, yes. I needed a cigarette, and it was the fastest way out. I've been trying to give up for months. The gum stopped working, so I tried the patches, but I missed holding something, you know? And now I think

I'm addicted to the patches too."

"Just go cold turkey," Emmy said. "It's the only way."

"You've given up?"

"Seventeen years ago."

"Wow, congrats." Hegler seemed to realise who he was talking to. "Sorry."

"What happened after you got your nicotine fix?" Alaric asked.

"I drove to the airport and handed my rental car back, then the limo service picked me up and took me to Irvine's friend's plane. That was when Irvine had me look at the painting. And I freaked! It wasn't a horse at all; it was a woman. And I thought Irvine would want me to go right back to the hotel, but he just told me to send him a photograph, and once he'd seen it, he instructed me to come straight home."

"Did you realise at that point the painting was stolen property?"

"No! I mean, I thought it was kind of odd, him paying for a horse and getting a girl, but he wasn't mad, so..."

"So you simply did as you were told?"

"Exactly."

"And when did you recognise the painting?"

"*I* didn't. Harry did."

"And who's Harry?"

"Harriet Carnes. Irvine's daughter. I helped Irvine to hang the painting on his bedroom wall, and then Harry walked in and hit the roof when she saw it. Started yelling at him, and Harry *never* yells. And then Irvine...his face went all weird. Sort of droopy on one side, and he couldn't speak properly."

Ah, shit. Alaric glanced at Emmy, and her long exhale said she understood what had happened too.

"The senator had a stroke?" he asked.

Hegler bobbed his head. "His nurse called the ambulance right away, but..." Hegler shook his head. "He was sick already, and now..."

"Cancer?"

"How did you know? Oh, right. You can't tell me."

"Sorry."

Hegler took out a navy-blue handkerchief and dabbed at his eyes. "Before that afternoon, Irvine had occasional periods of confusion, but now he's disoriented most of the time. And he talks to the woman in the painting. Dominique, he calls her. They kept him in the hospital for four days, but every time he had a lucid moment, he insisted he wanted to come home. Harry arranged for nurses to visit, but even so..." Hegler gave a loud sniffle. "Irvine can be a grump sometimes, but he's become like family to me."

"I'm sorry for..." Alaric almost said "your loss," but the old coot was still alive. "I'm sorry for intruding at this time, but that painting has to go back to its rightful owners. And we'll need to speak with Harriet."

"I understand." Hegler took a sip of his drink and grimaced. "The coffee's awful here. You should try the place along the street. Or I can make you a fresh cup back at the ranch. Harry has a wonderful coffee machine. She says that if she's got to get up at five a.m. to see to the horses, she needs caffeine pumping through her veins."

"A woman after my own heart," Emmy said. She'd taken one sip from her mug and left the rest, so it must have been truly terrible. "Ready to go?"

"Now?"

"No time like the present."

As Emmy led the way out of the café, a bud of hope swelled in Alaric's chest. They were so close to *Red*, he could practically smell the paint. This time, they wouldn't let her go.

CHAPTER 6 - ALARIC

"HARRY? THESE FOLKS are from the FBI."

Harriet Carnes was younger than Alaric had expected. The senator had turned seventy-one last November, but his daughter didn't look more than twenty-five. The family resemblance was clear, though. They shared the same sharp jaw, the same assessing blue eyes, and although the senator's hair was more salt than pepper now, it had been the same glossy mahogany as Harriet's when he was younger. And while Harriet might have been small in stature, it appeared she'd inherited her father's imperious attitude. Chin high, arms folded, that haughty expression... Yes, Harriet was definitely a Carnes.

"Do you have a warrant?"

"We were hoping to have an informal chat. Do we need a warrant?"

She raised an eyebrow at Stéphane, just the faintest quirk. He nodded.

"Yes, the painting. I couldn't lie."

Harriet sighed and dismounted her high horse with a little more grace than Hegler. "I thought you'd come, but I didn't realise it would be so soon." The tremble in her voice betrayed her polished act. "Daddy's going to be... He'll be..."

"Be what?" Alaric prompted.

"Devastated. He'll be *devastated*. I don't suppose you'll believe me, but that's the only reason the painting's still here."

"It's true," Hegler put in. "Harry was going to send it back to the museum when...when..." The colour drained from his cheeks as he realised what he was about to say. "Oh, darn it."

He leapt forward with a handkerchief as a single tear rolled down Harriet's cheek, but she waved him away and used a sleeve instead, tucking her shoulder-length hair behind her ears before she straightened and faced up to Alaric.

"My father's dying, Mr.... I didn't get your name."

"Call me Alec."

"Alec. My father's sick. He might last a week, he might last a month, but he doesn't have long."

"I'm sorry to hear that."

Words were inadequate.

"Daddy...he's never been the easiest man to live with, but in recent months, he's become even more difficult. Unpredictable, but in his lucid moments, still sharp. He waited until I was out of town before he sent Stéphane to pick up Dominique."

The same name Hegler had mentioned. "Why do you call her Dominique?"

"Because that's her name. The woman in the painting."

"I didn't realise anybody knew who she was."

Though many people asked, the artist had never revealed his muse's identity. The enigmatic redhead walking through the forest, half-turned as she invited all who saw her to follow, had remained a mystery to the art world.

"Few people did. My mother forbade anyone from talking about her. The affair happened when I was very young, but our old housekeeper filled me in on the details, God rest her soul."

"So who *was* Dominique?"

"Daddy's mistress. The only woman he ever truly loved, I suspect." Harriet suddenly turned away. "This is wrong. All wrong. None of this should have happened."

Hegler steered her towards the table at the far end of the kitchen. The thing was huge, at least twelve feet long, made from what looked like rough-hewn oak worn smooth with age. The kitchen didn't really fit with the rest of the house—it was homey, lived-in, while the other rooms Alaric had glimpsed as they followed Hegler through a maze of hallways could have come from a magazine spread.

Country homes of the rich and famous.

The paddocks out front fit with the model-home theme too. Lush grass manicured to within an inch of its life, white post-and-rail fencing, a couple of horses grazing for show. But from the kitchen window, Alaric spotted a beat-up old jeep with a dent in the side, and the pastures in the distance didn't look quite so green. A life of two halves?

He'd compare notes with Dan later. She was around. *Somewhere.* Emmy had tasked her with watching the comings and goings from Lone Oak Farm in case a misstep alerted the Carnes family to Alaric and Emmy's intentions and they tried to move the painting. It didn't seem as if that would happen, though, judging by Harriet's demeanour. She looked more defeated than anything else as she took a seat.

Rather than joining the others, Emmy headed for the massive stove and picked up the kettle. She'd spent most of the drive over reading emails, and Alaric hadn't been entirely convinced she was listening when he talked through the playbook—namely that he'd lead the conversation—but drinks were a good idea. Sharing a cup of tea or coffee built rapport.

"Why do you say it's all wrong?" Alaric asked once Harriet seemed slightly more...well, not composed, exactly, but the threat of tears had receded.

She suddenly sat up straight. "Do I need a lawyer? Does Daddy? He's not in any state to talk to you."

Oh, fuck.

"That's up to you," Emmy said, opening and closing cupboards in search of mugs. "But the powers that be are keen to avoid this becoming a circus, especially with the election coming up. Your father might have retired, but he's still an influential figure."

The change was instantaneous. Harriet Carnes went from nervous to angry in the time it took to thump her fist on the table.

"Of course, the damned election. We couldn't possibly cause an upset, could we? Why do you think Dominique's here in the first place?"

Emmy found cups rather than mugs and set them onto saucers. One, two, three, four. Stéphane looked as though he needed bourbon in his. He came across as a man who didn't handle stress well. The way he fanned himself with his hand reminded Alaric of Bradley.

"You believe your father got the painting because he stood down?"

"No, not because he stood down." Harriet's voice dripped with bitterness. "Because *she* stood up."

"She?"

"Kyla Devane."

Was Harriet saying what Alaric thought she was saying?

"Are you suggesting Kyla Devane stole the painting?"

"Not personally. But if you think that my father suddenly acquiring his unicorn and Kyla Devane receiving his endorsement aren't linked, you're not much of a detective, are you?"

The kettle started whistling, and Alaric took over while Emmy turned the stove off.

"So you're saying Devane, what, bribed your father with *Red After Dark*?"

"That's exactly what I'm saying."

Alaric tried hard not to groan out loud. The curse had struck again. All he'd wanted was a nice, easy recovery, and now *Red* had landed him right in the middle of a brewing political scandal. This case was just one long Möbius strip of clusterfuckery.

He considered the possibilities. The easy option, the *smart* option, would be to excuse themselves back to the "office" and then have Ravi retrieve the painting later. They knew precisely where it was, and security appeared to be minimal. Or Alaric could call in real FBI agents. If they didn't dither around, they could rescue *Red* before the senator breathed his last. So what was the problem? Well, neither of those alternatives got Alaric any closer to *Emerald*.

Which left option three.

"If that's true, then Devane's committed more than one crime. Handling stolen goods, bribery... President Harrison wants to stamp out corruption in politics, and if you helped to expose—"

Harriet cut Alaric off with a laugh. "You think Kyla got her hands dirty? Of course she didn't. She may be a monster, but she's not dumb."

Emmy slid a cup of tea in front of Harriet, and no surprises, she'd managed to find cookies somewhere.

"You sound as though you're speaking from experience. You've met Kyla?"

"Met her? I went to school with her. Ever seen the movie *Mean Girls*?"

Alaric hadn't, but he could imagine what it was about. Fifty bucks said Emmy hadn't watched it either.

But she nodded. "Kyla was one of them?"

"The queen bee. She always had to be the centre of attention, and if you crossed her, you'd pay. Senators are meant to be public servants. Kyla only serves herself."

"I see."

"Do you? If Kyla wins that senate seat, she'll spend her entire term pushing legislation for her own benefit. Or perhaps for her friends, if she has any left."

Carnes had resigned with almost five years remaining on his term. That gave Devane scope to do plenty of damage, and it wasn't easy to oust a senator once they'd been elected. Like that guy from Vermont who'd won by a handful of votes in a low-turnout year, for example. He'd gone on vacation to California—with a twenty-year-old blonde who wasn't his wife—and spawned a thousand internet memes when he punched a journalist in the face on Rodeo Drive. Still he refused to vacate his seat.

"Nobody commits a crime without a trace," Emmy told Harriet. "If we follow the trail..."

"Oh, please. Kyla swept up afterwards, trust me on that. And even if she did miss a few breadcrumbs, the elections take place in two weeks. I've seen how slowly the FBI moves. Remember that psycho sending letter bombs to politicians nine years ago? Our housekeeper *died*, and you people took nearly a year to catch him."

Hmm... How should they play this? Their FBI badges had opened the door, but now they were stuck in mud on the other side of the threshold. They needed to demonstrate they were on the same wavelength as Harriet. Convince her that they could work fast. The old man had to know something about *Red*'s origins, and if they caught him during one of his lucid periods...

Alaric opened his mouth to speak, but Emmy got in before him.

"Yeah, we're not FBI agents." Shit. What was she playing at? Her American accent had fallen by the wayside too. "We're private investigators."

Hegler spat out his tea. "But you said..."

"Actually, I never did."

He pointed at Alaric. "He has a badge."

"Five bucks on the internet. Pretty convincing, huh? I think they make them in China."

Tea slopped into Harriet's saucer as she pushed back her chair and stood, arms akimbo. "Get out of my house."

Emmy sat down instead, nonchalant as she sipped her tea with one pinky extended. "Let's talk instead."

Alaric put his head in his hands and groaned. Emmy had that devious glint in her eye, and he realised she hadn't mellowed with age, not one bit. This wasn't going to be good.

CHAPTER 7 - ALARIC

"WHY ON EARTH would I want to continue this conversation? You just admitted you've lied to me." Harriet glanced at her watch. "And I have a TV crew due here in half an hour. Somebody has to try and undo the damage my father did."

Emmy dodged the question. "Kyla's a devious bitch, yeah?"

"Didn't I just say that?"

"Tell me, whose chances would you rate against her? The FBI? Or another devious bitch?"

Harriet didn't answer, but she did drop her arms to her sides.

"The way I see it, you're fucked. Rumour says your father's made bad business decision after bad business decision, and now he can't leverage his senate position to borrow more money. How much does this place cost to run? Ten thousand a month? Fifteen? When will the cash run out? If you sell many more horses, you won't have enough breeding stock left for next year."

Oh, shit. Was Emmy right? The pieces all fit, although Alaric would never have put it quite so bluntly.

Hegler's mouth dropped open. "No, that's not right. Tell her, Harry."

Harriet didn't so much sit back down as collapse

into the chair. "I..." She cleared her throat and tried again. "I can't. Stéphane, I'm so sorry. I know I shouldn't have kept this from you, but..."

"How bad is it?" he whispered.

"Daddy borrowed against this place. If I don't find a hundred thousand dollars by the end of June, then the bank wants to foreclose. Until he got sick and I started going through his paperwork, I had no idea. I mean, I should have guessed when he wouldn't replace Julio after he left last year, or Austin, but... I don't know what to do. I've been paying people out of my savings for the last two months, but they're almost gone. And now Kyla's back, trying to ruin my life."

"We'll be homeless?"

"I'm doing my best to prevent that. Or at least to delay things. If Daddy has to leave this place before his time, it'll kill him. He's living in the past now. Every time I go into his room, he's talking to Dominique." She met Emmy's gaze. "Please, I know you have to take the painting back, but is there any way you could wait until...until he's gone?"

They'd broken her. Harriet had gone from strong to sobbing in the space of ten minutes. Dammit, Alaric hated this part of the job. Bringing down people who deserved it was satisfying; ruining a woman trying to hold her family's life together hurt.

"I might have a solution."

Everyone looked at him.

"There's a fifty-thousand-dollar reward on offer from the Becker Museum. When we return *Red*, the cash is yours."

Harriet's glimmer of hope turned to confusion.

"But I don't understand. Why would you give up

your money?"

"Maybe we're just Good Samaritans."

"I don't believe that."

Alaric's turn to sigh. "It's a long story, but *Red After Dark* wasn't the only painting stolen from the museum that day, and it's not the main target of our investigation. Have you heard of *The Girl with the Emerald Ring*?"

Hegler nodded. "When we realised what Irvine had done, we looked up the details of the robbery. *The Girl with the Emerald Ring* was the most valuable painting taken, wasn't it?"

"It was. We've been trying to retrieve her for a number of years, and right now, this is the best lead we've got. Just know that we don't much care about *Red After Dark* or the reward. Our only goal is to get *Emerald* back where she belongs. Help us, and we'll help you."

Harriet's voice rose as nerves got the better of her. "But we know nothing about *The Girl with the Emerald Ring*. My father's never mentioned it, or any of the other paintings."

"No, but whoever gave *Red* to your father might have information, and they must have communicated with him somehow."

"What, and you want to interrogate Daddy? He's gone downhill rapidly since last week. This morning, he didn't even know who *I* was. I very much doubt he'll be able to tell you anything."

"There are other ways. If we can get into his phone.... His emails... Have you ever heard your father mention the School of Shadows?"

"The School of Shadows? What's that? A training

camp for spies or something?"

"It's the name of a group of art thieves," Alaric told them. "Nobody's ever been able to identify the ringleader, but rumour says they've been responsible for some of the biggest heists in the last four decades. Not only *Emerald* and *Red* but a Van Gogh, a Monet, works by Cézanne, Rembrandt, da Vinci... The list goes on."

"I don't recall him ever mentioning any school. Stéphane?"

Hegler shook his head. "It's not a name I remember either."

"My father never confided in me, Alec. Is your name even Alec?"

"Close. It's Alaric. Alaric McLain. And this is Emmy."

"Alaric." Harriet let out a long sigh. Her expression was pained. "I guess I could give you Daddy's phone."

Hegler didn't seem hopeful. "I don't think these people used the phone."

"What do you mean?" Harriet asked the question before Alaric could.

"There was a gentleman who came to the house unexpectedly a week before your father sent me to England. While you were in town. He brought a fruit basket and said he was an aide to Senator Schuman, but why would anyone deliver a gift by hand all the way out here? The more I think about it, the more certain I am that he was the one who started the ball rolling. Irvine was different after he left. Happier. Remember we thought it was the change of medication?"

"Did you call Senator Schuman to check?"

Hegler looked sheepish. "What was done was done.

I didn't see how it would help."

Harriet patted him on the hand, the gesture supportive rather than affectionate. Alaric reconsidered his age estimate. Harriet had to be closer to thirty if she'd gone to school with Kyla Devane.

"You're right. It doesn't matter."

"Actually, it does," Emmy said. "We're trying to track down the people behind this scheme, and one of them was right here. What did the man look like?"

"Uh, older than the average political aide. I guess in his early fifties? Or maybe his late forties? Most of us are worn out by the time we hit thirty. His hair was thinning, though. Probably due to the stress."

"What colour was his hair?" Alaric asked.

"Medium brown."

Alaric glanced at Emmy. Had she had the same thought? Hegler's description fit Dyson, the last man they'd known to be in possession of *Emerald*. Alaric had crossed paths with him eight years ago and only lived to tell the tale thanks to Emmy's shooting skills.

She shrugged. "Could be."

"Could be what?" Harriet asked.

"That description matches a suspect on our list."

"Well, great. You want Stéphane to pick him out of a line-up?"

"Unfortunately, we can't find him. Did anyone notice what vehicle he arrived in?"

"Sorry." Hegler shook his head again. "I don't recall seeing a vehicle at all, which is odd now that I think about it. But I could have missed a car, or possibly he came in a cab? Irvine called me into the sunroom right after the gentleman left, and as I said, he was in better spirits than he had been for weeks. We drank tea together, and Irvine told me the future was brighter. I assumed he meant politically."

"So really, we're no farther forward than we were before." Harriet rose to her feet and moved to the window. A mare and foal had come into view, waiting at the fence, ears pricked. "Dammit, this is their home. This is *our* home. I'll hand the painting back, of course, but even if they give me the reward rather than throwing me in prison, that's still only half of the amount I need to save the ranch."

Alaric got up to join her. "There's another fifty thousand on offer for *Emerald*."

"But I keep telling you, we know nothing about that."

Emmy took another sip of tea. Secretly, Alaric had always been envious of the way she stayed so calm under pressure. It seemed effortless to her, whereas he'd constantly had to fight to maintain a cool facade.

"Let's go through the chain of events again," she said. "A man came to visit the senator. Your belief is at that point, he negotiated an endorsement for Kyla in exchange for a stolen painting. If we apply Occam's razor, that probably isn't a bad assumption. The senator then dispatched Stéphane here to pick up *Red* from London, and at the same time, he released a video praising Devane. And that's where the theory falls apart. Why would the two sides trust each other? What would have stopped the senator from simply picking up the painting and keeping his mouth shut? The other party could hardly go to the police."

Good point. "What if he recorded the speech in advance?"

"A possibility. But if that was the case, then what

incentive did the other side have to deliver *Red*? There's no honour among thieves."

"Dyson always had a reputation for keeping his word until...you know."

And the outcome of that day hadn't been entirely Dyson's fault. One of Alaric's "team" had shot first, and then events just spiralled out of control.

"He's still a bloody criminal."

"Who's Dyson?" Harriet asked.

"Our suspect. Have you got any more cookies? I skipped breakfast."

Hegler headed for the nearest cupboard while Emmy continued.

"So, as I was saying, there had to be a safeguard in place. Stéphane, you mentioned that you called Irvine from the plane?"

"I did. Chocolate chip?"

"Perfect. I bet that your call was the senator's cue to hand over the recording. Do you know when it was filmed?"

"Neither of us heard a thing, did we, Harry? Frankly, I'm amazed he managed to record it at all. Before he got sick, he used to film his own sound bites for Twitter, but I still had to edit out the pauses and the mumbling."

"Daddy always was determined. When he set his mind on something..."

"I've seen the video," Emmy said. "Watched the whole thing half a dozen times last night on a big-screen TV. How long was it? Two minutes? And the quality was on point. That thing was made for broadcast. Even if your father managed to film it on his phone, the file must have been two gigabytes, which meant he couldn't simply email it. He'd have needed to use a file transfer site. Or..."

Alaric saw where she was going with this. "Or our culprit picked it up on a flash drive. You were both away on that day, but someone must have let the visitor in if your father wasn't able to. Who? Maybe they saw a car? Or something else that could help us?"

For the first time, Alaric glimpsed hope in Harriet's eyes. "I can ask. We've still got two ranch hands, and there would have been a nurse here from the agency. But I still don't understand—who are you people, and why would you help if it's not for the money?"

Emmy finished the last of her tea. She'd also managed to hoover up three more cookies in the blink of an eye. "As my friend here said, it's a long story. And not everybody is motivated by money. He wants to return *Emerald* in order to right an old wrong."

"And you? What do you want?" Harriet asked her.

Uh-oh. Alaric knew that smile. He hated that smile. That cold, cunning, malevolent smile.

"Me? I want Kyla Devane back where she belongs. In a spa or on a yacht or gracing some mid-morning chat show, not wandering the halls of the Capitol Building. Help us to bring her down, and when we find *Emerald*, the reward's yours."

"Emmy..." Alaric warned.

"Do we have a deal?"

"I... Well..." Harriet turned goldfish. "Obviously I'll do anything I can to help with the Kyla situation, but we only have a month and...and nine days before the bank forecloses. I don't—"

"Great. We'd better get started, then. Don't you have a TV interview to do?"

"Yes, but—"

"I'll have an associate stop by. Her name's Daniela, and she'll speak to your ranch hands and the nurse. Any idea where I can find Kyla?"

"You're going to talk to her?"

"Know thine enemy."

Ah, shit. Now Emmy was paraphrasing Sun Tzu. *The Art of War* was Black's favourite book, and if he was pulling the strings from behind the scenes, then things had the potential to turn ugly. *Uglier.* Was it too late to go back to Thailand?

"She has an estate near here," Hegler said, ever the helpful one. "It used to belong to her parents before they died, although I hear she remodelled extensively. But I don't think she'll be there right now—all the candidates have a debate this afternoon."

"Where?"

"The new convention centre in Frankfort."

Gee, guess where they'd be heading next? Although it could be interesting. Alaric had never seen Kyla Devane in person, and he was curious to see how she acted when the cameras weren't on her.

"What time?"

"The formalities start at four."

"Then we'd better head over there."

"I think it's ticketed, but I know plenty of people," Hegler said. "You'd better give me your number, and I'll find someone who can get you in."

Access really wouldn't have been a problem, but it was a nice gesture. Alaric handed over a business card and Emmy followed suit. Sirius Consulting and Blackwood Security. In the intelligence field, the two firms were the equivalent of a minnow and a blue whale respectively.

"Thanks." Emmy pocketed Hegler's card in return and turned back to Harriet. "So, what are you planning to say in this interview? Are you going to endorse Biggs?"

"Ugh, no way." She clapped a hand over her mouth, ashamed of her gut reaction. "I mean, no, I'm going to avoid that."

"What's so bad about Biggs?"

"He's been to a few of Daddy's gatherings. At the last one, he followed me out to the barn and propositioned me while his wife was inside with the children. My father might have made mistakes, but I'm fairly certain he never tried to take advantage of a friend's daughter. His only transgression was with Dominique, and my mother drove him to that."

"She was the neediest woman I've ever met," Hegler muttered.

What a family.

"So you'll be voting Democrat, then?" Alaric asked, half joking.

"If I vote at all. Aidan O'Shaughnessy's a centrist, and so am I. Our views aren't a million miles apart, but I can hardly come out and say that, can I? I'll come across as bitter if I back the opposition, and besides, I don't want to upset Daddy."

"Go with your heart," Emmy told her. "You've never considered running for your father's seat? It sounds as though you care."

"Me, run for office? Are you joking? I've seen enough politics to last me a lifetime."

CHAPTER 8 - EMMY

"THERE SHE IS," Alaric murmured. "Kyla Devane."

To give Stéphane his credit, he'd got us decent seats. We were three rows from the front, at eye level with Devane's stilettos as she strode to her podium with a tablet computer. She was wearing a pair of Giuseppe Zanottis if I wasn't mistaken—Bradley had educated me well. Those were thousand-dollar shoes, perhaps not the best choice for an audience made up of mainly blue-collar workers. The five-thousand-seat arena was full of red shirts for Biggs, blue shirts for O'Shaughnessy, and a particularly vocal contingent of yellow-clad supporters for Kyla. Thank goodness I'd worn black. I'd also worn a brown wig, which was itching, and a pair of plastic-framed glasses that could have been borrowed from Clark Kent.

"This is San Pellegrino," Kyla hissed at someone offstage. "I said Evian."

A young blonde dashed forward. An intern? "Ms. Devane, I'm so sorry."

"Just get rid of it. The Italians are *not* our friends right now."

Was she referring to the Italian ambassador trashing her plans for an import tax on Parmesan cheese and prosciutto? And if so, did she realise where her shoes came from?

I spotted Aidan O'Shaughnessy in the wings, sitting on a plastic chair with a laptop balanced on his knees, jacket off and tie loosened. Still tweaking his speech? Tsk tsk tsk. Surely he should have come prepared?

Actually... My phone pinged, and I almost choked on my popcorn. Black had tasked Nate with keeping me updated on Devane-related developments, and it seemed that Harriet had taken my earlier words to heart and backed O'Shaughnessy. I showed the news article to Alaric.

"Whoa. I thought she was gonna hedge her bets?"

"All or nothing, Prince."

And in that case, I'd forgive O'Shaughnessy for the last-minute adjustments. Perhaps he wanted to add something about cross-party support. A small smile played across his lips. Yeah, he'd seen the news.

Biggs, on the other hand, looked tense. He'd claimed the space at the other side of the stage, and every so often, I caught sight of him as he paced. Was that his wife with him? She seemed more concerned with keeping out of his way than with offering support.

The moderator appeared, microphone in hand, and Kyla smoothed the curtain of sleek mahogany hair that hung just past her shoulders. The front had been artfully twisted away from her face and pinned to the side. She'd gone with a navy-blue pantsuit today, which might have come across as conservative without the cleavage-baring top underneath. And was that necklace a real sapphire?

Tap tap tap. Sound check. The two men filed onto the stage and took their places either side of Kyla. Out of the three of them, she looked the most self-assured. Biggs had to be on the back foot after the twin snubs from Harriet and her father.

"Welcome, folks. It's great to see you here at the Jincheng Arena"—yes, Kentucky's newest venue was sponsored by a Chinese beer brand—"for what promises to be a historic debate. With the polls for the senatorial election balanced on a knife-edge, this is your chance to hear from our three candidates. We'll let each of them introduce themselves, and then we'll challenge them with questions on the issues y'all want to hear about. Kyla Devane, would you like to start?"

"Thanks, Marty." Kyla gestured towards the audience. "And thank *you* for coming today. It's wonderful to see so many friends from the place I call home." Cue rabid cheering from the yellow section. "So, why am I here on stage today? Well, there's nothing I love more than my state, my country, and the people who make it great. When I'm elected senator, I'll make real changes to the lives of Kentuckians. My background isn't in politics. I'm not a pencil pusher. Let's do away with all the red tape that stifles business and remove the wasted layers of bureaucracy. Mr. O'Shaughnessy wants to tighten up regulations, and Mr. Biggs... Well, he's a lawyer. What can I say?"

Laughter answered her question, and she carried on, flipping and flopping from point to point, ad-libbing from a speech somebody else obviously wrote. She wanted to increase police numbers but cut costs. Improve medical care yet do away with the rules governing health insurance. Give families more money in their pockets yet abolish the minimum wage. Did she give any specifics on how she might achieve these objectives? No, but she did throw some barbs at her opponents. Biggs's father-in-law was a crook, apparently, and O'Shaughnessy once punched a man in a college bar brawl, which clearly meant he was a violent thug. Good grief. Didn't everyone get into bar brawls? Oh. Just me? Okay then. Anyhow, Kyla was nasty. Even Biggs looked uncomfortable when she laid into O'Shaughnessy.

I tuned out during Biggs's spiel. Man, I hated politics. Even when I'd been screwing around with James, I'd avoided listening to his speeches. He used to practise them in front of the mirror, then ask me what I thought, and I'd thank my lucky stars Black had taught me to lie so well. How was Dan getting on? Her email update said she'd interviewed the ranch hands, and neither of them remembered anything useful. The agency was trying to get ahold of the nurse who'd been on duty that day. Irvine Carnes was sleeping, but Harriet had agreed Dan could speak with him when he woke up.

That was the popcorn finished, and I was still hungry. I laid my head on Alaric's shoulder.

"Is it over yet?" I whispered as Biggs handed over to O'Shaughnessy. "I'm so bored."

"You were the one who wanted to come."

"Yeah, but I've made my assessment now. Kyla's a bitch. Harriet was right."

We should've taken the opportunity to nose around Devane's place, not Carnes's. Maybe we'd find an art gallery? A row of stolen paintings, hidden away in— What the fuck? Alaric spat a mouthful of cola, and the entire auditorium gasped.

I looked up. Holy mother of...

O'Shaughnessy's facts and figures about Kentucky employment rates had been replaced by a video. Two men, grunting away as one thrust into the other's ass. Actually, scratch that. The one on the bottom was more of a boy. He couldn't have been more than fourteen. Fucking hell. It wasn't a cheap home movie, either. No, it looked professionally produced. The room was furnished expensively, even opulently, and both of the participants were well-groomed. The throes of...not passion exactly, because the boy didn't look happy to be there...whatever, they carried on for about ten seconds before someone hit pause. On a close-up. Testicles the size of gym balls filled the screen.

"Still bored, Cinders?" Alaric whispered, and I snorted before I could help myself. Some old woman in a scarlet jersey gave me a dirty look.

Up on stage, the candidates and the moderator were all frozen. The colour drained out of O'Shaughnessy's face, as was to be expected with his election hopes circling the drain. And perhaps his freedom too if that kid was underage.

But Kyla... Kyla's lips twitched in the faintest smirk.

Pleased at the death of her foe's political career? Or satisfied with her handiwork?

Her gaze flicked to the left, and I followed her line of sight. She was looking at a man. I only caught a glimpse of him, but he seemed familiar. Where had I seen him before? I was still puzzling over the question when the auditorium came back to life, and so did the AV techs. The screen went dark as the moderator stuttered into his microphone.

"Well, folks, I, uh, think we'll take a short break here."

The lights over the stage dimmed. Kyla strode off, chin high, and Biggs shuffled along behind her.

O'Shaughnessy didn't move. Was he in shock? Eventually, when the jeers from the crowd started, the moderator steered him away.

Who was that guy?

I used the confusion to slip past a security guard—not one of Blackwood's, I hasten to add—and headed to the spot where I'd seen him last. Where had he gone? A set of nearby stairs led down into the bowels of the building, and I trotted in the most likely direction.

"Why are we backstage?" Alaric asked from right behind me.

"I saw someone."

"Anyone in particular? Or just 'someone'?"

"A guy."

"That narrows it down."

"Where did Kyla go?"

Alaric stopped a harried-looking girl passing in the other direction. "Where can I find Kyla Devane?"

"Who are you?"

"Aaron Meister, *Bowling Green Daily News*. We have an interview scheduled. I'm not sure quite what happened out there, but it looks as though the debate finished early?"

"Yeah, I'm not sure either. Her dressing room's along that hallway, first door on the left."

"Thanks, ma'am."

I didn't waste time hanging around. If Kyla was going to have a conversation about the incident on stage, then I wanted to be first in line to overhear it. I spotted a clipboard on a nearby table and tucked it under my arm to give myself some cover. Was I too old to be an intern?

We rounded the corner, and I spotted my target

ahead. Dark grey suit, shortish blond hair with a fringe that flopped over his forehead, an aquiline nose, broad shoulders, and only six feet from the emergency exit. Shit.

"Ma'am, you can't come down here."

A two-hundred-pound gorilla stepped out in front of us, and I held up my clipboard.

"I'm just taking a journalist to Ms. Devane."

"She's not speaking to any journalists today."

"But my boss said—"

"In here, I'm the boss. And I'm telling you, she's not doing any interviews today."

Didn't matter. I had what I needed. The blond guy had turned, curious, and I recalled who he reminded me of. A guy I'd seen at a Navy reunion dinner I'd attended with Black, had to be five or six years ago now. Ridley? Radley? Something like that. He'd been Black's commanding officer before he joined the SEALs, and according to my husband, a Grade A asshole. Last I heard, he'd started up his own security company, although he operated at the other end of the market to us with cut-rate, dubious-quality contractors who I wouldn't trust to give out parking tickets.

"Sorry, there must have been a miscommunication. I'll go get it smoothed out."

And I also needed to call Black. I had a feeling he'd be very interested in the latest development.

Chapter 9 - Sky

"THERE'S BEEN A change of plan," Black said.

Day three of my new job, and I'd already drafted my resignation letter. The handwriting was a little shaky because I'd been too tired to hold the pen properly, but it was still legible.

So far, I'd run the equivalent of a marathon while Alex rode a trail bike alongside, lifted weights until I thought my arms were going to fall off while Black watched over me, turned black and blue through fight training, and possibly broken a toe when I tripped up the stairs in exhaustion. My ears were still ringing from shooting, and the amount of damage I could do with plants terrified me. I was never, ever eating anything cooked by Sofia. Carmen was also trying to teach me Spanish, but I couldn't remember anything except *joder*.

And now Black wanted to change things?

"Does it involve me running anywhere? Because I'm not sure I can crawl."

"I have to go to Kentucky."

Hurrah. Did that mean I'd get a lie-in? "Have fun."

"So you'll have a new trainer tomorrow."

Fucking fantastic. "Is he a sadist in his spare time?"

"Not that I'm aware of."

"Oh, good. Then he can't possibly be as bad as the

last trainer."

"Tell me again why we hired you? Because it wasn't for your charming personality."

"Right now, I'm not even sure."

Black's lips quirked. Was that meant to be a smile? So far, he'd been a miserable bastard, all "do this, do that, die if you want, I'm not picking you up." I had no idea what Emmy saw in him.

"You'll train with Alex as usual in the morning. Rafael's currently in Colombia, but he'll be back at some point tomorrow. He can pick up where I left off."

"How? By making me dig my own grave?"

"No, that's part of next week's plan. If you breathe your last this week, we'll just feed you to the cat."

Ah yes. The fucking cat. A woman like Emmy couldn't possibly have a normal pet, could she? No, she had a bloody jaguar. It had a fancy jungle enclosure out the back, but it preferred kipping on the sofa and mooching around the kitchen in search of scraps. Everyone else acted as if this was normal.

I was fairly sure Black was kidding about me being kitty chow, but I also didn't want to test him.

"Tell me again why I haven't run screaming from this place?"

"Because you like a challenge. Enjoy dinner, and I'll see you in a few days."

Enjoy dinner? It was nine p.m. and even my taste buds had fallen asleep. I almost went straight to bed, but I knew if I skipped eating, I'd pay for it in the morning. At least there was proper food at Riverley. Emmy's nutritionist really cared about our diets. I'd spent so long living on junk due to a lack of cooking facilities that steamed chicken and vegetables was a tiny slice of heaven.

I could have cried when I got to the kitchen and found I wasn't alone. Tonight, I was too tired to pretend to be sociable. But I also couldn't afford to alienate anyone in this new world, especially when I didn't know who they were.

"Hi."

"You must be Sky? I'm Hallie."

She knew who I was, yet I didn't know who she was. "That's me."

"It's good to finally meet you. And weird not to be the new girl anymore."

"You work for Blackwood too?"

"Yup. Started two months ago in the investigations division. Dan's showing me the ropes, but she's gone to Kentucky."

"Don't you have a backup trainer?"

"Nah, I just have a bunch of cold case files to dig into. You know, review them in light of new developments, blah, blah, blah."

I pulled the nearest pre-prepared meal out of the fridge without bothering to check what it was. The Post-it note stuck to the top said to heat for three minutes, and I used the time to open a can of energy drink and pour it down my throat.

"Wish I had your job. Apparently, Rafael's going to play drill sergeant tomorrow, so I might not make it through to the evening. Do you know him?"

"Rafael? Yes, I know him."

"What's he like?"

"Tall, dark, and grouchy. And also a little scary, but he has a kind heart."

"I'm not sure whether that description makes me

feel better or worse."

Hallie forked pasta into her mouth, chewing thoughtfully. She had a pile of papers spread out next to her—typed notes with what looked like photos peeping out from underneath. On the other side of the plate lay a notepad and pen.

"You're training with Emmy, right?" Hallie didn't wait for an answer before she continued. "I guess if you want to learn all kinds of freaky stuff, Rafael would make a good teacher."

That was something, at least.

"Are you still working?" I nodded at the papers.

"I got curious. This stuff was in with the other cold case files. How much do you know about what's happening in Kentucky?"

"They're looking for a painting. Two paintings."

"*Red After Dark* and *The Girl with the Emerald Ring*. Plus a missing pay-off—ten million dollars in cash and jewels. It just vanished. Poof. And after the botched exchange, *Emerald* disappeared again too. The perfect crime."

"Is there such a thing?"

"Well, *Emerald*'s still missing and so is the money. It's kinda fascinating. Before I got this job, I was a true-crime junkie, podcasts and documentaries, but now I'm right in the middle of things."

The microwave dinged, and I juggled the hot dish between fingertips as I carried it over to the table. I hadn't yet found a pair of oven gloves.

"Where do you think the money went?"

"Honestly? I have no idea. And don't forget, it wasn't simply stolen—it was swapped for a fake pay-off. Counterfeit hundred-dollar bills and diamonds in an identical briefcase."

I hadn't realised that part. "So someone was clearly organised."

"*Highly* organised. The briefcase was only out of Alaric's sight on four occasions. The first came after it was packed at FBI headquarters when he left it in his office while he used the bathroom. That was before he spent the night at Little Riverley. You're staying over there, aren't you?"

"Yes, but now I wish I wasn't. That walk's the last thing I need after dinner."

"Nobody'll mind if you sleep here."

Nobody except me. Changing rooms would mean admitting defeat, and I hated to lose. That was the only reason I hadn't quit.

"Nah, I can't be bothered to move my stuff." Which had grown to three or four suitcases' worth. I'd brought a single bag from England, but Bradley had already given me more clothes than I'd ever owned in my life. "So Alaric and Emmy *were* dating?"

"According to Dan. Emmy married Black for a green card, and they didn't...*you know* until much later. Which is weird, because I can't imagine either of them with anyone else."

"Me neither." Long term, I couldn't see any sane person putting up with Emmy's craziness or Black's psycho-ness. Was that even a word? "So the money could've got stolen from the FBI office or from here?"

"The FBI ruled out theft at their end, and Dan said nobody could have taken it from here. The security system at Little Riverley monitored every door and window, and nobody entered or exited all night. In fact, nobody came or went from the whole estate. There's a network of sensors that surrounds the entire perimeter. Apparently, there was a breach by a team of professionals a few years ago, but they only got in because some of the motion detectors had been obscured by undergrowth. At the time of the theft, the system had just been installed and everything was working perfectly. Plus there were two men in the guardhouse at the end of the drive and an additional roving patrol."

"What if it was the guards?"

"Questioned and ruled out. And they'd still have had to get into Little Riverley, don't forget. Would you want to try sneaking into Emmy's house?"

Not with the number of guns she kept handy.

"You said there were four places—what about the other two?"

"Alaric stopped for gas on the way here. Rather than lug the briefcase inside when he went to pay, he left it in the trunk. According to his statement, he could see the car from the kiosk, but for a minute or so, a panel truck parked in the way while he was waiting in line. The car alarm didn't go off, though."

The thieves would have had to be pretty organised to nick the cash in that tiny window.

"And the fourth place?"

"The pay-off for-painting exchange was meant to take place on a boat, and the sea was rough, so the crew hauled the briefcase on board first. Alaric said it was out of sight for maybe thirty seconds while he climbed up the ladder."

"So they could have swapped it?"

"Yes, but only if they had another briefcase already pre-packed with the fake pay-off. And more importantly, with the same three-digit combination set to open it."

There was one obvious answer. "So several people were in cahoots, right? Someone from the FBI, and either an accomplice at the gas station or one of the bad guys on the boat."

"That was the path the original investigation went down, but nobody found a link. It didn't help that most of the men on the boat died in the gunfight at the end. And it's still my favourite theory, although there is a fifth option."

"Which is...?"

"That Alaric took the money."

I barely knew him, but he didn't strike me as a low-down dirty thief. After a nasty incident when I was fifteen, I'd learned to listen to my gut more, and he didn't give off bad vibes.

"If that was the case, why didn't he just ride off into the sunset with the money?"

"I don't know the answer to that question," Hallie admitted. She finished the last mouthful of her dinner and put down her fork. "And I'm going to start by reviewing the FBI files. I don't trust them."

"You have the actual FBI files?"

Hallie put a finger to her lips as she got up to load her plate into the dishwasher. "Copies. Shh."

"Let me know if you find anything?"

"Sure. I'll be here all week—my roommate's gone to Colombia for a charity project, so I thought I'd take advantage of the facilities. Good luck with Rafael tomorrow."

Her tone said I'd need it.

As Hallie's footsteps receded along the tiled

hallway, I realised my own dinner was going cold. But I did feel more awake. Much as I hated to admit it, the *Emerald* mystery had me intrigued, and even though I should have been focusing on the basics, like, you know, staying alive, I also wanted to look through those files. Hallie had left a stack of folders on the table, no doubt ready for the morning. I opened the top one and began to read.

"Here, drink this."

Toby handed me a smoothie as I trailed Alex to the gym. Bless that man. Toby, not Alex. Alex was basically a mob enforcer with the empathy of a rabid bull.

"Thanks."

I'd need every scrap of energy. Rafael still hadn't turned up, so we were going straight from a ten-mile cross-country run to fight training. Alex informed me this morning's run had been "easy." Next week, I'd be expected to do the same route carrying a weighted backpack. The week after, I'd get a gun to lug as well. But for now, I dragged my heels into the gym at Riverley Hall and wished I had a time machine or even an invisibility cloak.

The gym was a cavernous space, a later addition in the same wing as the swimming pool. One end was filled with weights and cardio equipment, and at the other, mats had been laid from wall to wall. The whole room was lined with mirrors so I could see my fuck-ups from every possible angle.

"Today, we start to prepare for knife work, *da*?" Alex said in his thick Russian accent.

"You might as well stab me now and get it over with."

He didn't answer, just handed me a slim piece of polished wood. A fake knife. Oh, thank goodness. I might live to eat dessert this evening.

"Attack me."

Dammit. We'd already played this game without a weapon, and guess who kept losing? First, I'd come at Alex, and he'd flick me away like a piece of lint. Then he'd explain in excruciating detail everything I'd done wrong and teach me how to do the move properly. It worked—I couldn't deny it worked—but the beginning part where I got bruised to buggery stung like hell.

But what choice did I have?

I thought back to the lessons of the past few days. Alex had shown me how to block and feint, to use his own momentum against him and hit where it hurt. I went in low, keeping the "knife" back until I got close. At the last moment, I dodged, and...the asshole upended me. My breath rushed out in a whoosh, I heard material tear, and quick as a flash, he was on top of me. A Russian bear, but he moved like a cheetah.

Alex's weight pressed into me, and I couldn't kick him away because he'd forced his body between my legs. Then his hands wrapped around my neck.

"Cross your arms over mine," he instructed. "Grip my wrists and pump down with your elbows to break the hold. Do it, Sky. Do it."

But...but I couldn't. My thoughts darkened, and his words faded along with the bright lights of the gym as my mind took me back to another time. A living hell. And the next words I heard weren't Alex's.

"Fight harder, Sky. I like that."

I felt his hand over my mouth. Smelled the sickly aroma of alcopops as he exhaled, alcopops that I'd served him earlier. Hair tickled between my legs.

"Get off me!"

"Don't make this harder than it needs to be."

Was that Alex's voice? Or Brock's? I wasn't sure anymore. My cheeks cooled as someone breathed over my tears. It was happening again, wasn't it? Dammit, I'd worked so hard for so long to forget this.

Then the weight was gone, and I opened my eyes in time to see Alex flying through the air. And I mean flying. He hit the wall and sort of slid down it into a heap.

"*Chto za khuynya?*"

I didn't speak Russian, but I could take a good guess: what the fuck?

"She said to get off."

The voice came from behind me, a low rumble, calm but definitely threatening. Was that a hint of a Spanish accent? I tilted my head back and saw the shadow looming over me. Black had come back? No, wait. This man-mountain was younger.

"We were training," Alex mumbled, then coughed a bit.

"When a woman tells you to get off, you get the fuck off."

"I'm okay," I got out. "Is he okay?"

"He'll be fine."

The newcomer scooped me up and carried me right out of the gym before I could protest, leaving Alex struggling to his knees.

"Who are you?" I mumbled. "Why are you here?"

"I'm Rafael." He stared down at me with faint

incredulity. "Apparently, I'm here to mentor you."

CHAPTER 10 - BETHANY

"YOU BROUGHT YOUR dog?" Black asked. "Or does it belong to Alaric?"

I'd only met Emmy's husband briefly, a thirty-second introduction at Riverley, and he was the kind of man who made you clench your thighs and break out in a cold sweat all at the same time. I glanced around for help, but it was just me and the dog in the kitchen. She didn't have a name. Or any confidence, it seemed, because she yapped a couple of times, then slunk behind my legs when Black's shadow fell over her. I wasn't even sure how he'd got in. Had someone hidden a key outside for him?

"Uh, Emmy didn't tell you?"

"Tell me what?"

I gulped, my throat suddenly dry. "The dog...she... well, I guess she belongs to Emmy. Or Dan. Maybe both of them?"

"Fuck." He raised his gaze heavenwards. "Where *is* Emmy?"

"Still asleep, I think." It was six thirty a.m. and I'd only got up to let the dog out. "Her bedroom's the last door on the left upstairs."

It had been a late night for everyone yesterday. By the time the others got back, I'd already seen the news. One of the networks had carried the debate live, and I'd almost choked on a biscuit when the screen behind the candidates filled with unmentionables.

And apparently, the porn movie was an even bigger deal than I'd first thought. Not only was the Democratic candidate toast, but Senator Carnes's daughter had endorsed him right before the debate, so now she looked like a fool too.

There'd been one small glimmer of hope—the others had found *Red After Dark*. I could see they were trying to take that as a positive, and of course I was too, but the whole case had turned into one big mess.

"Is that coffee I sm— Oh. You're here early, Chuck."

Emmy had come dressed for action in black running tights and a tight purple T-shirt, but now she stopped in the doorway.

"What? Were you planning to rehome the dog before I arrived?"

"Not rehome, exactly. More like hide it."

"Diamond, we already have a dog."

"Yeah, but Lucy's getting on in years, and she can't do the long runs anymore. She needs a sidekick to stand in occasionally. You know, to take some of the pressure off."

"Barkley here looks as if she'd collapse if she went faster than a walk."

"Barkley? Oh, how cute—you gave her a name. Now we definitely have to keep her."

"Emmy..."

"Look, leaving her with her old owner wasn't an option. He was a mean old bastard, and besides, they don't let dogs into the emergency room."

Black groaned. "What did you do to him?"

"Absolutely nothing."

"Then what—"

"It was me." Dan appeared behind Emmy. "If I didn't fracture his jaw, I'm fairly sure I loosened a tooth or two."

"How's your hand today?" Emmy asked.

Dan flexed her fingers. "Much better, thanks. The swelling's almost gone."

"Stop changing the subject," Black said. "Why aren't *you* keeping the dog?"

"Because I'm usually out, and so is Ethan. There's always someone at Riverley."

"Georgia works at an animal shelter." Presumably, Georgia was a friend. "They rehome dogs every day. We donated a hundred thousand bucks last year—I'm sure they'd help."

"Aw, look at that face," Emmy said. "Isn't she adorable?"

Emmy crouched down, and the dog crept over to have her head scratched. Then—smart pupper—she tiptoed across to Black and licked his hand. At least Dan and I had given her a bath yesterday so she didn't smell quite as bad. Her wiry fur had turned from brown to golden as the shower stall went from white to yeuch.

"See?" Emmy's pleading expression turned to smug satisfaction. "She likes you."

"I'm not going to win this argument, am I?"

"Do you really want an answer to that? Hey, Barkley, you want bacon? Let's cook bacon."

Alaric appeared next, and I really wished I'd made the effort to tidy my hair instead of just scraping it back into a ponytail. He looked good enough to eat, and even though I'd tried to rationalise things—he was my boss, I was getting over a nasty divorce, all men were bastards, etcetera, etcetera, etcetera—I was still really bloody hungry.

I got busy pouring coffee for everyone to keep myself occupied.

"Alaric." Black gave a curt nod in his direction.

"Black."

"Is there a plan for today?"

"More or less. First, we're going out to Harriet Carnes's horse farm to try and talk her off a ledge. Dan's gonna stick around there to follow up leads on *Emerald* while Emmy and I look into porngate. From what I've heard, the laptop used for the presentation belonged to O'Shaughnessy personally, which means he has bigger problems than optics. The cops'll want to speak to him if that kid was under eighteen."

"I've arranged a meeting with O'Shaughnessy at three. His office. We have to go in the back entrance, if you'll excuse the pun. You've got to give whoever set this up credit—the holy grail of scandal is either a live boy or a dead girl, and their boy came prepubescent and in glorious technicolour."

"You believe this was a set-up?"

"You don't?"

"I haven't seen enough evidence either way so far."

"It's all a little too convenient. And if Eric Ridley was there... I don't believe in coincidences."

"Eric Ridley... Emmy mentioned you served with him?"

Black picked up a mug of coffee and took a sip before he answered.

"If there was one thing that got me through Hell Week during SEAL training, it was the thought of never having to take an order from that little shit again."

"He wasn't popular, then?"

"Ridley had his allies. Some people join the services to fight for a better world. Others want to learn a trade. Then there are men like Ridley—and I use the term 'men' in a purely biological sense—who simply get turned on by pulling the trigger."

"He was a renegade?"

"*I* was a renegade. Ridley was a bloodthirsty nutjob. It was only a matter of time before he caused serious damage."

"And he did do damage, I take it? What happened?"

Should I be listening to this? It seemed a bit above my pay grade, but nobody asked me to leave, and I was curious. There was no way I'd open my mouth about Alaric's secrets or Black's either. I knew how to keep quiet. I mean, when my ex-husband drove into my father's car after a drink too many, I hadn't said a word, although that was perhaps because they were both as bad as each other.

"He was commanding a Mark VI patrol boat off the coast of Syria when he came across a group of refugees in a dinghy. Rather than escorting them back to shore, his crew opened fire. Nineteen people lost their lives. The youngest was six years old."

"I'm surprised he's not in prison. Didn't he get court-martialled?"

"As I said, he had allies. He'd managed to find himself a team whose views aligned with his, namely that people from countries like Syria should be treated as vermin, and they all agreed that the refugees had opened fire first. And since the Syrians were dead, there was nobody around to contradict Ridley and his band of thugs."

"Did the Syrians have weapons?"

"Conveniently, the guns were deemed to have sunk."

"Nobody questioned that?" Alaric asked.

"Ridley's allegiances went up the chain as well as down. I wasn't sorry to leave that world. Fast-forward to his 'honourable' discharge, and he moved his mercenary operation into the private sector. Rumour says his new crew shot a civilian family in Afghanistan the year before last. Again, no witnesses."

"So what you're saying is wear body armour?"

"I'm saying watch your back or you might find a bullet in it."

I wasn't too keen on this new development. Last week had taught me that Alaric's job wasn't the safest in the world, but there was a big difference between facing off against a spurned lover armed with a kitchen knife and being stalked by a trained killer. We'd only come to America to look for a freaking painting.

But Alaric didn't seem fazed. "I'll take that under advisement. Are you sticking around?"

"For a few days at least."

"What about Sky?" Emmy asked. "You said you'd get her training started."

"I delegated to Rafael. It'll be character-building for him. I also drove through the night, so I need to get my head down for a couple of hours, and then I'll join you two when you visit O'Shaughnessy. Unless Alaric's too busy chasing paintings to go?"

Black's tone said he'd be more than happy if Alaric stayed behind. Where did the animosity come from?

"I'll be there."

"Have fun at the horse farm."

Black had made his disdain clear on the last two words, and I wasn't sure *I* liked him much either. What was wrong with a horse farm?

"Is there anything I can do to help?" I offered, more to annoy Black than anything. I already had my orders —monitor the company emails and send a holding message to each person until I could speak to Alaric. Start the search for summer holiday accommodation, a nice house so Rune could stay with Alaric while she was off school. Ensure there was food for dinner. Let the dog out.

But to my surprise, Alaric nodded.

"As it happens, there might be. Harriet lost some of her staff, and she can't afford to replace them. How do you feel about helping out with the horses for an hour or two?"

If I couldn't spend time with my own horse, the next best thing was pottering about with other people's. A morning at a ranch sounded fascinating. How did they do things in Kentucky?

"I'd love to lend a hand. Just let me grab a pair of boots."

CHAPTER 11 - BETHANY

"THIS IS YOUR dog?" Harriet asked.

Not really, so it seemed safest to avoid the question. "She's called Barkley. You don't mind us bringing her, do you? Otherwise she'd be left on her own."

"I love dogs. Samson, our blue heeler, he passed away two months ago." There was an air of sadness about Harriet, hardly surprising given the circumstances. "It feels like I'm losing everything."

"I'm so sorry," I said, my words totally inadequate.

Harriet led us into the kitchen at Lone Oak Farm, where a bunch of devices were laid out on the huge kitchen table—two mobile phones, a laptop, an iPad, plus a notepad full of wobbly handwriting, most of it barely legible. On the way over, Dan had told me she planned to check through them for clues.

"Here's everything I could find," Harriet told us.

"What are all the notes?" Dan asked.

"That's Daddy's jotter. He kept it on his nightstand. If he wrote anything down in recent weeks, it'll be on there." Harriet peeled a Post-it note off a pad and stuck it onto the scarred wood beside the jotter. "And these are the passwords. I've already been through everything myself, and I can't see anything unusual, but feel free to look again. Are you here to help Daniela?" she asked me.

"Oh, no, I'm not an investigator. Actually, I'm here to help you, if you'd like me to. Alaric thought you might need a hand with the horses?"

"You know horses?"

"I have my own back in England. A dressage horse. His name's Chaucer."

"We don't do much in the way of fancy stuff here. Most of our horses are trained for barrel racing and team roping."

I wasn't even sure what barrel racing and team roping were. The window over the sink gave a view of the paddocks behind the house, and I spotted a pair of foals beside the barn, nibbling grass behind a post-and-rail fence, plus a handful of older horses grazing in the distance.

"You breed as well?"

"That's my favourite part of the job—bringing on the babies. But this year... We lost one at birth, and I've had to sell some of the mares to make ends meet."

"How many horses do you have here?"

"Thirty-one of our own, plus another three geldings for training. Two stallions, eleven broodmares, eight colts, seven fillies, and three Arabians left over from Daddy's heyday. He liked to show them when he was younger, but we've gradually switched over to quarter horses. Nine live in the barn, and the rest are out at pasture. And we have a dozen Corriente cattle."

Thirty-four horses? I found it time-consuming enough looking after one. Where did Harriet get the energy? She was a good six inches shorter than me, and she didn't look particularly strong.

"Sounds like a lot of work."

That was borne out by her scuffed jeans and faded

shirt. She clearly spent a reasonable amount of time outside with the animals.

"It is, and now I only have Rodrigo left plus Rusty on the weekends when he's not at school. And Stéphane, of course, but he takes care of my father's affairs and the house, not the animals." She leaned in a little closer and dropped her voice to a whisper. "In fact, he's quite scared of them. You really don't mind helping?"

"Not at all." I'd only be sitting alone in a rented house otherwise, missing Chaucer. I wouldn't get to see him until the middle of June when I flew home to watch my little sister get married. "Where do you want me to start?"

While Dan got stuck into the investigative work, I headed out the back with Harriet. She proved to be easy company, and by the time we'd mucked out the horses in the barn and given them their lunchtime feed, I'd learned the basics of barrel racing—basically, you galloped your horse around three barrels in a cloverleaf pattern, competing against the clock. Team roping wasn't her main focus, rather something she did to stop the barrel horses from getting stale, and it involved two people on horseback catching a steer with ropes. Dressage seemed so much safer.

But the horses were docile, even the stallions, and although I was technically working, it felt more as if I were on holiday. People would pay thousands to wake up with that view—pastures and shade trees, and in the distance down a gentle hill, fields of tobacco and a winding river.

"This place is beautiful. Have you always lived here?" I asked.

"I was born in that bedroom up there." Harriet pointed at a window on the top floor of the house. "For as long as I can remember, all I ever wanted to do was breed horses. How about you? Did you always want to be... Uh, never mind."

She was right. No little girl grew up dreaming of a career as a PA, perhaps with the exception of being Girl Friday to a famous movie star or a billionaire—I'd binged romance novels as a teenager, okay? I understood how it worked.

"I wanted to event in the Olympics. But my parents sold my three-star horse while I was injured in the hospital, and that was the end of that."

Harriet gasped. "They sold your horse? Without you knowing?"

"I still miss him. My ex-husband bought me a dressage horse as a consolation prize, and between the physio and my father's constant browbeating, I didn't have the energy to fight."

"Were you injured badly?"

"I had to have my left ankle pinned. It wasn't even Polo's fault. A fox shot out of a bush during the cross-country, and he swerved to avoid it. I just fell off the side and landed badly."

"I broke both of my legs at different times when I was a teenager, and Daddy helped me back on again as soon as I could hobble. I even rode in a cast." She stopped sweeping for a moment and leaned on the broom handle. "I realise what you must think of Daddy. That he's a liar and a cheater and a thief. But he wasn't a bad father. I just didn't realise how awful he'd gotten with the money side of things. Mom used to take care of the finances. The money was hers, you know. Her father owned a bunch of local newspapers, and she inherited the spoils. That's why my father chose her over Dominique."

"The money?"

"This place was in trouble back then as well. A few bad winters, and they weren't sure they'd make it through another. My father was in love with Dominique, but he needed my mother. And Mom was so set on keeping her cowboy that she forgave him for the affair."

"What happened to Dominique?"

"She died. After Daddy ended things, her car went off a bridge. The police never determined whether it was an accident or suicide, but it broke my father. He changed. First, he sank into a depression, and when he was ready to face the world again, he'd become more... guarded, I guess. *Red After Dark* was always meant to be his. He'd paid a deposit. But Edwin Bateson, the artist, was also in love with Dominique, and after he realised she'd lost her heart to my father, he refused to hand the painting over. Daddy thought it had been destroyed until it turned up in the Becker Museum. I guess Bateson was short of money too. Or maybe he just wanted revenge? To keep Dominique away from my father forever?"

"That's such a sad story."

"It's what happens when you marry for money rather than love. Why do you think I'm still single? I'd rather live the rest of my life on the streets than defy my heart."

"I wish I'd met you twelve years ago. I needed to hear that then."

If I could turn the clock back, I'd have done a

moonlight flit with Polo and spent my twenties penniless but happy as a groom on somebody else's stable yard. Who knows? Perhaps I'd have come across a man like Alaric before both of our lives turned to crap.

"You mentioned an ex-husband—it was a bad break-up?"

"You could say that. I wasn't out on the street, but until Alaric gave me this job, I was in dire straits financially."

"How long have you worked for him?"

"Officially, this is my second day."

"Oh. Wow."

"Exactly. The afternoon we met, I basically screwed up his surveillance operation, and I think he felt sorry for me."

For a moment, Harriet just stared at me. Then she burst out laughing. In a heartbeat, I joined in, because it was a far better option than crying.

"We're both disasters," Harriet half giggled, half choked.

"Horses are better than men anyway. They don't screw my friends. Or their dental nursing assistants."

I'd never been able to confirm about the nurses, but for a pompous work-shy ass, Piers spent an awful lot of late nights at his dental practice.

"You married a dentist?"

"A cosmetic dentist. Honestly, I don't know what I was thinking. 'Darling, I'll do you a great set of veneers' was the worst pickup line ever."

"He really said that?"

"I thought he was joking. So I laughed, and then he laughed, but now when I look back on that evening, I think he was actually serious."

In the end, Piers had given me the veneers as a wedding gift. And goodness only knew what I'd do if I chipped one because it wasn't as though I could afford to get it fixed.

"A guy once invited me over to see his pet snake."

"Oh my gosh. You didn't..."

"I was eighteen, and thanks to my parents, my upbringing had been quite sheltered. So I thought a pet snake was totally cool, but it turned out to be more of a worm."

"What happened?"

"I also laughed. He didn't. Hey, do you want to try barrel racing after lunch?"

Did I? Hell yes. It looked a little scary in the videos Harriet had shown me on her phone, but I didn't ditch my old life only to stand on the sidelines of my new one.

"I'd love to, but isn't your father's nurse coming over to speak to us?"

Harriet's face fell, her earlier good humour wiped away in an instant.

"Sorry," I muttered.

"You're right, she is. Maybe tomorrow, if you come back?"

"Maybe."

I had no idea what tomorrow would bring.

After lunch, I met Harriet's father. Irvine Carnes ignored me completely, and he barely seemed to register Harriet's presence either. There were pictures of them together all over the house—the latest taken just a few months ago—but Irvine looked a decade older now. Wispy hair curled over his temples, and his voice was thin, almost inaudible. When he told Dominique they'd be together again soon, Harriet's eyes glistened, and I couldn't stop myself from giving her a hug when we got out into the hallway, professionalism be damned.

"Are you okay?"

"Not really. It's just hard, you know? Mom had a heart attack—one minute she was there, and the next, she was gone—and I was heartbroken because I didn't get to say a proper goodbye, but this slow decline is a hundred times worse to deal with."

"I'm sure Dan wouldn't mind talking to the nurse on her own."

"No, I should be there."

Barkley joined us too, curled up beside the kitchen table on an old horse blanket. She seemed to like being around people, which was a minor miracle considering the start she'd had in life.

Rosaria was a smiley middle-aged lady from a small town on the Mexican coast, so she said over drinks while we waited for Dan to finish a phone call. According to Stéphane, the senator didn't like Rosaria much, but Harriet said he wasn't keen on any of his caregivers. They reminded him of his own limitations.

Once everyone was settled with biscuits—cookies— Dan kicked off with the questions. I'd offered to take notes, but she said she was recording everything. Standard Blackwood procedure, it appeared.

"I understand you attended to Mr. Carnes the Wednesday before last."

"*Sí*, I checked the schedule. I was here."

"Can you talk us through your visit?"

"I come in the afternoon. Mr. Carnes, he tell me to go again, but he always say that. I made him lunch. Chicken and dumplings, but he didn't eat it."

"Does he usually?"

Rosaria bobbed her head, black curls bouncing. "Always. He might lose his thoughts sometimes, but he never lose his appetite before."

"Did you clear the food away?"

"*Sí*. And when I get back with his pills, he was out of bed, trying to button himself into a shirt. Then he told me he have a guest coming in half an hour."

Dan, Harriet, and I all looked at each other. Surely this had to be our courier?

"Did he say who?" Dan asked.

"No, and he also got the time wrong. The man didn't arrive until four o'clock. I was meant to finish by then, but Stéphane hadn't come back, and I didn't want to leave Mr. Carnes alone with a stranger."

Harriet managed a smile. "I appreciate that."

"So they were strangers?" Dan asked. "Not friends?"

"Not friends, I don't think. The man, he acted more like he was there to work. Said it was good to meet Mr. Carnes, and was he ready to get started?"

"Started on what?"

Rosaria shrugged. "Mr. Carnes asked me to wait in the kitchen."

"You didn't hear anything that was said?"

"*Lo siento*. No, I didn't."

So near, yet so far. But Dan didn't give up. Rather than act defeated, she gave Rosaria an encouraging smile.

"I'm sure you know more than you think. Let's start with the moment you realised Irvine's visitor had arrived..."

Dan walked Rosaria through the whole afternoon once, and then she did it again. Unfortunately, Rosaria had spent her time waiting in the kitchen on the phone to her niece rather than being just a tiny bit nosy about what was going on in Irvine's bedroom. The courier could have arrived by car, horse, or spaceship—she didn't have a clue. At least we knew he had a local accent.

"You said he was white, in his forties, with brown hair," Dan said. "Did he have any distinguishing marks at all? A scar? A beard?"

"I don't think so."

"Would you be able to describe him to a sketch artist? We'd pay you for your time, of course."

Rosaria agreed, but I suspected it was the promise of cash that persuaded her rather than a conviction that she could provide a good likeness. Then they went over the clothes again—jeans, a grey T-shirt, and one of those man-bags. Wait. She hadn't mentioned the bag the first time around. Dan picked up on it too.

"Could you tell me a little more about the bag?"

"It was a green colour. Khaki? And it had leather edges."

"What shape was it? Slim, for a laptop?"

"No, fatter than that. And shorter. Maybe a foot long?"

"Did it have a logo?"

"Not that I saw, but there was something stamped into the leather."

"Can you remember what?"

"Billington? Billings?"

"Billingham," I blurted. "They make camera bags, the expensive kind. My ex-husband had one."

All the gear, no idea—that was Piers. After he found out photography was harder than he thought, the camera spent several years languishing in the stair cupboard until it went obsolete. But the pieces clicked into place, and I saw from Dan's expression that her lightbulb came on at about the same time as mine did.

"Ah," she said. "I get it now. These people didn't just send a courier; they sent a videographer to make absolutely sure they got the footage they wanted. Which means not only do they have money, which we already knew, but they're seriously organised too."

"But how do we find this person?" Harriet asked.

"Simple. We know from the accent that he's from this area, so we get a list of videographers for hire in Kentucky. Then I'll start calling the A's with Bethany while you and Stéphane work your way backwards from the Z's."

Lovely. I hated talking to strangers. I nodded my agreement, but in all honesty, I preferred mucking out the horses.

Chapter 12 - Alaric

"WHO ARE YOU people? My campaign manager told me I should take this meeting, but I don't know who you are."

Siri, show me a man in despair.

Aidan O'Shaughnessy's unkempt appearance was a contrast to the well-groomed Blackwood/Sirius team. Emmy was back to the pantsuit, and Black was in a shirt and tie. Usually, he only dressed up for special events—was this an attempt at intimidation? If so, Alaric had to conclude it was working. O'Shaughnessy could barely look at the bigger man.

Black knew someone who knew someone who knew O'Shaughnessy's campaign manager, and that person had vouched for Blackwood as well as making the introduction. Ever the ruthless businessman, Black had negotiated a fee for their services, to be split seventy-thirty between Blackwood and Sirius. At least they were getting paid for this shitshow.

When they sat down, Black positioned his chair a foot farther back than Alaric and Emmy, and he made no move to speak. Was this some sort of test? Because Alaric would have no problem passing it. He'd dealt with a hundred O'Shaughnessys in his life.

"I think the more appropriate question is 'why are you here?'"

"Why *are* you here?"

"We had front-row seats for yesterday's debate."

"So, what? You're here to gloat?"

"The opposite, actually. We're here to work out how to undo the damage. The people of Kentucky deserve an above-board election, and there's concern that one of the parties isn't playing fair."

"Not playing fair? You know where I was before this? Getting interviewed by the police. They've taken my laptop to be forensically examined, and the media's talking about jail time."

"It was *your* laptop?" Alaric asked, to confirm the rumour. "Not an aide's?"

"No, it was mine. It's my habit to keep the final version of the speech and presentation on my own computer in case I need to make any last-minute adjustments. Communications move at a frantic pace these days."

"Any idea how the porn got on there?"

"Of course not! I never watch that stuff."

Liar. Alaric was watching O'Shaughnessy's face closely, and he blinked three times in quick succession before the second phrase.

Black, it seemed, agreed with Alaric's assessment.

"Really?"

Alaric couldn't see Black's face, but he could imagine those cold eyes fixed on O'Shaughnessy's. Black's irises very nearly matched his name, and the effect was unsettling.

"Well, not the gay stuff. And definitely not the kiddie stuff." His gaze flicked towards Emmy. "Just the...you know. The regular stuff."

Alaric took over again. "You watch it on your

laptop?"

"No, only my phone. And that video popped up right in the middle of my presentation. Talk about timing."

"Which leaves two possibilities." Alaric had discussed the problem with Naz earlier in the day, and Emmy had done the same with her team. Both had come to the same conclusions. "Either you downloaded a virus and got unlucky, or someone sabotaged your speech. How well do you know your staff?"

"It wasn't Malorie. She's been with me since the beginning."

"Malorie was in charge of playing the presentation?"

"Yes, and she's devastated. My wife had to drive her home."

"How's your wife taking this?"

"Yes, well..."

"She's not speaking to you?"

"It's been a shock for everyone. The police interrogated her too, you know. Kept asking how I behaved around the younger members of the family. As if I'd *ever* touch them."

He shuddered, and Alaric did believe he was genuinely disgusted.

"Did you speak to Malorie before she left?"

"She said the computer just went crazy. The presentation vanished, and nothing she clicked would make the video stop. Even when she closed the lid, it kept playing until she pulled the cable out."

So, sabotage then. It was a thirty-second job if Alaric had access to the laptop. Jam a USB stick into the side, wait nonchalantly as it loaded a malware file timed to activate while O'Shaughnessy was speaking... Each candidate had been allocated a time slot yesterday. Child's play to write a program like that, Naz said. They'd hoped to look at the laptop, but if the police had it, they were left with guesswork for now.

"When did the schedule for yesterday get announced? How far in advance did you know you'd be speaking?"

"We've known about the event for weeks. This debate was a big deal."

"And the running order?"

"That kept getting changed. At first, they wanted to do some sort of presentation to local veterans at the beginning, but then they switched it to the end, right before Elodie Bryan was meant to perform."

The cynic in Alaric said they'd saved the best part until last to keep people from leaving. Elodie Bryan was an up-and-coming country singer from Frankfort, and he'd been looking forward to her set himself.

"When did they finalise the timings?"

"Sometime in the morning. Around eleven o'clock? You'd have to check with my team."

"And where was the laptop then?"

"On the battle bus."

"The bus that takes you between campaign stops?"

"Yes."

"And who has access to the bus?"

"Just my team. But I'm telling you, none of them would have done this. And besides, my wife was there for most of the day, sitting in the chair right next to my desk. She wasn't feeling well."

It wouldn't be the first time a wife had sabotaged her husband, but it seemed an unlikely option. Meagan

O'Shaughnessy had always appeared supportive.

"Okay, so let's narrow it down to the times the laptop was out of sight of the two of you."

"The police already asked these questions."

"Would you mind going over it again?"

"Why am I even doing this? I still don't know who you're working for."

"Let's assume we're working for you."

Emmy chipped in. "The police aren't going to win you this election, Mr. O'Shaughnessy, but they'll sure as hell help you to lose it if you don't take steps to control the damage."

O'Shaughnessy had started off pale, but now he lost another shade of colour. "The only time the laptop was out of my sight was when I handed it over to Malorie."

"Then we need to speak to Malorie."

"I'm not sure she's in a fit state—"

Emmy tapped her watch. "The clock's ticking, Mr. O'Shaughnessy."

Malorie Sykes was a nervous blonde in her early twenties. This was her first job in politics after majoring in political science at the University of Kentucky, and possibly her last if she was involved in this monumental fuck-up.

"I only ran to the bathroom," she said. "I was gone, like, five minutes max."

"And you didn't take the laptop with you?"

"There's no place to put it in those bathrooms except on the floor, and..." Her ski-jump nose crinkled. "Yuck."

"So you left it...where?" Emmy asked.

"On a chair beside the stage. There were people around. Like, security people. I thought it would be okay, and when I came back, the bag was right where I left it."

"Security people?" Emmy slid a photo out of her purse, an old picture of Eric Ridley from his Navy days. Alaric wasn't sure whether Black had called in a favour to get it or sent in one of his pet hackers, but it was the best they could do on short notice. "Did you see this guy hanging around?"

"Kyla Devane's boyfriend? Sure, he was around. Why? Do you think he was involved in this...this... horror show?"

Kyla's *boyfriend*? This just got better and better.

"Devane's dating this man?"

"Well, yeah, I think so. I mean, isn't she?"

O'Shaughnessy leaned forward and plucked the photo from his intern's hand. Studied it. "I always thought he was part of her security team. Eric, right? He looks younger in this picture. Must be fifteen years older than her if he's a day."

"You're familiar with him?"

"Not really. I've seen him with her a time or two, and he introduced himself once." O'Shaughnessy tapped his head. "Never forget a name. It's been a blessing in this game."

Emmy turned back to Malorie. "What makes you say he's her boyfriend?"

"I... I... I'm not sure. I guess I just saw them standing real close, like...you know. And so I figured..."

"It's okay. We're not trying to catch you out here, only understand your thoughts. Gut instincts are often the right ones."

If Ridley was involved with Devane on more than a professional level, it certainly gave him an incentive to assist with a dirty-tricks campaign. The money he'd get for providing security services paled beside the influence he'd gain as one half of Kentucky's newest power couple. He'd had it all—means, motive, and opportunity.

The only thing missing was the evidence.

But now Black leaned forward, elbows resting on his knees.

"Diamond, when you saw Ridley yesterday, was he wearing gloves?"

Emmy closed her eyes for a moment, thinking. "No, he wasn't. And the convention centre was hot as hell. I only kept my jacket on because..." She glanced at O'Shaughnessy. No, best not to admit that she'd smuggled a gun past the metal detectors. "Never mind. Anyhow, gloves would have looked weird."

"Malorie, you mentioned a bag. Yet there was no bag listed on the police evidence log. What happened to it?"

Good spot. Guess that was why Black earned the big bucks. That and apparently having his tentacles deep inside the Kentucky police force's databases.

Malorie sat up straighter. "I... I don't know."

"Did you pick it up?"

"I think I put it in the box with the flyers. Everything was in chaos, and people were shouting, and..."

"It's okay, it's okay," Emmy tried to soothe her. "Where did the box end up?"

"Maybe on the bus? I have no idea."

Black looked straight at O'Shaughnessy. "Get me onto that bus. We'll also need your fingerprints for elimination purposes. Malorie's too."

O'Shaughnessy gulped and nodded. "Let me make a call."

Two prints. They found two unknown prints on the oversized metal zipper tab, one each side, thumb and finger by the positioning. Black had photographed the laptop bag in situ on the bus, careful to follow evidence collection rules in case their findings were ever needed in court, then they'd couriered the package to the nearest Blackwood lab in Cincinnati, where a team was on standby. They had the results by the time Beth served dessert. In terms of resources, Blackwood was Harrods to Sirius's Mom 'n' Pop general store.

But who did the print belong to?

The working hypothesis was that Ridley was involved, but Mack hit a snag when she dug his fingerprint records out of the FBI database—they were held there by virtue of his military service.

"They're smeared," she said. "Forensics says there's one small area that looks the same, but the rest is too smudged for a conclusive match."

"Why are they smudged?" Beth asked. Alaric was pleased to see her taking an interest in the case. "Did he sabotage them or something?"

Black shook his head. "Poor-quality prints are more common than you'd think. You get printed as a matter of routine at the beginning of your military career, and the people handling the process aren't always as careful as we'd hope. Estimates suggest around a third of prints on file have imperfections, some worse than others."

"So we can't prove that Eric Ridley was involved? Kyla Devane will get away with ruining a man's reputation?"

"No, he won't. It just means we have to get more creative."

Alaric was glad Black had chosen to fight on the same side as him for once. He wasn't sure what "more creative" meant, but he wouldn't have wanted to be in Ridley's shoes at that particular moment.

"Define 'creative,'" Emmy said.

Black held out a hand to her, and when she placed hers into it, he brought her knuckles to his lips and kissed them.

"Join me for dinner, Diamond."

"We just ate dinner."

"Thursday evening at the O Club."

"The O Club?" Beth's eyes widened, and Alaric realised where her thoughts had gone. *Not that kind of O, sweetheart.* But he liked the way her mind worked, even though he knew he shouldn't.

"Short for the Officer's Club. It's a hotel in Norfolk, Virginia," Black clarified. "And the day after tomorrow, it's hosting Destroyer Squadron Twenty-Six's annual get-together. Ridley will be there. He never misses an opportunity to dress up and brag about his conquests. I usually skip it."

"Then how do you know he goes?" Alaric asked.

Black glared at him. "I skim the newsletter."

After their recent run of bad luck, they deserved a break. And if Ridley *did* show up at the dinner as Black predicted, it would save them from following the man to restaurants, rallies, and other random places. Emmy laughed, then twisted Black's hand in hers and brought it to her lips in a return of his gesture.

"It's a date, Chuck."

Chapter 13 - Alaric

"YOU'RE NOT TIRED?" Alaric asked.

Beth had yawned three times since dessert, but rather than going to bed, she flopped onto the couch in the living room. Her blonde hair spread out along the top of the cushions. The two of them had spent little more than a day at Riverley, but that had been enough time for Bradley to cut it into layers and dye it a few shades darker. More than ever, Alaric itched to run his fingers through the silky strands.

"Exhausted, but it's only nine o'clock and my sleep pattern's all over the place. I thought if I watched a movie and then went to bed, it might help me to adjust to the time zone."

Emmy and Black had disappeared, along with Dan. Emmy had muttered something about a conference call, but whether that was just an excuse for some alone time with Black, Alaric wasn't sure.

"What movie are you watching?"

If his ex was doing her husband upstairs, Alaric didn't want to overhear, and the walls in the rented house weren't particularly soundproof. He knew that because Beth had been singing to herself in the shower this morning, and he'd heard every word. She could really hold a tune.

"I don't know yet."

"Mind if I join you?"

"I just said I don't know what I'm watching."

"Doesn't matter. I'm not ready to go to bed yet either."

Alaric left his unfinished glass of wine on the table. It had been a while since he was alone with Beth, and already he could feel the tension building. But he was a glutton for punishment, and when she shifted to the side and patted the seat next to her, of course he took it.

"There's so much on TV," she said, flipping through the myriad of channels. "By the time I find anything good, I'll be too shattered to watch it."

"Then let's talk instead. How did it go at the ranch today?"

"Is this your attempt at employee relations?" she teased.

"Something like that."

Fuck, every time he closed his eyes, she was back in his arms at that party. The party where he'd taken things way too far and made her come in front of her ex-husband. Although really, the ex had been an excuse. Alaric should have stopped before he got her off, but the asshole inside him had wanted to see her O-face, and he hadn't paused to consider the ramifications.

Actions have consequences, son.

His father's words echoed in his head, the culmination of a heated argument over Alaric's steadfast denial of the charges levelled at him. When he'd refused to admit to stealing the *Emerald* pay-off, his father had disowned him.

Everyone makes mistakes, son. A man owns up

and takes his punishment. Only a coward ducks the blame.

Bancroft McLain would rather have seen Alaric in prison than be branded the father of a weakling. Didn't he realise that all the put-downs, the constant criticism and the bullying, they'd only made Alaric stronger?

Don't you walk away from me, boy!

He hadn't walked, he'd run.

He'd punished Emmy for something that wasn't her fault, and he'd done a hatchet job on his own heart in the process. Never again would he put himself in a position where he could hurt another woman like that.

Which meant keeping his relationship with Beth on a professional footing. He cared about her too much to play with her emotions.

"The ranch was fun," she said. "Harriet and Stéphane are both lovely, Dan's friendly and so, so smart, and it was wonderful being around the horses all day. And Barkley—she's such a sweet dog."

And yet Beth didn't sound happy.

"But...?"

"But what?"

"You don't sound as if you had a great time."

"No, I did. Honestly. It's just... I guess..."

"You guess what?" Alaric pressed.

"I guess I feel guilty about that."

"Why?"

"Because I'm meant to be working. You're paying me, and I was messing around with horses."

"And work can't be fun?"

"Well, historically it hasn't been."

"There's an old saying that goes 'find a job you enjoy, and you'll never do a day's work in your life.'"

"I always thought that was a myth.

"Sirius has its moments—you already got thrown in at the deep end last week—but when we started the firm, we all agreed that our priority was to have a good work/life balance. Without going into the details—the other guys' stories are theirs to tell, not mine—the four of us have been through enough shit with work that we don't want to go down that road again. Sirius is profitable, and we each make enough money to be comfortable. I'm never going to be a billionaire like Black, but nor do I want to be. I just want to be happy." Alaric smoothed the hair away from Beth's face. "And I want you to be happy too, okay? If there's anything urgent for you to do, I'll let you know, but until then, have fun with Harriet. Oh, fuck. Don't cry."

"I-I-I'm sorry. You're t-t-too nice."

Too nice? No, Alaric was just trying to be a decent human being. It pissed him off that his attitude was unusual enough that it made Beth weep with fucking gratitude. That dick she'd been married to should have had her on a damn pedestal for the last decade, but instead, he'd torpedoed her expectations into the depths along with her self-esteem.

Alaric wrapped an arm around her shoulders because that was allowed, right? He was only offering comfort.

"Tomorrow's a research day for me, so I'll drop you off at the ranch in the morning. Judd mentioned having a report for you to format in the afternoon, but you don't need to sit around here all day while I make phone calls. Just keep an eye out for anyone visiting the senator, okay?"

Alaric didn't expect any further contact, but it

might make Beth feel useful.

"Okay."

"Hey, here's a movie with horses in it. You want more wine?"

"I'd better not."

He kissed her hair because as he said, he was an asshole, and then sat dead still when she rested her head on his shoulder. *Actions have consequences, idiot.*

A white horse pranced across the screen. Wasn't Beth's old horse white? Which reminded him, he'd promised to search for the beast, and he hadn't done a damn thing about finding it. He needed to speak to Naz and get the ball rolling. Tomorrow. He'd speak to Naz tomorrow. Tonight, he'd accept his punishment as a human pillow and watch a terrible movie with Beth.

Damn, this bed was uncomfortable. Alaric shifted, trying to avoid the lumps, then realised his mistake. He wasn't in his bed at all. No, he was still on the couch downstairs, and the lumps were partly Beth. She was lying half on top of him, her legs tangled in his, and when she shifted against his chest, burying her head tighter against his shoulder, her hair tickled his face.

The sensible thing to do—the gentlemanly thing—would have been to carry her upstairs and tuck her into her own bed. But despite his earlier words, Alaric was no gentleman.

He wrapped his arms around her, closed his eyes, and returned to his filthy dreams.

CHAPTER 14 - SKY

"LONG DAY?" HALLIE asked.

To hell with the vegetables. I needed comfort food tonight. Luckily, there was a dish of macaroni and cheese in the fridge, and I scooped half of it onto a plate before sticking it all back into the dish again and microwaving the entire thing.

"You could say that."

"Did you meet Rafael?"

Did I meet him? I'd embarrassed myself totally in front of him. I stared at the food going round and round on the turntable as memories of this morning made an unwelcome reappearance.

Rafael hadn't put me down when we got out of the gym. No, he'd carried on walking through the house and up the stairs to the next floor, where he'd dumped me onto a velvet sofa in the corner of what looked like a meeting room.

"Do you want me to get a doctor?" he asked.

"What? No!" I tried to force a laugh past the lump in my throat. "Why would I need a doctor?"

"Because you were having a panic attack."

"A panic attack? Don't be silly."

I'd thought I was over them. A year had gone by since the last one, since Lenny hugged me and stroked my hair and told me everything would be okay. That time, it had been set off by a man's cologne. He'd walked past us on the street, I'd caught a whiff, and *bam*! I was right back in the limo with my rapist again.

"I know what a panic attack looks like, Sky. A friend of my sister has them."

"Well, you clearly don't know that much, because that's not what it was. And I've got no idea why you brought me up here. Alex is gonna be pissed."

Rafael just pulled out his phone and tapped away at the screen for a few moments. What was he doing? Messaging Alex to tell him to go easy on me or something? Now I'd look like a wimp.

"Alex is booked onto a course this afternoon. He'll have to go to headquarters."

"What kind of a course?"

"'Staff motivation: how to get the most out of your team.' Now he'll be pissed at me instead."

Don't laugh, Sky. There really wasn't anything funny about the situation.

"Yeah, well, I'll still get into trouble. I'm supposed to be on a schedule here. Boxes to tick and all that."

"You'll stay on schedule."

"How? You just sent Joseph Stalin off for a lesson in bullshit, which, by the way, is a complete waste of time because Alex isn't exactly a team player."

"Because you'll do your close-quarters combat training with me this afternoon."

"With *you*?"

Rafael folded his arms, and his tanned biceps bulged under the flimsy sleeves of his T-shirt. I took in the rest of him. He was big, nearly as big as Alex, and his dark eyes were a whole lot more dangerous. Black hair, black clothes, black boots, black aura.

"What? You don't think I'm capable?"

Oh, I thought he was capable of doing *his* job. I just wasn't sure I was capable of doing mine.

"Yeah, but I thought you'd have better things to do. Like fighting orcs or eating kryptonite."

"What's an orc?"

"You haven't watched Lord of the Rings?"

One of Lenny's druggie pals had the whole set on DVD. I'd watched all three of the movies half a dozen times while the idiots went on their benders, in between checking for vital signs at regular intervals.

"I'm not big on TV."

Preferred his violence in real life, did he?

"Well, whatever. Just get the punishment over with, will you?"

Rafael smiled for the first time, revealing a set of straight white teeth. Whose ass did he kiss in the gene pool?

"Take a half-hour break, then meet me in the gym. Sky Malone..." He gave his head a slow shake. "My uncle was right. You're a real ray of sunshine."

His *uncle*?

Oh, shit.

After the way Rafael flung Alex against the wall, I'd expected to finish the afternoon with broken bones or at least a full complement of bruises. But he surprised me again when he lay on the floor.

"Let's do this differently. This time, you're the aggressor. Choke me. You look as if you'll enjoy that."

Choke him? Presumably he meant the way Alex had tried to choke me earlier. Thanks to the break, I'd had time to steel myself for what was to come. To block out the memories of the past and focus on the here and now. Which basically meant lying on top of Gulliver here. When I knelt between his legs, I could barely reach his neck without sprawling on top of him.

"Do I need a crash mat?" I asked. He could toss me like a rag doll if he chose.

"Not today. But pick a safe word."

"A safe word? What do you think this is? Fifty fucking shades of grey?"

"No, but I also don't want it to be fifty shades of black and blue." Rafael touched my forearm. "He bruised you."

"Emmy said that the more I bleed in training, the less I'll bleed in combat."

"There's more than one way to train. You'll get bruises later, but you need to understand the tools you have before you can learn to use them properly. And it's not just your body you need to keep in shape." He tapped the side of my head. "Up here matters too. Pick your safe word."

I could have come up with something awesome. Something funky and cool-sounding. But what popped out of my mouth was, "Piggles."

"Piggles?"

Rafael might have looked all boy-next-door handsome when he laughed, but I still wanted to slap him.

"It was a toy I had when I was little, okay? A cuddly —"

"Let me guess... A sheep?"

"Shut up."

"Piggles." He started laughing again.

"Yeah, Piggles." I had to own it. "What's your safe word?"

"I don't need a safe word."

"You think? What if I kick you in the balls and mistake your gasp of pain for pleasure?"

"Fine." He closed his eyes for a moment. "Butt-Head."

"Huh? You want me to headbutt you?"

"That's my safe word. Butt-Head. He was my pet goat when I was a kid."

"You had a pet goat, and he was called Butt-Head?" I asked, wanting to check I hadn't fallen into an alternate universe, one where I wasn't lying on an admittedly hot guy having just confessed to owning a cuddly pig named Piggles. Piggles had been my favourite toy until my father shredded him in a fit of anger. I forced those memories to the back of my mind too, my father's yelling and his fists. They were easier to push away than the rape. I'd had years' more practice.

"I did. And now we have our safe words, so choke me or I'll spank you."

"Did you read *Fifty Shades*?"

I tightened my fingers around Rafael's neck. Rather than break them, he crossed his arms over mine and gripped both wrists. Then he pushed his elbows down, forcing my arms to bend and my grip to loosen. Half a second later, he tipped me to the side, got one foot on my stomach, and pushed me backwards.

"That's what Alex was trying to make you do earlier. Again."

"You didn't answer my question."

"Did I read the book? Yes, I read it. I was curious."

"What did you think?"

I leaned over him again, and my hair brushed

across his chest where my ponytail had come loose. He fisted it in one hand and pulled me closer.

"I don't understand why a man would want a woman to submit to him like that."

"Well, that's something we have in common. I don't understand why a woman would let a man boss her around either." I started to push myself away from Rafael, then quickly remembered where I was. "Outside of work, obviously. I'm getting paid for this shit."

This time, he shoved me off with both feet.

"Don't hold back on my account," he told me.

"Fine, I won't."

"Again."

Okay, I was getting used to this. Crawling between his thighs didn't feel quite so weird anymore. I wrapped my hands around his neck again and squeezed harder. *Let's see what you've got, buster.*

He raised his pelvis, and I just caught sight of the oversized bulge before he hugged my arms and slammed his hips back down. Fuck! I didn't even have time to freak out. My arms felt as if they'd snapped, his shirt rode up, and I ended up splattered against his bare stomach, close enough to lick his belly button. Fortunately, I managed to resist.

"That's what you do if your opponent is stronger. Now, let's switch."

"Oh, brilliant."

"On your back, Sunshine."

"Sunshine?"

"Get too close, and I'll burn." His hands came to my throat. "Now, get me off."

Get him off? How? He weighed twice as much as I did. My mind went to entirely the wrong place before I remembered ·to cross my arms over his to break his hold. Rafael had been Mr. Nice Guy at the beginning of the session, but now he wasn't cutting me much slack. It took me two hip-bumps and a bit of a struggle before I managed to kick him away.

"*Bien hecho*."

"What does that mean?"

"Well done. It's Spanish."

"Where are you from?"

"Colombia. Again."

He didn't wait for me to get my breath back, just dropped his weight on me. But with him, I didn't panic, not the way I had with Alex earlier. All I had to do was mouth my safe word, and I trusted Rafael to yield. *Arms, hips, legs, kick.* With that trust came strength, and I was able to buck him off faster than the last time.

"Good. Again."

Rafael was a hard taskmaster, emphasis on the hard—his muscles were solid. But although he was tough, he was also fair. Yes, I came away with a few bruises, but I hoped he did too, and for the first time since I arrived, I thought that maybe I *could* do what was being asked of me. At the end of the session, I wondered if he might do a debrief, but he just announced I'd be running with Alex first thing tomorrow morning and then walked out. Talk about confusing.

"Yes, I met Rafael," I told Hallie. "He's..."

"Intimidating? Moody? Oh-so-serious?"

"He's big."

Hallie laughed. "Yeah, that too. Did the training go okay?"

"It was challenging." Not to mention awkward.

"I know the feeling. Dan's got me learning about science and procedures and legal stuff. And she tosses random questions into the middle of conversations to try and catch me out. 'Hey, where do you want to get lunch? And what's the half-life of Rohypnol?' I'm reading old case files in bed at night."

"Like murders and stuff? How can you sleep?"

"Oh, easily. I used to listen to true-crime documentaries to nod off, so this isn't much different. And next month, I'm starting a six-week secondment in the forensics lab, so I'll probably switch to textbooks for a while."

"Rather you than me. I think I prefer the bruises." I nodded towards the stack of files on the table beside her just as the microwave pinged. "Did you find anything new on the *Emerald* case?"

"Not a lot, and I'm beginning to understand why it went cold. Come and look at this video."

I took my dinner out of the microwave and juggled it over to the table. I *really* needed to find the oven gloves. Or even a tea towel. This place was so damn *tidy*. Back in London, the squat I'd lived in had shit everywhere. There was usually a tea towel or two lying on the floor. At Riverley, there was a full complement of shiny cutlery in a caddy on the table, and I burned my tongue as I took the first mouthful. Fantastic.

"Where's this video, then?"

Hallie angled her laptop so we could both see the screen. "This is the camera outside Alaric's old office at the FBI."

The footage was sort of a let-down. A younger Alaric walked through the door with a briefcase. Walked out again a minute later. Five minutes passed, and then he came back again. A grey-haired guy ambled in behind him, and the pair of them left pretty quickly, this time with Alaric carrying the briefcase.

"There you go," Hallie said. "That was the only time the briefcase was left unattended at FBI headquarters."

"There was nobody else in that room?"

"Alaric doesn't recall seeing anyone, and there were only two desks in there. The guy he shared with was on vacation that week."

"What about the grey-haired guy? Who was he?"

"Richard Latham. Alaric's boss. His statement says there wasn't anyone else in the office."

"What if they hid? Was there a closet?"

"The report doesn't mention that, but even if there was, the scenario would be pretty far-fetched. Nobody knew Alaric would take a bathroom break at that moment."

"Not for certain, but if he had a long drive coming up, it would be an educated guess. He was coming here, right? Where's FBI headquarters?"

"Washington, DC. It's a three-hour drive. Or two if Emmy's behind the wheel. Have you been in a car with her?"

"Yes. I'm thinking of taking out life insurance."

"Blackwood provides life insurance. When the HR lady found out I'd be riding with Dan, she made sure to give me all the policy details." Hallie thumbed through the paper file. "I guess I should look into the hiding-in-a-closet idea. Honestly, I'm starting to think the original briefcase was beamed up by aliens."

"What about last night's theory? That someone else in the FBI was working with the thieves?"

"That's the only other credible hypothesis left.

According to Dan's notes, four people besides Alaric knew the lock combination, but in the eight years since the incident, none of them have suddenly started spending oodles of money. Two are still with the FBI, one—Latham—retired, and the other quit to drive across South America in an RV."

"That doesn't sound cheap."

"I checked his Instagram. The RV's fifteen years old, and the guy's got a cult following for his 'travel on a shoestring' tips."

"Maybe it was one of the other three and they've squirrelled the money away for a rainy day?"

"One of the current agents, his sister has a GoFundMe for her kid's broken leg. He's been posting links all over his Facebook. Don't you think he'd have taken a few bucks out of his stash for that?"

"Okay, so that leaves two. Plus the possibility of someone at the gas station or on the boat, and have you double-checked whether an intruder could have snuck onto the Riverley estate? Undergrowth or no undergrowth, if people broke in once, they could have done it a second time. What if they blocked a sensor? I saw a movie once where the bad guy used a mirror to complete the circuit or whatever."

"I'll add it to the list. I just wish we had the briefcase. What if a member of the boat crew jammed the lock so it would open with any combination?"

"Is that possible?"

"I'm not sure."

"You could try asking Ravi. He works with Alaric, and I heard he's good at opening things he shouldn't."

"When Alaric comes back, I'll see if he can put me in touch. Any other brainwaves?"

"No, but I'll keep thinking."

Because this case was bugging me now. Emmy had called to say they'd found *Red After Dark*, but that was only one piece of the puzzle. Like Hallie, I wanted to solve the whole thing.

CHAPTER 15 - BETHANY

OH, HELL.

I'D been an idiot.

When I woke on the sofa in the middle of the night, wrapped up in Alaric's arms, I should have done the honourable thing—wriggled free, put a blanket over him, and tiptoed back to my bedroom. But did I? Did I heck. No, I'd snuggled closer, then mostly regretted it when we both woke at dawn. The awkward *"I'm sorry— no, I'm sorry"* conversation had been mortifying.

But I'd slept well. And I say "mostly regretted" because I couldn't be sure I wouldn't make the same decision again.

Now I had to try and act normal while I made coffee for everyone. Well, almost everyone. When I got into the kitchen, I found the coffee machine already on and the jug half-full. Voices came from outside, and I glimpsed Emmy and Dan sitting at the wooden table on the patio.

I was about to ask them if they wanted anything to eat when I heard my name. *Back away, Beth.* But I couldn't. Eavesdropping on conversations was a terrible idea, but growing up with my parents, it was the only way I'd had a clue what was going on, even if I frequently wished afterwards that I hadn't found out. I tiptoed closer.

"Yeah, Beth's sweet," Emmy said. "I'm glad she's landed on her feet."

Aw, that was nice of her.

"She's done more than land on her feet. I mean, if I didn't work at Blackwood, I'd apply for a job at Sirius. All that eye candy."

"Dan, you're practically married."

"So? I can still look. Ethan knows I'd never touch. Is Naz hot?"

"No idea. I've never met him. And Sirius isn't a fucking pick 'n' mix. Judd's a bloody lunatic and Ravi's gay, for starters."

What? I clapped a hand over my mouth to cover my gasp. Why didn't I notice these things? Ravi liked men? I mean, I'd assumed Stéphane leaned in that direction, but Ravi too? And in what way was Judd a lunatic?

"Ravi isn't gay," Dan said. "I caught him checking out my boobs."

"Well, Bradley reckons he is, and his gaydar's on point. And everyone checks out your tits, honey. *I* check out your tits. They're great tits."

"Yours aren't bad either, babe. I got a whole bunch of new underwear while I was in London. From Black Lily—you know, the place Max's fiancée owns? Have you been there? I bought one corset, and when Ethan saw it, he ordered me half of the store."

"I might have an outfit or two from there. But not corsets. How do you breathe in those things?"

Uh-oh. I heard footsteps coming down the stairs and hurriedly backed up a few steps.

"Ready to go?"

We had casual Alaric today. Well-worn jeans and a T-shirt since he'd be staying at the house for a while. I liked him in the sports coat, but this new look wasn't bad either. *Don't think of those arms around you, Beth.*

"Uh, almost. Do you want coffee? Or breakfast?"

"Wouldn't say no."

It was eight thirty when I arrived at Lone Oak Farm, just in time for a second breakfast courtesy of Stéphane. I'd happily muck out every day in return for Belgian waffles with whipped cream and maple syrup.

"Ready to get started?" Harriet asked after we'd finished our coffee. "Rodrigo's gonna feed the cows and fix some broken fencing while we do the horses in the barn."

"Why not?"

Yes, I liked my new job. And I also liked Harriet. She handled the horses firmly but kindly—exactly what they needed—and she was happy to chat too. Although inevitably, after we'd told our war stories and compared scars, talk turned back to the case.

"So you really think Kyla Devane planted that awful video?" she asked.

"Not personally, but Emmy thinks it was somebody working for her. Or maybe he's more than an employee? One of the witnesses thinks they crossed that line, although Eric Ridley's almost old enough to be Kyla's father."

"Kyla and an older man? That doesn't surprise me one bit. She was failing math in high school until she screwed the math teacher. Ditto for chemistry."

I went into a coughing fit.

"You okay?"

"Just swallowed a hayseed or something." *Or something*. "What, she was sleeping with both of them?"

"Yah-huh. What were they gonna do? Complain to the principal?"

I guess not. "Did you ever hang out with her?"

"No way. She was two years ahead of me, and I avoided her like the plague. All of my friends did too. Kyla Devane's a nasty piece of work, and she always has been. If she gets elected, it won't be thanks to anyone in this town. And you know what? She probably will get elected. Nobody's ever made her face the consequences of her actions. Never. She's brazen, but she's careful, and on the rare occasions she does get caught, she'll throw anyone under the bus to escape punishment."

"What else has she done?"

"When she was sixteen, she crashed her mom's car into Bubba Morten's pickup before she got her driver's licence. Daddy's little angel convinced her boyfriend to take the rap, except Jarrod had been drinking beer in the Tumbleweed Tavern all night, so he got arrested for DUI and locked up for six weeks while Kyla got a neck brace she didn't need and a mailbox full of sympathy cards."

"Didn't he tell the truth after?"

"Sure he did, when he realised he was going to jail. But Kyla sobbed a lot and Mr. Devane's lawyer painted Jarrod as a guilty man out to evade responsibility for his mistakes. Ironic, huh?"

"How do you know Jarrod was telling the truth?"

"Because one of my friends saw Kyla get out of the driver's seat."

"Did your friend tell the police?"

"No, because Jarrod was a jerk, and she didn't want to face the wrath of Kyla either. Cross her and you'll pay. Like the time Piper Simms got voted homecoming queen and Kyla was only a princess."

Dare I ask? "What happened to Piper?"

"Who knows? She vanished a week before the parade. That was thirteen years ago, and nobody's seen her since."

"Did the police look?"

"Officially, the sheriff's department searched, but guess who was the biggest donor to Sheriff Tucker's re-election campaign?"

"Was their surname Devane?"

"Good guess. Bribery makes the world go round. Anyhow, Kyla pretended to be really cut up about Piper's disappearance. They were supposedly best friends before the homecoming quarrel, but did she forgo the crown when she 'inherited' it? No way. And a month later, a note arrived from Piper, saying she'd moved to LA to pursue a singing career and she was having a great time."

"Did anyone compare the handwriting?"

"I heard it was typed."

"Wow. That's crazy."

"Yup. So you see, the stunt with my father was nothing for Kyla. She's had years of practice. I only hope your friends know what they're doing."

"They do," I assured Harriet, although I wasn't totally sure about that. The team of Emmy and Alaric had worked well against a muscle-bound psycho in London, but Kyla Devane was a whole other level of cunning. Now that I knew a little more about her past, I needed to warn Alaric what he was dealing with. "What do you think happened to Piper?"

"I have no idea, but I don't think she's belting out show tunes in musical theatre."

That's what I was afraid of.

When Harriet trundled off to empty her wheelbarrow, I tried phoning Alaric, but my call went straight to voicemail. Rather than leaving a long, rambling message, I sent him a text.

Me: Would you mind calling when you have a moment?

Could eighteen-year-old Kyla really have been involved in her friend's disappearance? For a homecoming crown? It seemed somewhat drastic, but then again, she might well have bribed a sick senator with an expensive stolen painting and then tried to destroy a rival with underage porn. Perhaps it was all in a day's work for everyone's favourite political candidate?

"Enough about Kyla," Harriet announced. "I need to check on Daddy, but do you want to try barrel racing after that?"

It would be rude not to. When in Rome and all that...

"You'll have to show me what to do."

"You can ride Bucky. *He'll* teach you."

"Bucky? That's not a nod to his character, is it?"

"Don't worry; he's a dream to ride. But his registered name is 'Who Gives a Buck?' Rodrigo bet me five dollars it'd get rejected, but I think the person who checks the forms must've been asleep on the job that day."

Who Gives a Buck? Yes, I was definitely going to be good friends with Harriet.

CHAPTER 16 - BETHANY

WHAT A RUSH!

Eventing had always got my adrenaline up, especially the cross-country phase, but a short-course round over fixed fences took seven or eight minutes while a run around the cloverleaf pattern took less than thirty seconds. Bucky was a 2D horse, which meant he was usually within half a second of the 1D, or fastest, time. Learning all the new terminology was like getting the pass key to a different world, but even with a western saddle instead of a smaller English one, the basics of riding were still the same. Harriet was of course much faster, but I didn't disgrace myself.

"Thanks so much! I feel like a traitor when I say it, but I haven't had that much fun on horseback in years."

She adopted a snooty pose, back straight and head up. "You think I should give dressage a try?"

"If you ever come to England, you're very welcome to sit on Chaucer."

Harriet glanced around the barn, which was in slight disarray before our end-of-day tidy-up.

"Thanks for the offer, but I doubt that'll ever happen. There's too much to do here. Want to ride another?"

I couldn't keep the grin off my face.

By the time five o'clock rolled around, I was tired,

but a good tired. After I worked on Judd's report, which incidentally, he still hadn't emailed me, I'd sleep well. Maybe I'd even watch another movie with Alaric? Not that I could tell you what last night's film was, who was in it, or anything about the plot.

I gave "my" second horse a pat and led him back to the barn. Chaucer would love it here—he was a big fan of summer, always seeking out the sun, and the acres of pastures would be his idea of heaven. But we didn't have this much space in England. Everything was smaller.

I was just shutting the stall door when my phone rang. Alaric?

No, Gemma.

"Hey, how are you doing?" I asked.

What time was it in London? Nine p.m.?

"Good, I think. Better than last week. I still... I can't believe..."

"That part of your life's done now. It's okay to move on."

"Move on? Are you serious? I'm staying single forever. I'm totally not cut out for dating."

"I didn't mean dating. Just finding new friends." What was that weird cry in the background? I had limited experience with children—unless you counted Piers—but it sounded almost like a baby. "What's that noise?"

"Uh, Feather?"

Feather? Feather was Judd's cat, a velvety grey British shorthair who wore a perpetual scowl and acted as if she owned the place.

"Gemma, where are you? I thought you were staying in my flat?"

"I was going to, but then Judd had to go to Switzerland for the weekend, and he asked if I'd stay to feed Feather, and she's so cute..."

Fair enough—Alaric had mentioned Sirius's previous PAs having to take care of Judd's cat when he went away, and since I wasn't in London, it was kind of Gemma to step in. But why did she seem so edgy?

"Are you okay?"

"Yes?"

She didn't sound sure. But the small talk was Gemma's way—whenever she didn't want to say something, she'd beat around the bush for a while until she worked up the nerve. I'd left London too soon, hadn't I? I should have stayed to support her. Four thousand miles away, all I could do was talk.

"It's Wednesday. Is Judd still away?"

"Uh, no. He came back."

Please, say she hadn't...

"Gemma, you literally said two seconds ago that you'd sworn off men."

"And I have. He's just...just..."

A lunatic? Emmy's earlier words echoed in my head. Dammit, I wished I'd been able to hear the rest of that conversation.

"He's just nice. Honestly, that's all."

"I'm worried about you."

"And I'm worried about you."

"With Alaric? There's really no need."

Gemma gave a little giggle, and I was glad to hear it. Perhaps things weren't as bad as I'd feared?

"Oh, no, I'm not worried about Alaric. Like, he's the gay best friend every girl wants. I meant with all the stuff in America. Judd said the people Alaric's after aren't very nice."

I'm sorry. What?

"Back up a bit. What did you just say?"

"The painting thing—Judd said the people who took it could be dangerous. I haven't seen any more dodgy art at the gallery, in case you were wondering. Hugo's had a cold the whole week, so he's been moping around and complaining instead of working."

"No, I meant the part about Alaric being gay?"

"You didn't know?"

"Well, I don't think he is." He definitely knew how to please a woman.

"Really? But I heard him...you know...with Ravi."

"What?" Was she serious? "When?"

"The first night I was at Judd's place."

"You must have been mistaken."

Although hadn't Emmy also thought Ravi batted for the other team?

"No, I don't think so. When we walked past the bedroom door, I could hear...uh..."

"Gemma..."

"Balls on flesh, okay? It's quite a distinctive sound. And Judd, he just chuckled and said that Ravi and Alaric were up to their old shenanigans again."

Alaric and Ravi? My knees gave way, and I slumped onto a hay bale. I felt sick. No, not at the thought of *that*. Rather, at the loss of a man I'd never truly had. I... I really, really liked Alaric, yes, in that way, even if I'd been in attempted denial. The big speech in England he'd made, the one where he'd told me he wasn't worth it... I'd thought that if I just stuck around long enough and showed him that he was, maybe things could be different. His words replayed in my mind. *I live in the shadows, Beth. I'm no Prince Charming. And I'm not the kind of man you throw your entire future away for. It's only a job.* Had he been talking about himself as relationship material? Or merely as an employer? I'd believed it was the former. At least, I'd wanted to believe it. But what if I'd been wrong?

Another memory popped into my head, of Alaric telling me he wasn't in the market for a woman. I'd assumed he meant work took priority at that time, but what if he'd been trying to tell me in a roundabout way that he preferred men?

"Beth?"

"Oh," was all I managed to say.

"Shit, I'm sorry. You like him?"

"Alaric's just a friend. Really. If he's happy with Ravi, then I'm happy he's happy." Desperate to change the subject, I latched onto something else. "What were you doing up with Judd in the middle of the night?"

A long pause.

"I was a bit upset. Everything...it just got to me. I was trying to stay quiet, but Judd must have superhuman hearing because he heard me crying and came in to check I was okay. And when I wasn't, he took me downstairs and made me hot chocolate. See what I mean? He's nice. And he looks out for me. He drives me to work every day and picks me up, and... and...that's the main reason I'm calling, actually. Judd said not to say anything, that he'd handle it, but..."

See? I was right, even though I wished with all my heart I'd been wrong.

"What happened?"

"Judd picks me up from the gallery, and he waits out the front in his car. Did you know he drives a

Jaguar?"

"No." And I didn't care either. "Gemma, what happened?"

"There was a girl standing outside this afternoon with a baby in her arms. Really nervous looking. And she asked if I knew an American man who'd been asking questions on the Bellsfield Estate."

Alaric. Or possibly Ravi. It had to be. And they'd been asking those questions right before we'd killed a man. Me, Alaric, Ravi, Emmy, Sky, and Gemma. We'd all been involved.

Shit.

"What did you say?"

"Nothing! I had no clue *what* to say. Judd got out of the car, and I thought he'd help me, but then this woman walked past on the phone—one of those hoity-toity types, you know the ones—and she wasn't watching where she was going. She just walked right into the girl. And the girl fell into the road, and there was a car coming..."

Now I felt even sicker. "The baby?"

"She tried to jump out of the way, but she lost her balance and kind of threw the baby. I managed to catch it, but Judd couldn't get to her in time." Gemma gulped back a sob. "She bounced off the car and hit her head on the pavement."

It was a good thing I'd sat down already. This whole case was jinxed. More than once, Alaric had muttered about the Becker paintings being cursed, and I was beginning to believe him.

"Is she okay?"

"I don't know. She's in the hospital. We followed the ambulance in the car, and the police were on their way, and I was panicking because what if she knows what we did and she tells them? And Judd told me not to worry, that he'd sort it out."

At that moment, I wasn't sure whether that was a good thing or a bad thing.

"What did he do?"

"Well, they wouldn't tell us anything at first because apparently they can only talk to next of kin. So he fibbed a tiny bit."

Uh-oh. "What did he say?"

Another pause, and I imagined Gemma biting her lip the way she always did when she got nervous.

"He told the nurse that the girl was his wife and the baby was his."

"He did what?"

"The good news is that we're allowed in to see her now—I'm his sister, by the way—but Alaric isn't answering his phone and neither is Emmy, so Judd basically made up a name for the girl because we have no idea who she is. Plus we also have a baby to look after. I don't suppose you know where Alaric disappeared to?"

"No, but he's meant to be coming to pick me up soon."

"Oh, thank goodness. Could you get him to call Judd? And don't tell him I told you any of this. We didn't want to worry you."

Usually, I tried to avoid swearing out loud, but "fuck" really was the only appropriate word in that situation. It just slipped out.

"Where's the baby, Gemma?"

"On the sofa. Judd's gone to the shop to buy food and nappies."

"Is it old enough to eat food?" And I couldn't keep calling the baby "it." "Is it a boy or a girl?"

"Neither of us has looked yet, but Judd found a growth chart on the internet, and we measured it with a ruler. We reckon it's about six months old."

Bloody hell. "He'll need to get formula as well."

"Uh, I'll tell him. He's going back to the hospital after to sit with the girl. Can you find Alaric?"

I spoke through gritted teeth. "I'll do my very best."

Emmy was right. Judd was an absolute lunatic.

CHAPTER 17 - ALARIC

BETH WAVED GOODBYE to Harriet, but as soon as she climbed into the passenger seat, her smile faded.

"Everything okay?" Alaric asked.

"We have a small problem."

"How small?"

"About two feet, I'd say." She closed her eyes and sighed as she leaned her head back. "Judd and Gemma...they've...well, they've kidnapped a baby."

No, he must have misheard.

"For a moment there, I thought you said Judd and Gemma kidnapped a baby."

"Yes, because they did."

"You'll have to start at the beginning."

"Gemma called me half an hour ago. A girl came to the gallery today, asking her about 'the American man who'd been asking questions on the Bellsfield Estate.' That's got to be you, hasn't it? Or Ravi?"

Yes, they'd been asking questions, but they'd been careful not to leave any evidence that the "suicide" of one of the residents had actually been a little less than voluntary. Could a reporter have gotten wind of Gemma's involvement? Unlikely—the death of a nobody on a run-down housing estate was hardly front-page news. But Gemma had dated the guy for months—had she made any friends there? Met any acquaintances who might know where she worked?

"Gemma didn't recognise her?"

"She says not."

"How did we get from a visitor at the gallery to kidnap?"

"The girl had a baby with her. And while she was talking to Gemma, some toff took offence to her being on the pavement, and she ended up getting hit by a car."

Getting closer... Alaric had a bad feeling about this.

"That still doesn't explain the baby."

"Well, I guess Judd was worried about the girl knowing too much, because he told the staff at the hospital that he was the father of her baby, and now he's at her bedside playing the concerned husband until she wakes up."

"Fuck."

"Funny, that's the exact word I used."

Judd's loyalty was unquestionable, and for that Alaric was grateful, but hot damn, couldn't he think things through for *once*? Alaric's stomach twisted into a knot because although he'd spoken to a dozen women with babies during their search for Gemma, only one had made a long-lasting impression. *Say it wasn't Hevrin...*

"Give me your phone." Alaric took a deep breath. "Please."

"What happened to yours?"

"Emmy dropped hers, so I lent her mine, and she left it on top of the car and drove off."

He should have known better. Emmy went through so many phones she got a bulk discount. Beth fished hers out of her purse, but when he moved to take it, she held on.

"Uh, could you not tell him I told you? Gemma said she wasn't meant to mention it."

Good thing Judd was in London. Alaric couldn't inflict grievous bodily harm if he was four thousand miles away, could he now? He punched in Judd's number, put the phone on speaker, and waited. One ring, two, three...

"What's up, babe?"

"Her name's Beth, not 'babe.' What have I told you about harassing the female staff?"

"I'm on my best behaviour. Scout's honour."

Right.

"So, how are things in London? Busy day? Have you been working with your usual *clinical* efficiency?"

Emphasis on the clinical. Judd's pause said he knew what Alaric knew.

"I tried to call you." He lowered his voice and echoed Beth. "There's a small problem."

"How small?"

"Five feet six and 35-25-35 at a guess."

For fuck's sake.

"Elaborate. And stop referring to women like they're objects."

"A girl stopped Gemma outside the Pemberton gallery today. Started asking questions about the Bellsfield Estate. About an American. Then some bitch in a designer suit barged her out of the way, and she landed in traffic."

"So you called an ambulance, right?"

Alaric already knew the answer, but he also didn't want to drop Gemma in it. Trust was important in this game.

"Yes, but what if she knows something about what went on last week? Gem's been through enough already, and you and Ravi don't want your names coming out. The cops are gonna question her when she wakes up."

"About the accident, presumably, not about the Bellsfield Estate."

"What happens if she lets something slip? Do you want to take that chance?"

Quite honestly? No. But when there was a child involved, that had to take priority, a fact Judd should have been well aware of after everything they'd been through with Rune. This was why Alaric's name was on her fake birth certificate rather than his.

"It's not just about us. Who's the girl? Does she have a name? Any ID?"

"I lifted her wallet, but all that's in it is ten quid and a bus ticket. Her phone got smashed in the accident. So for now, her name's Nada Millais-Scott, and her address is Curzon Place." Curzon Place was Judd's townhouse in Kensington. "The bloody receptionist wouldn't let me past unless I was next of kin."

"Nada?"

"The first name I thought of. She looks Middle Eastern, and I used to work with a woman from Iraq called Nada. I panicked, okay? There was a baby."

Middle Eastern. Alaric's worst fears were ninety percent confirmed.

"I'll need a photo to be sure, but she's likely to be Hevrin Moradi. She's a Kurdish refugee, and she was instrumental in leading us to Gemma. Where's the baby?"

"With Gemma."

"You can't just keep a baby, Judd. Social Services should be..." Alaric trailed off. Emmy had been in the foster system, and so had Sky. It hadn't been kind to either of them. Yes, Judd was an impulsive asshole, but he wouldn't abuse a kid, and between Blackwood and Sirius, they'd move heaven and earth to look after it. "Never mind. The baby's at your place?"

"Yeah."

"Do you know how to take care of it?"

"No fucking clue, mate."

"Are you at the hospital?"

"Next to her bed. I got her a private room."

"How is she?"

"She wasn't knocked out for long, but she was confused and crying when she came round, so they took her for an MRI and a CT scan to be on the safe side. Her arm's broken, but they reckon her head's okay. Now she's sleeping. I don't know what she's told them, but nobody's arrested me yet."

Good. Alaric had to take that as a positive, apart from the broken bone, obviously.

"But..." Judd continued.

"But?"

"I saw the X-rays. That girl's broken half the bones in her body at some point or another."

"Fuck."

"I told the doctors she used to race motocross bikes."

"Motocross? We're gonna need to work on your bullshit, buddy."

"Normally I'm good at it—you know that. This just threw me off balance. The baby and everything. Shit, it was a close call."

"What happened to the woman who pushed her?"

"She tried to walk off, but I grabbed her handbag and hung onto it until the police picked her up for questioning. No way was she leaving it behind, even if the self-centred cow did try to snatch it back while I was putting Nada into the recovery position."

"Hevrin."

"Right, Hevrin. About this baby..."

"I'll find someone who can help. Leave it with me."

Alaric hung up and leaned his head against the steering wheel. Why him? He could've gotten a nice, easy job pushing paper around a desk, but instead, he was left to wrangle former spies and bail women out of tricky situations.

"Why didn't you tell him to go to Social Services?" Beth asked.

"Because I don't want this kid turning into Sky. Foster parents are a mixed bag. Do you know anybody who might have a clue how to look after a baby?"

Beth thought for a moment. "I guess I can see your point about Sky. What about you? Didn't you help with Rune when she was little?"

"I wasn't involved with Rune in her younger years."

Cue the disapproving glare. Alaric had to take it. No way was he having a discussion about Rune's origins at that particular point in time.

"What about Dan? Doesn't she have a son?"

"Dan adopted Caleb when he was ten. And don't even consider suggesting Emmy—kids scare her more than small-arms fire."

"I guess I know the basics. My sister's eight years younger than me, and I used to help the nanny with feeding her and things."

"Call Gemma. Do what you can to assist while I drive us back."

Judd might have been sought after as a spy and an assassin, but as a nanny? No.

Back at the house, Alaric had hoped to see Emmy or even Dan, but the only person home was Black, sitting behind his laptop at the kitchen table.

"Anything new?" he asked.

"You could say that. This case is going from bad to worse. I should've stayed in Thailand."

Now Black looked up. "I'll gladly pay for the ticket if you want to go back there." One-way, of course. Asshole. "What happened?"

Alaric gave him a brief précis, and predictably, Black laughed.

"There's a woman in the hospital," Alaric snapped. "This isn't fucking funny."

"Yes. More absurd, I'd say. So, what do you need?"

"Do you know anyone with a baby? Gemma needs advice."

"I thought you were the man who knew everything?" Black's tone was mocking.

"I've never had to change a diaper before. Do you know anyone, or don't you?"

Finally, Black picked up the phone. "Georgia's got an eighteen-month-old daughter. I'll get her to call."

CHAPTER 18 - BETH

AFTER GEMMA'S REVELATION about Alaric, I'd been shocked, but by morning, I'd had time to think things through. Beyond the drunken fumble at my father's birthday party, it wasn't as though he'd shown any extracurricular interest in me apart from going out of his way to help turn my life around and being extraordinarily nice. Gemma was right. He was the good friend every girl wanted. Plus without the sexual tension constantly running through me, I'd be able to relax more. Stop worrying about what I looked like and what every little touch meant.

And another huge positive—he wasn't Judd.

"Any update on Hevrin?" I asked Alaric as we climbed into the car. We'd both decided to skip breakfast at the house since Stéphane had promised to make pancakes today. Alaric planned to work from the ranch. He said he could do with a change of scene, but secretly, I suspected the fact that Black had taken over the kitchen table had influenced his decision. According to Dan, Black was focusing on Ridley and his buried dirt.

The hospitalised girl had a name now, at least. Judd had sent a picture, and Alaric recognised her. With some help from a friend of Black's, Gemma had managed to change the baby and feed her, although she got slightly squicked out when the baby vomited. Totally normal, Georgia assured her. Gemma seemed pleased that she'd taken a vow of chastity.

"Hevrin's still sleeping, but the doctors don't seem to think there's a cause for concern."

On the medical front, at least.

"How do you think she found Gemma?"

"I don't know. Judd and I both spoke to Gemma last night, and she's adamant she never told anyone on the Bellsfield Estate apart from the dead guy where she worked."

"What if *he* told Hevrin? What if they were friends? What if...?"

"When I spoke to her, she said she didn't know him. And don't forget, she was the one who helped give him up. Plus I never even mentioned Gemma to her—I told her I was from the council, acting on a complaint about a cat."

"You only met her once?"

"Twice." Alaric blew out a long breath. "But I might have sent her a care package afterwards."

"A care package?"

"Food and some cash. She couldn't even afford groceries."

Why did that not surprise me? Alaric had a big heart.

"Could she have tracked us down from that?"

"Not without the investigative skills of Blackwood. I sent everything anonymously. And even if she traced the stuff to me, that still doesn't get her to Gemma."

It was a mystery, one we wouldn't solve until Hevrin decided to tell us. *If* she decided to tell us. And nobody was going to go against the doctor's advice and wake her prematurely.

All we could do was wait.

Stéphane and Harriet both greeted me with hugs when we arrived at Lone Oak Farm. The ranch was fast becoming my happy place, a home away from home in Chaucer's absence. The rolling pastures were balm to my soul. And yes, there were pancakes, a great big stack of them with crispy bacon and maple syrup. Beside the platter sat a jug of fresh coffee, and next to that lay two paper files, each an inch or so thick.

"What are those?" I asked Harriet. I'd definitely become nosier since I began working for Sirius.

"Remember those cases we discussed yesterday? Kyla's teenage horror story? Rusty's brother's a deputy, and I asked him to..." She put her hand over her mouth and coughed. "Borrow them. I got curious."

"We both did," Stéphane said. "Talk about liar, liar, pants on fire."

"Kyla's lyin' ass could send a rocket ship to the moon."

"What cases?" Alaric asked.

Oops. "I completely forgot to tell you last night what with...everything. I'm so sorry."

"How about you tell me now?"

Stéphane did the honours. "When Kyla was a teenager, she sent her boyfriend to jail and disappeared her best friend."

"We don't know that for sure," Harriet said. "The second part at least. The first part's a given."

"Mind if I take a look?" Alaric asked.

"Knock yourself out. Stéphane's also compiled a list of all the videographers around here, so we can start calling once we've mucked out the horses. He already sent the names to Dan, and she said she'd take A through G."

Alaric poured himself a large coffee and set his laptop on the table. "Looks as if we've got a busy day ahead, doesn't it?"

By lunchtime, we'd spoken to half the people on Stéphane's list, but all of them denied coming to Lone Oak Farm. Some hadn't even heard of the senator. Harriet had gone back out to the horses, and Stéphane was seeing to Irvine, who seemed happy to eat his lunch today. My voice was hoarse from talking, but Alaric still sounded smooth in every way.

"Is this what you do every day?" I asked him.

"Fortunately, no. I usually deal with intelligence gathering at a higher level. Take a break, sweetheart. Drink something."

"But there are still so many names left."

"A lot of these people seem to be busy filming in the afternoons. I think we'll have better luck trying again tomorrow morning, and I need to call Judd in any case."

Gemma had phoned in sick, and apparently Hugo wasn't happy since she'd also taken the whole of last week off. But when she pointed out that she'd most likely got her imaginary cold from his coughing and spluttering, he soon piped down. The baby was eating and pooping, she said. Mostly pooping.

Alaric propped his tablet up on the table, and I squashed onto the bench next to him. Urgh, Judd looked terrible. Had he slept at all since the accident?

"How's it going?" Alaric asked.

"I'd forgotten how bad hospital food tastes."

"Why are you eating hospital food?"

"I've been here the whole night."

"What about visiting hours?"

"What can I say? The nurses like me."

"How's Hevrin? Any change?"

Then we heard a weak whisper coming from the speakers. "Why does everyone keep calling me Nada?"

Judd's head whipped around, and in the background, I saw Hevrin for the first time. Slender with dark hair, fine features, and wires sprouting from both arms.

"Hey, you're awake," Judd said.

"Where am I?" She tried to sit up. "Where's Indy?"

"Indy's your daughter? She's fine. We're taking care of her."

Hevrin's voice rose in panic. "Who are you? Where am I?"

"You're in the hospital. A car hit you. And I'm... Well, it's a tad complicated. You were looking for an American man, and..."

Hevrin leaned forward, piercing eyes fixed on the screen, and then she seemed to relax infinitesimally.

"It's you?" she asked, and I realised she was talking to Alaric.

"Yes. I'm sorry I can't be there in person."

"I still don't understand what happened."

"You were talking to Gemma outside the Pemberton gallery when a woman got impatient and shoved you under a car."

Hevrin closed her eyes again. "I don't remember. I was going to go to the gallery, but I don't remember."

"My friend here came with you to the hospital, and he called you Nada because he didn't know your name at the time. None of us wanted to see your little girl taken in by the authorities."

"Did she get hurt too?"

Alaric smiled. "Not even a scratch. Gemma caught her."

"*Alhamdulillah*," she breathed, her voice barely audible.

"Are you up to speaking? Or would you like to see the doctors? Get them to check you over?"

"I've been through worse."

Alaric squeezed my hand under the table. "That doesn't make it okay."

"I can talk. I just wanted to thank you. That's why I came. And also to tell you that I'm not living in my flat at the moment. The food..."

Judd's brow furrowed. Guess Alaric had forgotten to mention the part about the care package to him.

"What happened to your flat?"

"The police are in it."

"Why?"

"There was a bad smell, so the council came. They took apart the plumbing and found... Eunice said it was pieces of leg. A person's leg. Then all the stuff we normally flush down the toilet got stuck behind it, and the blockage got worse, and the bathrooms near the bottom of the tower flooded. Some of the pipes run behind the walls in my flat, so now the police are pulling them down."

Oh. My. Gosh. I regretted the chicken I'd eaten for lunch because it nearly came straight back up again.

"They found body parts?" Alaric asked, and he

sounded incredulous too.

"That's what Eunice said. They didn't tell me much, just said I had to go."

"Go where?"

"To a bed and breakfast. In Ealing." She cracked the tiniest smile. "The hospital is actually nicer."

A door opened, not in the farmhouse but in the hospital. Judd's head turned to the side, and I heard a female voice.

"Mrs. Millais-Scott, you're awake. Good. How are you feeling?"

Hevrin looked puzzled, but only for a second.

"Much better, thank you."

The screen went blank. Wow. Working for Sirius was like living in a soap opera.

Alaric didn't say anything straight away, just poured himself a glass of water from the pitcher on the table. Me? I couldn't stop thinking about the body parts. If we hadn't found Gemma when we did, would that have been her remains in the drain? Despite the warmth, I shuddered.

"Don't think about it," Alaric said. "We did what we could. Gemma's safe, and that sick freak's dead."

"But somebody else didn't make it."

"Don't dwell on the past. It only ruins your future." He sighed. "I know, I know. Do as I say, not as I do."

Don't dwell on the past. Those were words to live by. Logically, I knew that, but still...

"At least Hevrin seems to be keeping the secret about that night." I tried to think positive.

"*Seems* to be."

Alaric's tone sent another chill through me.

"You don't think she will?"

"Right now? I don't know. I keep coming back to the logistics—how did she find us? She only lived on the estate for a month, and she's a refugee. She's got no network. No contacts. We gave her almost nothing to go on, and yet somehow, there she was."

"You're worried." He had lines on his forehead, and I ran a fingertip along one furrow. "Is there anything I can do?"

"No." He shook his head. "I'll speak to Judd later, but I think Hevrin Moradi's got her own secrets. And I doubt she'll share them before she's ready."

CHAPTER 19 - EMMY

"SO, WHERE ARE we?" I asked.

Black wanted to have a recap before we left for Norfolk because this case had more tentacles than a genetically modified octopus. Nothing was bloody simple at the moment—apparently, there'd been a training accident at Riverley and Alex had broken ribs, but Rafael sent a message to Black saying he was handling it. Thank fuck. I didn't have time to fix any more problems today, not with Dan, Alaric, and Bethany sitting at the kitchen table in the rental house, waiting to start. At least there were Danishes. Bethany had picked them up from somewhere.

"Damn dog," Black muttered as he uncapped his fountain pen. I looked under the table. Barkley was sitting on his feet, her chin resting on his knees as she waited hopefully for any stray flakes of pastry to drop. Black might have complained, but he still put down his pen to scratch her head as Dan started speaking.

"Let's start with the problem that brought us here— the painting. We've got two possible leads—the two men who visited Irvine here at the house. Stephané and the nurse have both worked with us to produce sketches. The man Stephané saw bears a vague resemblance to Dyson. See?"

Dan turned her laptop, where the screen showed

the newest sketch lined up beside the drawing produced eight years ago when Alaric and I worked with an artist after our Atlantic gun-fest. Irvine's visitor had been wearing glasses, and his hair was thinner, and his jaw was different. The same man? Possibly.

"It looks more like Nicolas Cage," Black said.

"Stephané admits he's terrible with faces. If this *is* Dyson, we're chasing a shadow. Which leaves the second guy." Dan clicked to another sketch, a much younger guy with a goatee. "Neither Harriet nor Stephané recognises him. Working on the assumption that he recorded the endorsement video, we called every professional videographer in a hundred-mile radius to see if they were involved, but so far, nobody's admitting to it."

"So far?" Black asked.

"Six of them didn't answer the phone, and one man I spoke to sounded evasive. We're following up, and I've got two interns from the Lexington office expanding the search radius to two hundred miles and also checking websites to see if anyone in the industry matches the sketch."

"Leave that ticking along. Priority goes to Devane right now, and by extension, Eric Ridley."

"Guilt by association?" Alaric asked.

"You could say that. Nobody hires a man like Ridley unless they're strapped for cash or shady, and Devane claims to be worth two hundred million bucks. My sources say it's more like fifty million, but that's still not an insignificant amount."

Her wealth came from family money—her father had been big in the aviation industry before his death nine years ago, ironically in a plane crash. By all accounts, Kyla had never done a proper day's work in her life, although she did have a thriving Instagram account and got paid big bucks to flog make-up and turn up to parties. Oh, and she'd presented a short-lived reality show where rich people and poor people swapped houses for a week. Rumour said she'd disinfected her shoes every time she set foot in the projects and once squirted a Black man with Purell before she allowed him to shake her hand.

Alaric tilted his head from one side to the other. "Plenty to hire decent security."

He ought to know—his parents were worth as much as Kyla, and they often had a bodyguard or two around.

"Precisely my point. Anyhow, I've had a word in the ear of a friendly reporter, and the American public will shortly be getting a reminder that Ridley was suspected of involvement in the murder of three little girls and their parents in Kandahar. Logan's on his way there to see if he can dig up any further information."

Alaric raised an eyebrow. "He's going to Afghanistan?"

"I don't believe Kyla Devane has an appropriate temperament to represent Kentucky in the senate, so it seemed worth the airfare."

Black might have framed his motives as altruistic, but I suspected there was a teeny bit of self-interest involved. His genuine dislike of Ridley had come through loud and clear in our conversations over the last two days. But Alaric seemed to swallow the explanation.

"I find myself in unexpected agreement."

Black ignored the jab. "I've also got our people in Syria taking another look at the incident off the coast of

Latakia, but since Ridley was officially exonerated, I'm not sure it'll help our cause to draw attention to it at this time."

"Which brings us back to Kyla herself."

"Yes. Assuming she *is* shady, it appears she's also careful. We can't find concrete evidence of any recent wrongdoing, just a whole lot of suspicious smears and rumours. It appears her ex-staff all signed NDAs, and she has a hair trigger when it comes to sending her lawyer after them. You mentioned you'd found something interesting, though?"

"It was Beth and Harriet rather than me, but yes. Kyla might not have been quite so discreet as a teenager."

Alaric told us about two incidents—one where Kyla's sense of entitlement was compounded by a boyfriend dumb enough to take the rap for her, fairly cut and dried, and another that sounded far more interesting. Black leaned forward an inch. He thought so too.

"Doesn't sound hopeful for Piper."

"No, it doesn't. Although nobody found her car either, and that's harder to hide than a body."

"You've reviewed details of the case?"

"Harriet 'borrowed' the files from the sheriff's archive. I've got digital copies of everything, although 'everything' isn't as much as you'd expect. Apparently, the sheriff at the time of Piper's disappearance was one of Daddy Devane's cronies. The current sheriff's more conscientious by all accounts, but he's got limited resources and sees no need to reopen a case colder than the dark side of an iceberg. Piper's grandmother still lives in town, according to Stéphane, but she's got a reputation for being a bit out there so nobody listens to her."

"Out there?" I asked. "In what way?"

"She believes Piper was abducted by aliens. Her buddies at the Saucer Syndicate stage a picket outside the Woodford County Sheriff's Office every year on the anniversary of her disappearance, although in recent years, it's turned into more of a general conspiracy theory-based rant."

"I see how that could be controversial. What about her parents?"

"Never in the picture, so Harriet says. When Kyla and Piper started hanging out in ninth grade, Piper was the ugly duckling, but smart, and Kyla just wanted someone to do her homework. Piper managed to stay in the clique as she blossomed into a swan, but there was evidently tension between the two of them, which culminated in the homecoming queen face-off."

"Wannabe royalty, tinfoil hats, and a body lying in a shallow grave. Maybe," Dan murmured. "All the makings of a good novel."

"Except this is real life," I pointed out. "But you know how you love a good cold case..."

"I also love sleep."

"You can sleep after the election. I'll make you hot chocolate and sing you a lullaby."

"Sing? You? I just said I liked sleep."

"How about I promise to keep my mouth shut instead?"

Dan sighed and drained the last dregs of her coffee. "Fine, send me the file."

Bradley had left me an outfit on the jet—a cocktail dress in deep purple, plain enough that I didn't look like a tart but short enough for me to play the part of a trophy wife. Yes, some outsiders knew I was involved with Blackwood, but I never liked to disclose quite how hands-on my job was. Far better to play dumb and let people underestimate me.

Black was wearing his old dress uniform, which, let's face it, was the only reason I usually went to these things with him. Not only did I get to stare at him in it all evening, but since our marriage had turned from a convenient sham into at-it-like-rabbits, I also got to peel him out of it at the end of the night. Bradley had booked us a hotel room nearby, thank goodness. Otherwise the cab driver might have got an eyeful.

"What's the plan, boss?" I asked. "Do you want me in full vapid-blonde mode tonight?"

"I think so, yes." Black cracked a rare smile. "You certainly look the part."

I threw a tube of mascara at him, but the asshole caught it.

"Ah, you want me to go as a drag queen?"

"Shut up, Chuck."

The O Club could have been any mid-budget hotel the world over—slightly tired decor, harried waitstaff rushing around, and an unimaginative menu created with a nod to profit margins rather than gourmet dining. The white tablecloth had a tiny hole in front of my place card, and my wine glass had a chipped rim.

But we were seated just one table away from Eric

Ridley.

He was angled side-on to me, his uniform now a little tight across the stomach, and since he kept turning away to talk to the brunette on his right—he hadn't brought a date of his own, she was somebody else's—that gave me plenty of time to check him out unobserved. He'd changed his hairstyle since I saw him last. Tonight, the top was slicked back, the sides shaved. But paying a visit to the barber didn't make up for his tendency to slouch. Every so often, he'd catch himself and straighten. Puff his chest out. He also liked the sound of his own voice. The others at his table struggled to get a word in edgeways, and I caught a couple of eye-rolls during a particularly long anecdote. Which fitted with Black's assessment that Ridley lacked self-awareness and thought the lieutenant's stripes he wore on his shoulders elevated him to demigod status.

I'd had a fair bit of practice at this shite, so I still managed to make small talk and eat as well as conducting surveillance. Also at our table of ten was another Blackwood guy, a former enlisted man who Black had recruited into our Boston office a few years after he and Nate started the company. Black did that a lot—snaffled up the good guys he met along the way—which meant our team was built on a solid foundation.

I went easy on the wine, watching, waiting for my chance. It finally came between dessert and the start of the charity auction when Ridley pushed his chair back and strode off in the direction of the bathrooms. The relief from his dining companions was palpable.

"Be right back," I whispered to Black, picking up the oversized handbag Bradley had sent for the occasion. Black caught my hand and kissed my knuckles, and the lady opposite swooned a bit. I couldn't blame her.

A moment later, I slid into Ridley's vacant seat and smiled at the brunette.

"Hi, I was just wondering where you got your necklace? It's really eye-catching." In a gaudy, plasticky sort of way. I lowered my voice a touch. "Plus I wanted to escape yet another conversation about ships' innards."

"You like it?" She sounded faintly surprised. "It was a gift from my husband." Ah, so she was wearing it under duress. "Honey, where did you buy my necklace?"

A faint look of panic crossed the man's face, which was made all the more amusing by the captain's stripes he wore.

"Uh, from the internet."

"Which site?" she asked. "This lady wants to buy one."

"I don't remember. There was an ad."

The brunette rolled her eyes. Men.

"Sorry," she told me.

"No problem." I picked up Ridley's three-quarters-full wine glass as if it were my own, careful to hold it by the very bottom of the stem as I took a sip. Ridley had wrapped his fingers around the bowl each time he drank. I'd been watching him. And at one point, he'd swapped the glass into his other hand while he accepted a business card from the guy opposite. "Nice to meet you, anyway. Do you happen to know where the bathrooms are?"

She pointed me in the right direction, which I already knew. Ridley passed me on the way, and I couldn't resist holding up his glass in an imaginary toast.

"Great evening, huh?"

"Sure is," he said automatically, then his gaze rose from my cleavage to my face, and he scowled when he recognised me.

I held my smile, sweetened it to saccharine as I carried on walking. Ridley and Kyla deserved each other.

Locked safely in a bathroom stall, I tossed the remains of the wine down the toilet, then set the glass on the closed lid. Forensics had never really been my thing, but I'd spent enough time in the lab to know how to collect a set of fingerprints. Sure, I could have sealed the glass in an evidence bag and left it to the techs, but if this set of prints was smeared too... We'd be back to square one. At least if I did the work now, I could have another crack at Ridley right away if it didn't pan out.

Carefully, carefully, I sprinkled graphite powder onto the glass, then gently brushed away the excess. Jackpot. Four fingers and a thumb near the bottom where he'd held the glass to drink, plus the same on the sides, and they looked pretty clear to me. Phew. I'd got both hands. Once I'd transferred the detail onto sticky tape and stuck the prints onto a piece of white card, I photographed them and sent the pictures to the Cincinnati lab. Black had put them on standby. We'd have an answer as to whether they matched the prints on the laptop bag by the time the charity auction started.

My job done, I wiped up the mess, stashed the evidence in my handbag, and strolled back to my husband. How long until we could leave? I'd rather walk a tightrope over a lava field than listen to another round of speeches, and my fingers were itching to get Black out of that uniform.

"Home time?" I whispered.

"Prints okay?"

"Yup."

He stood, a man of few words, towering above me despite my four-inch pumps. And we almost got away with it. A few nods, a couple of goodbyes, and we were almost at the exit when a bottle blonde in her late fifties stopped us, clipboard in hand.

"You're not leaving, are you?"

There were some moments when being a billionaire had definite drawbacks, and trying to sneak out of a function right before a charity auction began was most certainly one of them. Black never broadcast his wealth, but they knew he had money.

"We're just about to start our fundraiser," she continued. "Everyone was so excited when they saw your name on the guest list because we all know how much you *love* to support injured veterans."

"How about I just write you a cheque?" he offered.

"Where's the fun in that?" She looped her arms through ours, oblivious to the fact that I wanted to sew her lips shut. "You can come sit at our table. Linus, could you get extra chairs?"

"Someone kill me now," Black mouthed, but she didn't notice.

"Next time, you can bring Dan as your date," I muttered back.

Although I did change my mind half an hour later. Right after lot seventeen went up for auction, a signed football jersey from a player I'd never heard of. But it seemed Ridley had because he was locked into a bidding war with an admiral, and the price was up to sixteen hundred dollars and he was winning. Black waited until the last possible second, right before the hammer came down, before he raised his hand.

"Ten thousand dollars." He turned to stare right at Eric Ridley. "Your move, asshole," he murmured so only I could hear.

Oh, the way Ridley's cocky smile faded was worth the wasted hour. The vague confusion, the realisation, and finally the scowl that spread across his not-quite-so-smug face. Delightful.

The blonde woman started the applause, and soon everyone was clapping, even the admiral who'd been outbid. Everyone except Ridley, anyway.

"What are you gonna do with a football shirt?" I asked Black.

"Gift it to Admiral Nelson." Yes, that really was his name. "*Now* we can go."

Once again, we almost made it to the door, but this time, it was Ridley who blocked our way. Open the dictionary at the definition of "sore loser" and you'd find his ugly mug glowering back at you.

"I suppose you think that was funny," he snapped.

Black feigned puzzlement. "Are you referring to the ten thousand bucks I just donated to charity?"

"You know I've always been a fan of the Miami Dolphins."

"Actually, I had no idea."

"Just because Blackwood keeps losing out to EBR Group on contracts, there's no need to be petty."

"We're not interested in entering a race to the bottom. That benefits nobody."

"Bullshit. Blackwood's a bloated behemoth, that's why you're so overpriced. Too many has-beens like you at the top, sitting behind desks, collecting overinflated salaries. You've forgotten what it's like in the field."

Oh, what a load of bollocks. Comparing Blackwood to EBR was like saying that the only difference between a sweatshop and Louis Vuitton was that Louis Vuitton had more managers. Blackwood competed on quality, not price, and we weren't short of work. And as for suggesting Black kept his hands clean now... I had a feeling Ridley was going to find out just how dirty my husband could play, and soon.

But tonight, Black merely shrugged. "Sure, things change. Perhaps I enjoy finishing at five every day, then going home to my lovely wife."

"You're not the only one who can attract a pretty young lady," Ridley snapped back.

Did he mean Kyla? Had O'Shaughnessy's intern been right?

"And yet here you are alone."

"You always were an arrogant son of a bitch."

Black merely smirked. "Yet here *I* am with a beautiful woman and a football jersey."

"Fuck you."

Gee, that was original. The man certainly had a temper on him, didn't he? Black and I watched as Ridley turned on his heel and stomped back into the banquet hall, no doubt ready to inflict his foul mood onto the next victim.

"You know," Black said, his gaze heating as he looked down at me, "for once, I might actually take his advice."

CHAPTER 20 - ALARIC

"WELL, THIS OUGHTA set the cat among the pigeons," Alaric said.

Black worked fast, he had to give the man credit for that. The full forensic report had come in not long before midnight, and by the time Alaric's morning coffee was cool enough to drink, the results were already spreading online, thanks in no small part to O'Shaughnessy's campaign. Beth leaned over Alaric's shoulder and turned up the volume on a local news piece.

"Following Aidan O'Shaughnessy's dramatic fall from grace during Monday's senatorial debate in Frankfort, Kentucky, there appears to be a twist in the tale. Fingerprints belonging to Eric Ridley, a member of Kyla Devane's security team, have reportedly been found on a bag that held the Democratic candidate's laptop, the same laptop that was confiscated by police after it was found to contain underage pornography. Bruce Goddard, campaign manager for Mr. O'Shaughnessy, has confirmed to KSBC News that there is no reason why any member of Devane's staff should have handled the bag in question."

"Do you think that'll lose her enough votes?" Beth asked.

"Who knows? Give it an hour, and I expect the

Devane campaign'll come out with a rebuttal. Dispute the evidence, say O'Shaughnessy's lying because he's desperate, that sort of thing."

The fingerprint evidence would be enough to cast doubt in a criminal case, but in a trial by media? Voters were unpredictable. Really, they needed something more to tip the balance. Dan had gone to interview Piper Simms's grandmother with the dog riding shotgun—rather them than Alaric—and there was also Ridley's civilian atrocity to dig into. Alaric planned to call some of his contacts while Beth helped Harriet for an hour, but the bulk of his network was in Western Europe and North America, not the Middle East. Ditto for Judd, and Naz dealt with Eastern Europe. There were definite gaps in Sirius's coverage, but the firm didn't have the capital to facilitate a Blackwood rate of expansion. Only Judd was minted, and most of his money was tied up in family trusts. Growth at the moment was slow but steady.

Which was why he had to ask Beth to help out with the investigative work as well as organising accommodation for the next week since it looked as if they wouldn't be leaving anytime soon.

"I'll send the owner of this place an email right away," she said when he mentioned it. "Hopefully it'll be free for a while longer. If not, I'll find something similar."

"I'm sorry you can't stay with the horses all day today."

"Don't apologise—this is my job."

"But still..."

The guilt was strong, and with it came the realisation that Alaric didn't want Beth to make his travel arrangements and type his reports. He wanted her to play with horses all day, smile at him over dinner, scream his name as he fucked her, then curl against him while they slept. Even though deep down, he'd known the just-a-job story was bullshit, it was the first time he'd allowed himself to admit it, and the revelation hit him like a cannonball to the chest.

Fuck.

Could his feelings have reared their ugly heads at a worse time? Probably not. Not only were they in the middle of this Hydra of a case, but Beth had also distanced herself in the last couple of days. She'd clearly decided her role, and it was executive assistant rather than wannabe girlfriend. Since that night on the couch, she'd been the consummate professional, and Alaric had to afford her the same courtesy.

"Of course, yes, it *is* your job. A similar property will be fine. We're all used to packing up and moving around."

Beth's cheeks turned pink, and Alaric realised he'd put his foot in it yet again. She'd unpacked, hadn't she? Made herself at home. He kind of envied that optimism —even after her life got flipped on its head, she tried to put down roots, albeit shallow ones.

Alaric still put his toothbrush back in his suitcase after every use.

Predictably, the memo about professionalism hadn't reached every member of the Sirius team. At first, Alaric had been happy to see Judd sitting in his kitchen when he video-called him from the living room at Lone

Oak Farm, but that joy soon faded when he heard a baby cry.

"I thought Hevrin got discharged from the hospital last night?"

That's what Judd's latest email had said.

"Yeah, she did."

"So you took her home, right?"

"Mate, she's got a broken arm and a baby. I couldn't just drop her off in some shitty part of town and leave her to fend for herself. She needs help."

The words made sense, but not when it was Judd speaking them. His bedside manner consisted of flushing the condom and closing the door quietly on his way out.

"And you thought you'd be the best person to assist?"

"Nah, Gemma offered. Nada didn't even want to come, but Gem talked her round."

Gem? Nada? What, was he starting a bloody harem?

"Don't you mean Hevrin?"

"I guess I got used to calling her Nada in the hospital, and that's what her new passport says. She answers to either."

"She's not a fucking dog, Judd. And what do you mean, new passport?"

"The admin lady at the hospital wanted to see ID, and it was easier to call in a favour and get her a new passport than admit I didn't know what my own wife's name was."

"She's not your wife."

Alaric heard the cocky smirk in Judd's voice. "Our marriage certificate says otherwise."

"You've gone the whole nine yards, haven't you? What did you do, photoshop the honeymoon photos?"

"Nah, I only managed to get one good headshot before she got suspicious."

Deep breaths, Alaric.

"You've given her a whole new identity, and you haven't told her?"

"Need-to-know basis, mate. Although Mother heard about it on the grapevine and called with some awkward questions."

"I bet she did."

Stella Millais-Scott had spies everywhere, which was only to be expected for a woman who was second in command at MI6. She was also a ruthless bitch. Her boss, Sir Rodney Barrington, was rumoured to have suffered a minor heart attack last fall, and at the Millais-Scotts' most recent pre-Christmas gathering, she'd served up liver pâté, roast beef with all the trimmings, and crème brûlée. Alaric had felt his own arteries furring as he tucked in.

"Does that mean Hevrin won't be staying for long?" Alaric asked hopefully.

"I didn't tell Mother she was staying here. I just said we needed the spare ID for a job."

"And she bought that?"

"Who knows? She told me not to give Nada any money or bring her to family gatherings, reminded me yet again that my talents are wasted at Sirius, and then hung up."

Par for the course. Stella Millais-Scott made Black seem positively pleasant. Alaric would pay good money to watch the two of them go at it in a battle of wills.

"Well, speaking of your talents, I've got work for

you to do, work that doesn't involve women, forged documents, or making your mother dislike us any more than she already does."

"Buzzkill."

But Judd would help. He always did.

"Two and a half years ago, a former American Naval officer was involved in an incident in Afghanistan. His company got hired to search for a hostage, and somehow, a family of five ended up dead. Two adults, three children. He claimed they shot at his men first, that they were militia, but neighbours said the parents ran a bakery. Rumour says the wife got raped before she died."

"Man, that's bad. And the kids?"

"Someone tossed a grenade into their bedroom."

"Fuckers. Got a name?"

"Eric Ridley. EBR Group. Your contacts in the Middle East are better than mine, and I need any dirt you can dig up on the guy."

"Why? What's he up to?"

"It appears he's trying to meddle in a US senatorial election."

Judd gave a low whistle. "That porn thing? It was on the news last night."

"He works for one of the other candidates, and she's bad news."

"I'll get what I can, but I have to take Nada out to buy baby stuff first. Turns out those things need a *lot* of kit."

Although Alaric was annoyed that Judd was collecting women again, he couldn't deny that he'd have helped both Hevrin and Gemma in the same way if he'd been in London. He just had to hope that Judd didn't screw either of them, either physically or metaphorically.

"How's Hevrin holding up?"

"Hard to say. She's the quietest girl I've ever met. Gem's pretty freaked out by the whole dismembered women thing, though. She was crying again last night. But don't worry—a little of the old Judd magic soon changed that."

"Tell me you didn't..."

"Relax, I just made hot chocolate and watched a chick flick with her. Hmm... I think that might actually be the longest I've kept my clothes on around a woman. Which reminds me, how's our lovely new assistant?"

"Off limits," Alaric said through gritted teeth.

Judd guffawed. "To me or to you?"

"To both of us."

"You should consider changing your policy. If you got laid, maybe you wouldn't be so uptight all the time."

"Do some work, Judd."

Alaric hung up and let out an audible groan. Judd was good at his job—when he did it—but his personal life was a different story. He'd left a string of broken hearts from Tahiti to Timbuktu, and if he caused any more problems, Sirius's next hire would be a three-hundred-pound heavily tattooed babysitter named Butch.

"What's up?" Beth asked, walking in from the yard. "We're done with the animals, and Harriet said she'd look after Barkley while we're out asking questions."

Alaric rose halfway to pick a piece of straw out of Beth's hair. She smelled like the barn, but he didn't care. Horses were a part of her.

"Nothing you need to worry about."

"You realise when you say that, I only worry more?"

"Judd's just running Curzon Place like a halfway house. Hevrin's staying there as well."

"Oh, that's nice. She can keep Gemma company. How's her arm?"

The least of her problems if Mr. Millais-Scott got his teeth into her, or worse, his dick. But Alaric really didn't want to make Beth anxious.

"She's feeling better by all accounts. Ready to hit the road?"

Dan had spoken to Piper's grandma earlier. Barb Simms was the single mother of a single mother, and she still lived alone in the same trailer she'd shared with Piper after Piper's mom upped and disappeared. Runs in the family, she'd said. Never found a trace of either of them.

"What about the letter?" Alaric had asked Dan. "She didn't believe Piper sent it?"

"That was the only time Barb got angry. Said it was a low-down dirty hoax because Piper wanted to be a scientist, not a singer, and she only went to karaoke nights at the Tumbleweed Tavern because she wanted to fit in."

"Fit in with who? Kyla's crowd?"

"There were half a dozen girls she hung out with, and Kyla was one of them. Although it was a love hate relationship, apparently. Piper didn't like Kyla as a person, but she enjoyed perks that came with being her 'friend.' Cast-off designer togs, invites to the Devane family mansion, and latterly, boys."

"What did Grandma Simms think of Kyla?"

"She barely knew her. Piper never invited her to the trailer—probably embarrassed to—and the Devanes didn't exactly run in the same circles as Barb and her cronies," Dan said. "One of her pals turned up just as I was leaving, and he reeked of weed. An entire rock band could get high by sniffing his sweater."

"Did she give you anything useful?"

"Not much more than was in the file. Piper disappeared in broad daylight the Wednesday before homecoming. She felt ill in the morning and decided to stay home from school—just a cold, but she wanted to try and sleep it off before the dance. Barb went to work at the grocery store, and when she came back, Piper and her car had gone. At first, Barb thought maybe she'd gone to the pharmacy, but then it got dark, and she began to worry. The cops started canvassing the next morning."

"And we already know the rest of the story."

"Yes. Apart from her grandma, the last person to see her was a kid who watched her drive out of the school parking lot alone the previous day." Alone, not with Kyla or any of her other friends. Another symptom of the homecoming feud? "Anyhow, I've started canvassing the neighbours on Aspen Canyon, where Barb lives, but I want to go into town to check out the pharmacy angle, just in case. Can you and Beth carry on where I left off?"

"Just let us know who you've already spoken to."

"I'll email over a list. Although at this point, I'm beginning to think there's something in Barb's extraterrestrial theory. Nobody saw a thing."

Nobody saw a thing. Those words echoed in Alaric's head as he guided Beth towards the front door of the farmhouse, glancing towards Irvine Carnes's private wing as he did so. *Red After Dark* was still through there, and it was as if Dominique and *Emerald* were both laughing at them all.

CHAPTER 21 - BETH

GROWING UP, I'D always thought being a private detective was such a glamorous job. Sherlock Holmes, Magnum, Nancy Drew, Veronica Mars... I bet none of them spent two whole days traipsing up and down driveways in intermittent drizzle, asking questions that no one—absolutely no one—knew the answers to. Either the people hadn't lived there thirteen years ago, or they hadn't seen anything, or they couldn't remember back that far.

At first, Alaric and I had started off canvassing together, but after an hour or so, he let me take the lead on the questions, and when I didn't screw that up, I was finally allowed out into the big wide world on my own. He was twitchy, though, and I could understand why. If Piper *had* come to a nasty end, then her killer was still walking free. What if it hadn't been Kyla? Quite honestly, I struggled to believe that a teenager could not only murder a person, but also hide the body successfully for over a decade.

Which meant I was twitchy too.

Dan had dug up a voter registration list, and Alaric assigned me all the houses with either women or retirees listed as the only occupants. Plus I had to call him after every visit. So far, I'd worked my way down Aspen Canyon, a twisty road where ramshackle wooden homes and trailers nestled among the trees, and onto Lakeshore Drive. Alaric had twice as many properties to visit as me, but somehow, he was still farther ahead. I raised my hand to knock on another door.

"Hi, my name's Beth, and I'm working with a team of private investigators to—"

The lady stared at me. "You're English."

"Yes, from London. I'm just helping—"

"We don't like strangers around here."

On the contrary, all of her neighbours had been extremely welcoming. Half the pensioners had invited me in for cookies, and if I had one more cup of coffee, I'd never sleep again. Plus I really needed to pee.

"I promise I won't take up much of your time. We've been hired to look into the disappearance of a local girl, Piper Simms, and—"

"That was years ago."

Was I ever going to finish a sentence?

"Her grandma still can't sleep at night from wondering what—"

"Barb Simms thinks she got beamed up by little green men. You want my two cents? Look at that pothead she hangs out with. Homer. He always looks at my Lisa funny, don't he, hun?" She turned to the girl who'd materialised behind her, a redhead who didn't look more than twenty. The girl nodded. "See?"

"Thank you, that's very—"

"There, you've had my help. Now scoot. Some of us have got useful things to do." She began to close the door in my face. "You're hunting for a ghost. Waste of time."

Click.

Was it a waste of time? Who was Homer? I hurried

down the drive and dialled Alaric, feeling a tiny buzz of excitement. Was *this* what detective work was all about? Hours of tedium followed by a lead that might help to solve a murder?

"Everything okay?" Alaric asked.

"The lady I just spoke to, she told me about a man called Homer. Apparently, he's a friend of Piper's grandma, and he's a bit, well, creepy towards her daughter."

"Homer? Did you get a surname?"

"No, but she mentioned he smoked a lot of marijuana."

"Okay, I'll call... Wait. Homer? I bet that's a nickname for Bill Simpson. Dan already ruled him out. He went drinking the night before Piper disappeared and got arrested for urinating on a cop. Took him two days to sober up enough to make bail."

The spark I'd felt faded. "He peed on a *cop*?"

"Got confused, so he claimed."

"That must've been some bender." Homer made Piers look positively teetotal. "Have you found anything?"

"About Piper? No. But Kyla's campaign put out a press release about Ridley. They claim he merely moved the bag off a chair because he wanted to sit down."

"Really? Why would he need to hold the zipper for that? It doesn't ring true."

"You know that, I know that..."

"So what happens now?"

"Now things get interesting."

"What do you mean? They're not interesting enough already?"

"Ridley's got to know that O'Shaughnessy had help finding those fingerprints, and if he's smart, he'll realise Emmy and Black's presence at the reunion wasn't a coincidence. Which means we'll get front-row seats for the battle of Black versus Ridley. I may not always see eye to eye with Black, but I know who my money's going to be on."

"Is it too late to go back to London?"

I hadn't signed up for a battle, and although Black had been perfectly polite, he still scared me.

"Don't worry, I'll keep you out of the crossfire. Trust me?"

I might not have known Alaric for long, but yes, I did.

"I trust you. But don't forget I'll need to be in England in the middle of next month for my sister's wedding. Actually, maybe getting caught in the crossfire wouldn't be so bad—if I were dead, I'd have a valid excuse for declining the invite."

"You can't miss your sister's wedding."

"Just wishful thinking, I guess. Honestly, I could do without another dose of Piers, and he's bound to be there."

"Need a date?"

Was Alaric offering? Last time he'd volunteered as my plus-one, things had got rather…heated. Our relationship, such as it was, had changed completely since then, but my insides still clenched from thinking about it.

"Is that a good idea?"

His voice got lower. Huskier. Be dry my soaking knickers. "I promise I'll keep my fingers to myself this time."

I swallowed hard and nearly told him not to bother, then quickly remembered Gemma's revelation. Alaric liked men. He also happened to be an outrageous flirt who sometimes got carried away, but on balance, I'd rather deal with Alaric and my raging libido than horny groomsmen or that weird friend of my sister's fiancé who kept stroking my arm.

"In that case, I'll take you up on the offer. But if— when—Piers does show his face, you'll get bonus points for keeping your hand on my bottom."

I heard the smile in Alaric's voice. "I think I can manage that. Should we practise first?"

Oh, what had I done?

"No, we've got work to get on with. Shoo. Go ask your questions."

Yes, the job was boring, but I was smiling as I trekked up the next driveway. Alaric was fun, a genuinely nice guy. After a decade of walking on eggshells trying to please Piers, being around a man with a sense of humour was a refreshing change. Why were the good ones always gay?

I reached the house, a tiny cottage that had seen better days, and knocked on the wood siding next to the screen door. A grey-haired lady soon shuffled towards me.

"Hi, I'm—"

"The private detective? Marcy Belmont called to say you might come by. I don't know anything about the Simms girl, but I just baked cookies." She waved me inside. "Would you like coffee?"

Chapter 22 - Alaric

TWO DAYS, THEY'D spent canvassing, and they were no farther forward. Nobody heard anything. Nobody saw anything. Kyla had spent the afternoon cementing her reputation as a media darling by doing a meet-and-greet with veterans, notably with Ridley hovering in the background like a malevolent spirit. Rumour said that O'Shaughnessy had been scheduled to visit a school, but the principal cancelled at the last moment. So O'Shaughnessy went to an animal shelter instead. Cute puppies, y'all.

Did Alaric sound cynical? That's because he was.

"There." Black walked into the kitchen and tossed his phone onto the table. "It's done. Tomorrow, the media should put two and two together and realise that Devane's fuck buddy and the sick bastard accused of murdering an Afghan family and then burning their home to hide the evidence are one and the same man. Damn, I hate politics. What's for dinner?"

"How's the evidence of that coming along?" Alaric asked, and Black shot him a dirty look.

"Nothing concrete. That's the problem when he shoots all the witnesses."

"Playing devil's advocate, do we know he did it?"

"Firstly, there's circumstantial evidence. The weapons used, the method, and we know his crew was in the area. Secondly, it doesn't matter whether he did it or not. Our job is to muddy the waters around Devane. Taking down Ridley would merely be a bonus."

That. *That* second point was the difference between Blackwood and Sirius in a nutshell. Black would play dirty and do a hatchet job on a person's reputation if it suited his cause. That wasn't to say he had no principles whatsoever—Alaric couldn't imagine him taking money to, say, bump off somebody's business rival—but he didn't mind collateral damage in the pursuit of a higher goal. In this case, Alaric happened to agree that Eric Ridley was a problem, but he liked to think his moral compass pointed in the right direction most of the time. That was why he'd left the CIA, after all—it had become clear that their ultimate destinations were on different bearings.

At Sirius, they'd vowed to seek out the truth, then let the chips fall where they may.

Emmy didn't seem bothered by her husband's ethics. She was sitting on the floor petting the dog, who lay on its back with its legs waving in the air.

"I ordered takeout," she told Black. "Sushi and salad for you, pizza for all the regular people."

"What about dessert?" Dan asked.

"Cookie dough ice cream."

"I love you."

Beth had been rummaging in the fridge, but when she came back with a bottle of Coke, Emmy waved her away. Emmy's diet had always amused Alaric. She refused to touch soda, but she'd live on cheeseburgers if she could, and on a night out, she'd quite happily pour shot after vile shot down her throat.

"What's the plan for tomorrow?" Beth asked as she

topped off Alaric's glass.

"We've got a dozen houses left to cover, mostly people who were out the first time we called. Then I'll defer to Dan."

Dan rubbed the black circles under her eyes. "Honestly? I'm not sure where to go next. If Piper's disappearance was more recent, I'd suggest hiking with a cadaver dog, but so much time has passed... The LA office is checking locally, just in case Piper really did embark on a music career."

"What about Kyla?" Black asked. "Where was she on the day Piper disappeared?"

"I've been treading softly so we don't tip her off that we're digging into the case, but the owner of the beauty salon remembers seeing her. Back then, she was a nail technician working for the previous owner, and Kyla and Piper were both booked in for a manicure after school that afternoon. Kyla turned up on her own. Said Piper wasn't feeling well and she'd rebook if there were any open appointments the next day, but the lady never heard from her."

"Was Kyla at school that day?"

"I haven't found anyone who remembers either way."

"How about unusual movements? Disturbed earth? Trespassers?"

"There's nothing."

"There's something. We just have to find it. I'll come with you tomorrow."

"What am I doing tomorrow?" Emmy asked.

"Running off pizza."

Alaric's phone rang before Emmy could come up with a retort. Judd was calling via video link. Alaric retreated to the living room as the crunch of gravel heralded the arrival of a delivery driver.

"Can I call you back in half an hour? Dinner just arrived."

"You'll want to hear this."

Judd was using his "no messing around" voice. Clipped, professional, with the merest hint of underlying excitement. Alaric forgot about the pizza.

"What? Did you find something on the incident in Afghanistan?"

"Not Afghanistan. Syria. Or more precisely, two miles off the Syrian coast."

Judd fiddled with the camera, and it panned back to reveal a rather tense-looking Hevrin sitting beside him. What the hell was going on?

"You'll have to explain."

"Nada here overheard me mentioning Eric Ridley's name on the phone."

"Hevrin," Alaric said out of habit.

"Pretty sure that's not her name either, so I'm sticking with Nada." He gestured towards her. "Over to you."

"Eric Ridley is a monster," she said, and the steeliness in her tone shocked Alaric.

But he quickly adopted a neutral expression. "You'll have to start at the beginning."

Alaric felt a presence behind him, and he didn't have to look to know it was Emmy. She moved like a cat, and he smelled the faintest hint of whatever shampoo she'd been using this month. Let her listen. He had a feeling this would concern all of them, and it would save him from explaining everything twice.

"Eight years ago, Eric Ridley and his men shot

nineteen Kurdish refugees in the Mediterranean Sea. He called them vermin. It was fun for him."

"I'm aware of the incident. He claims the victims shot at his boat first."

"*Hara*! They were unarmed civilians."

"*Hara* means bullshit," Emmy murmured, although Alaric could have guessed.

"That's not what the investigation said."

"The investigation was a sham. They only found what they wanted to find."

Granted, Alaric hadn't spent much time with Hevrin, Nada, whatever her name was, but she'd always seemed meek. Quiet. And today? Today, she sounded angry.

"How do you know that?" Alaric asked.

A shrug.

"Nada wants to help with the Ridley sitch," Judd cut in, "but she has trust issues."

Could anyone blame her? Alaric had seen the way she lived. At one time in her life, she'd lost everything, everything except her daughter anyway.

Alaric tried again. "We just want to make the world a better place for your little girl to grow up in, but we can't do that alone."

"What did Eric Ridley do now?"

"Why do you think he's done anything else?"

"Because he's evil. As long as he is breathing, he is dangerous, and still he is walking around free."

"We're trying to do something about that, but so far, we can't find enough evidence."

"Your people erased the evidence."

"My people?"

"The Americans." She tugged her fingers through

her hair. "I don't know why I am even talking to you. I shouldn't be here."

"What evidence? What Americans?"

Silence.

"Hevrin, we want to help. We have the same goals. I may be American by birth, but all I want to do is find the truth."

"Your government does not want to know the truth."

"What makes you say that?"

"They were told Eric Ridley was lying, but they were more concerned with good publicity. Photo ops, hearts and minds, American troops riding in their trucks through towns where there is nothing left—nothing—and then patting themselves on the back when they return to their base because they didn't die that day."

"Who told them he was lying?"

And how did they know? Who exactly was Hevrin Moradi?

Judd turned to her. "Alaric's right. We only want to help, I swear. And none of us work for the government, not anymore. Alaric, Naz, and I used to, but we all quit for exactly the reason you said. Governments don't always do what's right."

Hevrin stayed quiet for a full minute.

Finally, she spoke. "The SDF. The Syrian Democratic Forces. Their representatives told US contacts what happened, and the Americans said they were mistaken. Then the witness's village was bombed, and I do not believe that was a coincidence."

Now Emmy stepped forward. "What witness?"

"Who are you?" She leaned closer to the screen. "I saw you on the Bellsfield Estate. With Alaric, the night

Ryland Willis fell off the South Tower, and I do not
believe that was a coincidence either."

Ah, shit.

A hundred thoughts flew through Alaric's head. His
first instinct was to deny, deny, deny. Deny everything.
Although there wasn't enough evidence for a conviction
—of that he was confident—none of them wanted an
investigation into the Bellsfield debacle. But to deny
the truth was to insult Hevrin's intelligence. She was
smart, that much was clear. They needed to gain her
trust, not prove her fears were right—that everybody
lied.

"Ryland Willis came out of the same mould as Eric
Ridley."

"Yes." Hevrin looked surprised, probably because
Alaric hadn't tried to bullshit her. "I don't know exactly
what he did to Gemma, but I saw her that night, and I
see her today. It was bad. And then there are the body
parts they found in the pipes... He deserved his fate."

"He did."

"If I'd smelled the decomposition sooner, perhaps I
could have stopped him. But I had a cold for several
weeks, so I couldn't smell anything, and then when I
did report the problem, the council told me it was
probably a dead rat."

Another snippet of information to add to the list—
Hevrin was familiar with death. Plus her neighbour on
the estate had told Alaric that Hevrin didn't like to rock
the boat in case it affected her asylum application.

"It wasn't your fault."

"My head tells me that is true, but my heart... When
I left Syria, I only wanted to live in peace, but the
Bellsfield Estate is a war zone all of its own." She

turned to Judd. "Thank you for letting me stay here. I'd forgotten what it was like to sleep for an entire night."

"Any time." Judd shifted uncomfortably. This month had to be the first time ever that he'd had adult females stay in his house but not in his bed. It amused Alaric to see him off balance.

"Feel like telling us how you found Gemma?" Alaric asked. "We've been curious."

If he could get Hevrin talking about something unrelated to Ridley, maybe she'd feel more at ease?

"How would you do it?" she asked.

Push the question back onto him. Nice.

But Alaric humoured her. "I'd most likely ask Eunice if she knew where anyone connected with Ryland worked."

"I did. She didn't. But she recognised Gemma's picture, and so I knew she was his girlfriend."

"Picture? What picture?"

"Almost every phone has a camera now."

Hevrin had taken photos of them that evening? It bothered Alaric that he hadn't noticed, and judging by Emmy's pissed-off expression, she wasn't happy about it either.

"But don't worry," Hevrin continued. "I've deleted them now."

Which only offered a small measure of comfort.

"That doesn't explain how you found her at the gallery."

"Eunice said she used to see Gemma and Ryland in gym clothes together, plus she knew he drove a blue Honda. So I found it in the car park, and on the back seat, there was a class timetable for Workout World, so I figured they might both be members. All I had to do was look up Gemma's details on the computer there, then visit *her* neighbours until I found one who knew where she worked. Eunice watched Indy for a few hours."

All she had to do. Hevrin said this as if playing detective were perfectly normal.

"How did you access the computer at the gym?"

"I stuffed tissue into a plughole in the ladies' locker room, then turned on the tap and told the guy at the desk the sink was overflowing. He took ages to find a mop, probably because I'd moved it."

If Alaric hadn't been crazy over Beth, perhaps he'd have fallen a tiny bit in love with Hevrin.

Wait a second. What was he thinking? He already had Emmy in his life, not to mention her whole posse of X-chromosomed loonies. The last thing he needed was another sneaky female driving him insane.

Meanwhile, Judd was looking at Hevrin with newfound admiration.

"Do you want a job?" he asked.

Actually, that wasn't the worst idea he'd ever had.

But Hevrin shook her head. "I'm not allowed to work until my asylum application is processed. I don't understand it—people here, they complain that the government gives us money, yet we're not permitted to earn it for ourselves."

"Okay, so how about this... You lend us a hand with this Ridley thing, and you can stay in the spare room while your asylum application goes through. We get info on a scumbag, and you get to avoid World War Three for a while. Win-win. Uh, how long does an asylum application take?"

Emmy scrawled a note to Alaric. *You don't know*

who she is.

"Years, maybe."

"That long? Right. Okay."

"I can't expect to stay in your home for all that time. But just until the police let me back into my flat...it would be nice."

Alaric scribbled back, *I know we want her on our side.*

Emmy gave a one-shouldered shrug. She couldn't argue with that.

"Will you help us?" Alaric asked.

She nodded towards Emmy. "Who is she?"

"Emmy. She's an old friend of mine."

"Eric Ridley's trying to interfere in a US senatorial election," Emmy said. "The last thing any of us want is for more people who think the way he does to get elected to positions of influence. We're trying to bring down his candidate, but we've only got nine days to do so. If you know something that could help, we'd very much appreciate hearing about it."

"Eric Ridley should be in jail."

"I'd dearly love to put him there, but we need your witness."

"There are too many Ridleys in your military. They protect their own. From privates to the president, they protect their own."

"James Harrison wasn't the president when Ridley shot those people."

"Men with power, they are all the same."

"Not true. But I think you know that. Study thine enemy, right? President Harrison's been pushing for more support for the Kurdish people, but he keeps getting stymied by Congress. Which is why it's even more important to block a psycho from sitting in the senate for the remaining five years of Senator Carnes's term."

"The witness must be protected. She's been through enough."

She? On second thought, given his current company, that fact shouldn't have surprised Alaric in the slightest.

"She was on the boat that night?"

"She swam a mile and a half back to shore as her family lay dead. I spoke to her extensively. Even months later, she still heard Ridley's voice in her nightmares, giving the order to shoot."

"Where is she now?"

"Now? I do not know. She went to live with an uncle, but they had to keep moving because of the war."

"We can send a team to get her," Emmy offered. "We have people nearby."

"No, you cannot. She's terrified. She trusts no one."

"If we're going to get Ridley his just deserts, we need her statement. Did you record the conversations when you spoke to her?"

"Yes, but I do not know what happened to the videos. Everything got destroyed. Our base, our people, our equipment." Hevrin gulped back a sob. "The Turkish air force, they bombed us in the night, and then the army came. I should have known, I should have alerted people..."

Judd put an arm around her shoulders, trying to offer support as she broke down. For a man who treated women like objects, this was way, way out of his comfort zone.

"What should I do?" he mouthed at the screen.

Alaric was just about to suggest tissues when the doorbell rang. Judd fiddled with his phone, checking the cameras.

"Oh, fuck."

"Who is it?"

"My mother."

Fuck indeed. "Isn't it almost midnight there?"

"Eleven o'clock. She's probably on her way home from work."

"Hide Hevrin. She does *not* need an interrogation from your mom."

Even the most casual conversation with Stella Millais-Scott felt like the Spanish Inquisition.

"Gemma?" he called. "Gem? I need a hand here."

The screen jostled, leaving them with a view of Judd's living room as he went to deal with yet another problem.

Emmy just chuckled. "Wow. Life with Sirius has more drama than a senatorial debate."

CHAPTER 23 - ALARIC

"WHAT HAPPENED LAST night? Or can't you tell me?" Beth asked as they left Lone Oak Farm late on Sunday morning. Even with three cups of coffee inside him, Alaric could barely keep his eyes open. He'd only managed to snatch two hours of sleep.

Plus he felt guilty for leaving Beth in the dark last night, but things had gotten kind of intense, especially after Judd's mother turned up. Of course, with Stella Millais-Scott being Stella Millais-Scott, she hadn't just taken Judd's claim of a fake marriage for a job at face value, and she'd done some digging. Dodgy passport photo in hand, she'd ventured into the bowels of MI6 and consulted Gwyneth.

Judd had told Alaric about Gwyneth years ago. While the CIA relied on a network of supercomputers and millions of dollars' worth of software to identify unknown subjects, MI6 also had Gwyneth, a fifty-something chain-smoker with an eidetic memory and OCD. Woe betide anyone who interfered with her filing system. Anyhow, Stella had consulted with Gwyneth, who thought that Hevrin-slash-Nada bore an uncanny resemblance to a top SDF intelligence officer known only as *al Ghazal*. The Gazelle.

The Gazelle had gone missing over a year ago, presumed dead after Turkish forces blew up a Kurdish base, a move that led to a diplomatic disaster and more coalition ground troops being deployed. Confronted by Stella, a tearful Nada, as they'd now agreed to call her, had broken down and admitted fleeing after her husband was killed in the bombing, convinced that with the Turkish army on the move, she and her unborn baby would be next.

Then the arguments had started.

Stella began asking questions; Nada didn't want to answer them. Judd told his mother to back off, and when she didn't, he threatened to throw her out of the house, physically if necessary. The baby started crying. Stella pointed out that "Hevrin" had lied on her asylum application form, and the authorities wouldn't look on that too favourably, but perhaps if she cooperated, someone could put in a good word. Gemma called her a mean-ass bitch, and Judd pointed out that as far as the world was concerned, Hevrin was in fact Nada Millais-Scott, and he'd introduce her to the family as his wife if Stella didn't leave her alone.

Because Judd had forgotten to turn off his webcam, Alaric, Emmy, Black, and Dan had front-row seats for the whole argument, which as arguments went, had been pretty spectacular. If someone had thought to hit record, they could have shopped it as the pilot for a new reality show. *MI6: Behind the Scenes.*

Halfway through, Emmy had grabbed a couple of cold pizzas and a bowl of popcorn, and when the squabble showed no signs of abating, she'd hopped onto the internet. Only when the Deliveroo guy turned up at Judd's door with a "Congratulations on Your Marriage" cake for him and Nada plus a bunch of sour grapes for Stella did they remember they had an audience.

"Can we focus on the important things?" Black asked, and Stella's face would have put a gargoyle to shame.

With Black leading discussions and James Harrison joining the call on a secure line, everyone had agreed they had a common goal: to bring peace and stability to Northern Syria. The region had problems, and not all of its own making.

World leaders had hindered the provision of aid and troops to the area for their own political ends, an issue compounded by the previous US president meddling with the military justice system. As a result, both morale and discipline had suffered. In recent years, the situation had settled somewhat, but President Harrison acknowledged there was still work to be done. Cowboy outfits like EBR Group weren't helping matters—in volatile situations, they acted as a match to the powder keg, and those gathered for the discussion concurred that hauling Ridley before a military judge for his past transgressions would send a message that such misdeeds would no longer be tolerated.

In the early hours, they'd hashed out a plan, one which nobody liked but everybody agreed was necessary. Nada and Judd would be taking a trip to Syria. Nada hadn't wanted to go. She hated the thought of leaving her daughter, she didn't trust Americans, and there were people in Syria who'd kill her on sight. But Alaric saw in her eyes that she wanted justice for those who had died. Judd wasn't keen to go either because he hated working for his mother.

But going they were.

Their objectives? To find a cache of documents and data Nada's husband had once hidden as a bargaining chip, plus locate the teenage girl who'd witnessed Ridley's atrocities and convince her to testify against him. That was why Nada needed to go, why she couldn't just give Judd directions to the cache and stay at home—she knew the witness, and if anyone could gain the girl's trust, it would be her.

Stella was facilitating their exfiltration and providing a nanny, Harrison had offered witness protection for anyone who needed it, and Blackwood was sending Logan, one of Emmy's core team, to assist. They had four days. If they took any longer, there wouldn't be enough time for the wheels of justice to turn before the senatorial election, and with the search for Piper close to a dead end, they'd be relying on guilt by association to turn the public against Devane.

"Some of the discussions got a little sensitive," Alaric told Beth. Technically, he shouldn't have been present either since his security clearance had lapsed, but Black hadn't objected and he seemed to be in charge. "It turns out that Nada has a background in intelligence we didn't know about, so she's assisting with the overseas investigation of Ridley."

"Wow, really?"

"She and Judd will be out of contact for a few days."

"They're not doing anything dangerous, are they?"

"They'll be fine."

Alaric had to believe that. Nada feared her lack of recent training would let her down. As she'd pointed out, "The *alkaliba* who pushed me in front of the car would never have caught me off guard like that two years ago." So Stella had swung a punch at her to see what happened, and quick as a flash, Nada got her in an armlock. It was the first time Judd had smiled all evening.

"I'll keep my fingers crossed they manage to find something since we don't seem to be having much luck, do we? Are we going back to do the rest of the houses on Lakeshore Drive?"

"Yes, but let's stop at that diner we passed yesterday for some food first. I'm flagging."

"Good idea. Breakfast wasn't the same without Stéphane, was it?"

Stéphane had taken Irvine to church in the morning, and the senator hadn't looked at all well. In Alaric's non-expert opinion, Irvine would be talking with the big man in person soon. Harriet had wanted to go with her father too, but one of the horses in the barn looked colicky, so she'd walked the nag around in circles while Beth helped the two ranch hands with the mucking out. Chores at that place were never-ending, a bit like this damn case.

"No, toast and cereal wasn't a patch on pancakes."

That was what Beth ordered when they got to the diner. A stack of pancakes with maple syrup and crispy bacon. Alaric opted for sausages, biscuits, and gravy, and he'd also have to fit in a run later if he wanted his pants to do up tomorrow.

A late breakfast at the diner was a welcome respite from the trials of the last few days, made even better by the company. But a yellowed map on the wall made Alaric think of the old days once again. He'd always wanted to drive from coast to coast, meander from Maine to South Carolina, then back up to Chicago and west along Route 66 to California. Long ago, he and

Emmy had discussed making the trip, but a lack of vacation time meant they'd done nothing more than talk.

"How do you feel about taking a road trip?" he asked Beth.

"For the case?"

"No, after the case. I know you want to get home to see Chaucer, but maybe later in the year?"

"In America? With you?"

"That was the general idea."

"Like two friends on holiday?"

Friends? Deep down, Alaric had been hoping for more, but he'd take what he could get.

"Exactly that."

"What about work?"

"I think the boss'll let you have time off."

Beth's face blossomed into a wide smile. "Uh, okay then. Later in the year. Can we drive some of Route 66? I suggested we do that for our honeymoon, but Piers said it was called flyover country for a reason and booked us a trip to the Maldives instead. Which was lovely, don't get me wrong, but there was an awful lot of beach and not much else."

"The scuba diving's great."

Beth shuddered. "I don't even like swimming. When I was little, I went paddling in the sea in Barbados, and something touched my leg. I haven't been in open water since, not unless you count the time Polo dumped me in a pond at our first one-star event."

"Tell me you have a photo of that."

"Worse. There's a video." She looked sheepish. "I bet you're a great scuba diver."

"I worked as an instructor for a while when I lived

in Thailand. It's really not as bad as you think. Visibility's better underwater than on the surface, and whatever touched your leg was more likely to have been a plastic bottle than a shark."

"Logically, I know that, but I'm still sticking with the hot tub. Even just trundling up and down Lakeshore Drive gives me the heebie-jeebies."

Okay, the lake it was named after was pretty murky, he'd give her that. And he liked the hot-tub idea as long as she was in it too.

"People pay extra for that view."

"I'd rather live in a broom cupboard." She clapped a hand over her mouth. "Oh, heck. I shouldn't joke about that, not after what happened to Gemma."

"Gemma's okay. I spoke to her last night. At least with Nada's drama, she's got a distraction from her own problems."

"Every cloud has a silver lining?"

"So they say. Are you going to finish those pancakes?"

Beth slid her plate in his direction. She'd only managed to eat half a portion. "Help yourself. I need to use the bathroom."

He watched her go. That ass... What the hell had he been thinking, suggesting a road trip? He'd never be able to keep his hands off her if they were stuck in a car together for two weeks, just him and Beth. Dammit, he was in trouble.

CHAPTER 24 - BETH

NEXT TIME, I'D order from the children's menu. I'd only been in America for a week, and my jeans were already getting tight. If I hadn't been doing the horses, I'd have needed to go up a size or perhaps start wearing elasticated waistbands. Portions just weren't the same here.

I looked in the mirror above the sink and cursed under my breath. Why hadn't Alaric told me I had straw stuck in my hair? Lucky Mother couldn't see me —I'd gone from socialite to scarecrow in under a month.

"Excuse me?"

Was someone talking to *me*? I turned, drying my hands on a paper towel, and found a redhead standing there. Where had I seen her before?

"Yes?"

"You spoke to my mom. At our house."

Ah, now I remembered. Lisa? Her mom had been the grouchy lady who thought Piper was murdered by a cannabis user. The guy who peed on a cop. I still wasn't sure how anyone could mistake a police officer for a urinal. Up close, Lisa looked older than I'd first thought, maybe twenty-three or twenty-four.

"Yes, I did, yesterday."

"About Piper?"

"Yes."

The girl fell silent, and it seemed as though she was sizing me up. Did she want to tell me something?

"Do *you* know anything about Piper's disappearance?"

The girl glanced furtively towards the closed door. We were alone in the bathroom, and I began to feel uneasy. She should have been talking to Dan, not me.

"It weren't Homer. He only looks at me funny 'cause he's stoned."

Oh, phew. Was that it? "Don't worry, we've already ruled him out. He had an alibi for the time Piper went missing."

"Have you spoke to Kyla Devane?"

A chill ran through me.

"Why do you ask that?"

"I saw them together that afternoon. Sort of, anyway. But you can't tell my folks, okay? I was supposed to be in school."

"I won't say a word." At least not for now. What if Lisa was a witness to a murder? She'd have to speak to the police, wouldn't she? Perhaps even testify. "What do you mean, you sort of saw them together?"

"In their cars. Piper was driving in front, like fast, and Kyla was real close behind."

"You're sure it was them?"

"It was their cars. Piper's Honda had a dent in the door from where Ricky Maidlaw reversed into it in the school parking lot—my sister went to school with Piper and she told me—and Kyla had a fancy red BMW convertible her daddy bought her. Nobody else in town got one like that."

"Where were you? At home?"

"When I was a kid, I had this den in the woods. I used to go there some days to get away from, you know, stuff. It was right by the road."

"Which direction did they drive in?"

"This way. Towards town. I figured they were late for class, or maybe they were going to the mall. Kyla sure did shop a lot."

"Why didn't you say anything before?"

"If my pop knew I'd skipped school, he'd have killed me. I know I should have told someone, but..." She chewed on her lip, and from the redness, it looked as though that was a habit. "You promise you won't tell him?"

The quake in her voice told me she was still scared of the man, and it was then that I noticed the bruise peeking out from under her shirt collar, a purplish splotch that must've been a few days old. She followed my gaze and caught me looking.

"I promise. Are you okay?" I asked. "There are people who could help you. I could make some calls, find..."

But she was already backing away. "Just keep me out of this. You promised."

Then she was gone.

Holy. Shit.

Okay, detective work was back to being exciting. This was like a roller-coaster ride. I had to tell Alaric. Lisa was nowhere in sight when I hurried back to our table, and somehow, Alaric had managed to polish off half a portion of pancakes in my absence as well as clearing his own plate. Where did he put it?

"We need to leave," I whispered.

"Why? What happened?"

"I'll tell you in the car."

To give him his credit, he didn't question me further, just left enough cash to pay for our meal plus give the waitress a handsome tip and steered me outside.

"Don't keep me in suspense," he said once we were safely ensconced in the SUV.

"There's a witness. Well, maybe. She saw Piper and Kyla on the afternoon Piper disappeared."

"Who?"

"Lisa, uh, Handley, I think? I'll need to check the list. I saw her at a house on Lakeshore Drive, and just now she was in the bathroom."

"The redhead?"

"How did you guess?"

"Because she ran out of there like her heels were on fire. What did she say to you?"

I recounted the conversation to Alaric, careful not to leave anything out. I should buy one of those digital recorders like Dan had. Funny how easy it was for my brain to get confuddled in the heat of the moment.

"That's everything?" Alaric asked.

"I believe so, yes. What should we do to help that poor girl? Call the police?"

"It's not that simple. She'd most probably deny everything, and then she'd be in even more trouble."

"We can't do nothing. What if her father hurts her badly? Or worse?"

"I didn't say we'd do nothing, but we have to watch our steps around here, and until election day, Kyla's our priority." Alaric stared over the steering wheel, talking almost to himself. "Piper and Kyla drove towards town, fast, but why? What was so important? A manicure? We know Kyla got there, but what happened to Piper?"

Laughter wasn't quite the answer I expected.

"What? What's so funny?"

"It's been staring us in the face. We must've driven right past her a dozen times."

"I don't understand."

"The lake. Piper's in the damn lake. They weren't late for class—the pair of them had a fight and Piper took off. Kyla chased her. One little tap, that's all it would have taken, either on purpose or by accident. Either way, she covered it up. I bet someone repaired a dent in Kyla's BMW not long afterwards. A fender bender. Fifty bucks says she claimed a scumbag ran into her car in the mall parking lot and didn't leave a note."

"But...but... No. You really think she ran her best friend off the road and then went to get her nails done? Only a psychopath would do that."

"That's exactly what I think."

I considered the logistics. In many places, Lakeshore Drive ran right next to the water, rocky drops interspersed with clumps of trees and the occasional grassy picnic area. I'd seen fishermen trying their luck, sitting on the banks late in the afternoon with cans of beer beside them. The houses on the other side of the road were set back among the trees, and traffic was light.

"I guess it could have happened. But how will we find out?"

I feared I already knew the answer.

"There's only one way—someone's gonna have to go down there and look."

CHAPTER 25 - ALARIC

THE SUN WAS kissing the horizon when Alaric climbed out of the water with Knox, one of Blackwood's new recruits, trailing behind him. Knox was a former Navy SEAL, and Alaric's air consumption was embarrassingly poor in comparison.

Emmy and Nick were waiting on the shore, already changed into civvies.

"Anything?" Emmy asked.

Alaric shook his head. "Not unless you count a shopping cart and the remains of a bicycle."

Looking for a black Honda Civic along three miles of dark shoreline was never going to be an easy task. A storm on Wednesday had stirred up silt, and there were times when Alaric could barely see his hand in front of his face. He was beginning to understand Beth's reluctance to go near open water.

"Then let's call it a day. We've lost the light now."

Nick nodded. "I agree."

Nick was also a former SEAL, as well as being a director of Blackwood and another of Emmy's exes. This trip was turning into something of a reunion. The good news was that Nick made better company than Black, and the better news was that Black wasn't in Kentucky anymore.

The slightly worse news? Black had taken off to

search for Ridley, who'd been keeping a low profile since news of his possible involvement in the Afghanistan massacre hit the headlines at the weekend. Although Kyla was standing by her man. At her last rally, she'd made a touching speech explaining that Ridley had merely defended himself against terrorists trying to kill him. He was a hero. Members of the opposition just didn't support American troops and were determined to smear an honourable man in any way possible, and wasn't that the real tragedy? Her words went down well with her audience, and now sound bites of Kyla pledging allegiance to the military while standing in front of the Stars and Stripes with her palm on her chest were circulating on social media.

They were losing the battle. Devane was far better at PR than her opponents.

After that day, one might have expected to see Ridley standing proudly by her side, basking in glory, but no. He'd gone to ground. Why? As far as Alaric could ascertain, there were three possible reasons.

The first was that he'd gotten wind of what they were doing at the lake. He had to know Kyla played dirty, and maybe *he* was trying to distance himself from *her*? Or—another plausible scenario—he was on a spying mission. Several times over the last four days, the team had spotted people watching them from the road or occasionally creeping closer through nearby trees, curious about what they were doing.

They weren't publicising their purpose, of course. In fact, they'd done quite the opposite. Blackwood had supplied a panel van to use as a base, complete with logos for the non-existent Freshwater Eco-Survey. Whoever painted it had done a nice job. Inside, it was set up with comms equipment and an area to change, plus seating for the team to rest between dives. No bathroom, though. Emmy hated peeing in her wetsuit, so she was making regular trips to the trees and moaning like hell about it.

But despite the subterfuge, they'd had to come clean with the local sheriff. They'd been worried he wouldn't cooperate, but on the contrary, he seemed only too happy to wash his hands of the case and hand it over to someone who gave a shit while he focused on the important things in life, such as the department's annual summer barbecue. Smoked mutton, anyone? Alaric trusted the man when he said he wouldn't mention their intentions to Devane, but he didn't have quite the same faith in the deputies. According to Harriet, some of them were relics from the days when Daddy Devane's crony ran the department. Probably bought and paid for.

Hence the members of the dive team were constantly on their guard, and Alaric hadn't complained when Emmy insisted Beth stay at Lone Oak Farm with Harriet and Barkley.

And the third possible reason why Ridley had made himself scarce? That was to do with Syria. Alaric didn't yet know the full story because a nurse had confiscated Judd's phone, but the upshot was, the witness had arrived in the US with Logan yesterday while Nada and Judd were back in the UK. Their roles had been reversed, and now she was sitting at his bedside in the hospital while the doctors sewed his arm back together. Apparently, Logan had offered Nada a job, but Judd said Sirius was keeping her and he'd marry her for real if necessary. Damn.

And the best part? Following a preliminary interview with the witness, the NCIS was very keen indeed to talk with Ridley and his men. The three still on active duty had been rounded up already, and it was possible that word had gotten out to Ridley that he was a person of interest. Even though he'd left the Navy, he was still subject to the Uniform Code of Military Justice because he received retirement pay from the government.

Emmy took the weight of Alaric's air tank while he wriggled out of his BCD. The lake water smelled vaguely fishy, and duckweed clung to his regulator.

"Fuck, it's cold down there."

"There's coffee waiting in the van. I might see if I can get us drysuits if we're gonna be here much longer."

If only. Kentucky wasn't known for its scuba diving. They were having to get their tanks refilled in Lexington, but the centre there only had a basic range of equipment. In early June, the water temperature was in the mid-seventies near the surface, which meant wetsuits were fine for recreational diving but got damn chilly during a time-consuming underwater search.

"After that dive, I deserve bourbon."

"I need a beer," Knox said. "Did you see that fish?"

"What fish?"

"Was it a catfish?" Emmy asked, flicking the duckweed away. "A massive one came out of nowhere earlier, and let's just say I'm glad I've got a knife."

"You had to use it?"

"No, I punched the damn thing and it swam away, but I felt better knowing the knife was there."

"And you didn't think to warn us?"

"I was worried you might chicken out if I did."

Seriously? "It's a damn fish, Emmy, not a great white," Alaric said.

"Don't you watch *River Monsters*? A catfish can kill a man, and they grow to ten feet long. Oh, and sometimes they're venomous."

"You're not really selling tomorrow's outing."

"Ah, yeah, sorry." She pulled a vicious-looking knife from a scabbard strapped to her thigh. "Want to borrow this?"

"Thanks, but I'll pass." Alaric had his own knife, albeit a smaller folding one. "Have you seen my towel?"

Nick appeared with towels for Alaric and Knox. "Here you go. Look on the bright side, we're halfway done."

Halfway done with the lake, but they only had three full days until the election. Alaric wouldn't need a knife at this rate, he'd need a flashlight, because those promised to be very long days indeed.

"I thought you were never coming back," Beth said. "You look exhausted."

Alaric tried not to let on how tired he was. "I've had better days. Did Harriet bring you home?"

"No, Dan picked me up. She was on her way here from Lexington."

"Where I..." Dan gave them jazz hands. "Found the dude who fixed Kyla's car."

"Really? He remembers?"

Alaric had been convinced that lead would pan out to nothing.

"Yup. And you know why he remembers?"

"Why?"

"Because Kyla complained about the cost. Said there was no way a new bumper should cost that much, but it was a German import, and those things are never cheap. Plus he had to knock out the dents and respray the hood, and the cherry-red was a custom colour."

"He's certain it was Kyla?"

"He recognised her from the TV. Said he and his wife are voting Republican no matter what Mr. Carnes says."

"Did he get curious as to why we're asking about Kyla?" Emmy queried. "We don't want the news getting out too soon."

"I told him my dad recognised her on the TV too, and he swears she was the woman who ran into his beloved truck all those years ago. Even now, he grumbles about it every Thanksgiving, and he's determined she's gonna pay for the damage. Walt recalls Kyla claiming a moron drove into her BMW outside the mall..." It was satisfying to be right, Alaric thought. "And he's promised to go through the boxes of papers in his basement to see if he still has the original invoice."

Emmy gave Dan a high five. "Nice work, slut."

"Thanks, bitch."

"Slut?" Beth whispered. "Bitch?"

"Terms of endearment."

"Right." Beth didn't seem convinced. "Do you want dinner yet? I didn't have time to cook, so Dan and I stopped off on the way home and picked up Mexican. Everything's keeping warm in the oven."

"I need to take a shower first."

Beth crinkled her nose. "Thank goodness. I didn't

want to say anything, but…"

"I stink, I know. Give me fifteen minutes. Actually, make it twenty—I want to check in with Judd."

"How is he? Have you heard any more from England?"

"Just that he's out of the hospital." He'd texted Alaric on the trip back to Curzon Place. "To tell you the truth, I'm more worried about Nada. She's been through a hell of a lot this week."

From the Bellsfield Estate to a war zone via the emergency room. That was enough to shake anyone up, and she still had Stella Millais-Scott to contend with.

Alaric took a quick shower, although he'd have preferred to stand under the hot water for an hour or two, then towelled off. Sweats were the order of the day. He rarely wore sportswear outside the gym, but he didn't have the energy left to button a shirt. If he lay on the bed, he'd never get up again, so he sat at the desk in the corner of the room to call Judd.

"And? What's the story? Start at the beginning."

"Nada's Wonder Woman and Xena Warrior Princess rolled into one. I think I'm in love."

"You're in lust. That's different. And you'd damn well better keep your hands off her."

"Don't worry, I will. She still misses her husband. Plus she told me if I made a move, she'd cut my balls off."

Yes, Alaric was definitely a little bit in love with Nada too.

"What happened?"

"It was all going swimmingly. The Brits choppered us in, then we tagged along with a group of US Marines until we got near our destination. Nada had a driver lined up to meet us, an asset of hers from the old days, and he took us to get Nada's documents and then on to the witness. The hardest part was convincing Hanifa to come with us. She was terrified, and her family didn't want her to go, but they were living in rubble. In Syria, they could never stop running. What future did she have there?"

"Not much of one, unfortunately."

"Precisely. And they want Ridley to pay."

"So what went wrong?"

"You know Murphy's Law, mate. We drank tea. Hanifa packed a bag. The driver took us to the pickup point, and the Americans came by on patrol as scheduled. Then a mile up the road, the fucking convoy drove into an ambush and all hell broke loose. It's been a while since I got into a proper gunfight."

Same for Alaric. And he had no desire to get into one again.

"What happened to your arm?"

"The other guy ran out of ammo, so I went in for the kill, only my gun jammed, and it turned out he had a knife. Nada clubbed him with her fucking cast, then shot him in the head."

"Hot damn."

"Exactly what I said. Be still my beating heart."

"How's Nada holding up now that you're back?"

"She says she's never leaving London again. My mother promised this would be a straightforward trip—no drama—so Nada's pissed off with her, and that's an understatement. And Mother's due here any minute, so I have to go and mediate."

"Good luck with that."

"I don't need luck, I need body armour."

When Judd hung up, Alaric closed his eyes and took a long breath. He hated this part of the job. Yesterday, he'd almost lost two friends, one old and one new. Sirius was supposed to be a safe venture, trading in information rather than bullets, in secrets rather than body parts. Technically, Judd had been freelancing for MI6 on the Syria job, but still... They were playing a dangerous game.

At times, Alaric wanted to flip the board and walk away, but he'd already done that once, and trouble still found him. He didn't choose this career. It chose him.

"You okay?"

He looked up to see Emmy standing in the doorway, wet hair hanging over her shoulders.

"Yeah."

"You seem pensive, that's all."

"It's this damn job."

"The diving?"

"No, all of it. Sometimes, I wish I could quit again. Go back to the beach and bum around for the rest of my life."

"Then why don't you? As long as you leave an email address this time, I won't kick your arse."

"I've come to the conclusion that the job won't let me quit."

Emmy's cocky expression faltered, and a second later, it was replaced by a sad smile. When she spoke, her words were so soft Alaric could barely hear them.

"Welcome to my world, Prince."

CHAPTER 26 - ALARIC

"WHERE'S BLACK?" ALARIC asked on the way to the lake on Saturday morning. "Any new leads on Ridley?"

Emmy took a sip from her family-sized mug of coffee. "One of Mack's alerts pinged. Ridley got a speeding ticket on the way to Memphis two days ago."

"Memphis?"

"He's got family there, but so far, he hasn't shown up near any of their homes. We're watching them."

"We're watching them, and they're watching us."

The onlookers had been up by the road again yesterday, hovering from dawn till dusk. A local reporter had approached the dive team after lunch, wanting photos and an interview for a story on local ecology, and a fisherman complained they were scaring the bass away, but apart from that, their unwanted audience stayed silent. At times, it felt as if Piper's spirit were watching them too. Alaric got the same prickly feeling every time he looked at Dominique in *Red After Dark*.

Had Ridley's men been among the crowd? Dan had mingled, taking photos for Mack to analyse. If Beth had been on the shore, Alaric wouldn't have wanted to leave her alone, just in case, but Dan could take care of herself, as could Emmy and Nick. They knew the score. He had to take comfort in that.

"Mack hasn't identified any known adversaries so far, and she's good at what she does."

"I know."

Still, having Ridley lurking in the background was concerning.

"Maybe we should get a couple of extra people here? To keep an eye on things?"

"You think we need bodyguards?"

"No, but..."

"I already thought of it, okay? But the Kentucky office doesn't have any spare manpower at the moment. There's some sort of virus going around, and everyone's busy puking."

"Just watch your back."

"I always do."

That's what Emmy said, but if Alaric had known what was to come, he'd have handcuffed her, thrown her into his trunk, and driven them both far, far away.

What was the time? Alaric's stomach said one o'clock, but his watch said eleven. Why did tiredness always make you hungrier? He checked his air—down to forty bar. They should head up soon, but since Knox still had sixty bar left, Alaric was willing to push the envelope a bit.

Then he saw it.

Just the faintest outline to his left at first, a line too straight to be organic. The roof of a vehicle. He turned on his flashlight. For the most part, they'd been diving without lights because the beams reflected back off the silt and blinded them, but as he got closer, the glow illuminated a dark car, filthy from years underwater and covered in detritus. He tapped on his air tank with a metal clip to alert Knox.

It was a car, but was it Piper's car? The shape looked about right for a Honda Civic, but in the gloom, it could have been brown or grey or blue or burgundy.

Twenty bar left.

Alaric and Knox swam around the rear of the car, and even with the build-up of sediment around the bottom, the dent on the left-hand panel was clear to see. Knox used one gloved hand to rub at a patch in the centre of the trunk. A silver H gleamed back at them.

Who would break the news to Piper's grandma?

Alaric didn't want it to be true. He didn't want this car to be a vibrant young woman's final resting place. To be sure, he wiped a clear patch in the slime on the driver's side window and peered inside. He'd expected to see a dead girl, but he still jumped when empty eye sockets stared back at him, the tattered remains of a blouse still floating around bony shoulders.

They'd found her. They'd found Piper Simms, and now Kyla would pay.

He gave a thumbs up to Knox—not signifying good news but rather a diver's signal to ascend. Together, they started the slow trip to the surface, pausing for a three-minute safety stop at five metres to reduce the risk of decompression sickness. Nobody had time for a trip to a hyperbaric chamber right now.

The next step would be raising the car. They'd warned the sheriff to be ready for that possibility, but nobody had confidence the man would actually deliver, so Blackwood had a crane on standby. They couldn't simply winch the vehicle out—the shoreline was a sharp drop rather than a gentle slope, and Piper must have been going at some speed when she entered the water because she'd ended up thirty feet out among clusters of rocks. If they could get paint fragments that matched Kyla's car from the dent in the back of Piper's, plus the invoice from the auto body repair shop and a statement from Beth's witness, it might be enough.

But they only had two days to do it.

Alaric forgot how tired he was as he unclipped his fins and used the rope they'd tied to a tree to haul himself up the rocky incline to the van.

"Emmy?" No answer. "Nick?"

The silence unnerved Alaric, and his chest tightened. For the first time in days, there was nobody watching, and even the birds had deserted them. But he began to breathe again when Nick emerged from the truck, a phone pressed to his ear.

"We found the car."

"Just a second."

That was it? That was Nick's reaction? Six days, they'd been looking for the damn vehicle, and a call was more important?

Wait. *Why* was the call more important?

Alaric dumped his BCD and tank, then unzipped his wetsuit. The tight neoprene felt cloying on land, even more so when it combined with the fear gripping his throat.

"What happened? Where's Emmy?"

Nick looked as if he'd rather be anywhere but by the lake at that moment.

"Uh, she got kidnapped. But chill, it's okay."

Alaric gave his head a shake. Could he have decompression sickness after all? Hallucinations were a symptom, weren't they?

"For a second there, I thought you said Emmy got kidnapped."

"Yeah, she did."

No, that wasn't right. Emmy couldn't have been kidnapped. She was carrying a machete, for fuck's sake.

"Is this a joke?" Knox asked. "Because it's not funny."

"It's no joke. Ridley's men have been keeping an eye on us, and I guess they realised we were getting close to the car because they decided we needed a distraction."

"Why are you just standing there? Didn't you try to stop them?"

"We need to find Ridley, and that's probably where they're taking her. So we figured the best idea was to stand back and give them a clear run."

Alaric's guts threatened to heave their contents all over the grass. "And when you say 'we,' you mean...?"

"Black and Emmy."

"Why the hell didn't she tell me?"

"Look, I suggested she should, but she said you'd try to stop her."

"Of course I damn well would have. Eric Ridley's killed two dozen people in cold blood. We need to go after her. Which direction did they head?"

Alaric had a gun in the truck. He might not have killed anyone in a few years, but assassination was like riding a bike. Satisfying and good for the planet. Dammit, why wouldn't the wetsuit come off? He gave up trying to tug it, grabbed his knife, and began hacking through the neoprene.

"Relax. The shadow team's with her."

Oh, so that made everything okay.

"Can she communicate?"

"No, they knocked her out with something, but she's wearing a tracker."

Alaric forced himself to breathe. He knew Emmy's capabilities. Alert and conscious, she'd stand a good chance—no, an excellent chance—of getting herself out of whatever predicament Ridley had planned for her. But out cold? All bets were off.

"What if she's dead already?"

"We're monitoring her vitals. She's fine."

"For now. If Ridley realises what you've done..."

"As I said, there's a team with her. I'm going to join them, and I'll call you when there's any news."

"No, you won't, because I'm coming with you."

"Black said—"

"I don't give a fuck what Black said. The man's had it in for me for years, and if he thinks I'm going to stand by while he leaves Emmy in danger, he can damn well think again."

"He won't let anything happen to her."

Black might have been the grandmaster of three-dimensional chess, but sometimes, Alaric thought he cared more about winning than about the wife he claimed to love. And Emmy could be too gung-ho for her own good.

"The only way you'll stop me from coming is to knock me out too."

Adrenaline had heightened Alaric's senses, and he felt Knox step closer behind him. But a barely perceptible hand gesture from Nick stopped the younger man in his tracks.

"Fine. You can ride shotgun. But if you interfere, I'm dumping you at the side of the road because *I* won't compromise Emmy's safety by letting you go on some half-cocked rescue mission."

"Fine."

Nick nodded to Knox. "Stay here, buddy, and don't let anyone near that car."

Chapter 27 - Alaric

BLACKWOOD WAS UNDERSTAFFED my ass.

Alaric realised now that Emmy had been playing him the whole time. The reason the dive team had been so light was because she'd *wanted* to get abducted. All those trips to the woods to answer the call of nature? She'd basically been issuing an invitation to Ridley's goons.

And now she was unconscious in the back of a sedan, trundling east along I-64 at five miles per hour under the speed limit with a rotating surveillance team of eight cars—including Alaric and Nick's Tahoe—following behind. Black's shadow team had seen Ridley's men bundle Emmy into the trunk of their Chrysler, her wrists and ankles tied with yellow cord, limp with a hood over her head. They'd ditched her watch, but she'd swallowed one backup tracker and had another sewn into her bra, and both indicated her pulse was steady at fifty-three beats per minute. Alaric's hadn't dropped under a hundred for the three hours they'd been driving.

"Is that your phone buzzing?" Nick asked.

"Huh?" Yes, it was. Alaric dug it out of his pocket and almost groaned when he saw Beth was calling.

"Hey, sweetheart."

"Is everything okay? Dan's not answering her

phone, and I thought you'd be finished by now."

"Something came up. We may be back a little later than planned."

"Did you find the car?"

"Yes, this afternoon."

"Well, that's great." A pause. "I mean, it's terrible for Piper and her family, but at least they'll know what happened to her. How long until the sheriff can get it out of the water?"

"We're working on the logistics at the moment."

"Should I stop at the grocery store?"

"Actually, we might just fill up on snacks. Do you think Harriet would let you stay with her tonight?"

"Probably—you really think you'll be that late?"

"The special election is in less than three days."

Muffled voices sounded, then Beth came back. "Harriet says it's fine to borrow her guest room. Just call if you need me for anything?"

What Alaric needed was to hold Beth in his arms, then bury himself inside her, but he kept those thoughts to himself. And even though he hadn't told her any outright lies about what he was doing, he hated keeping her in the dark.

"I will. Enjoy your evening, and I'll see you tomorrow."

Nick chuckled as Alaric hung up. "Nicely done."

Asshole. "You told your wife you were watching a football game tonight."

"Because I didn't want to worry her, and Lara's my girlfriend, not my wife. Although I'm planning to pop the question. Do you know anything about rings? Rule of thumb says to spend a month's salary, right? But I'm not sure Lara would want to wear a boulder on her finger."

Alaric really wasn't the best person to ask. The one time he'd bought a ring, it had been a three-carat purple sapphire. A diamond hadn't seemed appropriate since that was Black's pet name for Emmy. But what did it matter? Shit happened, so he'd never given it to her.

"Can we focus on the task at hand?"

"This magical mystery tour? Sure. Wanna make a bet on where we're going? My money's on the cabin."

Blackwood's research team had been busier than they'd previously let on, and they'd come up with three possible destinations so far. Ridley had once been stationed at the Naval base in Norfolk, and Black recalled he'd owned a cabin in the area. Chances were he'd held onto it. Heading north on the map past Fredericksburg, the Devane family had a country retreat near Lorton. Kyla's father and his father before him had used it as a base for the commute to DC. And heading south, an old newspaper article showed that Ridley's grandparents used to live near Greensboro, North Carolina. They'd both passed away, but so far, nobody had found a record of their property being sold. The team would know more when the convoy reached Beckley—Ridley's men would most probably turn onto I-77 if they were going to Greensboro.

"I'm going with the Devane estate," Alaric said. "High walls, plenty of privacy. Remember Ridley's doing this to protect Kyla."

Like Nick, Alaric didn't believe the timing was a coincidence—the enemy had snatched Emmy just before he found the submerged car. Ridley knew exactly where Piper's body was because Kyla had told him. The pair were closer than anyone had initially suspected.

The radio crackled. "Ana, drop back. Nick, you take over."

Alaric recognised some of the names spoken over the radio. Ana was Emmy's half-sister. Xavier was another ex-boyfriend, former Israeli special forces if Alaric's sources were to be trusted. Dan was along for the ride too, the little traitor, plus Carmen, Nate's wife. The big mystery? Where the hell was Black? He was using his wife as bait for a psycho, yet he wasn't in any of the chase cars. Neither was Nate, and the pair of them had been joined at the hip since their Navy SEAL days.

They were up to something.

Nick increased his speed a touch, passing Ana and her shadowy passenger in their battered Volkswagen. The car might have looked one ride away from a junkyard, but Alaric didn't doubt that it was a different story under the hood. That engine was no clunker.

The Chrysler came into view, silver in colour, two years old with no dings, dents, or scratches. Nondescript. If Alaric had needed to select a vehicle for transporting a kidnap victim, he'd have chosen something similar. Following the pattern set by Blackwood, he and Nick would stay in sight for twenty minutes or so, then swap again.

"We're approaching Beckley," Nick told everyone.

The unnamed controller took over. "Carmen, you go west on I-64. Isaiah, take I-77."

Carmen and Isaiah were in front of the Chrysler at the moment. Whichever route it didn't take, that driver would turn around and join the back of the tail. In the

FBI, Alaric had been involved in many surveillance operations, but budgetary constraints rarely allowed them more than three cars to rotate. Blackwood Security had thrown a lot of resources at today's proceedings, which made Black's absence all the more notable.

The screen built into the dash showed the red dots of Carmen and Isaiah peeling off left and right. Where would the Chrysler go? Eeny, meeny, miny, moe.

"Looks like we're sticking on I-64," Nick said for the benefit of the others.

Virginia it was. Which meant at least four more hours of worry.

Still, they got the chance for a bathroom break. They were fourth in the procession when the Chrysler pulled into a gas station, and the controller told Dan and Cade to carry on past. Nick slotted the Tahoe into a dark corner of the lot, which doubled as Big Al's Discount Cars, while the Chrysler pulled up at the farthest gas pump. Ana arrived soon after, taking the spot closest to the kiosk.

"We could get Emmy back right now," Alaric muttered. "That would be the sensible thing to do."

"Wouldn't go down too well with the big man."

"He's not even here."

"A hundred bucks says he's not far away."

"Aren't you worried Emmy might get hurt?"

Alaric was fucking terrified. Judging by Emmy's steady pulse rate and lack of communication, Ridley's men had given her a long-lasting sedative. She was in no state to fight back.

"Always, but I've worked with Black for long enough to trust him. If he says to hold back, then we hold back. You're not gonna try anything stupid, are you?"

It was damn tempting. Alaric had a gun, but he didn't fancy his chances against Nick, let alone Ana. In a previous life, Ana had been known as Lilith. Naz knew Lilith by reputation, and he'd warned Alaric to avoid her at all costs.

"No, I'm not."

The Chrysler's driver was a squat, tough-looking guy with a scar curving up one side of his neck. He kept his jacket on despite the heat, which meant he was probably carrying a weapon. The passenger looked more like a salesman—wiry with glasses, wrinkled slacks, and a button-down shirt. The driver finished pumping the gas, and then the pair of them headed towards the kiosk.

"They're gonna stop for coffee," Ana murmured. "And the fireplug says he needs to take a slash."

"I'll go," an unknown voice said. Ten seconds later, a brown-haired guy unfolded himself from the passenger seat of Ana's Volkswagen, stretched the kinks out of his back, and sauntered into the kiosk after Ridley's team.

"Rather him than me," Nick muttered.

"I'd have volunteered to get that asshole alone in the bathroom."

"No, I mean having to spend that much time with Ana. Samuel Quinn lost his mind when he hooked up with her. The man must have balls of fuckin' titanium."

That was Ana's boyfriend? Gee, and he looked so normal.

Staying in the front seat of the Tahoe was one of the hardest things Alaric had ever done. He itched to run over to the Chrysler, to force the trunk open and pull Emmy free. But he didn't. Not only because of Nick and Ana and Black, but because Emmy had made her decision, and even if Alaric disagreed with what she'd done, he had to respect it. Respect her and her abilities.

"Oh, hell." Just when he thought things couldn't get any worse, they did. A relic of a motorhome pulled up beside the Chrysler, blocking their view. Memories of the *Emerald* fiasco came rushing back. Alaric hated being out of sight of the target car, but at least the goons were still in the kiosk, chatting as they got coffee from the machine at the back then headed for one of three tables near the front window. Talk about unprofessional. Did they have no sense of urgency? The short guy laughed as he added sugar and stirred. Alaric felt as if his own sense of humour had departed for good. "Move the RV, asshole."

"We're okay," Nick said. "We can see in front and behind. Nobody's coming or going."

But the newcomers' presence totally ruled out rescuing Emmy. Until that moment, Alaric had held onto a modicum of hope that somebody would come to their senses and abort the mission, but they couldn't very well haul an unconscious woman out of a car with an audience.

"Yeah, great."

The couple in the camper seemed to be in no hurry as they climbed out. *Were* they a couple? Or father and daughter? The guy was in his mid-forties at a guess, and he'd forgotten to shave for at least a week. His Hawaiian shirt was out of place in Kentucky, as were his flip-flops, but he didn't give two hoots as he chatted with his blonde passenger in front of the hood. At first glance, Alaric thought she might've been Emmy, but a closer look told him she was a year or two younger, her nose thinner and her chin sharper. Then she lit up a cigarette. Emmy had quit smoking years ago.

Nicotine addict or not, the woman was in better condition than the rust bucket of an RV. A pair of denim cut-offs showed off shapely legs, though they weren't as good as Beth's. The girl blew her companion a kiss as he walked to the gas pump. Definitely not father and daughter, then.

"When our targets leave, Evan will take over as lead car," the controller ordered. "Ana, slot in behind Isaiah. Nick, you'll have five minutes if you need to get gas or take a comfort break."

Time seemed to slow as Alaric waited. The blonde pranced into the kiosk to pay and came out with an armful of candy. When the RV departed, the Chrysler was exactly where the goons had abandoned it, sitting in semi-darkness since one of the lights in the overhead canopy was out.

"They're leaving," Nick said. "Everyone ready?"

Murmurs of affirmation came over the radio. The others would have had a chance to stretch their legs out of sight while they waited, to relieve themselves in the undergrowth and take on water for the next part of the journey. Surveillance sucked.

It was midnight when they reached the Devane estate in Fairfax County. Ten-foot-high walls surrounded a two-storey house set in twelve acres of manicured grounds. They couldn't see the building in the dark, but

Mack had emailed satellite photos of the property plus pictures of the interior she'd found on Kyla's Instagram account and in the society pages back when Kyla's parents used to host parties there.

Nick parked the Tahoe under the sweeping branches of a weeping willow, out of sight of vehicles passing on the road. The other Blackwood drivers were all in the vicinity, no doubt doing the same thing. Now what? Was Ridley inside already? If so, Emmy was in ever-increasing danger. With eight two-person teams, they had enough manpower to go in and get her out. Why were they waiting?

"Xav will enter the property to take a look," the controller said. "Everyone else, hold the perimeter."

Alaric's phone buzzed again. He didn't need the distraction, but what if it was Beth? He'd never forgive himself if she had a problem and he ignored it.

She'd sent him a message.

Beth: Have you seen this?

Two links to breaking news stories followed. He clicked on the first.

Has Kyla Devane's past come back to haunt her?

In a stunning revelation, local sources in Woodford County have reported that the body of senatorial candidate Kyla Devane's teenage rival has been found in a submerged car just miles from her home. Homecoming Queen Piper Simms disappeared two days before her big day, handing the crown to Devane.

This reporter has been told by a representative of Blackwood Security, the company central to the search and recovery operation, that a dent in the back of Piper's car suggests she was run off the road. Could this be linked to rumours that Devane was seen driving erratically on the afternoon Piper vanished?

Oh, hell. If Kyla and Ridley realised her secret was out, that could send them over the edge. Alaric almost didn't want to click on the second link.

An unnamed military source has today informed us that Eric Ridley, a former Navy lieutenant who rose to prominence this week thanks to his role on senatorial candidate Kyla Devane's security team, is wanted for questioning by the Naval Criminal Investigative Service regarding an incident that took place in Syria eight years ago. Ridley was previously cleared of wrongdoing in the shooting of nineteen Syrian citizens found in a boat off the coast of Latakia, but we understand that new evidence has now come to light.

"Nick, have you seen this?"

"Seen what?"

Nick leaned closer to look at Alaric's phone. He read both articles in silence, then straightened.

"Shit. This could be a problem. Our profile of Ridley says he's volatile when provoked. Who knows what he'll do if he thinks Blackwood's out to get him?"

Xavier's voice came over the airwaves. "There's a second car parked around the back. Hood's still warm."

For the first time, Nick's voice held a hint of stress. "We need to get Emmy. If Ridley's in there..."

"Stand fast."

Was that Black? It sounded like him, but where was he?

Alaric couldn't hold his tongue. "Your wife's inside a building with a lunatic."

"She's—"

A gunshot cut him off. A large-calibre weapon by the sound of it, coming from the house. What the hell? A moment passed in complete silence, everyone frozen. Then a blood-curdling scream came from the same direction, quickly followed by two more gunshots.

"I'm going in," Alaric said, his own gun already in his hand.

"I said, stand fast."

This time, Black's voice came from close by, not over the radio. A second later, he materialised from the darkness with Nate at his side and a phone held to his ear. Who the hell had fired the shots? Not Black or Nate—they hadn't had time to cover the distance from the house.

"H-h-hello? Police? I wanna report a murder." He'd injected more than a hint of fear into his voice. It was the most emotion Alaric had ever heard from the man. "Yes, a murder. My boss just went crazy and shot two of my colleagues and our client." Wait. *Kyla* was dead? "His name? It's Eric Ridley. Be careful, okay? He's got a gun. ... Yeah, he's at the Devane estate on Willow Tree Road. Hurry."

Black hung up as the Hawaiian shirt guy from the gas station dumped a limp body onto the ground in front of them. A man in jeans and a dark-coloured bomber jacket. Black tucked the phone into the unconscious stranger's pants pocket, then straightened.

"Sweet dreams, motherfucker." He peeled off his gloves. "Xav, get back in the car. Everyone move out."

"Where the hell is Emmy?" Alaric asked.

"I'm here."

Her voice was weak, and Ana was half carrying her, but she was alive. "How'd it go? I slept through the whole thing."

"The wicked witch is dead." Black ignored Ana's glare as he picked Emmy up and cradled her in his arms. "Time to go home."

This wasn't just the fucking twilight zone, it was the full-fledged dark side.

"What the hell happened?" Alaric asked.

Black smiled, and honestly, that was scarier than his usual cold expression.

"Assassination's so much cleaner when you avoid pulling the trigger yourself, don't you think?"

"What do I think? I think you're crazy. You played Russian roulette with Emmy's life."

"No, I took a calculated gamble. Ridley's predictable. A small man with a big ego who shoots first and considers the consequences later." His tone hardened. "Now, move *out*."

CHAPTER 28 - ALARIC

THE FIRST SIRENS sounded as Black's team drove away from the Devane estate, each vehicle taking a different route out of the area. Alaric spotted the RV turning south towards Tennessee. Who *was* that guy? He voiced the question, but the Blackwood employee behind the wheel shrugged, and if Dan knew the answer, she was keeping her mouth shut.

"Did you know what Black was planning?" Alaric asked her.

"With Kyla? He said he was going to pick her up as an insurance policy, but I didn't know he was planning the switch. The original plan was to get Emmy out, then tip off the NCIS as to where Ridley was."

"What if he left the property in the meantime?"

"Yeah, no, that wasn't gonna happen."

"Why didn't anyone tell me?"

"Because you were supposed to be back in Kentucky. Nick only brought you because he understands what it's like to have little pieces of Emmy embedded in your soul."

Alaric had never thought of it that way, but it was true. Once you'd spent any time with Emmy, there was no escaping the effect she had on you. The memories stuck with you forever, good and bad.

In the front seat, Dan took a call, listened for a

moment, and then hung up.

"They caught Ridley."

"Did he get far?" Alaric asked. "Was anyone hurt?"

"No, he was still at the house. Cradling Devane's body, apparently. Seems her death hit him hard."

It occurred to Alaric that perhaps he should feel sorry for the man. After all, he knew what it was like to lose a woman he loved, albeit under very different circumstances. But Ridley had shot Kyla thinking she was Emmy, no hesitation, no mercy, which left Alaric struggling to muster up any sympathy. If Ridley hadn't been a murderous thug, maybe he'd still have his girlfriend.

"I'll send flowers to the funeral. Any word on Emmy? How's she feeling?"

She might have been alive, but she'd spent several hours unconscious and who knew what they'd drugged her with?

"Seems okay. She sounds properly awake now, anyway. The doctor'll check her out when we get back to Riverley."

Turned out they'd gotten a new doctor during Alaric's time away. Before, Black used to bribe some guy from the emergency room at Richmond General whenever Blackwood needed a hand with discreet medical care. His replacement was a thirty-something brunette, and judging by the looks Evan gave her, he wanted to volunteer for a check-up instead of Emmy.

"What happened to Dr. Beech?" Alaric asked Dan.

"Oh, he's still around. He heads up the ER now. We use him if anything big comes up, but we brought Kira on board to help lighten the load."

When Emmy turned to walk into the living room—

or rather, one of the living rooms—Alaric saw the telltale burns from a stun gun. Two small dots on the back of her neck. She'd have heard Ridley's men approaching, and yet she'd acted oblivious and allowed them to incapacitate her. Alaric couldn't decide whether she'd been incredibly brave or monumentally stupid in following Black's plan, and it *was* Black's plan. There was no doubt in Alaric's mind whose idea today's adventure had been. That stun gun could have been a silenced .22. A double-tap to the head, that's all it would have taken, and Black's next job would have been picking out a casket.

Which was precisely what Alaric said when he found himself alone in the kitchen with Black a half hour later. Nobody else would stand up to the man, and he needed to be told a few home truths.

"Could you pass me a glass?" Black asked. "A tumbler's fine."

"Emmy could have died today, you asshole."

"Is that a no?"

Alaric's hands balled into fists at his sides. If he'd have opened the kitchen cabinet, Black would have got his damn glass squarely in the temple.

"If you want to risk someone's life, make it your own."

"Emmy's life wasn't at risk."

"You couldn't be sure about that."

"Not with absolute certainty, but close to it." Black reached past Alaric and opened the cabinet. "I'd drink out of the carton, but Emmy would kill me."

Alaric marched to the fridge and grabbed the orange juice. "Here, go right ahead."

Black just barked out a laugh, took the juice, and

poured himself a glassful.

"I spent a year serving under Ridley. A year working out what made the sadistic bastard tick, what made him mad, and what I could get away with. The main things I discovered? He let his ego get the better of him. Palm his ID card, and he'd search the whole barracks because he was too proud to admit he'd screwed up and lost it. And he was as vindictive as he was predictable. Play a prank, and he'd make everyone pay. We did so many damn push-ups it was a miracle the ship sailed anywhere." Black flexed the biceps of one arm. Was that meant to intimidate? "Guess I should thank him now."

"*You* played the pranks?"

"We took it in turns. The enlisteds thought of it as a sport."

"I didn't think you had a sense of humour. And your past doesn't excuse what you did today."

Black put down the juice and ticked off the points on his fingers.

"I was certain he'd snatch Emmy. It was the obvious move, and we deliberately left her wide open. And I knew he wouldn't kill her, not right away in cold blood. He needed her as leverage. As a distraction. Remember, he knew me too, and he was well aware that if he harmed her, I'd hunt him down and gut him like a pig."

"But he *did* try to kill her."

"Only with provocation." Black shook his head and tutted. "Ridley never could control his temper. And I'll admit, that reaction was the part I was fifty-fifty on. I thought maybe he'd take the hood off before he pulled the trigger. But the rest...perfectly foreseeable."

"How? You didn't know he'd even put a hood on Emmy. Or that his men would stop for gas."

"Beg to differ. When we had to transport POWs in the Navy, Ridley insisted on hooding them every single time because he was a sadistic motherfucker who'd never pass up a chance to breach the Geneva Conventions. He said war shouldn't have rules. And that's what he considered Kyla's campaign—a battle. So it stood to reason that he'd hood Emmy. Don't look at me like that—you know damn well she trains for these eventualities."

Yes, Alaric did know. He'd accidentally witnessed a session of theirs once, the torture of the woman Black claimed to love.

"That doesn't make it right."

"Merely necessary. And of course they were going to stop for gas—Ridley doesn't have strong links to Kentucky, and the safest place to stash Emmy was out of state. Plus he wanted to get us all well away from the election circus. After we retrieved Emmy, it was just a case of pushing the right buttons. Ridley's vain, and he values his reputation, even if he does his utmost to trash it. Once he saw the negative news coverage, he was always going to snap. I was the obvious culprit for the leak, and therefore he'd want to punish me by hurting the thing I hold dearest."

"Emmy's not a *thing*."

"It was a turn of phrase. Anyhow, the job's done now. You should stop living in the past."

Oh, Alaric should, should he? Perhaps if the past hadn't had such an impact on his life, he'd be able to move on. Speaking of which...

"Funny you should bring up the past, because you

know what today's escapade reminded me of? The stop I made at the gas station with *Emerald*. Strange how the cash and diamonds disappeared right around that time, wasn't it?"

Black squared up to Alaric, arms folded. His tone remained mild, but his eyes were two glittering chips of granite.

"Are you accusing me of something?"

"I'm just saying the similarities were rather striking."

"That's because I used your screw-up as inspiration. Perhaps if you'd been focusing on your job instead of fucking my wife, you wouldn't have lost track of the cash."

"Well, she had to get what she needed from somewhere, and you weren't giving it to her."

"Deflecting, are we?"

Alaric drew himself up to full height, which was unfortunately six or seven inches shorter than Charles Black.

"I'm saying your priorities are messed up."

"That's rich coming from the man who left Emmy without a word eight years ago."

"Enough!"

Emmy's voice was soft, but there was no mistaking her annoyance. Alaric and Black both stepped towards her at the same moment, then glared at each other.

She held up a hand. "Can we all agree I feel like shit tonight? Good. Then stop bloody arguing."

"Sorry," both men said in unison.

How much of the disagreement had she heard?

"Alaric, I took a calculated risk today, and that was my choice. But I trust Black's judgement, and I trust him to have my back. We've been at this together for almost two decades now. All the training, all the challenges I face, that's my choice too. Sure, I could retire, but even though I might keep breathing, I'd be dead inside." She touched Alaric gently on the shoulder, almost a caress. "But I appreciate you caring."

"I just want you to be happy."

"And I am. You deserve happiness too, Prince. Black's right—forget the past and look to the future."

"I'm not giving up on *Emerald*."

"You know what I think? I think *Emerald* will be found when she wants to be found. In the meantime, don't sacrifice tomorrow for a ghost." She linked her arm through Black's. "Get some sleep. I know I need to."

Alaric hated to admit it, but what Emmy said made sense. Hadn't he wasted enough of his life chasing after a shadow? With that thought, he took out his phone to message Beth. He'd updated her during the ride to Riverley, but a quick "goodnight" message wouldn't go amiss. He was feeling weirdly positive about Sirius, about the time to come, about his feelings for a certain English lady who definitely wasn't Emmy. At least, he was until he glanced at the screen and saw seven missed calls.

CHAPTER 29 - BETHANY

"JUST LEAVE HER alone!" I snapped, sounding disturbingly like my mother. "Have you got no compassion?"

In England, if one of your nearest and dearest had a medical emergency, the hospital staff whisked them away for treatment and then a doctor came out to speak to you. Here in Kentucky, they sent an accountant instead. The cold-hearted dragon didn't seem too concerned about Irvine Carnes's survival, more by his ability to pay.

"It's hospital policy. We have to obtain financial information from all patients. Does he have insurance? What about Medicare?"

I snatched the bloody clipboard. "Leave it with me. I'll get your sodding forms filled in."

Perhaps I could ask Stéphane at an appropriate moment? Harriet was in no fit state to answer a hundred questions. I had no idea what Medicare was, but surely the senator must have some sort of health coverage?

The woman gave me a dirty look, then turned on her heel and stomped off to find her next victim. I let out a long breath. This evening had been a horror show, and considering the number of parties I'd been to where I'd had to haul a plastered Piers out to the car while apologising profusely to Surrey's finest, that was saying something.

Not so long ago, we'd been eating a late supper at Lone Oak Farm, a cosy affair with Harriet, her father, and Stéphane, who seemed to be practically family. Barkley was curled up on the old horse blanket, waiting for scraps. And everything had been going fine. Irvine appeared reasonably lucid, and he'd laughed along with the others at my expression when Stéphane informed me we were having a three-way for dinner. Luckily, that turned out to be three-way Cincinnati chilli—spaghetti with spiced meat sauce and shredded cheddar cheese— rather than an adventurous sexual experience. Although secretly, I'd always been kind of curious about the other type of three-way too, just perhaps not with Harriet and Stéphane plus the senator watching.

Then, as Stéphane was explaining a four-way—a three-way plus chopped onions—and a five-way (add kidney beans), Irvine's face started drooping on one side. He tried to excuse himself from the table, but when he gripped the edge to stand up, he lost his balance and fell over.

"Oh, shit," Harriet whispered. "It's another stroke."

Stéphane fumbled for his phone. "I'll call an ambulance."

I'd never seen anyone have a stroke before, although I had wished it on Piers several times. The worst part was the helplessness. Irvine was still breathing, and every so often he mumbled something unintelligible, but all I could do was support Harriet while she comforted her father. Stéphane went out to the road with a torch to wave down the ambulance.

And now we were at the hospital. Harriet was

squashed into the corner, curled against Stéphane's side, alternately sobbing and staring blankly at the wall. It didn't look good.

What was in these forms? I could manage the name and address, but I didn't have a clue about Irvine's social security number or medical history.

"Hey."

Oh, thank goodness. I threw myself into Alaric's arms without thinking, then realised what I'd done and tried to extricate myself. But he held on tight.

"I thought you wouldn't be back until much later. Weren't you at Riverley?"

"Nick flew me here in Emmy's jet. How's Irvine doing?"

"Nobody'll tell us. Whenever I ask, the receptionist just says to wait here. Sorry I kept calling—I didn't know what else to do."

I was more or less alone in an unfamiliar country with an unfolding crisis on my hands. Stéphane, usually the model of efficiency, seemed shell-shocked too. After the doctors had wheeled Irvine away, he'd whispered that this looked a lot worse than last time.

"You did exactly the right thing."

"Some pushy woman brought these forms. I can't ask Harriet or Stéphane to fill them in, not now, but what if the hospital won't treat Irvine otherwise?"

"They'll treat him. We can deal with the paperwork later. How are you holding up?"

"I'm fine."

"How are you really holding up?"

I buried my head against Alaric's shoulder so he wouldn't see my tears. Did Sirius do regular staff appraisals? I sincerely hoped not because I was the worst employee in the history of the world.

"It was just such a shock. Irvine fell down, and then the ambulance took forever to get there."

"What can I do to help?"

"Isn't that meant to be my line?"

"Not today, Beth. We're a team, remember?"

He kissed my hair, and I took a deep inhale, his cashmere sweater soft against my cheek. Alaric smelled of man and laundry soap, two of the most comforting things imaginable at that moment.

"Could you try asking again if there's any news? You're more authoritative than me."

Alaric glanced across to the desk in the far corner. The old battleaxe was still there, guarding the entrance to the kingdom while she played solitaire on her computer. I'd caught a glimpse of her screen the last time I ventured over there.

"Sure. Give me a minute."

I expected him to prepare for a fight with the receptionist, but as he neared the desk, he straightened, squared his shoulders, paused to say a few words, and then strode right on past. What the hell? No buzzers went off. No sirens sounded. The woman just returned to her game as if nothing had happened.

Ten minutes passed. Fifteen. Twenty. At twenty five, worry morphed into full-on fear, and I was soon shaking worse than Harriet. She was sobbing now, full of remorse for not spending enough time with her father, even though she'd needed to keep the farm going. Had Alaric been arrested for trespassing? Half an hour later, a doctor dressed in scrubs walked towards us, a stethoscope around his neck. Finally we might get some news, but I felt too sick to concentrate on anything but my missing boss.

Wait. Why was he heading towards me rather than Harriet? He peeled the paper mask away from his face, and I almost slapped him.

"What are you doing?" I hissed at Alaric.

"Getting information?"

"By imper—" I realised I was speaking too loudly. "By impersonating a *doctor*?"

He even had a bloody name badge. *Dr. Patterson, Consultant Dermatologist.* And one of those little paper caps too.

"You said you wanted information."

"I meant to ask the receptionist!"

"I've seen her type before—more backbone than a hardened terrorist. She'll never talk."

A nurse walked past. "Doctor, do you know where Mrs. Montell went?"

"Sure, she's in cubicle seven."

The nurse walked off, and I narrowed my eyes.

"Is that true?"

"Of course. Cubicle seven's right next to the nurses' station. Mrs. Montell and I had a nice chat while I waited to use the computer." Alaric's face turned serious. "I should talk to Harriet."

"You have news?"

He nodded, and I knew from his expression that it wasn't good. Stéphane already had his arm around Harriet's shoulders, and I squeezed one hand as Alaric crouched in front of her and took the other.

"Harriet, your father's had a massive brain haemorrhage. They're investigating possible treatment options at the moment, but it doesn't look as if there's much they can do. I'm so sorry."

Well, Alaric certainly passed the test for bedside manner, although that didn't make the revelation much easier to take. All the colour drained out of Harriet's cheeks.

"There's nothing? What about surgery?"

"With the size of the bleed, there's likely to be too much damage for surgery to be viable."

"I-I-I don't know what to do."

"He's on life support. I expect they'll let you see him soon."

"To say goodbye? We may not have seen eye to eye some of the time—well, most of the time—but I still love him. I can't... I can't..."

"You'll be able to take all the time you need."

"Time? I don't have time." She checked her watch, a utilitarian digital with a chewed strap courtesy of one of the yearlings. "It's six o'clock. The horses..."

"We can take care of the horses." Alaric gave me a slightly worried glance. "Right?"

"Right," I said. "And I can bring you some personal items if you need to stay here. Or I could swap with Stéphane later if he needs to go back to the farm?"

"Best that Stéphane sticks around too," Alaric said. "And I should go before someone decides to ask me a medical question I can't answer."

Stéphane nodded his agreement. "I'll take care of Harriet."

"Coffee first?" Alaric suggested.

"I think that's a good idea."

I knew my way around the kitchen at Lone Oak Farm now, so I put the drip machine on to brew. Sunday meant that Rusty would be working but Rodrigo had the day off. Rusty didn't ride, and he wasn't as knowledgeable as Rodrigo, but I could ask him to check the cattle and the horses in the paddocks at least.

That left Alaric and me to do the barn. Nine horses to muck out and feed, plus three to ride—the two stallions and a youngster who always had too much energy. I was running on empty by the time we finished.

"Breakfast?" Alaric asked.

With Stéphane providing moral support at the hospital, there was no spread waiting for us when we staggered into the house, and the thought of opening the fridge made me groan.

"I don't have the strength."

"When did you last eat?"

"A few mouthfuls at dinner last night."

"I'll make toast." Alaric waved at the old sofa in the corner. "Put your feet up."

"But I'm supposed to be *your* assistant."

"In that case, I'm ordering you to sit down. Does Harriet really do all this herself every day? With just one other guy?"

"Yes. Stéphane looks after the house and the senator. I'm not sure how she's going to cope when he leaves."

"He won't leave."

"But he's *Irvine's* assistant. And Harriet can't afford to pay him anymore."

"Stéphane's not here for the money. He's in love

with Harriet."

"*What*?"

"You don't see it?"

"No! I mean, I always thought Stéphane was gay."

"He's not gay," Alaric said mildly. "I'm good at spotting that sort of thing."

Because it takes one to know one? Once again, I felt a pang of sadness. The good guys were always unavailable, one way or another.

"That's, uh, I guess that's good news. But she's still going to struggle for money."

"Don't forget *Red After Dark*'s through there in the bedroom, and there's a fifty-thousand-dollar reward. Without wanting to sound callous, Irvine isn't going to need Dominique anymore. In fact, it makes me twitchy to think of a painting that valuable hanging on the wall in this house."

"Nobody knows it's here but us."

"Correction: nobody but us and the bad guys. It's served its purpose now—I wouldn't put it past them to take it back."

"You think we should move it?"

"For now, I'll put it somewhere more discreet than Irvine's bedroom wall, but I think the sooner it's back in the Becker Museum, the better for everyone. Unless..."

"Unless what?"

"Never mind. What do you want on your toast?"

"Anything but Marmite."

"You're safe—not so many people eat that over here."

How long did bread take to toast? One minute? Two? Whatever, it didn't matter. I was asleep in thirty seconds.

Chapter 30 - Alaric

A MONTH AGO, Alaric would have left *Red After Dark* on the bedroom wall. Enigmatic Dominique—the perfect lure. If the thieves took the bait, Sirius and Blackwood could reel them in.

But that was then, and this was now. Alaric wouldn't put Beth or Harriet in harm's way, not even for *Emerald* herself. Perhaps Black *was* right—that was painful to admit—and Alaric needed to stop living in the past? They'd retrieved one painting, and as soon as he worked out how to return it without tarnishing Irvine Carnes's name, Harriet would get fifty thousand dollars of reward money. If she needed more, he had some savings he could lend her. Nice though it was to have a cushion of cash to fall back on, he didn't need a fortune to be happy.

The toast was cold now. Dominique was hidden. Alaric scooped Beth up in his arms and carried her to the guest bedroom. Tempting though it was to lie down beside her and close his eyes, he made himself back out into the hallway. He'd be fine on the couch.

But damn, he loved that woman. The only problem was, how did he tell her?

"I'm sorry I fell asleep."

Alaric turned to see Beth in the living room doorway, wearing a bathrobe with her damp blonde hair hanging past her shoulders. Usually she tied it back. He'd just finished speaking to the sheriff from Devane's hometown about the young redhead who'd led them to Piper Simms. The man had promised to look into the situation. Discreetly. Her father was a well-known asshole, and the sheriff felt it was only a matter of time before he violated his parole.

"Not a problem."

He could get used to seeing Beth like that every morning. A little tug on the end of that belt...

"Do you want coffee? I'm just going to make some, and then I need to feed the horses again."

"With hay? I already did that."

"But how did you know...?"

"I used to help Emmy with her horse occasionally. Breakfast and dinner in a bucket, hay four times a day or he kicks the door. Did I get it right?"

Beth nodded. "You and Emmy are close, huh?"

"We've known each other for a long time."

The TV on the wall caught Beth's attention. Not surprising—Alaric had been watching the news for the last half hour, and apart from the rumours of Carnes's ill health, it had been remarkably entertaining.

"Is that...?"

"David Biggs? Yes." The Republican candidate.

"Who's that chasing him?"

"His wife."

From what the reporters had pieced together, it appeared the pair had gone out for dinner on Saturday night, to some Italian place in Frankfort. The restaurant had been promoting a special offer—write a review and get ten percent off the bill. Mrs. Biggs liked to save pennies, it seemed, because she'd hopped online to earn her discount, only to read the review above hers first. Glowing, five stars, and the reviewer had even included a photo of her and her friends enjoying their meal. And in the background of that photo was David Biggs, and the woman he was enjoying a cosy meal with was... Well, that was still under discussion, but she definitely wasn't Mrs. Biggs. The argument had been something to behold. Cell phone footage from several angles showed Mrs. Biggs throwing dessert at her husband, then whacking him over the head with her purse.

And it didn't end there. When the cops arrived, a drunk Biggs had waved a gun at them before cussing out half a dozen officers and getting arrested.

Not bad for a man who'd run on a platform of family values and respect for law enforcement. The irony was strong with that one. All they needed was a genuine O'Shaughnessy scandal before polling day and they'd have the full trifecta.

"My gosh," Beth said.

"We've played our part now. Forget the election. It's time to focus on the future."

"Is there any word on Irvine? Did you speak to Harriet?"

"I spoke to Stéphane. Irvine's on life support, and Harriet's going to spend as much time as she can with him while they run some final tests. I volunteered your services to help out for a few days. Is that okay with you?"

"Of course. *You* don't mind?"

"We've agreed it's sensible for me to return the painting in the near future, and I can do that alone."

"You won't get arrested, will you?"

"Definitely not." Beth still looked worried, so Alaric reached for her hand. "Trust me?"

"I trust you."

Alaric couldn't keep the smile off his face. Despite everything they'd achieved—taking out Devane, bringing down Ridley, solving Piper's murder, and finding *Red After Dark*—Beth's words and the concern behind them were the highlight of his month.

CHAPTER 31 - SKY

"OH. YOU'RE BACK." The words just slipped out.

Emmy sat up on the weight bench and wiped the sweat off her face. "You sound disappointed. Worried you might have to do some work now?"

"I've been doing work."

"With Rafael, apparently. What exactly happened to Alex?"

Rafael hadn't given her the low-down? I thought he'd have recounted my failings in excruciating detail. Or had he, and Emmy just wanted to see if my story matched up?

"Uh, Alex was kind of...sitting on me, and Rafael thought I didn't look too comfortable, so he hauled Alex off and threw him against the wall."

"So it was Rafael who broke Alex's ribs? I thought it was you. Now *I'm* disappointed."

Chances of me damaging Alex myself? Zero. The guy was built like a tank.

"It was an accident," I mumbled. A King Kong versus Godzilla accident. *Please, don't ask any more questions.* "How was your trip? Did you get the paintings back?"

"We sort of got one of the paintings back."

"Sort of?"

"We know where it is, but Alaric promised we

wouldn't return it until the person died."

"Is it with that senator?"

"Yup."

"I saw the news this morning. They said he's dead."

"Not quite, but he hasn't got long left."

"So I guess the painting can go back soon?"

"It can."

"What about the other one?"

"The investigation stalled again. I expect we'll let the dust settle for a day or two and then take another look."

"What dust?"

"You said you were watching the news—did you see Kyla Devane died?"

"Some crazy employee kidnapped her and shot her."

"Yeah, well, long story but he thought she was me. It's been an interesting week. But it's done now, so we can get back on track. How's it been going with Rafael?"

"I can't wait for Alex to come back."

Emmy barked out a laugh. "That bad?"

"Alex is brutal. Rafael is more…sneaky."

"In what way?"

"Last week, he made me go running. And after we'd slogged through the woods for about ten miles, he just vanished. Poof. Gone. I had to find my way back by myself. Hey, it's not funny."

"I'm laughing because Black did exactly the same thing to me. And you found your way home, didn't you?"

Home. Hearing Emmy say the word hit deep. This *was* my home, more so than any of the squats in

London, and it certainly beat the time I'd spent with my father and my years in foster care. The question was, how long would I be able to stay?

"Yeah, I got here."

Took me a few hours, a bunch of wrong turns, and a twisted ankle. I'd jumped into a truck for the last couple of miles. The driver didn't know—I just climbed on board when he stopped to move the branch I'd dragged into the road. Getting off was a bit dicey, but I'd managed to tuck and roll onto a grassy verge when he slowed for a corner.

And that wasn't the only stunt Rafael had pulled. Yesterday, he'd challenged me to a shooting match, and the arsehole swapped my ammo for blanks. Lesson learned: always load my own gun, or at least check the magazine.

"How about the rest of your training? The non-physical stuff?"

"I can swear in Spanish, and I'm never eating salad again."

It was far too easy to switch the rocket—or arugula, as Sofia kept calling it—for water hemlock, or the spinach for belladonna.

Emmy laughed. She knew exactly who'd been giving me lessons.

"I hate to tell you this, but Fia could just as easily slip ricin into your mac and cheese."

"In that case, I'm gonna buy all my food from McDonald's from now on."

"Good luck with that. You'll have to get it past Toby first."

"I'm training to be a spy. Sneaking junk food past a nutritionist should be easy."

"You think? He's got a sixth sense when it comes to saturated fat."

"Can I at least go out for dinner with Hallie one evening? I know I'm meant to be studying, but I can do extra the next day."

"One night a week, as long as the work gets done."

"Will there be a test?"

"Sure. I'm gonna drop you off in Uruapan with no money and no passport and let you find your way home."

Was Emmy joking? I hoped so, but I had a worrying feeling she was serious. And I already knew from Carmen that Uruapan was a hotspot in the Mexican drug war. Rival cartels had been taking it in turns to behead people and leave the corpses strewn around the city.

"Did you have to do that?"

"I got dumped in Acapulco."

Shit.

"It'll be a very quick meal. No alcohol whatsoever."

"You've been spending time with Hallie, then?"

"She's been staying here while her roommate's away. We've been looking at cold cases together."

"Really?"

"Just over dinner in the evenings. Don't worry, I haven't been skiving off all the other stuff. But it beats watching TV while I eat."

"What cases have you been looking at?"

Emmy added another weight to the stack and lay back on the bench. Fuck, she was pressing a hundred and ninety pounds. I could only do a hundred and ten. Plus she managed to talk while she did it rather than sucking in air like an asthmatic.

"The murder of Jaden Haan, the kidnapping of Mila Carmody, and the *Emerald* theft."

"The girlfriend killed Jaden. We've just never been able to prove it. And *Emerald*, huh? Find anything new?"

I had to agree with her on the Haan case. The girlfriend was as cold as liquid nitrogen. I'd watched videos of her police interviews, and she gave me the creeps.

"Not new, exactly. We just talked over all the evidence."

"And?"

I laid out the first theory we'd come up with. "There are two FBI agents we couldn't find out much about— Alaric's old boss and another guy. What if one of them was in cahoots with a member of the boat crew and gave them the combination so they could get an identical briefcase? Or another colleague who didn't have the combination could have told them what the briefcase looked like, and they could have jammed the lock on the fake so it would open with any number? We were going to ask Ravi if that's possible, but he hasn't been here."

"Even if it was possible, they couldn't have been sure they'd have the opportunity to swap the briefcases."

"The report said the boat was a scalloper rented for cash and Alaric had to climb a ladder up the side. Why that type of boat? If they'd brought a yacht, he could just have jumped onto the platform thingy at the back. I looked at pictures."

Emmy lowered the weights and propped herself up on her elbows, barely breathing hard.

"Or he could have asked them to drop the rope and then used it to strap the briefcase to his back. It just so happened that he didn't."

"They could have refused to drop the rope."

"Which would have aroused suspicions. We'd have backed off."

"Okay, so maybe it was Alaric himself. He had the means, the motive, and the opportunity."

"What motive?"

"Money. Doesn't everyone want to be rich?"

"Alaric was already rich."

"The file said he earned, like, seventy thousand dollars a year."

To someone like me, that was a hell of a lot of cash, but I still wouldn't class him as rich. There was a big difference between seventy grand and ten million.

"Putting aside the fact that Alaric's never cared about wealth, if his parents hadn't disowned him over the *Emerald* debacle, he'd be in line to inherit fifty million bucks."

"Oh." *Fifty million.* Wow. "Guess that blows that theory out of the water."

Emmy lay back and started her next set. "Yeah, it does."

"So that only leaves one option."

"Which is?"

"The money was stolen from your house."

"I thought you said you'd read the file?"

"I did."

"So you'll know how tight that place is buttoned up. CCTV, movement sensors, contact sensors, pressure sensors."

"What if there was a power cut? You were, ahem..."

"Fucking?"

"Yes, that. Would you even have noticed?"

"Firstly, we have a backup power supply, and secondly, I like to leave a light on so I can see who I'm doing."

"Okay, so what about the tunnels?"

The weights clattered back onto the stack, and Emmy knifed up to a seated position. "Who told you about the tunnels?"

Uh-oh. I hadn't realised they were meant to be some massive secret.

"Does it matter?"

"Bradley? Alex? Luke?" A pause, and boy was that stare intense. Her eyes were the oddest colour. More violet than blue. "So, it was Luke. You need to work on your poker face, sweetheart."

"Me and Hallie were asking about the previous break-in, okay? He didn't just volunteer the information." I liked Luke. Apart from Hallie, he was the only other person at Riverley who seemed vaguely normal. I didn't want to get him into trouble. "Don't have a go at him. Please?"

"I'll just remind him about the importance of discretion."

"Fine." As long as she didn't hurt him. "But what if that's the answer to the mystery?"

"It isn't."

"But—"

"The tunnels run between the two main houses, the garage, and the guest house. The entrances are hidden, and the buildings themselves are alarmed, just the same as Little Riverley. So yes, someone could have theoretically snuck into my house through the tunnels, but they'd still have had to breach the perimeter first. Think of it as one massive unit rather than four separate structures. It's all part of the same system. If one part's armed, it's all armed."

"What if they turned off the alarm in one of the other buildings?"

"They'd have been on camera going inside, and there'd have been a record of the deactivation. Plus they'd have had to sneak past me. And again, no motive."

"One person had a motive."

"Go on."

"Black."

Emmy snorted as she stood. "Puh-lease. You seriously think *he* did it?"

"I'm objective enough to see the way he acts around Alaric. Jealous doesn't even begin to cover it."

"You're saying I'm not objective when it comes to doing my job?"

"Yes."

Oh, Emmy didn't like that, not one little bit. I half thought she might take a swing at me, but somebody needed to say those words. Hallie had already told me she wasn't going there. Emmy took a step closer, then seemed to catch herself, and the fire in her eyes turned to ice. I swear the irises actually went bluer.

"You're wrong. Black wasn't even in Virginia that day." She stalked towards the door, then turned. "Where's Rafael? Don't you have work to do?"

"He'll be here any minute."

"Well, stop slacking and get on the fucking treadmill."

Chapter 32 - Emmy

"SHE'S NOT WRONG," Ana said softly from behind me.

For fuck's sake. I really didn't need this right now. I carried on walking, but Ana followed.

"Do you make a habit of listening to other people's conversations?"

Ana caught up and gave me side-eye. Okay, stupid question. Of course she eavesdropped. We both did.

"I find curiosity has benefits, especially when one of the participants in the conversation isn't listening themselves. Sky's right. You're not objective. The past clouds your judgement."

Ana was right. I hated to admit it, but she was right. Sky was new to Blackwood, and apart from Ana, she was the one person in the household who had no loyalty to Black. I had to admire Sky's thought process if not her conclusion.

"If anyone had a motive for framing Alaric for the theft, it was Black," Ana continued. "You should applaud Sky for having the guts to tell you the truth, not punish her because you don't want to hear it."

"Fine, I'll tell her to swap the treadmill for the Jacuzzi."

"How about we focus on the more important issue?"

"Which is...?"

"The theft."

"What? You think Black did it too? I know it wasn't him."

Ruining Alaric's life and career had, by extension, impacted on me and my happiness, and Black wouldn't have risked hurting me like that. Not to mention the fact that I'd ended up being shot at during the handover.

"Why? Because he told you so?"

"No." Come to think of it, he'd never explicitly said he didn't do it, but that was perhaps because I'd never asked. "Didn't you hear me say he wasn't even here?"

"Where was he?"

"On a job."

"Where?"

"North Carolina. Wilmington."

"Alone?"

"No, he was with Pale. They flew back the next day."

Pale was one of Black's long-standing partners in crime. Along with Nate, they'd been three of the four original Horsemen of the Apocalypse, a group of elite assassins used for jobs considered more or less impossible. After White died, the Horsemen had expanded to include me and a handful of others, but due to politics and the fact that trained killers were renegades by nature, the group was more or less dormant now. Officially, anyway. But Pale, Black, and Red were still tight. Case in point—who had Black turned to when he needed to rescue me from Ridley's clutches? I'd woken up in the back of an RV to find Pale's weathered face looking down at me. He ran his own team now, but he'd always help out an old buddy in a pinch.

"You saw them?"

"They landed on the airstrip out back. By that point, me and Alaric had already been used for target practice off the Virginia coast."

"What if he got back early and left again?"

"Ana, why are you doing this?"

"Because somebody has to ask these questions and you're not going to. We know whoever stole the money was bold as well as cunning, and who's the most capable person you know?"

She did have a point there. Fine, we'd go through this stupid exercise so I could point out the flaws in Ana's arguments, and then maybe she'd stop acting like a bitch with a bloody bone. The thought process might even shake some other ideas loose.

"Okay, brainstorm away."

She looked kind of surprised at my acquiescence but led me into Riverley Hall's gallery. Four stone pillars stood in front of the four windows, each with a rearing horse atop it. Black, Red, White, and Pale. The white horse had a black ribbon tied around its neck.

"Why the change of heart?"

"It's easier to get this over with, and then we can focus on the real problems like you said." I dropped onto one of the sofas, squashy beige leather that kind of hugged you as you sat. They were far more comfortable than the harsh-angled white ones in my gallery over at Little Riverley. The paintings were different too— classic oils and watercolours that contrasted with my abstract modern acrylics and sculptures. "How would you have done it?"

"I'll let you answer first."

"For years, I always thought it was a combination of Alaric's boss and the crooks. I never liked the guy, but in all the time we've been watching him, he hasn't put a foot wrong. No fancy holidays, no expensive cars, no drugs, no alcohol, no hookers. He fishes on the weekends."

"But?"

How did she know there was a "but" coming? Sometimes, her thought patterns were too close to mine for comfort.

"But just lately, I've been wondering whether Alaric *could* have had some involvement."

"Despite what you told Sky? What makes you say that?"

There was no judgement, only curiosity.

"Honestly? Because we've more or less ruled out everything else, and a few weeks ago, I found out..." I closed my eyes for a moment because I still couldn't believe he'd omitted to tell me about such an important part of his life. "I found out he has a daughter. A fifteen-year-old daughter."

"That's...unexpected?"

"Understatement of the year. And I keep thinking that if he kept me in the dark about that, what else didn't he tell me?"

"Maybe he had a good reason?"

"We dated for eight months. He'd made noises about transferring to the Richmond field office so we could spend more time together."

We'd even looked at houses in the area. Not for me to move in with him, because that would have been a big step—*too* big a step—but I could definitely have seen myself staying over.

"What if he didn't know he had a kid? Sam didn't realise for two years that he was a father."

"That was different. You were locked in a jail cell and you also thought he was dead."

"I'm just saying that the mother might not have told him."

"I guess it's possible," I grudgingly agreed. I'd been trying not to think about the logistics. What was the girl's name? Did she look like Alaric? "But that still doesn't change the fact that he told his personal assistant of *one week* all about her and he didn't so much as mention her to me."

"*Mudak.* And stealing the contents of the briefcase would have been straightforward for him."

"Yes. But I'm still struggling with a motive. It cost him far more than he would have gained. His job, his reputation, his inheritance."

Me.

And why would he still be looking for *Emerald* if he'd been responsible for letting her slip through his fingers back then?

"So who *did* gain?" Ana asked.

I was getting better at this. "Black."

"Assume for a moment that Black is the culprit. In the same way that it would have been easier for Alaric than anyone else to replace the pay off, Black has the advantage when it comes to breaking into his own home."

"But he'd still have to bypass the security system, and it's monitored in real time by the Blackwood control room."

"Every door?"

"Yes."

"Every window?"

"Yes."

"What about the roof?"

"Pressure sensors." Ever felt all the colour drain out of you? It's like a slow chill that starts at your hairline and works its way downwards through your forehead, nose, cheeks, and chin. "Except..."

"Except?" Ana asked. "What's wrong with your face?"

"Around that time, we had a new roof put on the guest house. The tiles were old, and... It doesn't matter. But the sensors got removed and replaced too, and each building has an escape hatch onto the roof."

"So somebody could have climbed up onto the roof?"

"No, that's not possible. We have cameras at the roofline."

"What about dropping down?"

"From where?"

"A tree?"

"There aren't any trees tall enough, not nearby."

"A plane? You say Black arrived in one."

"Is that even feasible?" We stared at each other. Both of us had made plenty of parachute jumps, but the guest house roof wasn't all that big. "It was daylight when me and Alaric went into the bedroom, and the windows face the stables, not the guest house. I suppose... I suppose that theoretically, someone could have landed there."

And Black had known the bare bones of the FBI operation. On the phone the evening before, I'd mentioned that Alaric would be bunking at Little Riverley overnight, although he'd arrived earlier than I thought he would.

"Were the sensors replaced before or after the theft?" Ana asked.

"I can't remember. When do I have time to organise building work?"

"Would Bradley know?"

"About the roof, sure, but I doubt he'd have got involved with the sensors. That's Nate's domain."

"So we have to ask Nate?"

"We're not asking him. Are you crazy? He'd go straight to Black and ask him why I wanted to know."

"There must be some kind of record. Emails, text messages... Nate wouldn't just turn up one day with a pile of sensors."

"Probably, but Nate's got more layers of security on his devices than you have on your house."

And considering even Quinn set the alarms off on occasion and he lived there...

"Well, somebody needs to find those details."

"Fuck." I wasn't a bloody hacker. Mack could do it. Or possibly Agatha, but I didn't want any of our Blackwood clan getting involved. Asking them to split their loyalties wasn't a route I was willing to go down. There was only one person I could ask. "I'll speak to Luke. He might be able to help."

That would still be hella awkward since he was married to Mack, but we had history and he owed me favours.

Ana squeezed my hand. "And if the timing fits, you know what we have to do."

Go and sob quietly in a corner somewhere? Because if Black *had* been involved in the theft, it meant he'd lied to me—perhaps by omission, but it was still a lie. I thought back to the way he'd defended Alaric for failing to tell me about his daughter. Had he been feeling guilty because he'd done a similar thing?

No, I couldn't quite see it. Black didn't *feel* guilt. It was one of the traits that allowed him to do his job and still sleep at night.

Stay objective, Emmy.

"Yes," I told Ana. "Somebody needs to make a test jump."

CHAPTER 33 - EMMY

"TELL ME AGAIN why I'm doing this instead of, say, Mack?" Luke asked. "Or you know, just asking Nate to do a search on his inbox instead of us digging through years' worth of archives."

"It's a potential personnel issue. I don't want anyone from Blackwood involved at this stage in case it turns out to be nothing."

"The old 'no smoke without fire' gossip."

"Exactly."

"What did they do? Steal roof tiles?"

"At the moment, I'm not sure they did anything."

"Okay, I'm in. Give me the time frame again?"

"Eight years ago. Early summer."

I paced the den in Luke and Mack's apartment. I didn't go over there often, and I'd brought a box of cakes from Mrs. Fairfax as a cover story. Would it be rude if I ate one? I suspected Bradley visited from time to time, though—the army of throw pillows lined up on the floor next to Luke's leather couch was a dead giveaway, as was the sparkly pot of pens that was about to fall off the edge of the desk. I nudged it closer to the nearest monitor and picked up a mini chocolate muffin.

"Don't drop crumbs," Luke told me. "Not on the keyboards, anyway."

"When you have kids, they'll get crumbs

everywhere. And toys, and mud, and baby vomit."

"Mack told you?"

"That you're trying for a baby? No, she just said you were looking for a house with a yard, and it seemed like the logical explanation."

Plus she had two assistants now. If she wanted to take maternity leave, it was the ideal time. Not that I could see her staying away from a computer for six months or even six hours. She'd probably be coding in the delivery room.

"I suppose it is. You're not upset?"

"Why would I be upset?"

"I guess... I guess because of our past?"

"We broke up over three years ago, and I don't even want kids. Just don't expect me to babysit."

Yes, I was fine. My husband might have ruined my ex-boyfriend's life and nearly gotten us both killed, but everything was tickety-boo.

"We're planning to get a nanny."

"I'm not really sure what I'm supposed to say. Good luck? Have fun?"

"Hey, here's the email." The relief in Luke's voice was evident because neither of us wanted to have *that* conversation. "Twentieth of June, Nate said he'd come and fit the new roof sensors the following Friday when he'd returned from Mexico."

Right. He'd been away, hadn't he? It was coming back to me now. A carnival in Carmen's home town and her little brother's birthday bash. And when had the *Emerald* shit gone down? On the twenty-third.

Fuck.

"Thanks."

"You don't sound happy. Is that everything you

needed?"

"I really appreciate you doing this." And at that moment, I was thinking perhaps I'd been a little hasty in ditching Luke. He wouldn't pull this next-level shit with Mack. No way. Sure, he was boring, but he'd never parachute onto a roof then creep through a tunnel and steal ten million bucks. "Please, just keep it between us?"

"I won't lie to Mack if she asks a direct question, but I won't volunteer any information either. Good enough?"

"Good enough."

See? Luke was a straight shooter.

My heart sank faster than the elevator as I made my way to the basement parking garage. For a moment while I waited on the top floor, I'd considered opening a window and taking the quick way down. If Black *had* done this, the entire foundation of my world would be shaken. He was my rock. My mentor, my lover, my friend. I'd put my life in his hands a hundred times, a thousand, and I could only do that because I'd thought the trust between us was absolute. Now? Now, I wasn't so sure.

Last night, I'd had to lie beside him in bed, make love to him as if nothing had happened. When he asked what was wrong, *I* was the one who'd had to lie and tell him Ridley's drugs had left me feeling weird.

Damn him for forcing me into this position.

Ana was waiting for me back at Little Riverley. But before I could go inside, I had to get past the truck in my driveway.

"What the hell is this?"

Tension hummed through me, and I didn't need any more shit to deal with. Enough was enough. One of the security guards who usually manned the gates was standing beside said truck, watching with his hands on his hips as the driver lowered a BMW coupe from the back. Not a bad vehicle, admittedly, but what was it doing outside my house?

"Your new car?" the guard asked. He must have caught my puzzled expression. "You didn't know about it?"

Last time a car turned up unexpectedly like this, it had been a late birthday present from Black, but my fake birthday was last month and my real birthday wasn't until December.

"Are you sure it's come to the right place?"

"It's got your name on the plate."

What the fuck? I took a look, and sure enough, the vanity plate read "E BLK." It also had a picture of a horse on it.

The driver stopped what he was doing and fetched a sheaf of papers from the cab. "Paperwork says it was ordered by a Mr. B Miles. Friend of yours?"

I. Was. Going. To. Kill. Him.

Or at least, I was when he came back from New York. I took out my phone and pressed speed dial two.

"Bradley, why is there a BMW on my driveway?"

"Oh, excellent, it arrived."

"That doesn't answer my question."

"You have three gas guzzlers, and we should all be doing our bit to save the planet. So I got you an electric car."

Give me strength. We'd had this discussion the other day. Bradley wanted me to go green. I pointed out that if I was driving somewhere in a hurry, I needed to fill up with gas, not wait hours for a battery to recharge. He said he'd look into battery ranges and charging times, which in Bradley's world clearly meant just go out and buy a damn car.

"I thought you were going to research this."

"I did. But what better way to test a car than to drive it around? You'll love it. The seats are heated, and if you press the button on the steering wheel, the cupholders pop out."

"It has a vanity plate. I don't do vanity plates."

Because how was I meant to run surveillance if the target could look in their mirror and literally see who was following?

"The gentleman at the auto dealership threw those in for free."

Arguing about the car was pointless, I realised that. If Bradley had decided I was having a fourth car, then I was having a fourth car, and I had to concede that the other three drank petrol like I drank gin. But my patience was at breaking point that day.

"Get rid of them."

"Okay, okay, I'll have them changed. How about the horse? Can the horse stay?"

"Just get me plain, regular, bog-standard plates."

Did anything else want to try me?

Ana was laughing at the window when I made it inside, and I scowled at her.

"It's not fucking funny."

She schooled her features into something more appropriate. "I'm sorry." One corner of her lips quirked. "You make dictators nervous, yet your assistant runs rings around you."

"Shut up." A long sigh escaped. "We need to talk."

Immediately, she grew serious. Funny how tradecraft kicked in, wasn't it? No phone calls, no text messages, no emails, even while my life got flushed down the toilet. And we went outside to speak in case Bradley had bugged the fucking house again. Luckily, he didn't seem to have listened in on our initial conversation, or the whole world would know about our suspicions by now.

"And?" Ana asked.

"The timeline fits."

She didn't say anything, just hugged me. Ana wasn't a touchy-feely person, not at all, but she gave good hugs when the need arose.

"I spoke to Sam," she murmured. "He'll make the jump."

"I thought we were keeping this between us?"

"Sam won't say a word. And besides, I didn't tell him the whole story. As far as he's concerned, he's just helping us to settle a bet."

That wasn't entirely untrue. I wasn't thrilled about another person being in on the secret, even marginally, but I trusted Ana's judgement, perhaps more than I trusted my own at that moment. The jigsaw was finally coming together in the most horrible way, and all I wanted to do was flip the board.

"When?"

"Anytime you want. He's working from home this week and next."

"I'll have to check the schedule. We obviously can't do it with Black watching, or Bradley, or anyone else who might talk." We'd basically have to clear the estate. A logistical nightmare. "I'll need a few days."

"Take as much time as you want. It's been eight years—another week or two won't make a difference."

But it would.

Because every minute was another sixty seconds that I'd have to spend acting normally while I was falling apart inside. The nine months when I'd thought Black was dead were actually easier to deal with, and I'd had a full-on breakdown back then.

I found out just how difficult things were going to be when Black arrived home half an hour later. Was it too early for a drink?

"Missed you."

He leaned down to kiss me, a kiss that quickly turned heated. If I closed my eyes and blocked out the dark clouds hanging over us, if I didn't *think*, perhaps I could forget the knife that was inching its way between my ribs?

"Missed you too."

I wasn't lying. My heart craved him, even if my head wasn't so sure.

"I thought we could go flying this afternoon. It's been a while."

Oh, shit. Did he know? My spine stiffened as a reflex, and I willed myself to relax.

"I was planning to check on Sky in the gym and then go for a run."

"Take a day off? You've earned it after the weekend."

"I had too many days off in Kentucky. And too many carbs."

"Too many carbs? I never thought I'd hear you utter

those words."

"Well, you live and learn, don't you?"

"I could do with a run too. We can go out for dinner afterwards. Something healthy. How about that new sushi place downtown?"

Next time, I needed to think before I opened my damn mouth.

"Sure, sounds great. Meet you on the terrace in half an hour?"

This time, he picked me up for a kiss. I wasn't small, not by normal standards, but beside Black, I always felt tiny.

"Don't be late."

We parted ways, and as soon as he disappeared around the corner, I sagged against the wall. Maybe I was overreacting? Just because Black *could* have committed the crime didn't necessarily mean that he *had*. But deep down inside, I knew what I'd been denying to myself for years—that Black was the best suspect. In the immediate aftermath, I'd discounted the possibility, and nobody else had pushed me to consider it. Of course they wouldn't. Black had an alibi, and the execution of the theft was perfect. I'd have expected nothing less.

But now Ana was here, and Sky, both looking at the case with fresh eyes. I barely knew Sky, but she was smart, and I trusted Ana implicitly. My whole life, I'd scoffed at the idea that blood was thicker than water, but then I'd met my half-sister and we'd just clicked. Bonded over a shared hatred of our father and the fact that our pasts had followed eerily similar paths despite us growing up on different continents.

When I got to the gym, Sky was on the mats at the

far end, sparring with Rafael. I paused in the doorway to watch them, and it was as if I'd stepped back in time eighteen years and looked into a mirror. A young girl who didn't have a clue what she was doing being schooled in the lethal arts by a man who choreographed death like a ballet.

I cleared my throat. "Can I have a minute?"

"With who?" Sky asked.

"You."

Rafael didn't speak, just stalked silently past me and vanished along the hallway. The Grim Reaper reincarnated as a panther. I'd kidnapped him once. Wasn't sure I could manage it a second time.

"What?" Sky asked. She didn't look at me.

"I need to apologise. For being a bitch yesterday."

"You saw where I grew up. You think I'm not used to that shit?"

"Yes, but you shouldn't get it from me."

Now she met my eyes. "Forget about it."

That was as close to an acceptance as I was going to get.

"So..." I picked up a pair of hand wraps. "What did you learn while I was away?"

"A detour to the office won't take long," Black said.

"For the last time, I don't need to see Dr. Kira again."

My husband stood in the bedroom, half-dressed—flannel slacks on the bottom half, nothing on the top. Ordinarily, I'd have lain back on the bed and enjoyed the view, but this wasn't an ordinary day.

"You were drugged, Emmy."

"Most likely with ketamine and a side of benzodiazepine. That's nothing. And it's worn off now. I just scrapped with Sky in the gym then ran ten miles, for crying out loud."

"You're out of sorts."

"I'm tired, that's all."

"Do you want to stay in tonight?"

Yes, but that would only lead to even more questions.

"Let's just have a quiet dinner out and an early night." A sigh escaped my lips as he tugged on a T-shirt. "A girl's gotta eat."

Damn Black for making this harder.

When he was in work mode, he took no prisoners, and more often than not, he pushed me to the point of pain and beyond. But in husband mode, he still made me swoon even after fifteen and a half years of marriage. Yes, we'd only been a proper couple for three of those years, but he'd always been a gentleman and tonight was no different.

As Black topped off my drink and pressed his thigh against mine under the table, I wondered if it was too late. Could I pretend the last two days hadn't happened? Besides me, only Ana and Sky truly suspected Black's duplicity. I'd already shut Sky down, and Ana would drop the matter if I asked her to. *Emerald*'s trail had gone cold. It would be easy to back off and let her fade into the night again.

It would also be wrong.

Alaric had only ever tried to make me happy, and he'd suffered for it. Somebody needed to make things right, and that somebody had to be me.

But for tonight, I buried all the fear and sadness along with my head in the sand, and when Black took my hand at the end of the evening and led me upstairs to bed, I let him undress me and caress me and bury himself inside me. And as the moon rose ever higher and the stars twinkled over the balcony, I thought back to my childhood, to the mother I hated so much. When I was little, maybe five or six years old, Julie Emerson had told me that people like us weren't destined to be happy. I'd spent my whole life trying to prove her wrong, but maybe it was time to accept that just for once, on that single point, she'd been right.

CHAPTER 34 - BETHANY

"THANK YOU SO much. I'll be sure to pass on your condolences."

I took the covered dish and carried it into the kitchen. Hmm... Where to put it?

Alaric looked up from his spot at the table.

"Tell me that's not another casserole."

"The lady said it was biscuits." But not cookie-biscuits. These were scone-biscuits, and I knew which I preferred. That wasn't to say we didn't have plenty of cookies too. They'd been arriving all day.

Harriet had been at Irvine's bedside late last night when the doctors turned off his life support, right after the results of the election came in. Aidan O'Shaughnessy took the senate seat, although the news barely merited a mention on TV. It was playing second—or rather fourth—fiddle to Irvine's tragic demise, David Biggs's impending divorce, and Eric Ridley's denial of any involvement in Kyla's death. Apparently, he'd just walked in and found her like that.

Alaric shuffled the dishes around to make space for the new offering, and I grabbed the ringing phone.

"Harriet?" a lady asked.

"No, this is her friend Bethany."

"It's Wilma Turner—one of Harriet's neighbours. I'm so sorry to hear about Irvine. If Harriet needs anything... A casserole?"

"We've got plenty of food at the moment, but thank you for the offer. If you have any spare time, though, Harriet would love some help with the animals."

"The horses? I don't know a thing about those beasts. I could pick up groceries or do laundry?"

That was everyone's story. We had enough food to sink an aircraft carrier, a rota set up for washing and ironing clothes, and even a lady coming over to vacuum. But nobody had the time or the inclination to muck out.

"Fetching groceries might be useful. Could I take your number and phone you back?"

She read it out, and I added it to the list. I'd turned into Harriet's assistant rather than Sirius's, but Alaric didn't seem to mind. He'd even answered a few calls himself. Harriet was sleeping now, and I was beginning to think Alaric was right about Stéphane—he hadn't left her side since the ambulance ride to the hospital.

And Alaric had barely left mine, apart from when he slept on the sofa at night. Harriet, Stéphane, and I had taken the three upstairs bedrooms, and nobody was going to suggest Alaric sleep in Irvine's wing. It was too soon. Harriet was raw. Raw with pain at losing her father and also with guilt that she'd spent more time with the horses than with him during his final weeks.

The funeral would be next Monday. Open casket, which freaked me out a bit because we just didn't do that in England. In the absence of other offers, Alaric had agreed that I should stay until after Irvine's cremation to support Harriet while he saw to the return of *Red After Dark*. Although the senator had a small life insurance policy, it would take a while for the money to come through, and Harriet needed cash now more than ever. Hopefully by the time I had to leave, the reward would have been paid and she'd be able to hire an extra pair of hands to help on the farm.

I worried in case the owners or the FBI thought Alaric had stolen the painting himself, but he assured me it wouldn't be a problem. No matter, if it came to it, I'd come clean about my part in the whole affair no matter what it cost me. I owed him that much.

"Everything's arranged," he announced, leaning back from his laptop. "I'll leave for Boston tomorrow morning."

"Are you flying?"

"No, driving. Stéphane says you can borrow the truck if you need to go anywhere here."

"Isn't it a long way by road?"

"I'll break it into two—here to Richmond tomorrow, Richmond to Boston on Friday. Emmy said I can use the guest house, and I need to drop their luggage off anyway. And the dog."

Apparently, Black had grudgingly agreed to them keeping Barkley. Not that he had an awful lot of choice in the matter—the pooch had made her feelings quite clear by falling asleep on his feet every evening in the rental property. Speaking of which, with everyone else having unexpectedly returned to Virginia, we couldn't justify shelling out for a four-bedroom house for two people. Hence we'd packed everything up and decamped to Lone Oak Farm. Not only was it cheaper, I liked seeing the horses from my bedroom window when I woke up. When this episode was over, we'd look at finding a new place for the rest of the summer so

Rune could come and stay. Alaric and I had to go to England for my sister's wedding on the sixteenth and of course pay a visit to Chaucer, then we'd pick up Rune and fly back to the US after that.

Dammit, *I'd* look for a new house, not *we*. That was my job, not Alaric's, even if he did seem to be acting more like a friend than a boss at the moment.

The phone rang again.

"Lone Oak Farm."

"Is this Bethany Stafferton?"

Stafford-Lyons, but it was close enough.

"Yes, speaking." The man sounded young, friendly, with none of the dripping sympathy I'd been accepting since the news got out. Nearly every caller had been a woman. "Who am I speaking to?"

"Joel Schumacher."

The name sounded vaguely familiar, but I couldn't place it.

"I'm sorry, I—"

"HiCam Videography?"

"Oh, yes, of course."

Was he one of the people who'd been on holiday? I scrabbled for a pen and paper. And my list with all the scribbles. Where had I left it?

"Looking for this?" Alaric whispered.

I nodded gratefully. Schumacher... HiCam... There he was. I'd called him near the beginning and left a voicemail.

"Mr. Schumacher—"

"Joel."

"Joel, thank you so much for getting back to me. We're trying to track down the person who recorded an announcement by Irvine Carnes several weeks ago."

"Why?"

The lies were coming much more easily now, and I wasn't sure whether to be proud or disappointed in myself.

"Harriet Carnes—Irvine's daughter—she knew somebody had visited to film her father, but he wasn't able to tell her who, and she's concerned in case there's money owing. So she asked me to make some calls to check."

"Oh, don't you worry about that. He paid up front."

"Mr. Carnes?"

"No, his assistant."

Huh? "Stéphane?"

"Nah, the other one. Edwin. Strange guy—he wouldn't do a wire transfer, insisted on mailing an envelope full of cash."

Edwin? Weird. The artist who painted *Red After Dark* was called Edwin. A coincidence?

"Mr. Carnes doesn't have another assistant," I blurted before I realised I shouldn't have said that. *Think, Beth!* "Uh, perhaps Edwin's part of his old senatorial staff. I wonder if we should be reimbursing *him* instead? Do you know what he looked like?"

"Never met him in person."

"I don't suppose you've got his surname? Or a phone number?"

"Edwin told me I shouldn't talk about the job with anyone. But you're family, right?"

"I work for Harriet. Perhaps I could get her to call you? It's just that she's a little upset after her father's death."

"Saw that on the news. He was a nice old guy, a bit tense but, you know, friendly. Anyhow, Edwin didn't give a surname. And he always called me. Blocked his number too, except for the last time. I guess he forgot. Are government people always like that?"

"In my experience, they can be a bit cagey."

Especially when it came to their mistresses, if my father's friends were anything to go by. Most of them had at least two phones, and some had two names as well—one for their wife and one for their bit on the side.

"Yeah, so I wrote the number somewhere. A piece of paper... Someone probably paid Edwin though. He seemed pretty organised." Muffled scratching was followed by a wail. "Eh, my kid's crying. If I find the number, I'll call you back, okay?"

The impatient part of me wanted to demand he keep looking *right now*, but I couldn't afford to alienate what could be our best lead.

"I'd really appreciate it."

"Wait, here it is." He reeled off a number, and I wrote it down. "I'm sorry about Mr. Carnes."

"I'll pass on your condolences."

Wow. My heart was going three hundred miles an hour when I hung up. Had I just managed to get a lead on the people who stole *Emerald*?

CHAPTER 35 - EMMY

SKY'S PERFORMANCE WAS improving. Rapidly. Staying ahead of her on runs was no longer a breeze, and I didn't have to hold back so much in fight practice. On Saturday, I'd challenged her to a race to the centre chimney of Riverley Hall, climbing up the outside of the building, and she'd damn near beaten me.

Rafael wasn't a bad teacher, or so it seemed. His methods may have been a little unorthodox, but they worked. No carrots or sticks; he preferred the psychological approach. Every time Sky asked a question, he came back with more questions until she worked out the answer for herself.

Yesterday, I'd seen them lying out on the back lawn. When I asked Sky later what they'd been doing, she said they were visualising the climb up the building so that next time she could do it better. *Picture every move, every handhold, and then see yourself at the top.* Did it work? Well, when I watched her having another go, she'd certainly seemed fast, and that was borne out by our race. When Black was teaching me to climb, he'd made me stand at the bottom of the cliff, building, whatever and work out the best route up. Rafael's method made Sky exercise her memory at the same time. Two birds with one stone and all that. Not bad.

But today, Sky's burgeoning perceptiveness wasn't doing me any favours.

"You've done well this morning. Why don't you take the rest of the day off? Go into town or something?"

"Rafael said he'd run through sniper practice with me this afternoon. Carmen cancelled at the last minute."

Carmen had cancelled because I'd surprised her, Nate, and their son, Josh, with a trip to a children's science fair in Florida. Josh loved gadgets, just like his father. I'd also sent Toby to visit his sister in Idaho, encouraged Bradley to go shopping in LA, and given Mrs. Fairfax the day off. The grounds team didn't work on Mondays. Dustin, my horse's groom, rarely spoke to Black—he was a man of few words—and an emergency evacuation drill at Blackwood HQ had got rid of everyone else except for the roving security patrol and the guards at the gates. They were familiar enough with my shenanigans that a bit of fancy flying and somebody jumping out of an aeroplane wouldn't raise any eyebrows.

But Sky and Rafael... They were another problem.

"Sky, that wasn't a request. If it helps, think of it as an exercise. You've got to come up with a convincing enough story to get Rafael away from this place without arousing his suspicions."

"Why? What are you going to do?"

I stayed quiet, and I was both pleased and resigned when she put two and two together and made sixty-three. Yup, Sky was smart.

"Is this about our conversation last Sunday?" She nodded, almost to herself. "The whole estate's quiet as a grave. Everybody's gone, and you've been grumpy as fuck all week. It is. You want to test shit out, don't you?"

"Once again, you've proven why I was right to hire you. About Rafael...?"

"Okay, I'll do it. I'll do it because I like Alaric and for some unknown reason I like you."

"Thank you." Then I changed the subject to an easier one. "How's Lenny?"

"Yeah, he's doing good. Says that hospital you put him in is more like a hotel. It's even got satellite telly and a dinner menu."

At the price I was paying, I'd expect nothing less, but at least he was recovering from his past indiscretions.

"Bet he's charming all the nurses too."

"And a woman called Julie?"

Ice formed around my heart. Damn Sky and her intuition. My mother was firmly off limits. I didn't even want to think about that bitch, let alone talk about her.

"Don't fucking go there."

Sky must have heard the barely controlled animosity in my voice because she offered a hesitant smile.

"I'll get Rafael to drive me into Richmond. Tell him I need new boots or something."

"Do me a favour—get him to stay and have dinner with you as well."

My earlier hopes of letting *Emerald* fade into darkness had been scuppered when Beth came up with a new lead. A phone number. I was beginning to suspect that

Alaric was right and *Emerald* was cursed because she'd sure screwed up both of our lives from the moment she came into them.

I'd had Mack run the number, and surprise, surprise, it came back as unregistered. A burner phone. But she'd been able to access the call history, and over the past two months, it had been used seven times. Four times to call our videographer, once to call a Chinese restaurant in Norfolk, again to call an automated banking service, and finally to call a feed store in the small town of Penngrove, just south of Chesapeake. Two connections to the same area—Norfolk and Chesapeake weren't all that far apart—and the call to the feed store interested me. It had lasted four minutes. Nobody called a feed store for that long unless they were interested in buying animal feed, and if they were buying animal feed, it stood to reason that they had animals nearby. Had we found the mysterious Edwin's hidey-hole? Nobody thought it was a coincidence that the fixer shared a forename with the dude who'd painted *Red After Dark*, and who was up to his eyeballs in dodgy art?

Dyson.

I'd agreed to travel to Penngrove with Alaric when he was set to go. Maybe it would lead to something and maybe it wouldn't, but we had to try. Black was gonna be pissed about me taking off, but if today's parachute experiment went the way I feared it would, he had no right to feel upset.

"Are you ready?" Ana asked.

"Nope."

But Sam was. He'd checked and repacked his parachutes in the ballroom at Riverley Hall, put on his jumpsuit and helmet, and strapped a camera to his chest to record what he said was possibly the dumbest thing he'd ever done.

The plan called for Ana to sit in my bedroom at Little Riverley while I flew Sam overhead in the Pitts Special I kept in a hangar beside our grass airstrip. I rarely used the little plane. I'd bought it years ago for aerobatics, but life was all work and no play at the moment. We'd make several passes, going higher each time, and when Ana told me over the radio that she could no longer hear the noise from the engine, Sam would jump.

Of course, skydiving from a Pitts Special was a challenge in itself. To prepare, we'd consulted YouTube, which suggested the best approach was for Sam to hang onto the framework by the top wing while I inverted, then drop away. That way, he wouldn't strike the tail. I was beginning to understand his "dumbest thing I've ever done" comment now.

Fortunately, Sam was an experienced skydiver. He threw himself out of planes on the weekends for fun, a concept I struggled to understand. Sure, I jumped out of planes too, but only when it was absolutely necessary.

After a final briefing beside the plane, Ana hefted her and Sam's daughter, Tabby, onto her hip and headed for the house. The lack of a babysitter meant we were training her young. I strapped myself into the pilot's seat, and Sam climbed into the back.

Was it too late to drive to the airport instead? A last-minute break in New South Wales seemed remarkably appealing.

An hour later, it was all over—the experiment, the jump, and quite possibly my marriage. Sam had landed on the very edge of the guest house roof and cracked his shin on a stupid weathervane—another of Bradley's additions—but he'd still hit the target. I'd deactivated the rooftop sensors, and it had only taken three minutes after landing for him to descend into the guest house basement and hobble through the tunnel to Little Riverley. None of the cameras or the other sensors caught his entrance. We'd found out how the pay-off *could* have been stolen, but the question was, did it go down that way?

Finding out for sure would be our next challenge. After Sam had taken Tabby back home and the plane was tucked safely back in its hangar, I slumped onto the couch in my living room with Ana and poured myself a large gin and tonic. Fuck knows I needed it.

"Now what?" she asked.

"I'm thinking of becoming an alcoholic."

She took my glass, opened the window, and poured the contents into a bush outside.

"*Nyet.*"

"Well, do you have a better idea?"

"We need to either prove or disprove our theory."

"No shit, Sherlock. How?"

"You said Black used a friend of his as an alibi. Pale? We should talk to him."

I laughed and laughed and then I laughed some more. "Not even you could persuade Pale to talk. He's part of Black's posse, not mine. He, Black, and Nate will always cover for each other."

Pale looked like a beach bum, but if you fell for the act and crossed him, you'd soon find out the error of your ways. I hadn't worked a job with him before, but Black and I had joined him for a morning of surfing a year or two ago in California, and we were hanging out on the beach—which made Black twitchy because he hated doing nothing—when some perma-tanned prick in budgie smugglers with muscles bigger than his brain accused Pale of ogling his girlfriend. Probably that was true, but there was no need to start a fight over it. First, we ignored him, but the asshole wanted to look like a big deal in front of the bunch of ladies lying out nearby, so he shoved Pale. Big mistake. Black and Pale both caught the guy under the chin with synchronised uppercuts and knocked him out cold. Then Pale turned around and asked if any of the girls wanted to go out for dinner. A perky blonde young enough to be his daughter gave him her number because under the Hawaiian shirt and baggy shorts, he still kept in shape and he had one of those faces that only got better with age. And Black was happy because Pale went home to take a shower so we didn't have to sit on the beach anymore.

"If we can't crack Pale, there's only one option left," Ana told me.

"I know."

Fuck, I knew. And I hated it.

I hated it because I'd have to confront the man I loved. I'd have to look him in the eye and ask him if he'd lied to me. Would he tell the truth or lie again? If he lied, it was over. I only hoped that after eighteen years of knowing him, I could tell the difference.

Chapter 36 - Emmy

WORK NEVER STOPPED, and no matter how much I longed to curl up under my duvet and hide from the world, I still had to go to the office for a late meeting. Some government guy wanted me to do a job. I wanted to sit at home in yoga pants and eat ice cream, so I quoted him an outrageous fee and he bloody agreed to it. See? My life was jinxed.

I finally got around to checking my messages and found one from Sky, asking if she could come home yet. She'd sent it at eight p.m. last night. Shit. I fired off a quick apology, deleted a text offering me free casino chips, then ignored everything else. Finally, I headed for the gym at headquarters. Punching something would help.

By the time I got home, Black was already there, complete with takeout from Claude's, Richmond's best French restaurant. Usually, that was a cause for celebration, but my appetite had deserted me.

"Dinner?" he asked.

"I'm not hungry right now."

He closed the distance behind me and dug his thumbs into the knot of tension in my shoulders. Mmm. That felt good. I closed my eyes for a second, enjoying one last moment of bliss.

"How about we take a swim instead?"

In our own home, swimming didn't tend to involve clothing and usually led to other things. But I couldn't afford to get sidetracked, not tonight.

"I thought we could watch a movie."

"A movie? Sure."

I headed for the movie theatre before I chickened out, but Black caught my hand.

"Don't you want to change first?"

I looked down at myself. Okay, so a tailored pinstripe dress and stilettos weren't exactly typical moviegoing attire, but it was now or never. No distractions.

"I'm fine in this."

"Okay." His tone said he wasn't convinced. "Do you want snacks? A drink?"

A bottle of wine would be nice, but I'd promised Ana I'd be good. Her spare bedroom was ready and waiting in case I needed to get away from home tonight. She'd taken Sam to the hospital to get his shin X-rayed because it had swollen up and gone a horrible purple colour—once again proving that this whole fucking nightmare was cursed—but she'd be back later.

"I just said I wasn't hungry."

The movie theatre at Riverley Hall was usually a comfy, cosy place, but tonight, a chill washed over me as I stepped through the door. The big screen at the front of the room glowed grey as it waited for me to press play on the clip I'd cued up earlier. A picture painted a thousand words, right? So a video should be good for a million. I couldn't speak anyway. My throat was too dry.

Nine sofas—three rows of three—sat on three levels, complete with cushions and fluffy blankets. Vintage movie posters decorated the walls, and a drinks cooler hummed in one corner. A table held bags of candy Toby hadn't yet got around to confiscating, and because Bradley had done the decorating, there was a vase of fresh flowers too.

Black dropped onto the middle sofa and patted the seat beside him.

I sat.

Felt sick to my stomach as I pressed play.

Raw footage from Sam's jump flickered across the screen. The roll. His release. The ground rushing towards him, a lurch as he adjusted his direction, and finally, the slate tiles of the guest house roof filling the lens. Black's arm dropped away from my shoulders. I'd never known him to be scared before, not once, but that night, I smelled the fear seeping from his pores.

And then I knew the truth.

"What's all this about?" he asked mildly, but he couldn't hide the tension in his voice.

Our guess had been right on the money.

"I don't think I need to explain."

His voice softened to the faintest whisper. "I didn't plan to do it."

"Oh, right, it just happened, did it? You simply tripped over the briefcase and decided to replace the contents with a bunch of fakes?"

"I came home early because there were things we needed to discuss. And then I realised *he* was there, and I heard you fucking, and..."

"You thought you'd destroy him and then lie about it?"

"Technically, I never said I didn't do it."

Oh, that prick... I shoved him in the shoulder and

stood up.

"Don't treat me like an idiot. You offered to head up the investigation into the theft and then conveniently didn't find anything."

Black stood too, and I wished I had a stepladder.

"I spoke to people. Made sure the FBI didn't prosecute."

"Oh, gee, so because Alaric stayed out of prison, that makes everything okay, does it?"

"Clearly not."

"For once in your life, can't you show some empathy?"

"I...struggle with that."

"No kidding. You almost got me killed that day. How does that make you feel?"

"I had no idea you were going with him. If I had..."

"You'd have come clean?"

"I'd have stopped it somehow."

"People died, Black. Alaric lost everything. I lost a man I cared about." I sucked in a breath and stared my husband straight in the eye. "Who I still care about. And now I've lost you too."

"Emmy, I—"

"Shut up! Your jealousy's a monster. Sure, you had feelings for me back then, I get it. But instead of growing a pair and telling me, you sabotaged nearly every relationship I got involved in." I ticked off on my fingers. "Take James, for example. Rather than risking us getting back together, you engineered him into the presidency and bribed a woman to marry him. A woman, I hasten to add, who you were fucking at the time. You think I didn't know that? Yet you don't see me losing my shit every time you're alone in a room with Diana, do you?"

"James wanted to marry you."

"So? Did *I* want to marry *him*? No. After everything that happened—" I swallowed down the sob that threatened to burst out as I recalled the nightmare of a week that had ended my relationship with James Harrison. "After everything that happened, marriage was never an option. And you're still an asshole to him even now, eleven years later."

"Because he's still in love with you."

"Fucking hell! It takes two to tango, and the last contact I had with his balls was when I planted my knee in them. You're irrational! And what about Gideon? You had him reassigned to Paris."

"It was a promotion."

I closed my eyes and forced myself to take a deep breath.

"That's not the point. You split us up on purpose. And Alaric... Where do I even start? You knew I liked him. A lot. At least with James and Gideon, you gave them a consolation prize, but you ruined Alaric's life!"

"I tried doing it the nice way first. Why do you think he got assigned to the overseas art squad? But he just kept coming back. And..." Black's turn to compose himself. "And I kept asking myself, what did he have that I didn't?"

"Nothing. He had nothing that I wanted more than I wanted you."

I tore a hand through my hair. A clump snagged on wedding ring number two and ripped out from the roots. Ouch, fuck. Alaric was an amazing guy, but if it had come down to a choice between him and Black, it would have been Black. Always Black. Except maybe today.

"There must have been something," Black said, a dog with a damn bone. "I remember the way you looked at him."

"Fine." I narrowed my eyes, irritation getting the better of me. "You're really that desperate to know? Then I'll tell you. Alaric was the master at giving it to me up the arse. The king of anal. Is that what you wanted to hear? Oh, and he didn't take himself so fucking seriously all the time either."

Black's eyes glittered, and I wondered if I'd gone too far. Winding him up was like poking a sleeping bear with a really big stick. But I just couldn't stop.

"And above all, he was a friend. Newsflash: I have lots of friends. You never get jealous when I go out with Sofia, and I hate to tell you this, Chuck, but if I was gonna fuck around behind your back, I could just as easily do that with a woman. So it's the dick, right? You got scared in case Alaric had a bigger fucking dick than you."

"Emmy, shut up."

He sounded annoyed. Well, I was pissed off too. Pissed off that Alaric's life had been ruined, and angry that I hadn't realised Black's role in the affair sooner. How could I have been so blind?

"Screw you."

"Really? You want that? I'll show you who's got the biggest dick."

He spun me around, reaching for my zipper, a move he'd pulled a hundred times before. But today, I batted his hand away. He growled and fisted a handful of fabric, and my dress tore as I sidestepped away from him. Top to fucking bottom, and Black was left holding the remains of my outfit. A fine piece of Italian workmanship that turned out to be.

"Get the hell away from me. You're not fucking your way out of this mess."

"We can talk about this."

Now he grabbed my arm. I tried to unpeel his fingers, but he wouldn't let go, so I did what came naturally. Hit him with a right hook. He staggered backwards and fell against the side table, but his eyes quickly focused again, and he didn't flinch when the vase wobbled and crashed to the floor. Quick as a flash, he threw me backwards onto the sofa, but I kicked his legs out from under him on the way down. It only took me a second to roll sideways and get into a fight stance, but what was left of my bra pinged open and sagged around my chest. I flung it at Black as he scrambled to his feet. Of course, he ducked.

"Diamond, what are we doing?"

Black was looking for an opening, a way to subdue me, but I was in no mood to listen to his bullshit. When he dropped his gaze for the merest fraction of a second, I knew he was going to go for my legs. Getting me flat on the floor was his best option. So I ducked under his guard before he could make a move, grabbed his shirt for leverage, and kneed him in the bollocks. Normally, that would have been counterproductive, but today I didn't care. Buttons flew everywhere as his shirt ripped. Black gave a satisfying grunt, then tried to tackle me but missed when I leapt back.

"I'll tell you what *you're* doing. Proving you're the world's biggest dick."

When he began to straighten, I raised one foot, not bothering to temper my fury as I booted him in the chest with a stiletto. He fell back onto another sofa, and this time, he didn't get up. My spiked heel had left a red mark on his chest, right over his traitorous heart. Good. He deserved it.

"I'm sorry," he whispered.

"You absolute fucker."

Even if he forged each letter from steel and honed every edge until it was razor sharp, "sorry" didn't cut it. For a moment, I was tempted to go in with a left hook as well.

"Diamond..."

"Don't think you can talk your way out of this either."

"Just—"

"Enough!" I strode towards the door, holding my head high as I fought the urge to cry. In a final insult, the elastic on my flimsy silk knickers gave way, and they floated to the floor. "Don't even think about coming near me."

"Emmy?"

At first, I thought it was Black who'd spoken, but as I blinked back tears, I saw the blurry outline of Alaric standing in the doorway. Fuck. *Fuck, fuck, fuck.* How much had he heard?

"Are you okay? I came to talk over the case, but I heard shouting..."

"I'm fine. Perfectly, wonderfully fine."

I took one last glance at Black, sitting motionless in semi-darkness, and pushed past Alaric. Horror turned into devastation as I walked and then ran through the house, barely noticing when I smacked my bare hip bone on the edge of a door. I had to get out of that place. *Get home to Little Riverley, call Ana, scream.*

I was fumbling with the lock on the front door when a hand closed over mine.

"Get off me!"

"Cinders, you can't go outside like that. Here…" Alaric tucked his sport coat around my shoulders. "What happened in there?"

"I don't want to talk about it."

"Okay." Alaric shrugged, accepting, always accepting. "But if you think I'm letting you run upset into the night, you've got another think coming."

"I need to get out of here."

"Then I'll walk you home."

CHAPTER 37 - ALARIC

WAS EMMY CRYING? Emmy never cried. She seemed to have loosened up a bit emotionally since the old days, but tears? What the fuck had happened in that room? Was there trouble in paradise? Alaric had never seen Black look so...contrite.

Turned out the iris scanners didn't work when Emmy's eyes were watering. Alaric leaned forward and stared into the lens himself, and the bolts securing Little Riverley's front door shot back with a muffled *thunk*.

"What can I do? I hate seeing you like this."

Emmy started to wave him away, but when she held up a hand, they both saw it was shaking.

"Shit," she muttered. "Pour me a glass of wine."

"Alcohol isn't the answer."

"Where have I heard that before?"

At a guess? Toby with an outside chance at Ana.

Alaric nudged Emmy inside and closed the front door behind them. Gee, this wasn't awkward at all, standing in front of his half-naked ex.

"Let's find you some clothes."

When Emmy made no move towards the stairs, Alaric pressed the button for the elevator. The fact that she didn't complain was a testament to just how unsettled she was. Usually, she hated the thing, and anyone caught taking it got forced to do push-ups as a penalty.

"Don't worry, I won't tell," Alaric promised as they climbed on board.

She didn't even acknowledge his words.

The last time Alaric had been in Emmy's bedroom, on that fateful visit when *Emerald*'s pay-off had disappeared, the decor had been blue and white. Today, it was earthy tones—browns, creams, and beiges—complete with a driftwood sculpture in one corner. What was it? An ostrich? A canoe?

"It's called 'Dragon Fruit,'" Emmy said when she saw where he was looking, followed by a sniff. "Bradley bought it from some bohemian artist in Portugal."

"Aren't dragon fruit normally pink, spiky things?"

"The front end's a dragon and the back end's a banana. The sculptor's doing six months for possession now." Pain filled her eyes again. "I guess I should get dressed."

"Do you have pyjamas?"

"I... I don't know."

"You don't know?"

"There's probably a pair somewhere, but..." She shrugged. "Usually, I sleep in a T-shirt and a pair of Black's boxers, but tonight...no."

That must have been some bust-up. Alaric was curious as hell about the circumstances, but he also knew Emmy would never talk if she didn't want to. She'd done drill after drill as a prisoner of war, stress test after stress test, and she'd protect Black the way a momma bear protected her cubs even if he wasn't her favourite person at the moment.

Alaric's jacket slipped off her shoulders, so he

darted into the walk-in closet and grabbed the first thing that came to hand—a sparkly pink dress completely unsuitable for the occasion—and quickly tugged it over her head. Actually, *was* it a dress? It barely came to mid-thigh. Hard to tell.

And that wasn't the only problem. He headed back into the closet, which was bigger than the first apartment he'd rented in Thailand, and rummaged through the drawers. Wallets, purses, a selection of firearms... Eight drawers in, he found a selection of underwear, not the sporty stuff she used to wear but frilly, lacy lingerie, each set in its own compartment. He grabbed a black bra and panties and tossed them out the door.

"You'll need these."

And pants. She needed pants. Skinny jeans, or leggings, or...yes, this looked like a cross between the two. And that shawl would work as a cover-up. When he'd first met Rune, she'd been a quivering mess for weeks, and she'd liked to wrap herself in a blanket. Even now, she resorted to scarves and big, bulky jackets whenever she felt insecure.

"Here you go." He emerged into the bedroom just as Emmy tugged the panties up her legs, and he hurriedly averted his eyes. Yes, he'd seen it all before, but that was then and this was now.

"Good thing I waxed, huh?"

Even joking, she still sounded sad, and when Alaric tried to wrap the shawl around Emmy's shoulders, she shrank back.

"Cinders, I won't hurt you. I promise."

"You already did," she muttered.

He deserved that.

"And I'll forever be sorry, but I'll never do it again."

"Thanks, but you can go now."

That stung. After the way he'd run out on her, he deserved to be pushed away, but it still stung.

"I'm not leaving you alone. Who can I call? Who do you trust?"

"Right now? No one except Ana, and she's out."

"What about Dan? Mack? Nick? Sofia?"

Emmy shook her head. Why not them? They were her oldest friends. Alaric's synapses fired, and suddenly he understood. Shared loyalties. They were Black's friends too.

"If you want space, I can sit downstairs."

"Just leave. You lied to me. Everybody lies."

"Cinders, if I could turn the clock back, I would, but I can't. I left you, and I'll always regret that, but I swear I never lied to you."

"Oh, really? So you...what? Just completely forgot to mention your daughter the whole time we were dating? Even if you weren't with her mother, surely you knew she existed?"

Alaric laughed. He couldn't help it, even when Emmy gave him the mother of all glares.

"You're talking about Rune?"

"Unless you have *two* daughters?"

"Emmy, Rune isn't my biological daughter. I didn't tell you about her because I hadn't even met her at that point."

Now Emmy raised her eyes and met his gaze.

"Then what...? Did you *adopt* her?"

"It's a long story. How did you find out about Rune?"

A shrug. "Sources. Are you going to tell me the

story? Or is it a big secret?"

"I've been waiting for the right time. We've both been so busy, and..." They'd been finding their way back into each other's lives slowly. Truth be told, Alaric had been on tiptoes, sticking to business for fear that Emmy might slam the door in his face. And there'd always been somebody else around. Black, or Beth, or Sky, or Emmy's staff. But that wasn't a great excuse. "I should have made the time."

"Seems our communication could do with some improvement all around."

Alaric held out a hand. "Then let's talk. But not here —too many bad memories."

If Black was being a prick, then Emmy could do with getting away from Riverley too. He'd probably bugged the place, and if not him, then Bradley had a habit of planting clunky surveillance devices he bought from internet spy stores. Weekly sweeps picked them up for the most part, but every so often, one slipped through temporarily. Alaric didn't exactly want their private conversation, their secret thoughts, broadcast to all and sundry.

Emmy put her hand into his. "Okay. Where are we going?"

"I'll drive."

They often used to sneak out to CJ's Diner in the old days. CJ's served the best cheeseburgers, and the high-sided booths kept private conversations safe from prying ears. Eight years had passed since Alaric last set foot in there, and the place hadn't changed a bit. Same wood-panelled walls, same faded red vinyl seating, same crackly jukebox. Even the same waitress, although her hair was mostly grey now.

"I haven't been here in forever," Emmy murmured as Alaric led her towards "their" table—the one right at the back, nestled beside an ancient cigarette machine. An *Out of Order* sign was taped over the coin slot.

"What can I get ya, hun?" the waitress asked, no hint of recognition in her eyes.

Alaric already knew what Emmy would have. "Two cheeseburgers with everything, two portions of fries, one of onion rings, a diet cola, and a sparkling water."

Emmy always said that if they split the onion rings, they could also split a dessert afterwards. Calories shared were calories halved. They'd spent hours in this place, talking and laughing about nothing in particular, but tonight, Emmy could barely muster a smile.

"They've got chocolate orange cheesecake." Alaric nodded towards the glass counter at the front. "I bet it's the same recipe."

It had been her favourite. If he'd ever mustered up the courage to give her the ring he'd bought all those years ago, he'd planned to hide it in a slice.

"I'm not that hungry."

"See how you feel later. So, you want to know about Rune?" If Alaric kept talking, that meant Emmy wouldn't feel pressured to. "It all started five years ago in Phuket. I'd been travelling more or less constantly until then, doing odd jobs, meeting people, but I figured I'd spend the winter in Thailand for a change. The past couple of years before that, I'd headed back to Europe to ski, but diving seemed like a fun alternative. I passed my IDC—Instructor Development Course—

and rented an apartment near the beach."

"At this particular moment, I'm tempted to do the same."

"Don't be too hasty, Cinders. Was that the first proper argument you've had with Black?"

She nodded.

"Then let the dust settle. It'll blow over."

"I'm not so sure."

"You two were made for each other. We might both have tried to deny that once, but with time comes clarity."

Emmy looked dubious, then turned away and began rearranging the table accoutrements. The napkin dispenser, the cutlery caddy, the ketchup, the salt and pepper—she wanted everything lined up just so. She only normally got OCD over her weapons.

"Anyhow, I spent my days either underwater or hanging out near the beach, and I hooked up with Ravi."

"As in hooked up, hooked up?"

Alaric nodded.

"And now? You're still together?"

"Mostly just for work, but occasionally we fool around. We agreed that as long as we're both single, it's preferable to sleep with each other rather than picking up strangers to satisfy a physical need."

"Thanks. I just won fifty bucks off Dan. She said he wasn't gay."

"You'll have to split it—he goes both ways."

"Dammit."

"He broke up with his ex-girlfriend three months before we met. They were meant to travel to Thailand together, but he decided to go alone rather than waste the ticket."

"And what's Ravi's background? A gymnast with a B&E habit?"

"Close. He grew up in the circus. His parents were both acrobats, but now they're doing life for burglary."

"Harsh."

"He's always been cagey about exactly how they were caught, but I suspect he was there and got away. They'd been forcing him to help out with the family business since he was a kid."

"And now? He's gone straight?"

"He had until we started Sirius. When I met him, he was working as a bartender in a dive on the backstreets of Patong. I was there, waiting for him to finish his shift when it all started."

"When what started?"

When what started? The rest of Alaric's life.

Chapter 38 - Alaric

"WE'VE TAKEN TO calling it 'the incident,'" Alaric told Emmy. "Judd and Naz were there in the bar too, drinking. Well, Naz was hunched over his laptop. And Judd was hitting on a girl who was actually a guy. Ravi and I made a bet on how long it'd take him to notice."

"How long *did* it take?"

"He never found out because that was when the *incident* happened. A man walked into the bar with a girl, and I was trying to work out what she was to him. Girlfriend? Daughter? She seemed too young for the former, but who would take a kid out to a shitty bar in the early hours?"

"A bad, bad parent."

"Exactly. He sat with another man who'd been there for a while, they had a conversation that sounded more like an argument, then the girl left with guy number two instead. And she did *not* look happy."

"I'm getting a bad feeling about this."

"That's precisely what I said to Ravi. We didn't understand a word they said, though. My Thai was limited to diving terms, getting directions, and ordering food, so Ravi asked his boss if he knew the man, and it turned out he did. He came in once a week, once every two weeks, always with a different girl. The bar was a handover point for sales."

"Shit."

"I think I said that too. But you know me—I couldn't just leave it."

"That was one of the things I always liked about you."

"Past tense? Ouch."

"I still do like that about you." Emmy managed a tentative smile. "So, what happened?"

"I followed the original guy. The seller. Cut the head off the snake, right? But after a couple of minutes, I realised I wasn't the only one who'd had that idea."

"Judd?" Emmy guessed.

Alaric nodded. "I didn't know who he was or why he was there, but I recognised *what* he was by the way he moved."

"An operator."

"And surprisingly not a bad one."

"It's like he has two modes—James Bond and dickhead."

Succinct, yet entirely accurate. "That about sums him up."

The drinks arrived, and Alaric paused to take a sip. The diner had changed from plastic to paper straws, proving the place wasn't completely stuck in a time warp.

"Thanks, sweetheart," he told the waitress, ignoring Emmy's eye-roll when the woman giggled.

"Food won't be long, hun."

She swished off in her pink dress and sensible shoes, and Alaric picked up the story.

"So I saw Judd, he saw me, and it was weird—we'd never met before that night, but we didn't need words to know that we were both up to the same thing. He stayed one side of the street, and I stayed the other, and we followed the seller to a go-go bar. The Angels Playground. No apostrophe, and no paradise either."

"Classy."

"Definitely at the lower end of seedy. Girls in neon costumes, waitresses dressed as schoolgirls. We went in and had a few drinks. Watched the dancers. None of them looked underage, but we both knew what we'd seen. At that point, we still hadn't talked much—I told Judd I was a scuba instructor, and he said he was writing a screenplay. Turned out neither of us was lying, but nor were we being entirely truthful."

"Judd's writing a screenplay?"

"Yeah, but don't tell anyone. Especially his mother."

"What's it about? Have you read it? Is it any good?"

At least Emmy seemed slightly perkier now. If Rune's story took her mind off whatever had happened at Riverley, Alaric would talk the whole night.

"He's written half a dozen, actually, all under a pseudonym. Sci-fi romance. One even got made into a movie."

"What movie?"

"*Stellarium.*"

"I haven't seen it."

"It's surprisingly good. Give it a go."

Emmy sort of...shrivelled. Fuck. "I think I'll be skipping movie nights for a while."

"Even with me? I'll bring popcorn. And M&Ms. We can make s'mores if you promise not to set fire to the marshmallows this time."

A tiny smile. "Maybe."

"Maybe" was better than an outright "no." "Anyways, back to the Angels Playground... We watched the dancers, and every so often, one of the waitresses would lead a guy through a door at the side of the stage."

"For extra services?"

"That was our assumption. But we didn't get to find out that night because the club closed. Four a.m. was kicking-out time, so we went back to the bar. Ravi's boss wouldn't say much because he was scared. The men who sourced the girls were bad news, and he didn't want any trouble."

"So you decided to investigate yourselves?"

"We did, and by that point, Naz had come over to see what was going on. He didn't like the look of the men either, and while they were talking, he'd checked out just who was hooked into the bar's Wi-Fi network."

"Naz is a hacker? You've never said much about him."

"Yes, he's a hacker, and he shies away from the limelight, probably because he's officially dead."

"He faked his own death?"

"Since the Bratva wanted to kill him, it seemed like a sensible idea." The Russian Mafia didn't mess around. "By day, he was a government guy—GRU—but at night, he poked his nose into the wrong servers. Ended up bringing down a network of corrupt politicians."

"I see how that could be a problem."

"Now he's got a new name and a Norwegian passport." Among others. "And that night, he came up with another name for us. Sunan Thungchunkoksoong. We couldn't be certain who it belonged to, but the guy who took the girl had been busy on his phone while he waited for his 'friend' to arrive, so that seemed like a good possibility. And here's the funny thing about Thai surnames—they didn't exist until 1913. Thai law says that each family has to take a different surname, and everyone using a given surname must be related. So not many people share the same full name."

"Bet that makes police work easier."

"Sure, if you can find a cop who isn't corrupt. It made our work easier too—Naz found the guy online in five minutes flat. A local businessman. He ran a catering supply store. Family man. Wife, two kids, and he'd just taken possession of a young Thai girl. So, by then there were four of us and two problems."

"Here you go, hun."

The waitress was back, complete with a tray of food. Had the portions always been that big? Emmy's burger was the same size as her head. The instant the waitress set her plate down, she covered her fries in ketchup and stuffed a couple into her mouth. Thank goodness. Emmy without an appetite was unnatural.

"And?" she asked. "What happened next?"

"We decided that walking away wasn't an option. And we had two things on our side: time and ability. Judd had just quit his job at MI6, I was freelancing, so was Naz, and Ravi didn't much like working at the bar anyway. Judd rented us a bigger apartment, and we set about learning everything we never wanted to know about the Thai sex-trafficking industry. Starting with another visit to the Angels Playground." Alaric closed his eyes for a moment, remembering what he didn't want to. "That place was sick."

"Did you go as a punter?"

"We all did. It seemed the best way to work out what was going on. Ravi drank too much and puked in the toilet, and his girl made him tea. Naz claimed he'd gotten confused and just wanted a massage. Judd couldn't get it up. For real. Didn't even have to pretend."

"And you?"

"Me? I got Rune."

Alaric would never forget that first meeting. He'd asked for a girl on the younger side, expecting a teenager. Not barely ten-year-old Rune, cowering on the far end of a dirty single bed in a negligée. When she saw him, she tried to smile, and someone had obviously schooled her in the art of acting coquettish, but not very well. It didn't help that she was so thin he could see her ribs and obviously exhausted.

Instinct had warred with reason. Instinct told him to find the man who'd shown him into that room and break his fucking neck. But reason said they needed to play the long game, and the thugs who worked at the club were probably as replaceable as the girls.

"What you want?" Rune asked. "Massage? Suck? Love?"

"Let's talk. I want to talk."

He crouched down beside the bed, trying to make himself as small and unthreatening as possible.

"Talk?"

Shit, did she even speak English?

"Talk." He pointed at his mouth. "Words."

What was he thinking? She was half-naked. Feeling quite sick, he'd wrapped a grubby sheet around her in much the same way he'd done with Emmy earlier. That had scared Rune even more, and she'd tried to pull it off again.

"No, not allowed."

"You're not allowed to cover yourself?" He mimed wrapping himself up and shook his head.

"Not allowed."

Fuck, this was a nightmare. The kid had a bowl of condoms sitting on a table next to the bed. Alaric felt ashamed to have a dick.

"How long have you been here? Worked here?"

"Work here?" She held up a hand, all the fingers and her thumb extended. "Five year. Live here? Always." Tears welled up in her eyes. "I very good."

Bile rose in Alaric's throat. He might have retired from the assassination game, but he knew at that moment he'd do at least one more job.

From then on, the men who would become Sirius spent their nights in the red-light district. Daytimes were for research and planning and a few hours of restless sleep. Alaric forked out an obscene amount of Judd's trust fund for Rune's company each evening. He became the Angels Playground's number-one pervert. Handing cash to a pimp was uncomfortable, but as Judd had put it, they were confident of getting a refund soon.

One thing that became evident before long was that Rune was sick. She coughed from a constant cold, she had sores on her back that wouldn't heal, and each time Alaric saw her, she looked thinner, although he'd taken to bringing her snacks. They no longer had the luxury of planning for every eventuality. They'd have to go in sooner rather than later.

And they had. Naz jammed their communications, Ravi snatched Rune and got her the hell out of there, and the final score had been Alaric and Judd eleven, pimps and traffickers nil. Thanks to the cash they liberated, they'd even made a profit.

"Rune was a prostitute?" Emmy was as horrified as Alaric had been. "She'd have been what…? Ten?"

"Ten years old, but she'd experienced things no adult ever should."

"You took care of them?"

There was no need to ask who "them" was. The girls and the men who sold them, taken care of in two very different ways.

Alaric nodded. "Most of the trafficked women went back to their families, but Rune had been born in that place. Her mother was a sex worker, and her father was a client."

"What happened to her mother?"

"One of the older girls said she got beaten to death the year before. Or maybe two years before—time seemed to warp there. Rune had nobody, and she also had the beginnings of type 1 diabetes."

"So you kept her?"

"We couldn't just let her disappear into an orphanage. One of us had to claim her as ours. Ravi was on the young side, and she looks nothing like Naz, which left me or Judd. And can you imagine Judd taking responsibility for a child?"

Emmy's snort told Alaric everything he needed to know.

"So we brokered a new birth certificate with me named as her father and got her a British passport. By then, she was taking insulin, and she'd been living with the four of us for two months. And we'd worked out she was smart. Seriously smart. Her English was getting better every day, and all she wanted to do was learn."

"So where is she now?"

"At a boarding school in Hertfordshire."

"You sent her to *boarding school*?"

"It was her idea—she'd managed to read Harry Potter by that point, and science is her crack. We offered her the choice of living in London and going to a local school, but she had her heart set on Ridgeview Prep."

"And she's happy there?"

"She loves it. We take it in turns to visit."

Emmy reached out for Alaric's free hand. Took it in both of hers. "You did a good thing, Prince."

"We did the only thing we could under the circumstances. And strange though it may sound, Rune helped us as much as we helped her. Before that day in the bar, the four of us had been drifting through life, each convinced that we'd been dealt the worst hand ever. Rune helped us to put everything into perspective. It was she who suggested we keep working together. She thought we made a good team."

She'd also come up with their name. Sirius. The brightest star in the sky. Rune said she used to stare out between the bars on her window every night and wish upon the stars that somebody would rescue her.

"I think you make a good team too. What happened to the other girl, though? The one you saw in the bar?"

"Ravi found her hidden in a room behind Sunan's office. You know, keep your sex slave at work so your wife doesn't find out? Judd dropped him off a bridge."

"Good." Emmy managed a proper smile. "I'd have offered my services otherwise."

She fell silent, but at least she was eating. More than just picking too—she attacked the burger with a steak knife and ate more than her fair share of the onion rings. Although the circumstances were awkward as hell, Alaric still enjoyed spending time with Emmy. A quiet dinner. Just the two of them. It was nice.

The only thing nicer would have been if Beth were sitting opposite him instead.

How was she getting on in Kentucky? He'd spoken to her earlier as he drove back from Boston. The funeral had been every bit as bad as she'd expected— trying to comfort a devastated Harriet while fending off well-wishers offering fake sympathy. Apparently, Stéphane had nearly decked a woman who got offended when Harriet wouldn't speak with her.

"What are you thinking about?" Emmy asked, stuffing the last fry into her mouth.

"You first."

Boy, that was a heavy sigh.

"I'm thinking that I should take a lesson from Rune too. That no matter how shit this last week has been, at least it wasn't ten-year-old-in-a-whorehouse bad."

This *week*? So whatever it was had been building while Alaric was away. It had just come to a head this evening.

"Do you want a lesson from me too?"

"Not really."

"Well, you're gonna get one anyway."

Sometimes, tough love was needed.

"Hurrah."

"Don't run away from this one, Cinders. You've got a habit of that."

"Ha! You can talk."

"Which is why I'm qualified to advise. Speak to Black and clear the air. Don't let whatever happened fester and grow because you'll end up hurting yourself as well as him. I meant what I said earlier. You two were always destined to be together, no matter how much I once wished otherwise."

"He lied to me," she whispered.

"Then he's got a hell of a lot of grovelling to do."

Another long pause. Emmy was thinking, and Alaric wasn't sure whether that was a good thing or a bad thing. Sometimes, she'd mull over a problem and come up with a solution way out of left field. But tonight, she just smiled.

"I think maybe I'll have that cheesecake now."

"Two pieces? Or do you want to share?"

"Two pieces. What were you thinking about?"

"Beth." Since they were being honest with each other.

"You like her, don't you?"

"I do. I more than like her."

"And have you told her?"

"No."

"Why not?"

"I'm not sure it's a good idea. Firstly, I'm her boss, and secondly, I always promised myself I wouldn't get involved with anyone until I found *Emerald* and cleared my name. That fucking painting's cursed my life, and I'll always be on a crusade until it's found."

That and he was scared. Scared of rejection. Since the night on the couch, Beth had pulled back.

"Black's my boss," Emmy pointed out.

"Bullshit. Nobody's the boss of you."

"And how bossy do you feel towards Bethany? On a scale of 'I want her to rearrange my schedule' to 'she can spank me any day'?"

Alaric had to smile at that. "I'd hand her the fucking

paddle."

"Well, there you go. Just tell her. Don't make the same mistake I did with Black."

And the sadness was back. Further distraction was called for. Alaric waved a hand, and the waitress hurried over.

"Two slices of chocolate orange cheesecake, sweetheart. Is Milo's still open?"

"Comin' up. And Milo's is always open."

"Prince, we're not going dancing."

"What, you want to waste that sparkly top? Since we're reliving our misspent youth tonight, we're going dancing. Just try not to lose your shoes this time."

CHAPTER 39 - EMMY

"EMMY, YOU'RE GONNA have to help me out here."

I tried, honestly I did, but my legs refused to cooperate. Was that me giggling? Oh, right, it was.

"No more cocktails for you. Ever."

Alaric tipped me sideways and dragged me out of the passenger seat by my armpits. I made a half-hearted attempt to hop towards the house, but thankfully he picked me up bridal-style before I broke my ankle. I wrapped my arms around his neck and hung on. The driveway was rippling like a demented snake.

"Have I ever told you that I love you?" I slurred.

Honestly, after all the shit I'd inadvertently rained down on him, I didn't deserve his company, but the selfish part of me accepted it anyway.

"No, actually, but it's nice to finally hear it. Do you need to puke before I take you inside?"

I considered the question carefully. My stomach felt kind of weird, sort of churny, but—

"What the hell is going on here?"

Uh-oh. Ana looked *pissed*.

"I might have drunk a teenshy bit too much."

"I've been trying to call you. I was worried."

"Her purse is in the car," Alaric said. "I haven't heard her phone ring, but the music was deafening. If

I'd known you were looking for her..."

"Where's her other shoe?"

"No idea."

"Please don't maim Alaric. I forgot the cocktails and drank too much time."

Or was it the other way around?

"You definitely did *not* forget the cocktails."

Oops. Was Ana really mad? I wasn't sure I could disarm her while I was a bit tipsy.

"I'm sorrrrrrry. It was all my fault. And maybe the bartender's. He told me I have nice eyes. Do I have nice eyes?"

Finally, Ana...well, she didn't exactly smile, but she did look a little less like she wanted to murder someone.

"I guess at least you're happier than you were earlier."

My head lolled back, and boy, the stars looked really twinkly at whatever time of night it was. Or morning. Was it morning?

"Can you get the door?" Alaric asked.

I tried to ask what door, but the words went funny in my throat. Sort of fuzzy and sticky and too big for my mouth. Oh, look, it was all dark now.

What was wrong with my head? Was a piledriver doing a mating dance in my skull? The last time I'd felt this rough was after I got into a drinking competition with Pale and Black—who was on one of his rare cheat days —and lost. Badly.

Wait a second... Black. Pale. Those *bastards*.

Slowly, slowly, the events of yesterday evening came back to me, and that hurt worse than the headache. Black's betrayal, tempered slightly by Alaric's sweetness afterwards. I needed to apologise to Alaric, both with words for being such a mess last night and also with actions for what Black had done to him.

But first, I had to do something about this hangover. Where was my phone? I didn't remember bringing my purse home last night, but there it was on the nightstand. Come to think of it, I couldn't recall getting into these pyjamas either. Was drunk me better at finding things in my closet than sober me, or did I have help?

"Bradley?" I asked when he picked up.

"Oh, good, you got my message. Blue or green?"

"What message? Blue or green what?"

"The earrings, of course."

Who knew? Who cared? "Why don't you just get both?"

"Because you keep telling me not to do that. Are you feeling okay?"

"I might've had a tiny bit too much to drink last night."

"In that case, you need to take one Siberian ginseng capsule, sixteen hundred micrograms of prickly pear cactus extract, a piece of ginger—fresh, not dried or pickled—two borage lozenges, the recommended dose of Tylenol, a cup of milk thistle tea... Are you writing all this down?"

"Right now, I wouldn't even know which way up to hold the pen."

"I'll email you a list. And you need to have breakfast. Lightly burned toast, muesli, half a litre of orange juice, and plenty of water. Oh, and wear sunglasses."

"My brain's broken."

"You'd better fix it because if you being worse for wear means I can shop more, I see a lot more drinking in your future."

"Bad news. I've decided I'm going teetotal."

Bradley's squeak sounded like a mouse being run over by a bicycle. "Gotta go. I have jewellery to buy."

Bollocks, what had I done?

I stumbled into the bathroom and leaned over the sink as a wave of nausea hit. Hungover me stared back from the mirror. I'd cried my mascara off before I went out yesterday, which meant those big black smudges under my eyes were all natural. And my mouth tasted like I'd been chewing cigarette butts. Had I been smoking last night? I wouldn't have put it past myself.

Downstairs, I staggered into the kitchen. I'd been planning to make coffee and then go back to bed, but that plan flew out the window when I found Ana and Alaric waiting for me. Brilliant. I collapsed onto a stool at the breakfast bar instead.

"Uh, good morning?"

They glanced at each other.

"Is it?" Ana asked.

"I've had better."

She pushed a glass of orange juice towards me. "Drink this."

Had she been talking to Bradley?

"Sorry about last night," I said. Ana had been there for me after the fight, and what had I done? Made her anxious. "I turned my phone off in case Black tried to call, but I should've texted you."

"Forget it. I knew you could look after yourself; I just didn't want you to be alone."

"I had to get away from Riverley."

"I understand that." Ana checked her watch. "Do you need me this morning? I'm meant to go to the school."

"Is Tabby okay?"

"She's fine. The PTA asked me to help decorate the hall for the summer fair. Those people are more persuasive than hostage negotiators."

As the saying went, laughter was the best medicine. *Thanks, Ana.*

"You're going to Tabby's school to make garlands and stick crêpe paper flowers to the walls?"

"It's not fucking funny."

"Yes, it is."

"Why don't you join me, Auntie? I'll even let you use the glue gun."

"Sorry, I'm too busy dying of alcohol poisoning. Has anyone got Tylenol?"

Alaric passed me a fresh packet, then took a seat opposite. "I was going to make you a Bloody Mary, but your sister wouldn't let me."

"You've done quite enough damage already," Ana scolded, but she didn't sound as annoyed as she had last night. It was more of a warning not to let me get into that state again. "I'll come over after school unless I get arrested for murder."

"Is it possible to kill someone with a staple gun?"

"I'm not sure the carotid is close enough to the skin to bleed out from the staples themselves, but there's always bludgeoning."

"Or you could just staple their lips together so they

can't eat?"

"Or talk. That would actually solve my problem."

Alaric got up and herded Ana towards the door. "No killing, no maiming. Why don't you offer to paint instead?"

"It's definitely possible to kill someone with a paintbrush."

"I don't want to know. Off you go, have fun. I'll take care of Emmy."

Ana glared at him as she left, but at least no knives were thrown. I had to look for the positives in life, didn't I?

"So..." I started.

"Ana's right. I should have stopped you drinking sooner. One minute you were dancing, and the next, you were trying to lick the bartender's face."

"Ah, shit."

"He took it in good humour."

"Where's Sky? Does she know what a bad role model I'm being?"

"She was asleep when we got home last night, and she left early this morning."

Thank goodness. Training her would be so much harder if she knew I was a complete hypocrite. *Do as I say, not as I do.* I reached across the breakfast bar and gave Alaric's hand a squeeze.

"Thanks for being there for me. I needed your special brand of antidepressants."

"Just think about what I said, okay? Uh, do you remember what I said? About not running from your problems?"

"I remember. I'll talk to Black." Perhaps I could use another drink after all? "Will you talk to Beth?"

"I guess I'll have to man up and have that conversation. But we're meant to be flying to England tomorrow for her sister's wedding, so I might wait until afterwards. No sense in adding to the stress."

"She doesn't get on with her family?"

"You could say that. She's taking me as her plus-one to spite her ex-husband."

"Gee, look at us both with our normal, healthy relationships. Do you need to borrow a plane?"

"Thanks for the offer, but Beth already booked our tickets."

"When are you coming back?"

"Next Sunday. The wedding's this Friday, but Beth wants to see her horse, and Rune breaks up for the summer at the end of next week. I need to collect her from school, and she'll want to visit Judd before she comes here."

"You're spending the summer in the US?"

"With Rune, yes. I'm not sure how long Beth'll stay. Her horse is important to her."

"I've got eight stables, and only three of them are occupied. Just saying."

My horse, Stan—formerly known as Satan, which gives some idea of his character—had primo position next to the door. He also had double glazing, central heating, and a television courtesy of Bradley. Dustin's old mare was still ticking along, and Luke's sister, Tia, had brought one of her Arabians over from England a few months ago now that she spent most of her time stateside.

Alaric squeezed my hand back. "It's a bit early for that. We don't even have a place to stay."

"The guest house?"

"You and Black need space. I know I'm not helping matters."

"He'll just have to get over himself. This is my home too."

"Emmy, it's easier if we rent a place."

"Actually, I might be able to help out there. Remember before you left, you were looking at houses for sale near here? And I came with you?"

A flicker of sadness crossed Alaric's face, but only for a moment and then it was gone.

"I remember."

"And your favourite was that old brick-built place on the hill. The fixer-upper with the great views?"

"The foreclosure? Yeah, I still think about those views. They were straight out of a Clyde Aspevig painting."

"Well, I bought it and fixed it up." I stared down at the granite counter to hide the fact that my eyes were watering. Why was I so emotional at the moment? "I kind of hoped you'd come back to live in it."

"Cinders, I'm sorry."

"The past is the past now. We've both moved on." I forced myself to look at Alaric again. "But it's good to know you're around again. More than anything, I missed our chats."

"I'm just thankful you're still talking to me."

"Like you said, I understand the compulsion to run." Even now, I itched to drive to the airport. "Anyhow, the house... The people renting it moved out a couple of months ago, and it's still empty. Must be fate or something. It's yours for however long you want it."

The offer wasn't quite as selfless as it sounded.

Hillside House was six miles from Riverley, and I kind of liked the idea of having Alaric close.

"I'll pay rent."

"You bloody won't."

"Emmy..."

I folded my arms and stared at him.

"You're as stubborn as ever."

"Yup."

"Then what can I say but thank you?"

"You're welcome. Always. And are we still going to Penngrove to look for your art thief when you get back from England?"

I had to do everything I could to minimise the damage Black had caused.

"If you're busy, I can go alone."

"I'm coming." Those were words I hadn't said to Alaric in a long time, albeit in a very different context. "I'll get Sloane to rearrange my diary."

"You're positive?"

"Yes."

"In that case, I'll ask Beth to make hotel reservations."

"No, you two enjoy your trip. Sloane can handle the logistics."

Speak of the devil... No, not the devil. Sloane was more of an angel. And when I went back upstairs and checked my phone, I had five missed calls from her. Uh-oh. Five calls suggested either butt-dialling or panic. And Sloane was too fastidious to butt-dial.

"What's up?"

"Black sent an email ordering me to clear his schedule."

"How long for?"

"Like, forever. I thought it was a mistake, so I called him, and he just said it was no mistake and that he had some issues to deal with. What am I supposed to do? Should I move everything to you and Nick and Nate? Aw, Nate's gonna go crazy if I do that."

"I'll talk to Black, okay?"

"Thank goodness." Sloane took a deep breath, and I pictured her composing herself. "Uh, is there something I can help you with?"

Hell, she was going to hate me. "Yeah, I need you to clear my schedule..."

CHAPTER 40 - EMMY

BLOODY HELL. IF I thought I'd looked bad this morning, that was nothing compared to Black. Rumpled clothes, messy hair, a day's worth of stubble, a swollen jaw... Had he slept at all? Now he was sitting at the kitchen table in Riverley Hall, staring at a slice of cold pizza as if it held the answers to life. A small pile of dog biscuits sat next to the plate, and Barkley rested her head on his knee. Turncoat.

"Hey."

Black's head snapped up. Boy, those eyes were bloodshot. Had he been on the sauce too?

"You came back."

"Yes."

"Diamond, I'm so sorry. For what I did last night and for what I did eight years ago."

And so he fucking should have been. If I'd been a regular girl, I'd have been packing my bags by now, but our relationship had always been physical in every way. The fight was just an extension of that. The jealousy? I understood that because I felt it too, albeit to a far lesser degree. He'd had other women, not quite in the same way I'd had men, but they'd still been there, lurking in the background.

And maybe, just maybe, when James had asked me what I thought of the whole marrying-Diana-and-running-for-president thing, I possibly might have told him it was a fantastic idea even though I hated it. Why? Because although Black had once complained that Diana was too clingy, she was the one woman he'd brought back to Riverley with him. He thought I didn't know that, but I did.

I knew who some of the others were too. And even now on the rare occasions I came across one of them, I still felt that hot little bud of fire in my belly, the primal instinct to shove them over a damn cliff. But I didn't. Perhaps because in the past, I'd had to cope without Black for the best part of a year, and I knew I could survive alone.

I'd be miserable as hell, but I'd survive.

All of which meant I could forgive Black for what he'd done to me, but not for what he'd done to Alaric.

"Sloane said you told her to clear your schedule."

"How can I work? I can't even think straight right now."

"You weren't thinking straight yesterday either. I'm half surprised you didn't splatter Alaric against the wall."

"I wanted to," Black admitted. "I was angry. Angry at him for being here, angry at you for leaving with him, but most of all, angry at myself for driving you back into his arms."

"Back into his arms?" Oh, for crying out loud. "Is that what you think happened?"

"Didn't it?"

"For fuck's sake, you've got to stop thinking that way. Alaric saw a distressed woman and helped her because that's the kind of man he is. We went out for dinner. We talked. Alaric told me he was in love with

Bethany, and I told him he should be having that conversation with her and not me. He told me I should talk things through with you instead of running away from my problems again, so here I am. Happy?"

"He brought you home. Stayed the night."

"What did you do? Spy on me? Can't you just let this go? He brought me home because I drank so much I couldn't walk. Ana was there too, last night and this morning. I have no idea if she stayed over as well because I was unconscious. If this is how you're gonna react every time I spend five minutes with Alaric, then we've got even bigger problems than I thought. And let me tell you, Chuck, we've got some pretty big problems."

"I know." He closed his eyes and pressed the heels of his hands against his forehead. "I can't believe the way I treated you last night. The way I grabbed you. You're right—I *am* a monster."

"Look, you have a jealousy problem, I get it, and I'll take some of the responsibility for how far things went." My knuckles were a tiny bit bruised too. "You're not a monster. A fool, maybe, but not a monster. I'm more concerned with the past. Why did you do it? Why did you ruin Alaric's whole life? Did you plan it? Did you sit down and map the entire fucking path of his destruction?"

Black had always been a planner. A plotter. A schemer. But the thought of him jotting notes and calculating probabilities and working out timings made me sick to my stomach.

"I didn't plan it at all. I just...snapped."

"You snapped? And somehow happened to pull off the perfect fucking crime? Oh, and nearly got us both killed in the process?"

Black's worried expression turned to absolute horror. "I swear I didn't know you were going with him to the drop! If I had, I'd never have done it."

"So it was okay for Alaric to get killed? Just not me?"

"I didn't think he'd get on the damn boat. I figured he'd open up the case to check everything before he left here."

Because Black would have done exactly that. Check, check, and check again. He was meticulous whereas Alaric was more of a one-and-done guy. He did things once, and he did them carefully.

"So he'd *only* have lost his job, lost the painting, and possibly gone to jail?"

"I fucked up. Like yesterday, I wasn't thinking straight, and I panicked. I was...scared."

He whispered the word as if it were an intruder. A trespasser that had no place in his psyche.

"Scared of what?"

"That you'd leave me."

"I wouldn't have."

"You were looking at houses. He bought you a ring."

The first part I was well aware of, but the second part? That was news.

"A ring?"

"A fifteen-thousand-dollar white gold and purple sapphire solitaire ring. There's only one reason a man buys a woman jewellery like that."

"Shit."

The word slipped out, much the same way as it would have if Alaric had asked me to marry him all those years ago. Then the rest of my brain caught up.

"What were you doing? Monitoring his credit card statements? His email?"

Black's silence told me that was precisely what he'd been doing.

"For the love of fuck! Why didn't you just talk to me? Ask me how *I* felt? Yes, I liked Alaric a lot, but I didn't want to marry him." I closed my eyes and sucked in a ragged breath. "Not when it would have meant divorcing you. I couldn't have done it. Even after you coldly informed me our one and only kiss was a mistake, I still wanted you. If you felt the same, why didn't you just tell me?"

"I came home that evening to do exactly that. The job finished early, and I got a ride back—"

"With Pale?"

Black nodded.

"That lying cretin."

"I asked him to lie. He told me I was an idiot."

"He was right."

"I know."

"So, you came home..."

"I jumped out of the plane. I hadn't skydived for a while, so I figured it was a good opportunity to fit in some practice. Originally, I planned to land on the lawn, but a gust of wind blew me towards the guest house. I was going to correct, but then I recalled the security system had been partially deactivated and thought why not surprise you? So I landed on the roof and nearly broke my tibia."

Quinn wasn't alone, then.

"And you came through the tunnel?"

Another nod. "I saw the briefcase first. In the living room. And then I went upstairs and I heard you in the bedroom, both of you, and something in me broke."

"You switched the pay-off."

"Yes."

"How did you open the briefcase?"

"Trial and error. There were a thousand possible combinations, and Alaric picked five-one-five so I only had to go halfway."

Five-fifteen. May fifteenth. My pretend birthday, the one the whole world knew. The significance wasn't lost on me, and it probably hadn't been lost on Black either.

"Where did you get the counterfeit money? The fake diamonds?"

"I'd confiscated the money from a forger years before. Didn't quite know what to do with it at the time, so I kept it around for a rainy day. The cubic zirconias came from Bradley's craft room. I think he was using them to decorate lampshades or something."

"And the next day? You snuck away and got Pale to bring you back again?"

"Nothing that complicated. I hid in the woods next to the airstrip and just got him to land the plane. When I walked back to the house, everyone assumed I'd arrived that afternoon. Diamond, I'm sorry. If I could turn back time, I'd do things differently."

Of course he would, now that he knew actions had consequences.

"We'd all do things differently. But I can't just forgive and forget this, Black. The initial fuck-up in the heat of the moment, perhaps, but not the lies afterwards. All this time, we've worked as a team because our trust was absolute. But now? You've shattered it. How can I put my life in your hands when

I no longer have that belief in you?"

He didn't have an answer to that, but I had another question.

"How many more times have you lied to me? Skated around the truth? Thrown a few fibs my way?"

The silence stretched along with my nerves. How bad would this be?

"Once or twice, I told you a dress didn't suit you when in reality, it looked too good. And I might have thrown away a couple of gifts Gideon sent you from Paris. And I used to take the Christmas cards you wrote for James out of the mail every year and replace them with something more...corporate. I think that's it. And I had Gideon relocated to Paris, but you already guessed about that."

"You *think* that's it?"

"That's it," he said with a little more finality. "What can I do, Emmy? The thought of losing you..."

He turned away, and for a moment, it was me who felt guilty. Then my resolve hardened again. The other stuff Black had done was petty, but the level of maliciousness levelled at Alaric had been something else.

"I can deal with most of the stupid shit you do. The control freakery. The jealousy. Even you drugging me before our second wedding. But not the lies, Black."

"So where does this leave us?" His voice softened to a whisper. "Don't you love me anymore?"

Good questions, both of them. My heart would always love Black. Alaric was right—we were destined to be together. He completed me. But I couldn't just carry on as if nothing had happened.

"I love you, but right now, I don't like you very

much."

"That's still more than I deserve."

"Probably. I wish I had more control over my feelings when it comes to you, but sadly I don't."

"If it's any consolation, I think you cracked a rib last night."

"Good. And if you want my trust again, you'll have to earn it back. Do you realise what a horrible position you've put me in? I'll either have to cover for you and lie to Alaric or shop my own husband."

"I'll never be able to apologise enough."

"No, you won't. Words won't cut it."

"So what do you want me to do?"

"Fix it. Fix the mess you created."

"You mean get Alaric his old job back? I could try to pull some strings... And I can give him the money he lost out on."

"Oh, no. No way. This is one problem you can't throw cash at, Chuck. It's not about Alaric's job, and it's not about his inheritance. I mean fix his reputation."

"How can I do that?"

I stepped forward and patted Black on the arm, the first time I'd touched him since the argument.

"It's for you to find a way."

A single nod.

"You'll also have to change. You want me to trust you? Then you'll have to trust me too. Slay that green-eyed fucking monster."

Another nod.

"And call Sloane. You owe her more than an email."

"Okay."

"Plus I'll be away with Alaric the week after next. We're going to Penngrove because someone has to look for that bloody painting."

Black took a deep breath. "And in the meantime?"

"I'll be at my house. Feel free to call if you need anything work-related."

I tore myself away before I got tempted to stay. Black needed to know I was serious. He couldn't crap all over people I cared about and expect there to be no repercussions.

Yes, I'd survive alone.

Chapter 41 - Bethany

WHAT A ROLLER coaster of a month, and we were barely halfway through. I still had to endure the wedding of the decade, as my sister's matron of honour had billed it. And no, that wasn't me. I wasn't even a bridesmaid. Priscilla had, and I quote, "saved those spots for my friends." I didn't mind in the slightest—my sister made Bridezilla look positively charming—but I was getting a bit sick of all the "Ooh, Bethie, why aren't you in the wedding party?" nosiness as we waited outside the church. I hated being the centre of attention, and people kept staring at me when they thought I wasn't looking.

At least I had Alaric by my side. I'd missed him more than I had a right to after he left Kentucky. But he'd had to go to Boston, and by coming through with the reward money for *Red After Dark*, he'd staved off Lone Oak Farm's creditors for the immediate future. Harriet was still hurting, but the day before I left, I'd accidentally walked in on her in Stéphane's arms. Cue red faces all around. But I was happy for them, and I knew then that she'd be okay.

Gemma seemed to have come through her ordeal remarkably well too, even if she hadn't slept at my flat once. I very much suspected she hadn't been at home either. Last night, Alaric and I had gone to Curzon

Place for dinner with her, Judd, and Nada, and the three of them seemed quite at ease in the kitchen together. Enough that I'd had a whispered "What the heck?" conversation with Alaric and he'd taken Judd aside to ask what he was playing at. Judd swore nothing was going on. That he wouldn't dare to touch either of the girls, not in that way, but they seemed happy and he had spare rooms, so why not let them stay for a while? I had to admit he did seem to walk on eggshells around Nada. And Gemma was smiling a lot, which was certainly better than crying. Even baby Indy seemed to like him. Alaric had done a double take when Judd sat her on his lap.

"I've heard of the bride being fashionably late, but half an hour?" Alaric whispered.

"Par for the course."

This was Priscilla. She'd been late for her own birth, and things had only gotten worse since then. She was probably berating her hairdresser or something.

Alaric's arm tightened around my waist as Piers approached with Andromeda in tow. She must have misread the invitation—this was the wedding, not the hen party. Her hot-pink dress was at least six inches shorter than anyone else's, and her make-up was so overdone I had to squint to check she hadn't glued leopard moth caterpillars to her eyelids. I'd gone for pastel florals in an attempt to fade into the background, but Alaric had scuppered that plan slightly by gifting me a beautiful pair of shoes. Cream patent stilettos with pale pink ribbon woven around the top—far too expensive, but he said I deserved them after the trip to Kentucky.

"Surprised to see you here, Bethie," Piers said.

"Why? Priscilla's my sister."

"But you don't have much in common, do you?"

"I'm still expected to be here. I'm surprised you showed your face after the way you acted towards me."

"Now now, Bethie, no need to be hostile. You know Priscilla and Andromeda are friends. And I'm going into business with your father. We're going to open a new dental clinic. He's providing the property, and I'll manage the place."

"Good for you."

Piers looked Alaric up and down. "So, this is the boyfriend?"

"I thought we made that quite obvious when we saw you at Daddy's birthday party."

He leaned in closer, and yes, he'd been drinking already. "After the performance you put on, we all assumed you'd hired the man. I mean, who would do that sort of thing without being paid? And everyone knows he's fallen on hard times."

We assumed? Had Piers spread a rumour that I'd hired a freaking escort? Was *that* why people kept staring at me? The pig!

"No, Piers, hiring people for services is your bag, not mine."

Alaric pulled me closer to his side. "Buddy, if anyone's paying, it should be me."

He meant it as a joke, but his words left me cold as bad memories came bubbling to the surface. I backed away, trying to block out Piers's chortling. How had I ever married that man?

"Can we just go somewhere else?" I muttered. Like, say, the Scottish Highlands or the wilds of Mongolia.

"Beth, are you—"

Murmurs spread through the crowd as a Rolls-Royce drew up. Oh, perfect timing for once. Priscilla was here.

The ceremony was predictably over the top. A classically trained choir, half an orchestra, plus it turned out Krys Baxter-Ragsdale was allergic to the five thousand roses Priscilla had stuffed into the church, and she couldn't stop sneezing. Mother had given Krys dirty looks the whole way through, and I had a feeling the Baxter-Ragsdales would find themselves disinvited from any future gatherings.

"Thank heavens that's over," I muttered to Alaric as we exited the church. One advantage of sitting at the back was that we could get out first.

"You're not the only one who thinks so. Did you see the outline of a hip flask in the vicar's pocket?"

"No, really?"

"I almost asked if I could take a swig. Do women honestly like this stuff?"

"My wedding was awful. I wanted a small affair with close friends and family, but Piers insisted bigger was better, and by the time our mothers got involved, we had six hundred guests, photos in *Hello!* magazine, and a reception sponsored by Taittinger."

"There *are* some situations where bigger is better, but I'd agree that a wedding isn't one of them. What time does Priscilla's reception start?"

"Four o'clock. She wanted time to take photos and change her outfit and get her hair and make-up redone first."

"Are you okay to walk there in those shoes? Or do you want me to call a cab?"

"It's only five minutes away, and I've had plenty of practice."

Alaric offered me his arm, and we joined the throng trekking along the lane to my parents' estate. Sadly, there wasn't a handy pub we could nip into, and with the amount of rain we'd had yesterday, I couldn't hide along a footpath either, not unless I wanted to ruin my new shoes. And I loved those shoes.

A friend of my mother's fell into step beside us as we walked, and I was forced to explain my absence from the country club. From her incredulous harrumph, it seemed that having to travel for work didn't pass muster as an excuse for missing the charity golf tournament. Did I mention how much I hated golf?

When we got to the house, the first thing I did was grab a flute of champagne from a passing waiter. The second thing I did was remember I wasn't meant to be drinking and toss it into one of the many, many floral displays. Had Krys Baxter-Ragsdale gone home? I couldn't hear sneezing.

"Why did you ditch the fizz?" Alaric asked. "Neither of us is driving."

"You heard Piers earlier. I don't want a repeat of last time."

"Shame."

"Everyone thinks you're moonlighting as a gigolo. Doesn't that bother you?"

Alaric snagged two more drinks and passed one to me. "A glass won't hurt. It might even take the edge off. Come on..." He steered me towards the open French windows. "Let's go outside. Most of the vultures are hanging out by the snacks."

He was right—the terrace was quieter, even if it brought back memories of our previous shenanigans out there. My thighs clenched just from thinking about that evening.

"You didn't answer my question," I muttered.

"Do I care what people think of me? No, I only worry about the things that matter. And what matters is that I've got the prettiest girl at the party on my arm."

Heat rose up my cheeks.

"But I need to apologise," he continued. "My comment earlier was uncalled for, and I'm sorry."

"What comment?"

"The one where I suggested paying for your services. I felt the way you stiffened."

"Oh, no, no, it wasn't because of you."

"Then it was Piers? That jab you made about hookers being his bag? You caught him?"

I quickly shook my head. "Can we not discuss this? It's mortifying, and you're my boss."

"We're not at work today. This afternoon, I'm your friend above all else. If you want to vent, feel free."

"Please, no." I downed the Veuve Clicquot before I realised what I was doing. And if you're wondering how I knew it was Veuve Clicquot, the banners draped over the ice buckets were a dead giveaway. "Have you ever had a sexual experience so mortifying you wished you could sink into the ground?"

"Sure. You want me to go first? A few years ago when I was in France, I met a girl at a music concert, and some privacy seemed like a good idea."

"I'm not listening. It was a rhetorical question."

I pressed my hands against my ears, but then just for good measure, I removed one for long enough to grab Alaric's champagne and knocked that back too. And still he kept talking.

"So we meandered through the woods and found the perfect spot. Quiet, secluded, tucked away off the beaten track... And we got a little busy. Only to realise that nesting above our heads was a pair of ovenbirds, literally the only ones in the country, and what we thought was dense undergrowth was actually a cleverly disguised hide filled with twitchers. Some of them had cameras. Most of them had binoculars. One gent had a mild heart attack, which was how we found out. They all started panicking and someone called an ambulance."

I gasped and covered my mouth.

"You're kidding."

"No, I'm not. If you look at birdguru.com and search for ovenbirds near Antibes, you can still find a picture of my ass."

I absolutely wouldn't be doing that...until I was safely tucked away in the privacy of my own bedroom.

"What happened to the man? Was he okay?"

"Fortunately, I underwent a reasonable amount of medical training in a previous job, so I asked around for aspirin and then kept him comfortable until the doctors took over."

A bridesmaid walked past and gave me an odd look. I realised I was holding two champagne glasses up to my ears and hurriedly dropped my hands. Oops. Alaric was watching me closely, but what could I say? His tale was funny, whereas mine was more... Wait a second... What did he say?

"You were fooling around with a girl?"

He shrugged. "I'm forty years old, Beth. I've never been a saint."

"But...but I thought you were gay," I blurted. Oh, hell. I clapped my hands over my mouth, then mumbled through the and the champagne glasses. "Not that being gay isn't perfectly fine, of course. And I realise some men don't come out until later in life. My old showjumping trainer, he was married for years, but then he got divorced and moved to California with a guy who made magnetic horse blankets."

"What makes you say that?" Alaric asked mildly.

"The blankets? They sent me one as a gift."

"No, why do you think I'm gay?"

Oh dear. Was it too late to drown myself in the swimming pool?

"Because...because you dress well?"

"Beth..."

"Okay, okay. Uh, Judd might have mentioned it. To Gemma. That you were with Ravi. And Emmy said Ravi was gay and so I just assumed... Can I go home now?"

"I'm not gay, Bethany. I'm bi, and so is Ravi."

"What does that mean? Actually, forget I asked. I sort of know, I mean, logically..."

"It means I fall for personalities rather than body parts."

"Oh. Oh!" I thought about his words for a second. The champagne was already going to my head, so the cogs whirred kind of slowly. "That really sounds quite lovely."

"Lately, I've been more into women. Well, one woman. And not exactly *into* her, but..."

"Who?" I asked.

He didn't answer, just brushed his lips over mine.

"Feel free to slap me."

No, I didn't want to do that. I dropped the two champagne glasses into a flower border—they'd done their job now—and wrapped my arms around Alaric's neck.

"Can I kiss you instead?"

He didn't wait for me to make the first move. When our lips met, I forgot where I was and who might be watching and melted against him. My head screamed that smooching with my boss was a terrible, terrible idea, but my heart beat it into submission. My toes curled in my shoes as Alaric's tongue teased the seam of my lips, and I let him in on a sigh. Heat crackled in my veins as long-dead parts of me came to life.

Alaric was the easiest man to kiss. Hard and soft at the same time, gentle and strong. His hands parted, one sliding to my bottom and tipping me against his... Oh, wow. Bigger might not *always* be better, but I hoped I'd get the opportunity to experiment for myself. His other hand came to the back of my head, tangling in my hair and then tugging it sideways so he could feather soft kisses along my jaw.

Then he pulled away.

"Shall we skip the audience this time?" He glanced at his watch. "We've got an hour and a half to fill before the farce continues."

"You've got a sister of the bride to get into," I murmured, then my brain caught up with my mouth and I screwed my eyes shut, which did absolutely nothing to help. "Can you just pretend you didn't hear that part?"

"I could, but I'm not going to."

Holy hotness. I grabbed his hand.

"The stables. We can go to the stables. Nobody keeps horses here anymore, so they're empty. And I'm quite sure there are no ovenbirds."

Alaric chuckled. I loved that he didn't take himself too seriously.

"Lead the way."

The stable yard had eight loose boxes set in a U-shape, plus a tack room on the end of one row and a feed room on the other. The boxes were all shut up and probably a bit dusty, so I tugged Alaric towards the tack room.

"There might be an old blanket. Or a cushion for my knees."

"For...your knees?"

His filthy grin said he knew exactly what I was thinking.

"I'm not a bloody contortionist, all right?"

Nor was I very organised. I hadn't even considered that I might end up screwing Alaric, which meant I hadn't brought condoms. I was on the pill, but would he...

Alaric reached past me and yanked the tack room door open, and I was so busy imagining him sans clothing that it took a good few seconds for my brain to register what my eyes most definitely didn't want to see.

Piers's head snapped in my direction. "What the...?"

Wasn't that meant to be my line? His disappointing dick hung out of his fly, but I couldn't immediately see who he'd been boning because of the sheer volume of cream satin in the way. Hold on a second...cream satin?

My sister turned slowly, the shock on her face

mirroring mine. "Bethie, what are you doing here?"

Becoming a witness for impending divorce proceedings?

"What am *I* doing here? What are *you* doing here? With *him*?" I pointed at Piers. "He's engaged. And you just got freaking married!"

"Will you keep your voice down?" she hissed.

"Why should I? You've cheated on Tarquin within an hour of saying 'I do.'"

Why the hell had she even married him? Oh, right, because he was rich.

"If you had to sleep with Tarquin, you'd do exactly the same. He just sort of...lies there. A girl has needs."

"And you think Piers is the best person to fulfil them? You really need to get out more."

I might not have been all the way with Alaric, but one kiss from him beat an entire night with Piers hands down. It was like comparing Van Gogh to a toddler with finger paints.

"You're just jealous."

"Oh, please." Hold on, why was I even having this conversation? As a wise man once said, never argue with stupid people. They'd drag you down to their level and then beat you with experience. I couldn't fix Piers's flaws, or my sister's, and I didn't want to try. "On second thoughts, you know what? I'm done with this family. I'd rather spend time with people I actually like."

Andromeda knew Piers had cheated on me, and a leopard didn't change its spots. It shouldn't surprise her in the least that he was screwing Priscilla behind her back. And Tarquin was a conceited idiot. I turned to leave, but Alaric's grip tightened on my hand, and he stayed put.

"We're leaving," he said. What was that in his hand? His phone? "And I suggest you be very careful what you say about Beth in the future."

Piers bristled. His dick had gone limp now. Normal service: resumed.

"Are you threatening me?"

"Congratulations. You're not as dumb as you look."

"How dare you!"

"You've already hurt the woman I love once. Hurt her again and I'll squash you like the cockroach you are." Alaric waved a hand at Priscilla. "Please, carry on. Don't let us stop you."

Chapter 42 - Bethany

I SNUGGLED AGAINST Alaric in the back of the taxi. Although I wanted to wash my eyes out with bleach, at least catching Piers and Priscilla in the act meant we could escape early. No way would she complain about my absence.

"I can't believe you got pictures."

"Video, actually." Alaric leaned in and kissed my hair. "Definitely the most memorable wedding I've been to, for more than one reason."

And I couldn't believe he'd said he loved me. Did he mean it? Or was he just trying to hurt Piers? I didn't dare to ask.

"What happens now?" I whispered.

The driver was wearing headphones, and he nodded in time to the music leaking out. Good old-fashioned rock 'n' roll. He'd be deaf by the time he hit forty, but at least he wasn't listening to our conversation.

"Right now? Depends how daring you are."

Alaric's fingers crept up my bare thigh, and I gasped and clamped my legs together. "We can't!"

"Fair enough. Then I guess we talk until we get back to your place."

Talk. In that situation, teetering on the edge of everything I'd always wanted and despair, it was a word that struck fear into my heart.

"What do you want to talk about?"

"The future. Our future. I'm not sure the whole boss/assistant thing's going to work out for us."

"You're...firing me?"

"Hell no. I very much want you to carry on working for Sirius. But I can't treat you the way I would any other employee. The thought of you sitting in an office at Judd's place while I'm in the US... Speaking of which, I'm never going to hear the end of this. It's usually him who corrupts our staff."

"I'll come with you," I said quickly, then regretted my words just as fast. Did I sound too eager?

"What about your life here? Chaucer?"

"There's room in my heart for both of you."

Alaric kissed the corner of my lips and smiled. "Since I don't have a horse, you get the whole of mine."

"What about Ravi?" I blurted. "I know you were together recently."

"Gemma again?"

I was so bad at this. "Maybe?"

"Ravi and I have an arrangement. If we're both single, we'll take care of the physical side of things for each other. Since I'll no longer be single, that ends. But we'll stay friends, and we'll work together. Does that bother you?"

I considered my answer for a moment. Did it? Alaric had been honest with me, perhaps brutally so, but better that than the constant lies I'd gotten from Piers. Alaric trusted me with his secrets, and I had to afford him the same courtesy.

"Honestly? I'm not sure, but I like Ravi."

"Actions speak louder than words. I understand

that, and I appreciate your candour." He barked out a laugh. "Fuck, just listen to me. This sounds like a business meeting, and we're definitely not working today."

"What are you doing?" I asked as he wriggled out of his suit jacket and draped it over my lap.

"Shh."

His hand found its way back to my thigh, and this time, it crept higher.

"I'm not... We can't..."

He silenced my protests with a kiss. Guess I was more daring than I thought.

Oh, heck, the neighbours... My front door bashed off the wall and slammed shut as Alaric carried me towards the bedroom. After his antics in the cab, I was already hot and bothered, and I needed to get out of this damn dress. And my damp knickers too.

"The tie's got to go," I told him, desperately trying to reach my zipper. "And the shirt."

"It's all going except for your shoes. You can keep those on. I want the heels digging into my ass."

When Alaric unhooked my bra, he paused for a moment to study the tattoo over my heart. Piers had been furious when I got the name of my old horse inked there permanently, but Alaric dipped his head and traced the letters with his tongue.

"Usually, I'd hate seeing another man's name over your heart, but in this case..."—he pressed a soft kiss to the P—"I'll make an exception."

"I'll get yours done too," I blurted, then we both

tumbled onto the bed. Alaric ended up on top. I was kind of glad he was taking the lead because I was way out of practice here. Having to lie back and think of England while Piers pounded away had in no way prepared me for this.

But I must have been doing something right, judging by the tent in Alaric's trousers. Hell, that was more of a marquee. The marquee... We should have been sitting in there at this very moment, pretending to be happy for Priscilla and Tarquin. A giggle escaped.

"What's so funny?"

"I don't know what they're serving the other guests for the wedding breakfast, but I definitely got the better end of the deal with salami."

"Have at it."

Alaric rolled me, and I fumbled with his belt, then cursed the button and the zipper on his trousers when they wouldn't undo fast enough. Oh, wow, he trimmed down there. With Piers, I'd had to search for the toadstool among the undergrowth. Self-doubt hit, but when I hesitated, Alaric gently guided my head downwards.

"Don't overthink things, Beth."

I gave his cock a tentative lick. Then a suck. His groan told me I was on the right track, and for the first time in my life, I actually enjoyed giving a blow job. But Alaric stopped me before he finished, flipped me onto my back, and treated me to the dirtiest grin I'd ever seen.

"This is going to be good," I said, accidentally using my outside voice instead of my inside one.

"It's already better than good."

Holy hell! His tongue hit exactly the right spot, and

I screamed as I arched off the bed. My upstairs neighbour banged on the ceiling. Whoops. The stream of filth that flowed from my lips as Alaric went to town would have made a porn star blush, and I ended up stuffing my own knuckles into my mouth in an attempt to stop it. Didn't work.

"Oh, fuck. Fuck, fuck, fuck! I hate you. Just let me... Oh, oh! I adore you. You're a bloody monster. Don't you dare, I can't— Keep going! Stop, I'm— There, there! No! Sweet mother of..."

When I shattered for the third time, he finally let me rest. Every part of me was broken. I wasn't sure I ever wanted to be whole again.

"You've got quite a mouth, haven't you?"

"Sorry. I'm so, so sorry."

"I meant it as a compliment."

"You've ruined me. I mean that as a compliment too."

"Really? Ruined you?" Alaric nuzzled my neck, sweet and tender. "But I'm just getting started. Care to demonstrate your riding skills, Ms. Stafford-Lyons?"

"Maybe, I..." He flexed his hips, and that glorious cock pressed into my stomach. "I guess I could give it a go."

"Hold on... Let me find my wallet. I'm kicking myself for only bringing one condom now."

"I...I'm on the pill." Was that too forward? "And I got tested for everything after the hooker incident, so if you want to..."

"The hooker incident? Piers?"

Ah, crap. A flood of icy air drenched the room. "I'm not certain whether he did or he didn't. But probably."

"Beth, don't run away from me. We can talk about

anything, okay? It can't be worse than what we saw earlier."

"It sure felt that way." Alaric wrapped me up in a hug, and I knew at that moment that he was right. We *could* talk about anything. I took a deep breath. "It happened three years ago. Our marriage was already on the rocks. We hadn't had any luck in trying for a baby, and I'd taken to reading self-help books. One of them suggested ways to spice up a stale relationship, so I talked to Piers, and he agreed to give it a go."

That had been some conversation. A hurried negotiation over breakfast while he answered emails and munched on toast. I should have realised. Realised that if he couldn't give me his attention for something so important, our marriage was doomed and there was no saving it.

"The book said that we should each tell the other our deepest sexual fantasy, and then we'd act it out. Piers said he'd go first. He...he wanted me to dress up and meet him in a hotel room. Like a prostitute. Trashy outfit, slutty shoes, a coat over the top. And when it was over, he gave me money and kicked me out. I've never, never felt as worthless as I did that day."

"Sweetheart, I'm so sorry he did that to you."

"Thirty freaking pounds! That's all I meant to him."

I loved Alaric's soft kisses. The fluttery ones that danced over my cheeks.

"You're priceless, Beth."

I wanted to believe that. I really did, but... "It gets worse."

"How can it get worse?"

"Well, it was my turn, wasn't it? So I confided in him. I told him one of my deepest, darkest fantasies, and he laughed. Said I was disgusting and he wasn't a fucking faggot." I quickly remembered Alaric's sexuality. "Sorry. I'm so sorry. That's just what he said, and with such venom."

"From that comment, I can guess what you want, and I'll give it to you. Not today, but I'll give it to you. What else?"

"What else? Nothing. That was it. I knew that was the beginning of the end, and I never slept with Piers again."

"Piers is your past. This is your future. I meant what else did you want to do? You said you told him *one* of your fantasies?"

"Oh, I can't..."

"How can I make them come true if I don't know what they are?"

"We've only just met."

"Then we should start as we mean to go on, don't you think?" Those soft brown eyes locked onto mine. "If it doesn't involve kids or animals, I'm probably gonna be good with it."

"Well, one of them sort of does involve animals."

Alaric raised an eyebrow, and I covered my face with my hands. He gently removed them.

"Beth..."

"Fair's fair. You have to tell me one of yours first."

"Okay. I want to nail my secretary over my desk. Think you can help with that?"

"Yes, Mr. McLain, sir."

"Fuck. Tomorrow I'm buying a desk. Your turn."

I hurriedly shook my head to clear the image of myself sitting on Alaric's blotter with my legs spread. If I'd still been wearing my knickers, I'd have been able to wring them out by now.

"I want a man to catch me unawares in the hay barn. To bend me over a bale and take me from behind while we're still wearing our clothes. Then we just walk out as if nothing happened."

"Seems as though we're gonna have a busy day tomorrow."

"Are you serious?"

He wrapped my hand around his solid cock. "What do you think?"

"I think it's your turn."

"Mile-high club. Commercial flight." His eyes rolled back as I stroked. "I can't take this any longer."

I glanced between us. That thing had to be nine inches at least. "I'm not sure I could either."

"Beth, you're killing me, but at least it's a pleasurable death." Before I could blink, I was underneath him again. "Are you sure about this? Bare?"

"I'm certain."

I didn't ask whether Alaric was clean. I knew he wouldn't risk hurting me. And weirdly, his "arrangement" with Ravi made me feel better because if they were taking care of each other, then they weren't hooking up with random people they met in bars.

Alaric stretched me to the point of pain as he slid slowly inside, and I began to wonder whether fantasy number one was a good idea after all. But he gave me a moment to adjust, peppering me with those sweet, sweet kisses that sent shivers through me before he started to move. Oh, fuck again.

Earlier when I'd snapped at Priscilla, when I told her she should get out more if she thought Piers was decent in bed, I feared I'd been bluffing because I really didn't know any better. But now I knew I'd been telling the absolute truth. At this rate, I'd need to soundproof the ceiling. And the floor, and probably the walls too. By the time I fell back on the mattress, I'd found a new religion.

"I love you," I gasped, then regretted it as Alaric stiffened, and not in a good way. "Uh, too soon?"

"When you know, you know. I love you too."

A warm glow spread through me.

"Say it again."

"I love you, Beth."

"Again."

"I love you."

Piers had made me believe I was unloveable, but thanks to Alaric, I'd seen the truth. *Felt* the truth. The problem had been *us*, not *me*. But now I was part of a new "us," and I was free to become the person I'd always wanted to be.

"It's your turn again," he told me, pulling me closer so our hips pressed against each other. The tip of his tongue rimmed my ear before he murmured, "Tell me your deepest desires."

Uh, perhaps not.

"I don't need fantasies anymore. I've got reality."

"No, I think you should confess."

"You might hate me. I don't want to ruin this."

"Does it involve spanking?"

"No."

"Rope?"

"No."

"Candles?"

Candles? "No."

"Tell me."

So I did. I leaned forward and whispered my darkest thoughts into his ear, and his eyebrows shot into his hairline. Oh, shit. Had I broken us before we really even started?

Alaric blew out a breath. "Not quite what I was expecting. You're a dark horse, aren't you, my sweet?"

"Please, forget I said it."

"Forget it? Never. But maybe I'll just file it away for the moment."

Thank goodness. "It's your go again."

Now it was Alaric's turn to look nervous. "I'm not sure it's entirely appropriate given today's events."

"What happened to 'we can talk about anything'?"

He made a show of covering his balls with his hands before he answered, then he leaned in close to whisper the way I had with him.

"I want to fuck my wife in her wedding dress."

"Oh, that's an easy one," I blurted. *Stupid, stupid mouth.* "Uh, what I meant, without wanting to sound presumptuous, was that if maybe at some appropriate point in the future you happened to ask, I would definitely be willing to keep the dress on. Can I go and die quietly now?"

"As long as you do it in my arms. Out of interest, what would you consider to be an appropriate point in the future?"

"Huh?"

"A month? Two months?"

"Uh..."

"I'm not sure I can wait much longer than three."

Was he saying what I thought he was saying? My post-sex brain was still drowning in endorphins.

"Three months," I choked out. "Three months is good."

CHAPTER 43 - EMMY

"READY TO GO?" Black asked.

"Not remotely."

Over a week on, and I still hadn't forgiven him, not even a little bit, but he was trying. Very trying.

When I'd said to call me if anything work-related came up, he'd taken it to heart. He called me about work every five fucking minutes. And now he'd come up with the marvellous idea of the two of us heading to Penngrove to get a head start on the search for Dyson.

But I could hardly complain, could I? Not when I'd told him to fix things. Nor could I send him on his own because Alaric and I were the only ones who'd seen Dyson in the flesh. Well played, Black. Well played.

On the plus side, at least if I was away I'd be able to avoid the ever-increasing number of questions about why Black and I were no longer sharing a bedroom. First, I'd blamed it on my nightmares, and then I'd complained that he kept snoring.

Why didn't I come clean? Why didn't I tell people we'd had an argument? Because then they'd want to know what the argument was about, and if I didn't tell them, or they didn't believe whatever fake explanation I came up with, the rumours would start to fly. And I wasn't going to turn Black in. I'd almost lost him once, and even though I was really hacked off at him, I didn't want it to happen again. Not permanently. I'd had a week to consider things now. Blackwood employed too many people to risk it all by casting shadows on Black's reputation.

Two wrongs didn't make a right.

And do you know the crazy thing? The sick, sick part of me, the rotten little kernel in my brain that mapped out the paths to men's destruction, had to admire the elegance of Black's on-the-fly act. The simplicity. The sheer fucking balls of it.

The whole situation made my head want to explode.

So there we were, getting ready to travel to a dinky town near Chesapeake. Penngrove had a population of two thousand and change plus a pair of pot-bellied pigs who seemed to be the town mascots. In another masterful piece of planning, it turned out Penngrove only had one hotel. No penthouse, no suites. Of course, since we were a married couple on vacation, according to our cover story, Black had booked us one room with a king-sized bed. But I'd soon wiped the smile off his face when I informed him he'd be sleeping on the floor.

I'd toyed with the idea of taking a separate car, but again, that would be weird. Grrr. I shoved my last bag into Black's Porsche Cayenne. Couldn't put it off any longer, could I?

Oh, saved by the bell. I walked away from Black to take the call from Alaric, although that was probably pointless. Black no doubt had my phone bugged anyway.

"How's it going?"

I hadn't spoken to Alaric since he left. I'd been working on the "no news is good news" premise.

"We might need to borrow that spare stable."

We? "You told her?"

"No, I just thought I might take up horseback riding."

"I'm so happy it worked out." And I really was. After everything that had happened, Alaric deserved happiness. "I knew it would, though. You're a real catch. When are you coming back? Still Sunday?"

"We fly at ten a.m. UK time. Can we have a think about our trip to Penngrove? I know it's been eight years, but I don't want to leave it too much longer."

"Yeah, about that. We're planning to head there in an hour or so."

"Who? You and Dan?"

"Me and Black."

The long pause told me Alaric was as bemused as I thought he'd be. Probably a bit suspicious too, although thankfully, I had a plausible explanation.

"When it came to the choice of him coming with me or me going with you, he picked the lesser of the two evils."

"I guess I can understand that. Maybe he'll lighten up now that I'm with Beth?"

"Here's hoping."

"Emmy, I also want you to meet Rune."

I was looking forward to it, although I'd admit to being a teensy bit apprehensive. What if Rune didn't like me?

"Perhaps I could come over for dinner?"

"Yes, perhaps."

"On my own."

"Good idea." The relief in Alaric's voice was evident. He didn't want to inflict my darling husband on his daughter if Black was still being a prick, and I couldn't blame him.

"I should get her a gift. What does she like?"

"Science. She wants to get a PhD in molecular biology and help to find a cure for diabetes."

"Wow."

"Told you she was smart."

"I'd better not mention this to Bradley or he'll buy her a whole lab."

"Just a book or two will be fine."

"Do you need anything else? I'll get Bradley to stock the kitchen at Hillside House with groceries. And drop off a car." Was a little guilt kicking in? No, a lot of guilt. "The place comes with a gardener, and I'll check the pool's been cleaned. Does Bethany want to go horse riding? If she's feeling brave, she's welcome to borrow Stan. Or Majesty—Tia won't mind. But Majesty's out of the same mould as Stan, just not quite so nutty."

"Thanks for doing this, Cinders. I mean it. You've made coming back far easier than I feared it would be."

"I meant it when I said I was happy to see you. Beth's a lucky girl."

"We'll see you soon."

I could hear the smile in Alaric's voice, and it made me smile too.

"See ya."

Dammit, I couldn't put this off any longer. Once Alaric hung up, I traipsed back to the car. Road trip. Yay. I only hoped Dyson had gotten worse at hiding over the years.

Penngrove was a Hallmark movie come to life. Twee

little shops, a bakery run by two bubbly sisters, a cutesy library, a gallery full of local art, and an auto repair shop staffed by an impossibly hot mechanic, which we found out when the Porsche got a puncture driving past the Christmas tree farm. I smiled at the dude. Black saw me and shot daggers from his eyes. Realised what he'd done. Attempted to smile himself, and when that didn't work out, he tipped the guy a hundred bucks. I had to give him points for effort.

And we tried everything we could think of to find Dyson. After breakfast at the Penngrove Lodge Hotel each morning, we took Barkley for a walk around town so we could be nosy. Yes, Barkley. We hadn't intended to bring her, but she'd jumped into the car as we were leaving and refused to get out. Black cursed liberally, but he'd developed a soft spot for the mutt whether he admitted it or not.

A week into the search, we were still no farther forward. But we didn't have many clues to go on—just the call to the feed store, the fact that Dyson had a deep knowledge of art and an affinity for boats, and a possible fondness of Chinese food. Penngrove didn't have a Chinese restaurant, and it was twenty miles from the sea, which left art and animals. The feed store catered to everything from hamsters to horses, from geese to guppies, so there was no way to know whether Dyson kept farm animals or fish or feathered friends. And the art on show in the town was definitely on the amateur side.

I'd dyed my hair brown to lessen the risk of Dyson recognising me, and although Black's size usually worked against him on surveillance jobs, here it didn't matter so much because we weren't trying to sneak around. Plus Dyson had never seen him. Even so, he'd taken to wearing glasses and a day's worth of stubble. If anything, I was the one who should have been jealous because all the local girls kept staring at him, and the waitress in the diner had not-so-subtly written her phone number on the receipt. Dolly at the café paid him particular attention too, but I didn't mind that because she was about eighty and it meant we got free cake.

The other advantage? The café was right opposite the feed store, and Dolly saved the table in the window for us each lunchtime because she knew it was our favourite.

"I've made peach cobbler today, and apple pie," she told us when we walked in on Thursday, a week to the day after our arrival in Penngrove. Black had placated Sloane over the scheduling, but she was still juggling like crazy to keep us in town. We couldn't stay there forever. "And we've got fresh Chesapeake Bay crabs, big ones."

"Salad?" Black asked, the same as he did every day. "What about salad?"

Dolly's answer was always the same too. She laughed.

"A big man like you can't live on salad. I'll bring you ham biscuits."

"I'll need to have my arteries scraped when I get back," he muttered.

Things were still frosty between us. It reminded me of the weeks right after I moved to the US, those hellish days where I respected his abilities but his presence exhausted me. For sure he'd had more sleep than yours truly.

"Put me down for the apple pie. And the peach cobbler. And do you have any of those stoneground pancakes?"

I glanced at Black, daring him to challenge me, but he stayed quiet. Good plan.

"Of course I do, honey-pie. I'll fix them right up." She pinched Black's cheeks, and I turned my snort into a cough. "And I'll bring all the fixins with your ham biscuits, handsome."

"I think she likes you," I stage whispered as she swished off to the kitchen.

"If I were forty years older..."

We lapsed into silence. I'd taken to bringing a book with me so I didn't have to talk, and I bet Black was bang up to date with his emails. I breathed a sigh of relief when Dolly came back with the food.

"Eat, eat. What are you doing this afternoon? There's a classic automobile show over in Suffolk."

"I'm going to a painting class at the Marshall Gallery. We're doing dolphins."

Which should be fun since I couldn't draw for shit.

"Oh, you'll have a wonderful time. Who's teaching you? Loretta? She's such a talented artist. Quite young, but she went to some fancy art school in New York." Dolly pointed at a vivid landscape on the wall opposite. "That's one of hers."

Way to make me feel inferior. It was no Monet, but at least the boat looked like a boat rather than a tadpole.

"I'm looking forward to it."

"And what are you doing, sugar-pie? Are you gunna paint fishes too?"

"I'm taking Barkley to a dog-training class."

At the sound of her name, Barkley lifted her head. Dolly didn't mind her coming inside as long as she lay quietly under the table, and now the grey-haired woman picked a piece of discarded pie crust from an empty plate at the next table and held it out for Barkley to snaffle.

"But she's such a good girl already."

Black pulled Barkley's nose out of Dolly's crotch.

"Her obedience needs work. She's no good at staying where she's told."

Every evening, Black put Barkley into the new pet bed he'd bought and ordered her to stay. And every morning, he woke to find her squashed against his chest. Or draped over his legs. Or curled up on his pillow. If he overslept, she huffed doggy breath all over his face. She'd had some training—she knew how to sit, and give you a paw, and roll over—but her recall was non-existent, and if she started barking, stopping her was impossible.

"If anyone can teach her, then Dillon can. He's wonderful with animals."

"Do you know if there's anywhere I can ride around here? I'd love to see the scenery from horseback."

"That'd be Fletcher at Hope Valley Ranch. Ten years ago, the place was a ruin, but he's fixed it up good and now he offers trail riding. I'll find you his number."

"I really appreciate it. And are there any evening activities?"

Even another knitting class beat sitting around the hotel room with Black right now. We could bury our noses in our laptops, but we couldn't escape the awkwardness that shrouded us.

"The Penngrove Community Theater's putting on a

performance of *Much Ado About Nothing*."

I was beginning to think this whole trip was much ado about bloody nothing. Dyson was a ghost.

"Shakespeare? Lovely."

"Their patron's a big fan of the Bard. He spent time in England when he was a young man. I've got a brochure with all the details somewhere—I'll hunt it out, but let me go and get your lunches first."

"Diamond, we could just talk in the evenings," Black said once Dolly had disappeared.

"How does that help to fix things?"

"We might have to face the fact that Dyson won't be found. That this can't be fixed. Then what?"

"Congratulations. Now you know how Alaric's been feeling for the last eight years."

"I didn't mean for this to happen."

"And yet it did. I've got a horrible feeling your biggest regret is getting caught."

"That's not true."

I shrugged.

The truth was, I did think Black was sorry. And I did miss spending time with him the way I used to. But I'd put up with his petty jealousy for too long, and if I didn't teach him a lesson now, he'd never learn.

"Prove it."

We lapsed into silence until Dolly bustled back with enough food to sink a battleship. Black had been running with Barkley early in the mornings, but I'd stayed in the hotel room out of stubbornness. The bulge over my waistband said perhaps I should have a rethink.

"Here you go, sweetie-pie. Ham biscuits and pancakes with syrup and bacon." One portion had become two. Biscuits for both of us—which came with green beans and potato gratin—and the stack of pancakes was a foot high. A pig had given up its life for our lunch, and Canada was probably experiencing a maple syrup shortage. "And here's that brochure."

I wasn't a Shakespeare fan. I'd skipped school the year we were meant to study *The Merchant of Venice*, and consequently, I'd never developed an appreciation of his way with words. Nate had tried to educate me on more than one occasion, but I still preferred reading the Heckler & Koch catalogue.

What did Penngrove have to offer? *Much Ado About Nothing*, *Romeo and Juliet*, *Love's Labour's Lost*... Plus concerts by local bands, a stand-up comedy night, and a visit from an Elvis impersonator. And...

I started laughing. And laughing and laughing and laughing. Oh, hell. We owed Dolly the biggest tip ever.

CHAPTER 44 - EMMY

"WHAT'S SO FUNNY?" Black asked.

I jabbed my finger at a short paragraph on the back page of the brochure.

This year's performances are kindly sponsored by Killian Marshall, whose generous contributions have allowed the Penngrove Community Theater not only to survive but to flourish.

The photo above showed a man in his early fifties, slightly greyer around the temples than when I'd seen him last, and a fuck of a lot more composed.

"We've found Dyson."

"Killian Marshall? A local philanthropist?"

"Yup." A modern-day Robin Hood, it seemed. He stole from the rich to give to the poor. "I'll never forget that face."

Black blew out a long breath. "Thank fuck for that. I'll get the research team onto this. Then we can work out how to pick him up."

While Black pulled out his phone, I looked again at the picture. Dyson's expression was kind, benign, giving no hint that he was actually a master criminal. Did the townsfolk know where his money came from? I was betting they didn't.

"Diamond, who's driving your BMW?"

"Er, nobody?"

He held up his phone screen so I could see the message in red.

ALERT: E BLK - IMPACT SENSORS ACTIVATED

All of Blackwood's vehicles were fitted with a black box of tricks courtesy of Nate, and the BMW was no exception. Someone had crashed it? I couldn't say I was devastated, but who had been behind the wheel? Were they hurt?

"Well, somebody must have borrowed it. Where is it now?"

Black tapped away. "Three hundred yards from Riverley's main gate."

I began to get a bad, bad feeling about this. Riverley was on a quiet lane. Turn left out of the main gate and you'd be heading for Richmond, but turn right and you'd end up in buttfuck nowhere—just forests and fields plus a dozen or so houses, and we owned most of them. There wasn't a whole lot to hit. Unless the driver swerved to avoid an animal and drove into a tree, which Dan had managed to do on occasion, it was a tricky spot to crash in.

Black was already calling the guardhouse.

"Did Emmy's BMW just leave the estate?"

I shuffled my chair closer and leaned in to listen as the duty guard answered. Roy—I recognised his voice.

"Yes, a few minutes ago."

"Who was driving?"

"Well, Emmy was."

"Emmy's a hundred miles away."

"Are you sure?"

Ooh, bad move. Black's jaw clenched. "She's sitting opposite me. I think I know what my wife looks like."

"Sorry, I—"

"The BMW's been in a collision three hundred yards down the road, Richmond direction. Call the roving team. Get them to find out what happened. And tread carefully—this could be a trap."

"Yes, sir."

Black had gone through exactly the same thought process as me. If Roy had thought I was driving, then somebody else could have too, and thanks to my extracurricular activities, there were certain people who would rather I didn't see my next birthday. Sure, the crash could have been an innocent accident, but on the other hand...

"And we need to find out who was driving."

"I just started my shift, but I'll check the visitor log."

Oh, fuck. A fist clenched around my throat. "Don't bother."

Black raised an eyebrow.

"It was Bethany. I asked Bradley to lend her a vehicle, and she's got blonde hair. From a distance, in a moving car..."

Roy came back. "A Bethany Stafford-Lyons arrived in your car four hours ago. The 'purpose of visit' memo says she was there to see the horses."

Shit, shit, shit. How fast had Bethany been going? We kept the lane in good nick—no potholes, no overgrown bushes—and it was reasonably straight. And if I'd discovered one thing in the handful of times I'd driven that BMW, it was that it accelerated like a crazy-ass motherfucker. To sixty, it rivalled my Corvette.

I gulped down half a slice of apple pie because I had a feeling I wouldn't be eating again for a while, and Black dropped a hundred-dollar bill on the table.

"Are you leaving?" Dolly asked. "Is there a problem with the food?"

"There's a family emergency."

"Oh, sugar-pie, I'm so sorry to hear that. Let me box everything up to go."

I tucked the brochure into my handbag. "Really, there's no need."

Black's phone buzzed, and when he checked the screen, he grabbed my hand and pulled me towards the door. I didn't question it. Whatever grudges I might have been bearing, today they took a back seat to whatever was unfolding at Riverley. And from Black's furious expression, it was worse than I'd first thought.

"What?"

He bleeped the car open, then tossed me his phone as he jogged to the driver's side. There was a message on the screen.

Pale: Hearing rumours someone's escaped from the brig at Norfolk. They're trying to keep it quiet. Watch your back.

Ridley. Pale was still active military in some form or another. His exact status was hazy, but it made sense that he'd find out the news before us. A surge of adrenaline mixed with horror. *Focus, Emmy.* I'd long since learned to tamp down the panic and harness the rush it gave me.

"Well, I guess we know where the son of a bitch ended up. I'm driving."

Black didn't argue, just opened the door for me and carried on to the passenger side. Smart move. The drive from Penngrove to Richmond was a little over a hundred miles and usually took two hours. I planned to do it in a hell of a lot less. If Eric Ridley had come to take revenge for Kyla's death, there was no time to waste.

The phone connected to the car's speaker system, and Roy returned as I gunned the engine.

"The team's on their way."

"Hold them back. We suspect there's a felon involved. Consider him armed and dangerous."

"Understood."

The delay wasn't ideal, but better to pause, to take a breath than to send more people into a potential ambush. Our software allowed us to speak to more than one person at the same time, and Black's next call was to Rafael.

"Where are you?"

"In the gym with Sky."

"It's possible Eric Ridley's escaped, and there's been an incident in the lane outside. Since neither of us believes in coincidences, would you mind taking a look?"

"On my way."

I heard Sky's voice in the background. "What's going on?"

"Just stay here, Sunshine."

Sunshine?

Another second, and Matt's voice filled the car from Blackwood's headquarters.

"Control room."

"Take all our Richmond locations up to alert level one," Black instructed.

We used a scale of one to five based on the

DEFCON levels. One was as high as it got short of a full lockdown.

A pause. "Doing it right now."

I liked that about Matt. He didn't argue or question, he just acted.

"And send anyone from Emmy's Special Projects team who isn't in the middle of something critical to muster at headquarters."

Why headquarters, you ask? Because for all we knew, Bethany was lying dead and Ridley was hunkered down in the woods near Riverley with a sniper rifle. We needed to clear the way. Carefully.

"One second…" There was some murmuring in the background. "That's in progress."

"Send four of them to the end of Riverley Lane. Nobody comes or goes. We'll need the tech team on standby too. And investigations."

"What's happened?"

"Likely escaped felon. Eric Ridley."

"That guy from the news? Who killed the politician?"

"Yes. At this moment, Blackwood has one priority: locating him."

"Got it."

Dan was next.

"We're coming through from Chesapeake. Contact whoever you need to in order to clear the way because Emmy's not stopping."

Good choice. Dan had probably pissed off fewer cops than the rest of us and therefore had more favours owing. Black called a couple of his old Navy buddies and asked them to dig for information of the jailbreak, then Rafael came back.

"Car's empty. Looks as if it hit a tree. The airbags deployed."

"Any sign of the occupant?"

"No, but there's blood on the driver's door and crushed grass next to it." Which suggested a struggle. "A woman's purse is still on the back seat."

"What about another vehicle?"

"Not that I can see."

"Widen the search area."

Another fifteen minutes flew by. And I mean *flew*. The Porsche did its job, I did mine, and Black did his. Sky was babysitting Tabby while Ana helped Rafael to comb the woods. So far, they'd found no evidence of Bethany or Ridley, but fifty yards along the road, there were fresh tyre tracks behind a stand of trees.

At Riverley, Bradley was helping Mrs. Fairfax to prepare for the influx of visitors. Dustin was on the other side of Richmond getting a saddle repaired, Sam was at work, and the grounds team had been corralled in the lounge attached to the stables. Pale was apparently flying in from wherever, Nate and Carmen were on their way, and Dan had gone to the office to oversee the team there. Plus we'd had confirmation that it *was* Ridley who'd escaped. He'd killed one guard and injured another in the process.

Dan's name flashed up on the console.

"Your escort's waiting two miles ahead. You do still have that suite at the Giants, right?"

"You bribed them with tickets?"

We kept the suite for that very purpose.

"Yeah, cost us six."

"Fine, tell Bradley."

A minute later, a police cruiser pulled out in front

of us, matching my speed. *Thanks, Dan.* That was one less thing we had to worry about, but now we had a bigger problem.

"Somebody has to tell Alaric," I muttered. "I should make the call."

"I can do it if you want," Black offered.

"No, it'll be better coming from me."

Not that there was a way to make the fact that his girlfriend had been abducted sound anything less than awful.

"Hey, it's me."

"Hey yourself. How's it going? Did you find Dyson yet?"

He was half joking, but I was about to ruin his mood.

"Yes, but that's not why I'm calling. Where are you?"

"I had to go to DC for a meeting. We've had a flood of new business inquiries in the last week. Not sure where they've all suddenly come from, but we can't afford to turn them down." I had a good idea where the referrals had come from. Black's guilty conscience. "Wait a second... You're serious? You found Dyson?"

"Alaric, you need to go back to Richmond."

He knew straight away that something was wrong.

"Why? What's happened?"

"Bethany had a little prang in my car. There wasn't too much damage, but we can't find her."

"What do you mean, you can't find her? She wandered off?"

"We think she might have been taken." I had to do it. I had to tell him. "Eric Ridley escaped a few hours ago."

"What about Rune? Is Rune okay?"

Oh, fuck.

"Rune was with her?"

"I don't know. Maybe. Beth said they were going to see the horses at Riverley. Hold on, I'll call her."

Black was already on the phone, talking softly, updating everyone on a terrible situation that was now ten times worse.

"She's not answering." Alaric's panic was all too obvious. "I got voicemail."

"We'll send someone over to the house. We'll find them, I promise."

The question was, would they be dead or alive? Ridley was furious at us, he had nothing to lose, and he'd already killed four people this month. Plus he could be miles away by now.

When Alaric spoke again, it was in a cold tone I hadn't heard him use for years. This was Alaric the assassin, the man I'd first met on an undercover job over a decade ago, not the man who'd chilled out and lightened up once he quit the Agency and joined the FBI. There may have been a lot of uncertainties at that moment, but I knew one thing for sure. Eric Ridley was a dead man.

"I'm on my way."

CHAPTER 45 - BETHANY

"IS IT WORKING?" I asked.

"I think so. Okay, put me down now."

I loosened my grip on Rune, and she slithered back to the floor. We'd been trapped together before, but that had been fun, a visit to an escape room for her birthday, and this was hell. For the first day in the cellar, I'd been terrified, but I'd gone beyond scared and now my only focus was our survival. And to live, we needed to drink. Eric Ridley had left us with nothing. No water, no food, no blankets. When I'd told him Rune was diabetic, he just laughed.

"Nice try," he'd said. "Sure she is."

"No, really."

"Then you'd better hope Charles Black pays your ransom in a hurry."

What, so we could die quickly? Ridley had shown no interest in keeping us alive. And would Black even pay a ransom? He didn't strike me as the kind of man who negotiated with criminals. Alaric would look for us, I knew he would, but we'd travelled for hours to get here, stuffed into the boot of a car with our hands and ankles bound and hoods over our heads. He'd have to search half of the United States. I'd tried to leave him a clue that it was Ridley who'd taken us, but would he find it?

Meanwhile, we were on our own, apart from the rats that skittered around at night, anyway. We'd got out of our handcuffs pretty fast thanks to Judd—he'd taught Rune that it was a good idea to carry a universal cuff key, and she had one braided into her homemade necklace—but we were still stuck in a dingy basement. The only door had been locked with a key and then bolted from the outside for good measure. We'd both heard the rattle followed by the dull *thunk*.

The door might have been old, but it was solid. We'd tried to break it down, and all we had to show for it was bruised shoulders. On the plus side, my headache was easing now. I'd got a nosebleed when the BMW's airbag went off, and then I'd seen stars when Ridley cracked me over the head with his gun after I punched him by his car. My knuckles hurt too. At least Rune was in better shape than me, for now at any rate. Ridley had found her phone in her pocket and thrown it away, but he'd missed the little cross-body bag under her baggy sweatshirt. She wore it close, paranoid about something so important getting stolen, and she reckoned she had enough insulin to last her for two more weeks.

Would we survive for two weeks? Earlier, I'd almost given up hope, but Rune had given me a pep talk. At fifteen years old.

"Look." She'd smoothed out a piece of paper in the gloom. She kept that in her little bag too. "It's from Naz. Last year, he gave me a jar of stars for Christmas, and I opened one every day. Most of them had jokes on, but sometimes he reminded me how far I've come."

I squinted until I could make out the letters. The only light came from a ventilation grate roughly a foot

square, high above our heads. We couldn't escape
through it—even if we'd been small enough, metal bars
blocked our way.

> *You were born into darkness, but you became*
> *light. We all believe in you.*

"That's...that's...so lovely."

"Not every girl is lucky enough to have four fathers.
Naz also told me that the difference between a survivor
and a quitter is her spirit. My spirit's got me through
life so far, and I don't intend to die now."

"I... Neither do I."

Not when I'd finally found happiness. When I had a
man who would love me until the end of time. And
what would happen to Chaucer?

Last week in England, I'd finally got a taste of how
the rest of my life could be. It wasn't a vacation, but it
sure felt like one compared to my years with Piers.
Alaric had needed to work on a report—one of Sirius's
bread-and-butter projects, he said. Their client was
considering a move into new markets, and they wanted
to understand the pros and cons of doing business in
Ukraine—any problems they might encounter, that sort
of thing.

So I'd helped to organise all the issues and benefits
into a presentation as well as buying a new printer,
arranging travel to Vermont for Ravi, and a flight to
Vienna for Judd. Working hours were relaxed. If I
wanted to start early, then ride Chaucer in the
afternoon and do a bit more in the evening, nobody
minded. And of course I got to spend time with Alaric,
and Gemma too. She was still staying at Judd's, as was
the new girl. I hadn't quite worked Nada out yet. She
didn't say much, but she liked to cook in the evenings.

I didn't want to give up that life, and Rune wanted to go home too.

So we'd brainstormed and come up with our rudimentary water collector. It was raining outside—we could hear it hammering against the wooden sides of the house—so we tied my cotton sweater to the bars of the ventilation window with one sleeve trailing in a puddle outside and the other hanging inside over an old metal pail we'd emptied the spiders out of. And now I heard the most glorious sound in the world: the *drip, drip, drip* of water plopping into the bucket. Which was a whole lot better than what had plopped into the other bucket we'd found yesterday. We'd each had to take it in turns to answer the call of nature while the other turned her back. Old Bethany would have died from embarrassment, but new Bethany realised there were more important things than appearances.

Like staying alive.

And to do that, we needed food. Rune had a packet of glucose tablets with her for emergencies, but they wouldn't last long.

"What do you suppose is in those old mason jars?" I asked.

We'd spotted them when we explored our prison, stacked on wooden shelves screwed to the wall at the far end of the cellar, filthy, covered in cobwebs, with peeling labels. At that point, I'd still hoped Ridley might bring us something to eat, but two days after we arrived, there was no sign of him. The jars were the only possibility for sustenance.

Rune shuddered. "Either food or body parts. This place feels like a serial killer's lair."

As best as we could ascertain, we were in an

abandoned house in the middle of nowhere. There was no traffic noise, but the local wildlife seemed particularly active at night. Screams and grunts and cries were commonplace. A bear or a serial killer both seemed very real possibilities, as did Bigfoot. The place was straight out of a horror movie.

I cringed as I reached for a jar, then nearly dropped it when something skittered over my hand. Another spider? A centipede? A cockroach? Yuck. I wiped away some of the grime and held my prize up to the light. Orange blobs floated inside.

Rune stood on tiptoes to read the label. "Peaches. August eighteenth, 1982."

"Urgh. They're ancient. Probably full of bacteria."

"I'm not so sure. Alaric bought me a book on shipwrecks, and I remember scientists testing hundred-year-old canned goods they found underwater and concluding they were edible."

"Really?"

"The vitamin content had degraded, that's all."

In the absence of any other options... "I'd better try them first."

I popped the top on the jar, flipped it back, and gave the contents a sniff. What do you know? They actually smelled like peaches. I wiped my hands on my jeans and fished one of the slimy little suckers out of its juice.

"Wish me luck."

It didn't taste of an awful lot, which I guessed was a good thing under the circumstances. I gave a quiet whoop.

"It's okay! Can you eat them?"

"As long as I'm careful about the salt and sugar

content."

"Here, try one."

There were at least fifty jars stacked up, and if even half of them were edible, we could cope for a fortnight. As long as I didn't succumb to hypothermia without my sweater, that was. At least I'd worn a raincoat on my visit to Riverley—Rune and I could curl up under it at night. Would Alaric be able to narrow down our location? Would Black pay up? Or would Ridley come back and finish us off first?

CHAPTER 46 - EMMY

"WE FOUND HIM once, and we'll find him again," Black told Alaric, but fifty hours after Beth and Rune had been taken, we were worryingly short on clues.

We knew for certain that Ridley was our perpetrator, at least. The police hadn't been convinced at first because what escaped murderer would drive a hundred miles hell-bent on revenge instead of going to ground? A psychopath, that was who. We explained that, but they were still sceptical until we presented them with DNA evidence.

It was Barkley who found it. When we got back to Riverley, the first thing we did was stop to inspect the crime scene, and she'd escaped from the car, bounding around as a dozen people tried to catch her. We'd all been annoyed until she started barking at the ring she'd found in the grass.

Beth's ring. Alaric had bought it for her before they left London. Sparkling blue sapphires to match her eyes, a sort of pre-engagement ring, he said. Bloody hell. They were that serious?

Alaric had bent to pick it up, only for Black to smack his hand out of the way.

"Don't touch. It's evidence."

"There's blood on it." Alaric spoke in a choked whisper. "Beth's hurt."

"We don't know whose blood it is. Somebody get me a pair of gloves and an evidence bag."

A Rapid DNA test gave us the answer we needed—Beth had injured Ridley. Good on her. I only hoped his retaliation hadn't been too devastating.

We found Beth's phone in her handbag and Rune's smashed beyond the treeline, but what we couldn't locate anywhere was Rune's insulin. Alaric insisted she kept a supply with her at all times, and if she still had it intact, that might buy us some time.

Which let's face it, we desperately needed since we only had two solid clues. Firstly, we knew Ridley had stolen a dark green Toyota sedan back in Norfolk. The woman he'd carjacked was shaken but miraculously unharmed. However, nobody had seen the car since, and thanks to the story being front and centre on every news bulletin, the whole damned country was looking for it.

The second clue? Tennessee. We knew Ridley had been near Sevierville yesterday because that was where he'd sent the ransom note from. He probably thought he was being cute, submitting it via the comment form on Blackwood's website, but he most likely didn't realise we'd recorded the IP address of his device. And with that, Mack and her team of happy hackers were able to dig through networks and service providers to work out his phone's IMEI number. The idiot should have used a VPN. Unfortunately, he was tech-savvy enough to have turned his phone off, so we couldn't locate him right now, but he'd pinged off cell towers near Sevierville earlier, and that was where we were headed. I was in the helicopter with Black, Ana, and Alaric, and the rest of the team was coming by road.

Had we mentioned this little snippet of information to the police? Not exactly. We'd already gone the semi-legal route with Ridley once and look where it got us. He'd escaped. This time, we'd play for keeps. The cops were using their manpower to stake out the most likely locations as they saw it—anywhere Ridley had lived or had family or known acquaintances. Who was watching the Devane properties? Reporters and sightseers, that was who. Yes, still. Apparently, crime tourism was a growing phenomenon, which meant Ridley would be a fool to go near any of those places.

Of course, we still had the problem of what to do about the ransom request. The note asked for twenty million dollars in Bitcoin to secure the girls' release and said Ridley would be in touch. He'd wanted me, but when his plan went wrong, he'd adapted on the fly, and now he was using people I cared about as leverage.

Motherfucker.

Black didn't want to send the money. Not only because it would break Blackwood's policy and set a dangerous precedent, but because Ridley wouldn't know honour if it bit him on the ass, and on past form, he'd kill the hostages out of spite. But Black had offered the cash anyway. The final decision was up to Alaric. Whether we sent the funds or not, we'd hunt Ridley to the ends of the fucking earth.

"But will we be too late?" Alaric asked in response to Black's assurances.

We could be already. I squeezed Alaric's hand, and for once, Black didn't seem bothered by that.

"Let's try to stay positive."

Alaric looked haggard, hardly surprising since he'd had no sleep since Thursday and barcly catcn either.

He'd held up a lot better through the *Emerald* aftermath. I guess it only went to show what was important in Alaric's world—people, not work or material possessions.

"If I knew they were alive, I'd pay anything."

"What if we ask for proof of life?" Ana asked.

Standard procedure in a kidnapping case, but there was a slight hitch, as Alaric already knew.

"How? That motherfucker didn't give us a way to contact him."

Black hadn't said much on the journey. He'd been too busy thinking, and I let him get on with it. Now more than ever, we needed his insights.

"There might be a way," he said. "If Ridley uses the web form again, we can have Mack set it so any mention of cryptocurrency triggers a pop-up message. No proof of life, no money. If Beth and Rune are still alive, he'll comply because he needs the funds to run. His finances are in bad shape." Too much play, not enough work. "And if they're dead, we're no worse off."

"Could you not be so blunt?" I muttered.

"Sorry."

"Get Mack to do it," Alaric said. "Tell Ridley we need to hear from both of them. Beth and Rune. If they're still breathing, we take a chance and send the ransom."

CHAPTER 47 - BETH

"HE'S COMING!" RUNE hissed.

For the first time in three days, we heard footsteps. *Clomp, clomp, clomp* on the wooden floor overhead.

"Quick, put the handcuffs back on."

We'd discussed whether to leave our hands free or not, whether to try and escape by force if Ridley came back. But ultimately, we'd decided against it. Ridley had a gun, and in the confines of the cellar, we'd be sitting ducks. And if we left the cuffs off, he'd no doubt wonder how we'd undone them in the first place. Most likely, he'd search us, confiscate the key, and then put the cuffs back on, which would leave us in an even worse position.

I knew we'd made the right decision when Ridley called out from the other side of the door.

"Stand back, or I'll kill you."

We retreated to the corner and waited. Would he notice our rain collection device? Or the empty jars? Hopefully not—my sweater was navy blue, and the food was all at the other end of the cellar.

The door creaked open and Ridley's silhouette appeared at the top of the wooden stairs, gun in hand.

"Stinks in here."

"Where else do you expect us to go to the toilet?"

He ignored my words and tossed two bottles of

water in our direction. *Now* he thought hydration might be a good idea?

"Drink that, and then you're going to make a video."

"What kind of video?"

He threw a folded newspaper at me too. "Hold that up. You each give your name, the date, and say you're okay."

"What is the date?" I asked, just to check we hadn't somehow lost a day.

"June twenty-fifth. Hurry up—I don't have time to waste."

"And what if we refuse?"

"Then I've got no further use for you, so I might as well shoot you right now. The girl first. You can watch her bleed to death."

That was when I understood—Alaric had asked Ridley to prove we were alive before he'd pay a ransom. As long as we played along, he couldn't kill us, not yet. He might need us again, hence the water. I wasn't sure whether Alaric would actually pay the ransom or if he was just trying to buy time, but either way, he had a plan, and we had to play our part.

"All right, we'll do what you want."

The bottled water tasted like the finest champagne after what we'd been drinking. I offered half of mine to Rune, but she shook her head.

"You finish it."

"What are you whispering about?" Ridley asked. "Quit stalling."

I unfolded the newspaper and held it up. *The Washington Post*. Saudi Arabia was threatening war with Iran, and an experimental rocket promised to usher in a new era of space travel. At the moment, I'd settle for getting out of the damn basement.

Ridley almost blinded us with a torch beam, and I couldn't keep the tremble out of my voice when I spoke.

"My name is Bethany Stafford-Lyons. It's the twenty-fifth of June, and I'm okay."

"My name is Rune Andi Manette-McLain. It's June twenty-fifth, and I'm okay."

The light went out, but Ridley kept pointing the gun at us as he backed towards the stairs. I saw it in silhouette.

"Hey, can we have some more water? Food?"

He didn't answer, just jogged sideways up the stairs and slammed the door. The key turned in the lock with a loud *click*.

Brilliant.

I slumped against the wall, exhausted, and Rune undid our handcuffs again. We tucked them into our back pockets, ready to be put on again when Ridley came back. *If* he came back. Maybe we'd been abandoned for good? We'd barely slept, and we'd been rationing the food because we didn't know how long it would need to last. Rune's insulin was a bigger worry, though.

"How are you feeling?" I asked.

She managed a faint smile, but I could see it was an effort. "I'm all right."

"Rune Andi Manette-McLain. That's a pretty name. Is the Manette part from your mother?"

Rune had barely spoken about her past, although she had told me a little about Thailand and taught me a few Thai phrases to while away the time.

"No, Andi Manette is a character from a book. She and her daughters got kidnapped and imprisoned in a cellar. When Alaric sees that video, he'll know I'm trying to send him a message, and when he googles who Andi Manette is, he'll realise where we're stuck."

"That's genius." For the first time since we got captured, I felt a real flicker of hope. Rune definitely took after her father. "He'll need to narrow down the locations to search, but he's smart. He'll find us."

"We might not need to wait that long."

"What do you mean?"

Rune tiptoed over to the stairs. "I didn't hear Ridley push the bolt across. Did you?"

Honestly? I'd been so frazzled after the video, I couldn't say either way. But now that I looked, I couldn't see the telltale shadow across the tiny gap between the door and the frame.

"I don't suppose you know how to pick a lock?"

"Ravi taught me, but that one looks stiff. There might be an easier way."

She picked up the newspaper and hurried up the stairs. When she got to the top, she spread the pages wide and slid the whole thing under the door, leaving only a tiny corner on our side. Next, she took one of her syringes and wiggled the capped needle into the lock. I heard the key hit the floor on the other side, and when Rune pulled the paper back towards us, there was the key. Wow.

"Ravi taught you that too?"

Rune nodded. "Should we leave now? Or wait a while?"

I didn't know why she asked me—Rune was clearly the brighter one out of the two of us.

"Should we leave at all? We've sent a clue, and we've got enough supplies for another week at least.

Longer if it keeps raining."

"Ridley wants to kill us. If Alaric pays the ransom and doesn't get to us in time..."

Rune didn't need to spell it out.

But it was a risk. If we tried to escape and failed, if we got caught, then Ridley would be furious. The man had already murdered his own girlfriend, plus two employees and those people in Syria and Afghanistan, and Alaric said he had a terrible temper.

Could we afford to try escaping? Could we afford not to?

What would Emmy do in this situation? That was an easy one—she'd probably have tunnelled out of there with her bare hands already.

"Let's listen for a minute or two and see if we hear any more movement."

There was nothing but the wind outside, the occasional cry of an animal, and the familiar creaks of the old house settling. We had to leave, didn't we? Rune obviously thought so too. Until then, she'd stayed remarkably calm, but now she was twitchy.

"Stay behind me, okay?"

Rune nodded. At that moment, she looked very much like the child she was rather than the clever young lady I'd come to admire over the past few days. And I was scared stiff. My heart thudded against my ribcage, and I wondered whether I might die from a coronary rather than at Ridley's hands.

The door groaned as it opened, and we waited another minute, hardly daring to breathe in case he came back. Finally, we tiptoed out into a dingy hallway.

The house was abandoned—that much was obvious from a glance. Discoloured paper peeled from the walls, replaced by tasteless graffiti, the ceiling was covered in damp patches with the occasional hole, and the few pieces of furniture were dusty and broken. The good news? Half of the windows were either open or smashed, and the front door swung back and forth in the breeze.

Where was Ridley?

And almost as important, where were we?

We bolted out the front door and found ourselves in a clearing. The forest was doing its best to take over, but it hadn't quite won the battle yet. Which way should we go? There was no obvious path, in fact, no sign of civilisation whatsoever.

"There must be a driveway somewhere," I said. Ridley had half carried, half dragged us the short distance from the car to the house, but we'd still been wearing the hoods. "Let's go around the other side."

With hindsight, we should have taken our chances with the bears.

"What the...?"

Ridley's eyes widened in surprise when we rounded the corner right in front of him, while I imagined mine held abject horror. I turned to grab Rune, to run, but he reacted first.

"Stay where you are," he growled.

Instinct made me grab for the gun. It was either that or die. A bullet whizzed past my ear, deafening me, but I'd loosened his grip enough that the gun flew into a patch of stinging nettles.

"Run!" I screamed at Rune.

I was under no illusions that I'd be able to defeat Ridley, but if I could just slow him down enough for her to make a break for it, maybe one of us would survive.

If Rune went on to live a long and happy life, that was better than both of us dying in this wretched wilderness.

Ridley backhanded me, and I glimpsed his famous temper. Those cruel eyes gleamed maniacally as we fought for the upper hand. I got a knee to his balls; he grunted in pain and hit me in the face. I shook off the stars and stamped on his foot; he punched me in the stomach. I was losing, I knew that, but I just had to hold on for long enough for Rune to get away.

"You bastard," I hissed.

"Die, bitch."

He knocked my legs out from under me, and we grappled on the wet ground. It felt surreal, almost as if someone else were stuck in this nightmare and I was just watching. How long had we been fighting? It seemed like forever, and my strength was ebbing. I used one last effort to roll, but that backfired when Ridley got his hands around my neck. I couldn't breathe as his weight pressed down on me.

And the worst part? I'd never get to say goodbye to Alaric. To tell him I loved him one last time. To fuck him in my wedding dress.

I closed my eyes. I didn't want the last thing I ever saw to be Eric Ridley's sneering face.

Then he howled, a blood-curdling sound more terrifying than the animals we heard at night. In Ridley's own words, what the...?

My eyes sprang open to see Rune clinging to Ridley's back. He let go of my throat to claw behind himself, and I shoved him to the side with everything I had left.

"*Now* we run," Rune shouted.

She hauled me up, and I caught a glimpse of the syringes sticking out of Ridley's shoulder as we darted into the forest. A few seconds passed, and then I heard him crashing through the trees after us.

We ran. I twisted my ankle and a branch smacked me in the face, but still we ran. Rune cried out in pain as she tripped over a rock, and we kept going. Oh, hell! The ground disappeared out from underneath us and we slid down a muddy slope, landing in a heap at the bottom. The relative silence as we untangled ourselves made me pause. I couldn't hear Ridley anymore.

"Come on!" Rune said, tugging at me. "We can't stop."

"Shush a second. Where did he go?"

I had visions of him creeping up behind us, ambushing us when we least expected it.

"Perhaps he's dead."

"Dead?"

"I gave him insulin."

What? I thought she'd just stuck him with a bunch of empty needles.

"How much?"

"Maybe all of it. I'm not sure how much went in."

"All of it? Oh, hell. What about you? You'll need insulin. And how many glucose tablets do you have left?"

I might not have known a huge amount about type 1 diabetes, but I'd been reading up on it, so I was aware that stress and bursts of strenuous exercise could cause a rise in blood glucose. Rune's body didn't make the insulin to regulate the sugar level the way it should. Later, in the hours following, that level could drop precipitously, and she'd need carbohydrates.

"Three, and I had to do it. You need to go back to Alaric. I've never seen him as happy as when he's with you."

Oh, that sweet, sweet girl.

"Rune, you're the one who needs to go home."

She shrugged and tried to pull me along. "We have to carry on."

"What will the insulin do? If he just got a little?"

"It'll lower his blood sugar. If he got an overdose, he'll get dizzy and confused. His vision might blur, and he'll be jittery. But if he realises what I gave him and eats something sweet, it could be enough to counteract the effects. Come on, can you walk?"

My ankle hurt more with every step, but I nodded anyway. We had no choice.

"Yes, but which direction? What if we end up going round in a circle?"

"It'll be dark soon, so we can use the sun and the stars to keep us straight as long as it doesn't cloud over. But I don't know where we are. I don't know which way to go."

I heard the panic in her voice. Rune, I realised, liked to be in control. She liked order. There was an immense amount of knowledge locked up in her head, and a missing piece upset her.

"As long as we go in one direction, we have to hit civilisation eventually. A road, a trail, something like that. I think it's a tiny bit warmer here than in Richmond, don't you?"

Rune nodded.

"So Ridley probably drove us south. Which means we want to head north to go home."

I had no idea whether my logic would pan out, but

Rune seemed happier now that we had a plan.

"Okay." She pointed at the dense wall of green. "We have to go this way."

Now we were in a race, not only against Ridley if he was still out there, but against time. Would we make it to safety before Rune got sick?

CHAPTER 48 - ALARIC

ALARIC PACED THE hotel room. Emmy was doing the same, and they'd had to synchronise to avoid bumping into each other. She'd apologised a hundred times for Beth and Rune being snatched, and Alaric had never seen her so stressed.

"It should have been me who got taken."

"It shouldn't have been any of you."

"It was Blackwood who went after Kyla Devane."

"And it was Sirius who led everyone to Kentucky in the first place."

Alaric and Beth had befriended Harriet, and Alaric had wanted to see justice for Piper Simms as much as anyone. They'd all underestimated how unhinged Ridley would turn out to be. It just so happened that Beth and Rune had ended up paying the price.

The search team had spent the day canvassing the area served by the cell tower in Sevierville, but apart from a barista who thought Ridley might possibly have bought coffee and a panini to go on Friday, maybe, they had no leads. Ridley was as much of a ghost as Dyson.

The similarities between this week's events and those of eight years ago didn't escape Alaric. Both times, he'd been happy and lost everything. Both times, he'd found himself alongside Emmy searching for a needle in a haystack.

The main difference? This time, Black was being more cooperative. When the *Emerald* pay-off disappeared, he'd opened an investigation, but although he'd made the right noises, Alaric hadn't failed to notice his lack of enthusiasm. This time, he'd thrown the whole of Blackwood at the problem and cleared his entire schedule to head up the search himself.

Not that it was doing much good. Daylight was fading now, which meant another night without the girls Alaric loved.

"Rune's a tough cookie," Judd said from his spot by the door. "We know she is. And Bethany's no pushover either."

He'd flown in to help, as had Naz and Ravi. Naz was assisting the tech team back in Virginia, while Ravi was going through every property associated with Ridley, just in case he'd left a clue behind. But so far, no dice. Ridley hadn't sent proof of life either, and every minute that ticked by, another little piece of Alaric's heart died. He'd worked so fucking hard to rebuild his life, only for it to fall apart again. He wasn't sure he could do it a second time.

"Message from HQ," Dan said. "They've been monitoring the local police communications, and a camper reported hearing a shot fired in Great Smoky Mountains National Park. Said it sounded like a rifle or a large-calibre handgun."

"Are the police looking into it?" Black asked. "Isn't hunting banned in national parks?"

"Great Smoky Mountains is the exception, according to the research team. They have a wild hog control program. The cops said it's most probably the rangers chasing one down."

"What weapons do the rangers carry?"

"A .38 as standard."

"Who shoots a wild hog with a .38?" Emmy asked as she flopped back onto the bed. She'd been catnapping earlier, and Alaric had kept a very wary eye on her because her sleepwalking problem was no joke. She'd once destroyed his TV on a nocturnal meander, made all the more alarming by the fact he'd been watching it at the time. "I'd want a .44 Magnum, or better still, a shotgun, especially in the dark. But even if I had a twelve-gauge, I wouldn't be skipping through the woods tonight because it's pissing down."

"Want to check it out, Diamond?"

Grasping at straws? Perhaps. They'd already had three false alarms today—footprints around a derelict gas station that was most likely just kids, a stolen RV they'd found at a local chop shop, and one homeless gent whom they'd scared witless when they burst into a tumbledown shed. A member of Emmy's team had dropped him off at Target with five hundred bucks and an instruction to buy himself food and clothing.

"Sure beats sitting around here," she said. "Right now?"

Black nodded his agreement. "You, me, Ana, and Pale."

Pale. The guy from the gas station. He'd turned up too, along with a different girl—a redhead this time— and an even more garish Hawaiian shirt. Did the guy own any footwear but flip-flops? The chick was still out canvassing along with twenty or so other people. They planned to hit the dive bars, the flophouses, and the late-night convenience stores. The dealers. The fixers.

Ridley had to get supplies from somewhere, and maybe he'd tapped into the shadow economy.

Pale hadn't said much, and nobody had mentioned his background. Alaric could take a stab at it from the name—for years, he'd heard rumours about the Horsemen of the Apocalypse, a band of elite assassins. It wouldn't surprise him in the least if Black was a member, but this guy looked like the love child of a hippie and a hobo, so Alaric was by no means certain that his guess was correct.

And he'd be damned if Pale was going to look for Rune and Beth while he stayed behind.

"I'm coming too."

"That's not a good idea," Black said.

"I don't care whether you think it's a good idea or not. I'm telling you I'm coming."

"You don't—" Black started, but Emmy held up a hand.

"If we need to question campers, having an extra person along might be useful. But Alaric, if we have to go into the forest, Black's right—we're trained for this, and you aren't."

"Even him?" Alaric pointed at Pale.

Black nodded.

"Please, work with us on this?" Emmy asked.

Deep down, Alaric knew what she said made sense. Yes, he'd once have been an assassin by trade, but he'd specialised in the cleaner side of things. Investigation, infiltration, and a quick double-tap to the head when the time was right, not jungle warfare.

He also knew how hard Emmy and Black trained. Whatever bust-up they'd had the other week didn't seem to have affected their working relationship, and if anyone could find Ridley in the Smoky Mountains at night, it was them.

"Okay. I'll let you take the lead."

"Yeah, I saw him," the guy in the plaid shirt said, peering out from under an RV awning. The rain fell at a steady drizzle. "Yesterday? Day before? Comin' out of the shower. But I ain't seen him since. Is he the asshole shootin' out there? I told the cops it weren't no ranger. They use shotguns for huntin' the boar around here, and I know a shotgun when I hear one."

"We're not sure," Black said, wiping raindrops off the photo. "You're certain it was the same man?"

"Always was good with faces. What'd he do?"

"You haven't been watching TV?"

"Don't own no TV. Destroy your brain, those things."

"He's wanted by the police. Did you notice what vehicle he was driving?"

His friend waved a beer can. "Green sedan. Drove it over yonder." He waved at the far side of the campground. "I tried to tell him that wasn't the way out, but he cussed me somethin' proper and kept goin'."

"What's over there?"

"Don'know. I'm just here for the fishin'. Hey, Hank! What's along that track over there? The one with the 'no entry' sign?"

A third guy wandered out of the RV, his wide-brimmed hat decorated with fishing lures. "Go a mile, and you'll find an old house. The NPS used to store supplies there, but people kept breaking in so they abandoned the place. Ain't nothing there now but rats."

He'd got that part right.

"This is where we part company," Emmy murmured.

More than anything, Alaric wanted to charge down the track with his gun drawn, but he'd agreed to hold back. He didn't break his word. And this was one time being acquainted with Black could actually work in his favour. If anyone could defeat Ridley, it was that asshole.

"Just be careful."

"Always am. But if Ridley gets past us and heads back this way, would you mind shooting the fucker?"

As if she had to ask.

"It'd be my pleasure."

CHAPTER 49 - EMMY

BLACKWOOD USED A modular system for its gear, packed away in custom bags designed by Bradley. When he wasn't busy shopping and decorating, he did have his uses. We selected the essentials for tonight's excursion—first aid kits, survival equipment, emergency rations, water canteens, tech goodies, and of course, appropriate weapons.

Usually, my weapon of choice was a Walther PPQ, but tonight, I'd swapped it for an AR-15 fitted with a combined night-vision and thermal-imaging scope as my primary weapon. As a backup, I carried a P99 with tritium night sights plus a laser sight on the under-barrel accessory rail. We practised regularly in low-light conditions, and it was my favourite combination.

"Is my face okay?" Ana asked.

I smudged warpaint over a patch she'd missed. It was oil-based, which meant it shouldn't wash off in the rain. "Mine?"

"Good."

Black and Pale were ready too. I'd been a little surprised when Pale volunteered his services, but quite frankly, he owed us for that dodgy alibi he'd provided for Black, so helping with the search for Ridley was the least he could do. And if nothing else, it would be interesting to see how Black's old partner in crime operated. He'd semi-retired until he got talked back into the game not so long ago. Before we left the hotel, I'd quietly questioned whether he was the best man for the job, but Black had given a firm nod.

"That asshole moves like smoke through the trees, and wait until you see him track."

I found out what Black meant as soon as we started down the rutted path. I knew Pale was there in front of us, but I couldn't see him, not unless I used my night vision. The guy just *blended.* I understood at once where Black had learned his night combat skills, and holy hell, I needed Pale to teach me how to skulk like that.

Moving carefully, it took us a smidgen over an hour to confirm we were on the right path. Ridley had tried to hide the Toyota under the trees, but he hadn't done a great job of it. The tail lights gleamed when the clouds let the moon show for a moment. The licence plates had been changed, but the prison guard's uniform he'd stolen was lying on the back seat. We spiked the tyres just in case he tried to get away, then carried on to the old house. It had been beautiful in its day, two storeys with a small front porch and white siding, but now? It was a house of horrors, all shattered windows and yawning holes in the woodwork. We split into pairs— me with Ana and Black with Pale—and crept to opposite corners. From our positions, we could each see two sides of the house. We watched. Waited. Ten minutes passed, and then twenty. I controlled my breathing. Kept my heartbeat steady.

"Nothing stirring over here," Black said softly in my ear. We used satellite technology for operations like this, and our headsets linked to each other as well as to

Alaric and the team at Blackwood's headquarters.

"Quiet here too."

"Pale's going in for a closer look."

I switched my scope to thermal and saw his shadowy form melt out of the treeline. It seemed unlikely Ridley would have access to the same technology—jacking a car was one thing, but finding a handy-dandy military-grade scope right after he escaped from jail? Surely not.

Even so, I was tense as Pale approached the building.

Why didn't we just use thermal imaging to see who was inside, you ask? Because this wasn't the movies, and that shit didn't work in real life. Infrared couldn't see through walls. It couldn't even see through glass. For that, we'd need a handheld radar system, something like a RANGE-R or a Xaver. Did we have one? Yes. The problem was that they had a limited detection range—twenty metres max, depending on what kind of barrier was between the target and the device—and they worked best if you were right up next to the wall. Pale couldn't use it, not right away. He couldn't afford to get distracted so close to potential danger.

"Someone's been here in the last day or two," he said, pausing at the corner nearest to me. "There's flattened vegetation. Syringes too. Could've been junkies."

"Any sign of life?"

"No. I'll try the radar, but there's a basement."

Which we'd have to check out in person. Another quarter-hour passed before we considered it safe to approach, and the only signs of life we'd seen were the aforementioned rats, skittering across the front steps and running up the walls.

We'd drilled through building clearances a thousand times in the kill-house at HQ, and it seemed Pale had a training facility somewhere too. The four of us stacked up outside the front door, a pair on each side. When we went in, two of us would break left, two would break right, and we'd sweep the building, being careful not to cross fields of fire. Our primary goal at that point was to neutralise Ridley.

And we'd have achieved it if he'd been there.

There was evidence of his presence—food wrappers, empty drinks bottles, a sleeping bag—but no sign of the man himself.

Black and Pale materialised through the basement door. While Ana and I had searched upstairs, they'd done downstairs.

"Anything?" I asked.

"Somebody was imprisoned down there, and recently. We found empty jars, water bottles, a copy of today's *Washington Post*, and a sweater that looks the right size for Bethany."

Shit. Had we just missed them? If so, where were they? Ridley hadn't moved them by car. Not only was the Toyota still there, but we hadn't seen any fresh tyre tracks and our campsite buddies swore they hadn't seen another vehicle heading in this direction.

"They must be in the forest," Ana said, coming to the same conclusion as me.

Black waved a hand at Pale. "After you."

Picking up a trail was hard enough in daylight, and to this day, I didn't know how Pale managed to find the spot where our quarry had gone into the woods. He'd just stared at the trees, at the barely penetrable wall of black and grey and said, "There."

I saw the occasional footprint, half washed away in the mud, but for the most part, I just followed, staying alert for Ridley and careful to leave a ten-metre gap between Pale in front and Ana behind. Black brought up the rear.

"Three people came through," Pale said. "Two females in tennis shoes, one male in boots. They were all running."

"Do the sizes of the women fit Bethany and Rune?" Black asked.

"I'd say so, yes."

The going was slow. Rain hammered down, splashing through the tree canopy in big, messy drops, reducing visibility and threatening to wash away any clues. It was a race against time. We took several wrong turns and had to backtrack, and although I didn't let on to anyone else because Alaric was still listening in, I began to worry that we were too late. The Smokies covered hundreds of thousands of acres. If we lost the trail, it'd be like hunting for a contact lens in the ocean.

Pale stopped at the top of a near-vertical slope. Even I could see the broken branches, the crushed leaves where someone or something had crashed through. Fucking hell. They went down there?

He responded to my unasked question. "Pass the rope."

We hadn't gone much farther when Pale stilled. Not the "let me work out which way" hesitation I'd seen from him several times, but the instant rigidity of "fuck, there's a problem." I raised my scope and looked past him.

What the...? Was that Ridley? Judging by the size and body shape, it was definitely a man, and who the hell else would be running around in the wilderness at this time of night? Well, not running, exactly. He was just lying on the ground face up, arms by his sides. A ploy to lure us closer? Or was he injured?

I followed Pale's lead and faded back into the trees, and we covered the last forty metres at a snail's pace, careful not to make the slightest sound. I could feel Black and Ana behind me, but I couldn't hear them or see them.

A branch cracked. I resisted the urge to whip my head around and turned slowly instead, gun raised, finger hovering over the trigger. Did Ridley have an accomplice? After he'd killed two of his men, I'd kind of figured the rest would bug out.

Two eyes stared back at me. The interloper shared many characteristics with Ridley's goons—he was ugly, hairy, and he weighed about two hundred pounds—but he was only three feet tall with tusks and a snout.

The wild hog stared at me. I stared back.

Shit.

I'd never got into a punch-up with a pig before, and I didn't particularly want to start now. Did they attack humans? Remind me to insist on a proper briefing next time I decided to schlep through a forest at night.

I risked a glance sideways. Ridley's hands were empty. No weapon that I could see. Black came forward, darting the last few metres in case Ridley moved. But he didn't.

With the main threat neutralised, I fired a warning shot into the ground at the hog's feet. If Beth and Rune were still alive, I didn't want to kill them with a stray bullet. The beast turned tail and ran, hurtling through the undergrowth and vanishing into the darkness.

Phew. Crisis averted.

Black checked Ridley's pulse. "He's still breathing."

Unceremoniously, he flipped the motherfucker onto his front and pressed on the back of his head with one boot. Ridley woke up a bit, gurgling into the puddle, but he didn't seem to have the strength to fight back properly.

"We've found Ridley," I informed everyone not present.

"Alive?" Alaric asked.

"Just a minute…" Ridley had stopped moving, and this time when Black felt for a pulse, he smiled. "No."

"What about Beth and Rune?"

Pale was on the move again already, and this time we had one significant advantage. It didn't matter how much noise we made.

"Beth? Rune? Are you there?"

CHAPTER 50 - BETHANY

PERHAPS WE SHOULD have stayed in the cellar after all. Rune was drowsy, my ankle had swollen to the size of a melon, and even if we could have kept walking, the rain clouds had covered up the stars and we had no idea which way to go. And it was cold. Freezing. I was soaked through, and my teeth wouldn't stop chattering. I hugged Rune tighter as we curled against the base of a gnarled old tree.

"Stay awake," I whispered to her. "Just a little longer."

"I'm so...so tired."

We needed a miracle now. More than once, I'd almost drifted off, and I knew that if I fell asleep, I'd never wake up. If we died out here, would anyone even find our bodies? Or would we get eaten by one of the creatures that we could hear moving around in the forest?

Bang.

I'd been on the verge of passing out, but the gunshot jolted me back to life. Somebody was far too close for comfort. Ridley?

Rune let out a quiet sob. "Is it him?"

Please, no.

Although maybe a quick death would be preferable to a long, drawn-out demise.

"I don't know, but who else would be shooting out here?"

"We need to run again."

I tried to get up and almost passed out from the pain. Rune hauled on my arm, and I clawed my way up the tree bark. One step, and fire burned through my leg.

"I-I don't think I can even walk. What if we hide instead?"

"He'll find us."

Rune suddenly stiffened, and her fingers dug into my arm.

"What?" I whispered. "What is it?"

"I heard something. Shh."

And then I heard it too. The sweetest sound in the world, drifting from a distance on the chilly breeze. A woman's voice, and it was shouting my name.

"Beth? Are you there? Rune?"

"Over here!" Rune yelled. "We're over here."

I never thought I'd be glad to see four gun-toting commandos running in my direction, but how things had changed. Wait a second... Was that... Was that *Emmy*?

"Are you okay? Are you injured? You'll have to excuse the make-up."

I burst into tears.

"I need food," Rune said, staying remarkably composed. "I'm diabetic. And I need insulin, too. Beth's hurt her ankle."

"We've got glucose gel, raisins, and injectable glucagon as well as insulin. Beth, let's get some painkillers into you. Are you allergic to anything?"

"Assholes."

"Don't think there's any of those left around here."

"Eric Ridley... He was chasing us."

"He's no longer a problem."

"He's dead?"

She nodded. "We found him lying in the woods. Not quite sure what happened to him, to be honest."

"About four hundred units of insulin," Rune said.

Emmy looked at her with newfound respect. "You did that?"

"She's so very brave," I said.

"Do you want a job?" Emmy pressed a hand to her ear. "Ouch. Okay, Alaric says I'm not allowed to offer you a job."

"He's there?" I asked. "Alaric's there?"

"Yup. He was backstop in case Ridley went in the other direction. You'll just feel a little prick now."

For some reason, a vision of Piers popped into my head, and I quickly shook it away.

"Can I talk to him?"

Emmy removed her headset and passed it over. "The earpieces are custom-made, so they won't fit properly, but if you hold it close, you should be able to hear, okay? It's an open channel, so don't get too slushy."

I pressed it to my ears with both hands. "Alaric?"

"Fuck, it's good to hear your voice."

"I'm sorry for all this trouble."

"Sweetheart, it's me who should be apologising. I'm the one who got you into this situation."

"It wasn't you. It was that madman. And it's your friends who are here to help us, to save us... Uh, how are we going to get out of here? I can't walk."

"We're going to carry you," Emmy told me.

Somebody tucked a foil blanket around my shoulders, and I clutched it tightly around myself. Then lights came on, illuminating the whole sorry scene.

"*Carry me*? But it's miles. I think."

"Let us worry about that. Rune, will you be able to walk out of here once you've had some food? Or do you need a ride as well?"

"I can walk."

Half an hour later, I was hallucinating nicely from the morphine as Emmy helped me to lie down on the stretcher the men had made out of two saplings and several ponchos. They wrapped another poncho over the top, and everything got to me—the drugs, the relief at being rescued, four days with hardly any sleep—and I basically passed out. The last thing I remember was being hoisted into the air.

I woke I don't know how long later to the sound of singing. No, not singing. Chanting. The stretcher jostled in time to the words. I opened my eyes a crack and saw Rune beside me, riding on Emmy's back as we marched through the woods.

> *Superman's the man of steel,*
> *but he ain't no match for a Navy SEAL.*
> *Wonder Woman's fast as light,*
> *but an English bitch will win that fight.*
> *Iron Man is tough as fuck,*
> *but even he can get rusted up.*
> *Ridley was a massive dick,*
> *but he got slayed by a little prick.*
> *Heeeeey we're Blackwood,*

Get off your ass and follow us.

I'd follow these people anywhere just as soon as I could walk again. The pain had faded to a dull throb, but I couldn't see myself putting weight on my ankle anytime soon.

"Beth!"

Oh gosh, I recognised that voice. I turned my head to the other side and saw Alaric looming over me, and then I was in his arms, halfway in the air as he squeezed the breath out of me. I didn't care—after the death I'd been facing earlier, it would be a pleasant way to go. He loosened one arm enough to drag Rune into our little huddle, and then we were all crying.

"Beth," he said again, burying his face in my shoulder. "Rune. Fuck, I've never been so scared as when I found out you were gone."

"My next car's going to be a tank," I joked, then remembered what I'd done to the BMW. "Emmy, I'm so sorry I crashed your car. Something flew at us—it looked like a log—and I swerved to avoid it, and... I'll pay for the damage. Somehow."

"Oh, who gives a shit about the car? You and Rune are far more important than a heap of metal. At least the airbags went off."

"Don't worry about anything," Alaric murmured in my ear. "We can fix it all later."

"I could do with some ice for my ankle."

"You could do with going to the hospital," Emmy informed me. "Where's the car?"

"I brought them both up to the old house," Alaric told me. "All the hardware's in the Suburban—I'm assuming the Queen of Darkness'll want to make herself scarce."

The woman who wasn't Emmy glared at him but didn't argue. I didn't know her name. Nobody had introduced her, and she'd barely said a word in the woods.

"I'll take my leave as well," Black's friend said. "Don't forget to cancel the manhunt."

"And call an ambulance," Emmy added as she scrubbed at her face with wet wipes. She'd already stripped off weapons and goggles and removed a belt adorned with pouches. "Now that we look like search and rescue rather than a bunch of assassins, it's time to bring in the authorities, although I wouldn't exactly be devastated if we left Ridley's corpse out there to rot."

Neither would I. A funeral was too good for that man.

Black's friend glanced over his shoulder as he walked away, a faint smile gracing his lips.

"Won't be much left to bury once those hogs have finished with him."

Hogs? "What hogs?"

"Long story," Emmy said, grinning. "It can wait until later."

Later... I'd live to see later now, and the feeling of relief was so overwhelming I burst into tears for the second time.

Alaric quickly wrapped me up in his arms, and Rune as well. "It's okay. Nobody'll hurt you again. I promise."

"I thought I was dead. Everything was fading away, but then a gunshot woke me up."

Alaric lifted me into the front seat of one of the SUVs and reclined it so I could rest while we waited. Rune crawled into the back seat, tucked herself under a blanket, and fell asleep in three seconds flat.

"That girl," I whispered to Alaric as he sat on the door sill, gripping my hand. "She's the smartest, bravest person I've ever met. You've done an amazing job bringing her up."

"It was a joint effort."

"I know. We talked a lot in the cellar, and she told me stories. She said she has four fathers instead of one."

"Indeed she does. That's why I'm Alaric instead of Dad—she calls us all by our first names because having Dad, Pop, Papa, and Pappy would be confusing. Plus Ravi's only seventeen years older than she is."

"That doesn't upset you? That you're her father, yet she thinks of your friends in that way too?"

"Not at all. Why would I begrudge her their love and protection? But now... Now I'm hoping she'll have a mom too."

"Me?" I choked out the word, and the tears threatened to make a reappearance.

"Well, I was planning to put an ad on the internet, but if you're interested in the job..."

"Oh, gosh. I... I... Of course I am. I've always longed for children, and I never thought... But will Rune want that?"

"Yes," she mumbled from the back seat. Oops. Not quite as asleep as I thought. "Don't get mushy, Mom."

How could I not? The tears came yet again, and I hurriedly tried to wipe them away when Black materialised behind Alaric.

"Cavalry's five minutes out."

Alaric kissed me softly on the forehead before he rose to his feet.

"I know we've had our differences," he said to Black, "but I need to thank you for everything you did on this search. If you hadn't taken control of this operation..."

"As I've suggested before, don't dwell on what didn't happen. Focus on what you want to happen tomorrow." After a pause, Black held out a hand. "Truce?"

Alaric didn't answer straight away, but after a long moment, he nodded and shook. "Truce."

The first siren sounded in the distance, a high-pitched wail distorted by the trees. Well, my new life had certainly gotten off to an exciting start, hadn't it?

CHAPTER 51 - ALARIC

"TIME FOR BED?" Alaric asked.

Beth had yawned twice in the last two minutes, and the movie was finished.

"I just need to take a painkiller before we go upstairs."

It had been a long three days. Beth and Rune had spent the first of them at the hospital—a comprehensive check-up for both of them, plus X-rays on Beth's ankle. She had a hairline fracture as well as a horrendous sprain, but they'd strapped it up and given her the good stuff when it came to medication. Both girls' bruises were ugly—big purple welts—but they'd fade.

Then had come the hours of police interviews. Emmy's lawyer had kept them as short as possible, but the cops still needed to know the details, and the Navy too since Ridley had escaped on their watch. Nobody seemed bothered by Ridley's death. Reporters were lauding the "unnamed teenager" who'd been kidnapped at random along with her stepmom and somehow managed to escape from the fiend. Media outlets in Afghanistan and Rojava seemed particularly happy with the turn of events.

Beth and Rune had come back to the Riverley estate yesterday afternoon, both still exhausted. Black had offered the guest house again, and although Alaric would have preferred Hillside House and its privacy, the high walls and advanced security at Riverley won out for now. Rune needed it.

As Alaric had feared it might, Rune's stoicism in the immediate aftermath of the rescue had faded now that the immediate danger had gone. The same thing had happened in Thailand. She'd spent weeks fearful of being alone, terrified her old captors would come and snatch her back.

When they'd left the hospital in Phuket and taken her to the rented apartment, of course she'd said she was okay. She always did. Alaric hadn't needed a degree in psychology to understand that when they first met, she'd been afraid that if she put a foot wrong, they'd send her to an orphanage. They'd had to teach her that it was fine to have an opinion. Okay to rock the boat now and then. Rune had come a long way in five years, only for Ridley to knock her back again. But they'd work on it, the same way they always did.

Last night, Judd had slept on a fold-out bed by her window with a gun under his pillow, Naz stayed in the room next door to hers, and Ravi took the couch downstairs. This morning, she'd at least looked as if she'd gotten some sleep. Once again, they'd get through this together, and this time, they'd have help from Beth too.

Her tears had dried up, and she'd even joked about having the full set now that she'd broken both ankles. Resilient. That was the best word to describe Beth. Resilient and tired.

"I'll get you a glass of water."

"Wish it was wine."

"Did I mention I have a share in an Italian vineyard?"

"The estate you told my father about? I thought it was abandoned. You said it was just sitting there."

"Turns out it isn't."

"Ah." Beth suddenly smiled and nodded to herself. "You bought the vineyard with Emmy, didn't you? You were together once?"

"A long time ago. Are you okay with that?"

"I suppose. I mean, she's happily married now, isn't she?"

Married? Yes. Happily? Probably. Alaric nodded.

"So I guess I'm a little jealous. You seem to have better taste in exes than I do."

"I can't argue with that. And to answer your question, yes, Emmy replanted the vineyard without telling me. When your ankle's healed, we can take a trip there and drink all the wine you want."

Perhaps he'd even renovate the old house that came with it now he had someone to share it with.

"What about work?"

It was an excellent question. Alaric had long since come to the conclusion that there were more important things in life, but at the same time, he needed to earn enough to live on, and money had become more important now that his family was growing. He had to buy a house. Pay for a wedding. Keep a horse, maybe two if he somehow managed to track down Beth's beloved Polo. Give Beth and Rune everything he wanted them to have.

"Yes, I guess we have to do some of that. Unfortunately."

Beth laughed. "At least I can still type with my

ankle bandaged."

"I think you've earned a few weeks of sick leave."

"Honestly? I'd rather stay busy. And don't we still have a painting to look for?"

Emerald. The cursed painting that had started all this. At this particular point in time, Alaric was inclined to leave her to rot wherever she'd ended up rather than risk angering the gods again. But there was a tiny problem. He'd promised Harriet the reward money if they found that green-ringed bitch, and she desperately needed the cash.

"Do you think we should keep looking? *Emerald*'s jinxed. I don't want to risk my future with you by chasing after a ghost."

Maybe he could find another way to give Harriet the money? Emmy had mentioned that commercial production was starting at the vineyard this year—how much would that bring in? Alaric would gladly send Harriet every cent. But Emmy had also mentioned they'd found Dyson, and that made the decision even harder.

"I'll agree that sometimes it's better to cut your losses, but that painting's always going to haunt you. And it seemed as though we were getting closer. How about having one last stab at finding it? At least then you'll know you've done everything you can."

"I feel like she sucks out parts of my soul every time I get close," Alaric muttered.

"Well, I'll just have to put them all back again." Beth pulled him in for a kiss. "I love you."

The front door opened, and Ravi, Naz, Judd, and Rune burst in. The men had taken Rune over to the games room in the big house in an attempt to take her mind off things. Judging by her smile, it had worked to some extent.

"Busted," Judd said. "Get a room, mate. Ravi needs the couch back, unless you want to have a threesome."

Ravi laughed, and Rune poked him in the chest, but Bethany went bright red. Interesting. Alaric's mind flitted back to fantasy number three, and a seed of an idea planted itself. He'd meant it when he said he'd give her anything she wanted. Although for the first time, he also understood Black's insane jealous streak. At least he had that sapphire ring back on Beth's finger now.

"Okay, okay, we're going."

He carried her upstairs despite her protests, then got her a drink while she dressed for bed. Or rather, didn't dress. When he slid in beside her, she wasn't wearing a thing. Be still his twitching dick.

Or maybe not. Beth palmed him through his pyjama pants, and the temperature in the room rose a notch.

"Are you sure?" he asked. Keeping his hands off Beth had been hard, as had other parts of his anatomy, but he didn't want to push her.

"I'm sure. But I haven't been taking my pills for the last few days, so..."

Alaric almost suggested she didn't bother taking them ever again, but it wasn't the right time for that, not if they were continuing the search for *Emerald*.

"Bradley keeps the bedside tables well stocked. Flavoured or ribbed?"

"I have to choose?"

Oh, Beth. His filthy little temptress. He'd fuck her six ways from Sunday, Monday, and every other day of the week.

"No, sweetheart. You'll never have to choose."

"Been a hell of a week," Emmy said over breakfast.

She had three cups lined up beside a pain au chocolat—espresso, Americano, and cappuccino.

"Got enough caffeine?"

"Why choose?"

That was going to be Alaric's new motto. He could actually do with a coffee himself with the amount of sleep he hadn't got last night. Just thinking about it made him yawn.

Emmy pushed the espresso in his direction. "Here. You look as if you need this more than I do. What did you want to discuss?"

"*Emerald*. You really found Dyson?"

"Yes, we really did."

Emmy passed her tablet over, and Alaric found himself looking at a picture of the man who'd starred in his nightmares for eight long years. Killian Marshall. In the headshot, he didn't look like a master criminal. Wearing a collared shirt and V-neck sweater, he looked like the guy who shovelled snow off his neighbour's drive in the winter and barbecued for the grandkids in the summer. The caption framed him as a local philanthropist.

"Whoa. Not quite what I was expecting."

"We got a bit sidetracked so we haven't done much research yet, but Mack's found out the basics. Marshall was born in Penngrove, but he moved away to attend university—he read Art History at Cambridge."

"Smart guy."

"Yup. Then he did a year as an assistant at Sotheby's before moving to...care to guess?"

"Tell me."

"Pemberton Fine Arts."

"He worked for Beth's old boss? You're kidding?"

"I'm not."

Fuck. Alaric put his head in his hands and groaned. "That old bastard Pemberton's in this deeper than we ever imagined. If we'd just shaken him down in the first place..."

"It didn't make sense at the time. And by following Hegler, we ended up solving a murder as well as getting *Red After Dark* back and finding Marshall. Plus Marshall only lasted a year at the Pemberton gallery. He worked for another dealer in New York afterwards— Jago Rockingham—and if I had to guess, I'd say that's where he crossed the line. Rockingham was a major player twenty-five years ago, until..."

"He got shot in the head at his home one night," Alaric finished. He'd heard stories about Rockingham from his former boss on the FBI's Art Crime Team. Rockingham's client list had included bankers, musicians, politicians, actors, heiresses, oligarchs, and the odd Mafia boss. He'd been larger than life, attending every party and opening the Big Apple had to offer, always with a different girl on his arm. The police classed the murder as a burglary gone wrong, but there were rumours he'd double-crossed one of his clients.

Had Marshall taken over the shadier side of his business?

"Wonder if Marshall had a hand in the shooting?" Emmy mused. "Or was it merely a convenient accident?"

"I guess that's a question we'll have to ask him. But I need to take a week or two first. Beth and Rune, they've been through hell, and I can't just up and leave them right now."

"I don't suppose he's going anywhere. You and Beth are really serious, huh?"

"I'm going to marry her."

Emmy's eyebrows shot up. "Really? Wow. I'm really happy for you, both of you, but that's...sudden."

"It's right."

"Have you set a date?"

"Ten weeks, three days, and two hours. At least, that's when I'm gonna put the engagement ring on her finger."

"That's very precise."

"She said to ask her in three months. I have a countdown alarm set on my phone." Alaric took a sip of coffee. Fuck, that was strong. "You and Black seem to be getting along again. Is everything okay now?"

"He still has a few issues to work through, but he's trying."

Alaric had a feeling he was one of the issues. Black had been noticeably nicer to him since the fight, but he wasn't going to put Emmy in an awkward position by mentioning it.

"I'm glad. We both deserve happiness, Cinders."

"Sometimes, it feels like the universe is out to get us."

Yes, it did, but sometimes, the sun shone down.

"You versus the universe? I feel sorry for the universe."

Emmy drained her second cup of coffee and pushed her chair back. "Go be with your girls. Me and Black can start planning Operation Killian Marshall tomorrow."

F.A.S.T.

I just wanted to take a moment to remind you of the symptoms of a stroke. By remembering these and acting quickly, you might save someone's life:

F - Face drooping or numb. Is the person's smile uneven or lopsided?

A - Arm weakness or numbness. If the person tries to raise both arms, does one arm drift downwards?

S - Speech slurred or hard to understand. Can the person repeat a simple sentence?

T - Time to call the emergency services if a person shows any of these symptoms.

You can find more information at www.stroke.org

WHAT'S NEXT?

My next book will be *Spirit*, a Blackwood Security Christmas novella that slots in after *The Scarlet Affair*...

All assassin Emmy Black wants for Christmas is three days off work and plenty of junk food, but instead, she's left dashing around the country when her assistant comes up with yet another harebrained scheme.

Five girlfriends, four Christmas wishes, three crazy days, two exes, one jet...

Will it be happy holidays or hell on earth?

For more details: www.elise-noble.com/spirit

And Alaric, Bethany, Sky, and Emmy will be back in *When the Shadows Fall*, the fourteenth novel in the Blackwood Security series...

From shot girl to assassin...

When eighteen-year-old Sky Malone left England to work for Emmy Black, she realised her new job wouldn't be easy. After all, being Superwoman's sidekick wasn't a career you could half-ass.

In Virginia, she finds every day is a battle. Against exhaustion, against her tall, dark, and grouchy mentor Rafael, and against the ghosts of her past. And as if that isn't tough enough, after just two months, she's flung into the middle of an undercover operation that leaves her fighting not only for her place on the team but for her life as well.

For more details: www.elise-noble.com/shadows

If you enjoyed *Red After Dark*, please consider leaving a review.

For an author, every review is incredibly important. Not only do they make us feel warm and fuzzy inside, readers consider them when making their decision whether or not to buy a book. Even a line saying you enjoyed the book or what your favourite part was helps a lot.

WANT TO STALK ME?

For updates on my new releases, giveaways, and other random stuff, you can sign up for my newsletter on my website:
www.elise-noble.com

Facebook:
www.facebook.com/EliseNobleAuthor

Twitter: @EliseANoble

Instagram: @elise_noble

If you're on Facebook, you may also like to join Team Blackwood for exclusive giveaways, sneak previews, and book-related chat. Be the first to find out about new stories, and you might even see your name or one of your ideas make it into print!

And if you'd like to read my books for FREE, you can also find details of how to join my advance review team.

Would you like to join Team Blackwood?

www.elise-noble.com/team-blackwood

END OF BOOK STUFF

Is it awful that my favourite scene in this book to write was the fight between Emmy and Black? I love it when characters have arguments. If I could only write one romance trope for the rest of my life, it would be enemies-to-lovers because it's fun making people bicker and then so satisfying when they finally end up together. Oliver and Stefanie in *Rhodium*, Max and Lily in *Roses are Dead*, Iris and Marcus in *Demented*, Tai and Ren in *Copper*... Those books flowed the easiest.

Speaking of *that* fight, I think the initial version of Chapter 36 was the most controversial scene I've ever written—it was even more vicious originally, and half of my beta readers were like, "No way, he is *not* coming back from that." So I decided to tone it down a bit. Will Black manage to redeem himself? We'll see...

The main inspiration behind this book came from the world around us at the moment—politics seems to have polarised people around the globe. I never used to follow it, but over the last few painful years, it's become impossible to escape the fact that some people really don't have the temperament or the morals to make decisions on behalf of other people. Some countries have got lucky, but from America to Zimbabwe and almost everywhere in between, there seem to be some right twats in government. Fingers crossed the situation will right itself over the next few years or I don't think there'll be much of the world left. There. That's more than I usually say about politics, and quite enough.

So, where else did I get ideas for this book? A while ago, I read an article about a car that was spotted in a lake in Florida on Google Earth, and upon investigation, it turned out that the driver had disappeared twenty-two years earlier on his way home. He was still inside. I figured that would be a perfect (temporary) resting place for Piper.

And if you're wondering about Rune's reference to Andi Manette, that came from *Mind Prey* by John Sandford. His Lucas Davenport series is one of my favourites.

The final part of Alaric's story will be out at the end of the year, but before that, I thought we'd hop back in time a bit with a Blackwood Christmas story. I've wanted to write one for ages because when Bradley's involved, you know it's going to be chaos. *Spirit* will be out at the end of November :)

As always, huge thanks to the team that helped me with this book—to Nikki for editing, to Abi for the cover, to John, Lizbeth, and Debi for proofreading, and to Jeff, Renata, Terri, Musi, David, Stacia, Jessica, Nikita, Quenby, Jody, and Sandra for beta reading.

Chat again soon!
Elise

OTHER BOOKS BY ELISE NOBLE

The Blackwood Security Series
For the Love of Animals (Nate & Carmen - prequel)
Black is My Heart (Diamond & Snow - prequel)
Pitch Black
Into the Black
Forever Black
Gold Rush
Gray is My Heart
Neon (novella)
Out of the Blue
Ultraviolet
Glitter (novella)
Red Alert
White Hot
Sphere (novella)
The Scarlet Affair
Spirit (novella)
Quicksilver
The Girl with the Emerald Ring
Red After Dark
When the Shadows Fall (2020)

The Blackwood Elements Series
Oxygen
Lithium

Carbon
Rhodium
Platinum
Lead
Copper
Bronze
Nickel
Hydrogen (TBA)

The Blackwood UK Series
Joker in the Pack
Cherry on Top (novella)
Roses are Dead
Shallow Graves
Indigo Rain
Pass the Parcel (TBA)

Blackwood Casefiles
Stolen Hearts
Burning Love (TBA)

Blackstone House
Hard Lines (2021)
Hard Tide (TBA)

The Electi Series
Cursed
Spooked
Possessed
Demented
Judged (2021)

The Planes Series

A Vampire in Vegas (2021)

The Trouble Series
Trouble in Paradise
Nothing but Trouble
24 Hours of Trouble

Standalone
Life
Coco du Ciel (2021)
Twisted (short stories)
A Very Happy Christmas (novella)

Books with clean versions available (no swearing and no on-the-page sex)
Pitch Black
Into the Black
Forever Black
Gold Rush
Gray is My Heart

Audiobooks
Black is My Heart (Diamond & Snow - prequel)
Pitch Black
Into the Black
Forever Black
Gold Rush
Gray is My Heart

Printed in Great Britain
by Amazon